FOREST OF SECRETS

WHISTLER IN THE WOODS

FOREST OF SECRETS

WHISTLER IN THE WOODS

HOLLY KNIGHTLEY

For my mother

Contents

CHAPTER ONE
The Fog

Pleasant Mills, New Jersey: Present Day

"Where are we going, Teller?" Sammy Lopez asked uncertain, his pulse racing under his skin producing an anxious heat that kindled his body. The fire-like heat traveled to his head making him dull with a brain fever. His limbs resisted motion, as if his brain had slid down his backbone and was now in his feet, and his feet knew better. They moved to protect him, by planting themselves in the marsh.

Ivy answered with a pull to his hand, before whispering: "Deeper into the woods."

Reluctantly, the muddy wetlands released him, tugging on his sneakers as if it meant to keep them. Freed, he walked as close behind Ivy as he could, pushing back the branches of barberries with his free hand.

She appeared as a shadow, blending into the dense fog surrounding them like an ethereal apparition, more fake than real. It was as if she was a silhouette, a ghostly shadow of her former self, slipping through the woods as he fought against them one-handed. With every step they took she became more of the fog than of the Earth. Stepping on the heel of Ivy's sneaker, he was reassured she *was* real, but the farther they traveled into the woods the less he believed it.

"A little farther."

"Okay," Sammy tried to say back, his words stuck in his throat.

It had been nearly six months since the epic showdown with Chief of Police Devan Rainier at Pleasant Mills Church. He was dead, very dead, —the kind of dead that would not spawn a miraculous resurrection. He was in Hell, eyeless and far away from his granddaughter Rosa Littleton. Along with him, his accomplice Mrs. Lois Ball also bit the bullet, thanks to Pastor Uriah Leeds's good aim. But Jesse Richards was still out there and so was Japhet Dean Leeds, the Jersey Devil.

During the months that followed, there hadn't been one peep from JD—not one harmonizing tune piping out of the Pines. All was quiet—too quiet. It was as if he went into hibernation, retreating into the cold, dark woods that wrapped Pleasant Mills in a shadow of pitch pines and oak trees, taking the town with him along with Timothy Chen, who was still missing after being kidnapped. Not one bird chirped overhead, not one squirrel could be heard scurrying up a tree. The woods had gone still, and with the stillness, a mysterious fog rolled into the Pine Barrens clinging to the small river town like a dark shroud.

The local papers blamed it on pollution. The national news called it the result of global warming and an ever-thinning ozone layer. Scientists claimed that it was just happenstance that the fog settled over the protected lands of the New Jersey Pine Barrens. To which they conjectured, if we all did our part to live greener lives, with time, the dense fog would dissipate. But Sammy knew better. The fog was not the result of pollution or the ozone layer giving way. Hocus-pocus was in the air, and it was as thick as New England Clam Chowder.

And that's what Sammy thought as he followed Ivy Teller deeper into the woods that ran parallel to the Mullica River. Sammy felt like he was walking through soup and with every step farther he took, he was traveling deeper into the belly of the woods—asking for trouble.

"Ivy," he said, pleading, "I think we've gone far enough; we want to make sure we can get back to the kayaks."

"Just a little farther." Her voice came out drone and trance-like. The tone intensified Sammy's feeling of uneasiness.

Sammy continued with a low groan of protest. Ivy was usually not so spontaneous, and he had jumped at the chance to play along with her whimsy. He thought her motioning to the shore for a break was code for stop and make out, maybe more. Sammy had immediately agreed it was break time and pulled the kayaks to shore in haste, before going in for an urgent kiss. But Ivy had dodged Sammy's kiss. Instead of the make out session Sammy was hoping for, Ivy had taken his hand and methodically led him away from the tall grass of the marsh. She pulled him faster and faster into the woods, stepping as if she knew where every tree branch laid and where every tree took root. Sammy was blind to the forest, fumbling with every uncertain step, and Ivy his guide.

Sammy again allowed himself to be pulled along, his anxiety mounting the farther from the kayaks they went. The branches snapped under his weight and the muddy ground continued to tug on the soles of his sneakers with a sucking noise. He tried to calm himself by focusing on the nice weather.

Today was the first day of summer vacation. Jeffrey Lopez's suggestion to go kayaking at the river was met with cheers from his family and more so when Lindsey Lopez suggested to her son he invite Ivy.

Sammy had felt stuffed up all winter. Winter had become a seasonal vampire, sucking the life out of him. Since his kidnapping, Sammy hated tight spaces, not to mention the dark. Winter was symbolic for how he felt while he was being kept in Jesse Richards's underground crypt at Pleasant Mills Church and spring was his salvation.

Sammy had felt like his old self on the water that morning, gliding downstream in his kayak with Ivy by his side as the rest of his family enjoyed a picnic on the shore. The air was fresh, just breathing in a lungful made him feel healthier. It was true the fog was there, a reminder there was something not quite normal with Pleasant Mills, but the sun filtered through it, painting the river yellow as if they glided through liquid gold. It seemed like magic.

The little bit of his old self Sammy had gotten back that morning was again stolen from him as he breathed in the scents of tree mold and clay dirt.

His mind was instantly transferred back to Jesse Richards's underground crypt, where he clung to the floor of his earthen prison waiting to die less than a year ago. The blinding fog reenacted the darkness of the crypt, dulling his senses.

Just when Sammy thought he couldn't take it any longer, Ivy pulled him to her. Sammy's hand hit the rough bark of a tree scratching him, but he didn't mind, his mind was elsewhere as Ivy pressed a kiss to his lips. She had a way of doing that, making everything disappear with those lips of hers.

Nose to nose, he could see her face. Her dark eyes glinted as if they were made of precious stones as her soft, pink lips parted ever so slightly, beckoning him closer. Her dark hair blended into the fog like a watercolor in motion, the fog billowing around her in waves. She looked beautiful. He kissed her back with a newfound urgency, as if her kiss was air and he was suffocating.

Their heavy breathing seemed to bounce off the trees, rattling the leaves into a nervous chatter. Slowly, Ivy ran her hand down Sammy's chest before taking his hand in hers again. She tugged on it, leading him farther into the woods. He didn't object this time. He would let her lead him anywhere with the promise of more kisses. His heartbeat blocked out the stillness of the woods and his adrenaline drowned out the fear in the pit of his stomach.

"Just a little farther," she whispered in his ear, followed up by a kiss. "I think we should go just a little farther."

Sammy's foot got caught under an uplifted cypress root and he fell to his knees. He laughed, not entirely sure why. Ivy laughed too. She got down on her knees next to Sammy to kiss his mud bespattered face.

A light breeze shifted through the trees accompanying their laughter and carrying with it something foul smelling.

Ivy gasped, covering her mouth, "What's that smell?!"

Sammy was on his feet, trying not to breathe in. "Must be a dead deer or something." The moment was ruined and all of Sammy's anxiety came rushing back to him tenfold. "Let's head back to the kayaks."

"Agreed," Ivy said, getting to her feet and tucking her nose and mouth under the collar of her T-shirt.

"Great," Sammy said with a huff, spinning around. "What direction did we come from? With all this stupid fog I can't tell." He ducked below the layer of fog to look for their footprints.

He fell to his hands and knees.

"Sammy?!"

He didn't answer.

"Sammy . . ."

"It's Tim," he mumbled, barely audible.

"What?"

Ivy crouched next to Sammy; his face growing pale as the color drained from it. She tugged on his arm. He wouldn't budge.

"Sammy what the heck is wrong with you? Get up, let's get out of here."

"It's Tim."

"I don't know what you're talking about. *Him*? Him who? Let's go. I can't take the smell."

"It's Tim," he repeated, still not moving an inch. We found Tim."

Ivy squinted, straining her eyes to follow Sammy's stare. She saw Timothy Chen's putrefied corpse decomposing among brambles, saw the bits of skull poking out from under his skin, saw dead cloudy eyes and screamed. Birds fluttered from their seclusion in a fury of squawks as if Ivy woke the forest. The leaves rustled in the trees, gesticulating as if they themselves trembled.

CHAPTER TWO
The Letter

Sammy nearly collapsed on his bed. He felt a jolt to his stomach like Iron Mike Tyson just delivered a knockout body shot. It made his knees buckle and his head hurt. On his pillow lay a white envelope with the initials J.R. scribbled on it. Sammy recognized the handwriting right away. They were the same initials signed on the portrait of Japhet Dean Leeds, the portrait Ivy and he had found in Pastor Leeds's junk room, the one that unmistakably looked like his father. There was no mistaking this—the letter was from Jesse Richards, the painter of the portrait, former King of the now historical Batsto Village and the man who had befriended him to only later kidnap him for Jersey Devil food.

Time became a slow crawl as Sammy stared at the letter on his pillow. He stared so long and so hard the edges of the letter blended into his white pillow until only the initials J.R. were visible to his bloodshot eyes.

Sammy wanted to scream, wanted to call out for his father—for anyone. He hoped his sisters would come rushing in and save him from himself. He couldn't move. He felt paralyzed. The letter on his pillow meant that Jesse Richards got past his father's security system and was in his house—was in his room. He wasn't safe, none of them were. Since JD had told Sammy he would be watching him, he hadn't felt safe. His father had beefed up the security system at the house. He couldn't sneak to Ivy's or anywhere else undetected; still, none of his dad's high-tech gadgets eased his fear, nor did any of his grandmother's charms and enchantments promising protection. Every little thing made him jump—every noise, every shadow, and now he knew he had a good reason to feel that way.

There was a golden lining, at least that meant he wasn't losing his mind. His paranoia was justified. He was right to flush the pills from his therapist down the toilet to keep his mind sharp. Fear equated to self-preservation. Being numb to the danger that was very real would get him killed. It was that thought that stirred him to life. Sammy opened the letter. His trembling hands coerced him to place the letter on his bed to read it. Unbeknownst to him, he held his breath.

Sammy,

It's Jesse—Jesse Richards. Don't show this letter to anyone. Get rid of it as soon as you read it. Trust me. I know you have no reason to trust me. But you have to. I'm on your side. I couldn't help you before because of Devan.

Sammy paused to think of Devan Rainier—the old Police Chief, his father's best friend. The Pleasant Mills Herald named Devan Rainier Pleasant Mills's first serial killer, but before that he had been like an uncle to him, a trusted friend. If he couldn't trust Devan, he can't trust Jesse.

JD's been watching you, your whole family. He's obsessed—more than his usual obsessiveness. He's up to something—something big. I don't know what, but it involves Ivy. He's been snooping around her house. He's been in her room. Tell her not to leave the spare key under the doormat. Pull that macho boyfriend stuff I know you're so good at.

Sammy tensed, remembering Jesse threatening to hurt Ivy to get what he wanted—the jarred heart. He hated Jesse, that hatred boiling to the surface with the image of Tim from the woods. Jesse had helped do that to him, had played his part in Tim's murder. Sammy knew he would carry that picture of Tim with him for the rest of his life. He hadn't kept his promise to his friend, he hadn't saved him. Tim was dead. The smell from the woods stung his nostrils. He thought he was going to be sick, his stomach doing what felt like a somersault.

Don't try to contact me or find me. When I find out more, I will let you know. For what it's worth I'm sorry about Tim. I really am. And about Zac, Tyrone, and Louie too. I wished I could have helped.

Stay safe. And dammit Sammy, don't go into the woods.
J.R.

CHAPTER THREE
Jeffrey's Living Nightmare

Jeffrey Lopez took a deep breath in before knocking on his son's bedroom door. It had been one hell of a day, and he was exhausted. If he was being honest with himself, it had been a rough six months. He had been trying to balance his time between Sammy and his pregnant wife.

Lindsey and Jeffrey had wanted more children. They had tried for years after Sammy was born. When the twins were finally conceived, they thought they were blessed. When news of Hugo came, they thought it was a miracle.

Unfortunately, the good news also came with bad news. Lindsey's stomach cancer was back. She spent most days in bed passing off her illness as morning sickness. Jeffrey wished it was only the pregnancy draining the life from his wife, but he knew better. Lindsey's health was deteriorating, and he knew Lindsey's prognosis wasn't good. He could feel it in his bone marrow as if he had a sixth sense about these sorts of things.

As a couple, they had decided to forgo treatment until Hugo was born. They didn't want to risk hurting the baby. By then, there would be little that could be done to save his wife. He just prayed Lindsey would live long enough to get a chance to hold baby Hugo.

Lindsey and Jeffrey also decided not to tell Sammy and the girls she was sick. Lindsey didn't want to worry them. She wanted this time to be happy and full of smiles as they waited for their baby brother's arrival. Jeffrey agreed; however, the truth was wearing him down.

Jeffrey tried to keep his hopes up, but he didn't know how he would survive without his wife. He needed her—Sammy needed her.

"Come in," Sammy said, stuffing the letter from Jesse in his windbreaker pocket and plopping down on his bed.

Jeffrey took a seat on the bed next to Sammy. "You okay?"

"No."

"Stupid question, I know. You want to talk about it?"

"Not really, Dad."

"Okay, but later if you want to."

Sammy nodded.

"I know you have work tonight, but I was thinking after this afternoon maybe you should call out."

Sammy shook his head, his hair falling into his blue eyes. "I have to go to work. It's my last day before I start lifeguarding for the summer and they're short staffed. Besides, work will help me keep my mind off everything."

Jeffrey tucked his grown-out hair behind his ears. "I can understand that." Work had been Jeffrey's solace the last six months—problems he could deal with, problems he knew how to fix. "But I'm driving you," Jeffrey said, taking note of Sammy's still trembling hands.

Sammy attempted a smile. "Thanks Dad. I appreciate it."

Jeffrey got to his feet, tarrying by the bedroom door. "I'll be waiting downstairs."

"Hey Dad," Sammy called after him.

Jeffrey turned around. "Yes?"

"Did you check the cameras from today yet?"

"Yep, just finished before I came upstairs."

Sammy sat up a little straighter. "Anything funny show up?"

"No. Why, did something happen?" Jeffrey asked, his eyes narrowing in on his son. There was something in the way he asked.

"No nothing . . . after today I just feel a little jumpy, that's all." Sammy had wanted to tell his father about the letter the moment he saw it on his pillow, wanted to scream for him, but the shock of it had stolen his voice. Sammy's conviction to do the opposite of what Jesse asked of him waned when he saw his father's face. His father's handsome face looked ragged; his eyes webbed over in red. Today had been hard on Sammy and the same went for his father.

Detective Pearl Steele was hysterical at seeing her cousin dead. While Sammy remained silent in shock at seeing Tim, Pearl's response was the opposite and his father played a large role in calming her down. On top of that, his mother had a bad spell of morning sickness. News of the letter could wait till tomorrow. There was no immediate threat, besides what could his father do? They already had the best security system money could buy. It was, as Sammy always knew, out of their control.

Jeffrey walked back into Sammy's room. He crouched so they were eye to eye. "I'm not going to let anything happen to you. Trust me."

Sammy instinctively slid his hand inside the jacket pocket that stowed Jesse's letter. "I do, Dad. I trust you."

"Good evening, Mr. Lopez," Bob, the deli manager, said with a wave from behind the lineup of delicatessen specials. "See you finally got a haircut. You and your boy were starting to look like twins."

He waved back with a smile. "Sammy forgot his money for dinner. He's busy at the checkout, so I'm going to just put it in the breakroom for him."

"Go right ahead."

"Thanks, Bob."

He made a beeline for Sammy's windbreaker, pulling out the letter from Jesse and reading it to himself while he whistled. When he was done reading it, he returned it to where he found it along with a twenty-dollar bill.

12

CHAPTER FOUR
Disappointment

"**H**i Abby," Sammy said with a smile, happy to see his grandmother Anita Gomez when he opened the front door after work. Abby was short for abuela, a nickname Sammy had lovingly coined for his grandmother when he was a toddler and abuela didn't come out quite right.

"What's wrong with you child?" Anita demanded, gripping Sammy's arm a little too hard.

Sammy was accustomed to his grandmother accosting him but usually she wasn't so physical. "Nothing," he said, pulling his arm away from her and rubbing it. "Nothing, I'm a little upset that's all."

"And you should be," she said in a hiss, staring up at her much taller grandson. "This is your fault."

Anita had spent the day with Sammy's Aunt Francine, while the rest of the family went to the river, missing all of the drama. As soon as Fran dropped her off back home, Lindsey filled her mother in. Lindsey depended on her mother to help give Sammy emotional support, however,

Anita's way of providing emotional support was not what her daughter had in mind. Anita had traveled from Spain to live with the Lopezes. She was there to help Sammy come into his magic so he could protect himself. When the nice way was met with no result, her comforting turned to tough love.

Sammy's eyes glassed over. "Abuela . . . my fault?" He bit his tongue to hold back tears.

She nodded, her blue eyes cold like steel. "Well, Samuel Cameron what do you have to say for yourself?"

He hated it when she called him Samuel Cameron. That was his name, and he shouldn't mind it, but that was also the name of his uncle who went missing as a boy, a magical prodigy that he could never live up to.

With a lump in the back of his throat, Sammy shook his head. "I didn't do anything Abby."

"Exactly my point. You claimed to have had a bond with this boy. Promised to help him and now he's dead and it was your girlfriend who found him. It should have been you. You should have found him alive. If you would have tapped into your magic, you could have saved him." Anita hit her grandson's chest hard with her knuckles, her many rings, knelling against his chest. "All this time I've been working with you and there's nothing there. You just don't have it in you. I'm very disappointed. Never have we had such a weak witch in the family. You're undeserving of the family grimoire. I thought you were ready but you're not. Pull yourself together Samuel Cameron, before it's too late!"

Silent tears rolled down Sammy's cheeks. Hearing his father coming in behind him, he ran up the stairs to his room.

Jeffrey's eyes followed his son. "What's that about?" he asked Anita, hanging up his jacket.

"Just talking to him about young Timothy."

"Yeah, what a day . . . It was bad. Be grateful you were at Fran's."

"You need to stop babying him, Jeffrey."

Jeffrey breathed out through his nose, the sound resembling a whistling teakettle. "Anita, I don't need you to tell me how to deal with Sammy. Stay out of it. He found his friend dead today, give him a break."

"All you and Lindsey do is make excuses for him."

"Anita," he said firmly, "we have been through this, he's seventeen years old. He has been through Hell and back. As long as his grades are still where they should be, I'm happy."

"Grades," Anita said, throwing her hands in the air frustrated, her rings sliding down her skinny fingers. "Who cares about letters on paper?!"

"I do. Good grades mean a good college and a good college means he'll make a good living."

"Money," she said frustrated.

"Yes, Anita. Money. I want Sammy to do well in school and make good money."

"Money can't bring little boys back from the dead."

He gave her an incredulous look. "No, it can't, and neither can your silly spells, so back off."

She continued her assault with her eyes.

"Where's everyone?" he asked, ignoring her icy gaze.

Lindsey is resting in bed and the twins are tucked in for the night."

"How's Lindsey feeling?"

"She's the same, but Sammy's regressing."

"Anita, I'm warning you, leave Sammy alone. He has a lot on his plate. This is going to be a hard week for him with Tim's funeral and all. Try supporting him like the good old days. He could use his grandmother not a wicked witch."

CHAPTER FIVE
The Visitor

A chill stirred Sammy from his sleep. He pulled his blanket to his chest as his lungs expelled a cloud of visible air, his cold breath dancing around his handsome face before vanishing into the darkness of his room.

He heard a voice, strange, yet familiar as if it was speaking to him from far away. "Sammy." Sammy sat up in bed, yanking his covers around him and scanning the dark. He heard the voice again, recognizing it at once. "Sammy, over here."

Sammy's heart fluttered and his arms and neck pocked with gooseflesh as another chill traveled down his spine. "Zac . . . is that you?"

Sammy strained his eyes, not sure if he could trust what he saw. From the dark recesses of his room, Zachary Lewis stepped forward. Zac was wearing his go to Jersey Devils Football hoodie Sammy had last seen him wearing at the church lock-in before he went missing.

Sammy jumped out of bed, rushing to his friend, and wrapping his arms around him. "Zac! Zac, you're okay! We thought you were dead.

Where have you been this whole time?" Sammy was talking a mile a minute, keeping Zac in a bear hug. "So much has happened. Tyrone and Louie were killed. And Tim. You would've liked Tim."

Sammy shivered; it was as if the temperature in his room plummeted. Taking a step away from Zac, he rubbed his arms, trying to generate heat. Zac's face was cast in shadows, but it looked pale—too pale. It shone in his room like a white moon in the nighttime sky. "What's wrong?" Sammy said, closing the gap between them. Zac's countenance grew paler until his skin looked like cold marble. Dark bruises in the shape of half-moons settled under his eyes, aging him in an instant. "What is it?! What's wrong?!"

"Sammy, I think I'm dead." Zac's hands ran down his chest past the fruit punch stain on his hoodie to a darker stain—to a crimson one. It was blood. The blood came alive. It spilled over Zac's hands like a running spigot, hitting the floor with a splat. It filled the room with a metallic smell so strong Sammy could taste it in his mouth. "Sammy, help me. Please help me!"

Sammy woke up, his screams filling his room like a siren. He gulped large mouthfuls of air. He felt like there wasn't enough oxygen in the room and he was being smothered. He scratched at his neck with trembling hands before realizing he was alone in his room, and he was okay.

Jeffrey opened his son's bedroom door and turned on the lights, an action Sammy was grateful for.

"Sammy, are you alright?"

Sammy swallowed his tears, his mind going to the blood stain on Zac's hoodie. Zac, like the rest of his friends, had his heart torn out by JD and if he believed Jesse, eaten so JD could keep his mortal form. He wasn't surprised he dreamed of Zac after finding Timothy in the woods, it made all of his guilt and unhealed wounds fester.

"Uh huh," Sammy said, grunting it out. He couldn't say any more than that without his tears spilling over. He hoped his grandmother didn't hear him yell. How he wished he hadn't, but his dream was so real, everything was in such vivid detail, despite taking place in his dark room. All his senses were working overtime: the sight of Zac's ghost-white face, the feel of their embrace as they hugged, and the smell, the smell of blood was so rich.

Ivy put her earbuds in and turned up her music; she was restless. Her mind kept traveling back to the woods, back to Timothy lying amongst the fallen branches and leaves. She shuddered at the image of his ivory cheek bones protruding out of his gray skin, the rock-like look of his skinless knuckles, and his matted coal black hair.

She leaned against her headboard and attempted to count the cobwebs hanging from the attic ceiling. Every time a car passed by, the headlights caused the fine webery to glisten like cat eyes in the dark. "Eleven, twelve, thirteen." Ivy stopped counting. "Thirteen," she said again, running her hand over her lips nervously.

Her mind flipped back like an old movie, replaying the nightmare she first had months ago. Ivy saw herself clothed in a worn blue dress, her long hair being held back with a bonnet, as she delivered a baby on a stormy night. She recalled Deborah Leeds Smith smothering her thirteenth baby. Time seemed to stand still before the moment the infant breathed again, but not as a boy. "As a monster," Ivy whispered to herself. "A demon."

If Ivy was to believe her nightmare, that meant she not only gave JD his name, but she also played a part in his rebirth into darkness. He'd told her that much. Told her it was she *who brought 'him' back to life*. That was a hard pill for Ivy to swallow. That meant she was at the root of every bad thing he did. That meant she was responsible for the deaths of Sammy's friends, the good-natured Zac, Tammy's boyfriend Tyrone, and the polite and handsome Louie. And JD's latest victim, Timothy Chen.

Ivy had this funny feeling in her belly that rivaled an upset stomach after a double chilli cheese dog and a rollercoaster. She couldn't quite put her finger on it or give it a name, but it seemed oddly strange to her that they found Tim that afternoon, after all of the searches turned up nothing.

As she and Sammy had glided down the river, Ivy felt like the trees had called out to her, compelling her to come closer, as if they each had their own unique voices only she could hear. At this point, there was no denying she was a witch, although she still liked to lie to herself. She was good at lying, the very best, but she knew deep down inside where she hid all the things that scared her, it was not serendipitous that they found Timothy, it was magic—her magic.

Sammy's grandmother was right, Anita and Ivy were sisters in witch hood. After she gave Ivy the awkward soul cleanse in Sammy's bathroom, where she scrubbed her with an oversized brush like she was a muddy dog, Anita removed what Sammy called a witchy block, turning Ivy's perception of herself upside down. Anita's rigorous scrubbing and dyed herbs unlocked something in her. Ivy felt like she was hanging from the monkey bars by her feet seeing everything topsy turvy. She was seeing things in a different way, with different eyes. Ivy feared she was looking through the eyes of the woman she saw in her nightmare, an Ivy Teller from a different time, from a past she couldn't fully remember.

Ivy's memories were just out of reach for her. Her fingertips could never quite grasp a hold of the truth. Her brain felt like a delicatessen slice of Alpine Lace Swiss Cheese. There were large holes in her memories, even the ones she did have. It was just like how Pastor Leeds had described how he felt. Like he had no past, to only get a glimpse of it back each time JD murdered a child from the church. Ivy had no recent past. The mother and sisters she scarcely remembered last summer were less than an impression now. She couldn't even recall visiting her grandmother as a child and sleeping in the attic bedroom, scared.

All of that was lost to her. She had nothing but the strange dream of the Midwife, that she knew was more than a dream, it was a direct telescope into her past life. Ivy just hoped Pastor Leeds and she weren't linked, that her strange dreams weren't the product of Sammy's friends being murdered.

Ivy already knew she was tied to JD, she made him. It was she who somehow brought him back to life after his mother smothered him with a pillow. How much worse could things really get for her? Ivy reasoned a lot worse. She, like Uriah, didn't want to be the person they were in the past, didn't want the memories of what they'd done, but they had them, or at least part of them. It frightened Ivy to think what happened with JD after her dream ended. It frightened her to think of the emotions the Midwife felt while she gazed into his dreamy brown eyes and thought how beautiful he was even while covered in his parents' blood. It frightened her how one minute she was terrified of a demon to only be in love with the man.

Ivy turned up her music. There was nothing the rock 'n' roll gods could do to soothe her, but it was worth a try.

Ivy and Sammy hastily made their way up the old staircase to Ivy's room while Mary took an impromptu nap on the couch.

"You sure Grams won't wake up?" Sammy whispered. He had his sneakers off and took to the old staircase on his tippy toes, taking care to make sure the floorboards didn't squeak.

"Nothing to worry about. When her head goes back all the way like her neck is snapped in two, she's out for the count."

Ivy wrapped her arms around Sammy as soon as she closed her bedroom door. He squeezed her tightly. He felt safe in her arms and Ivy relished the feeling of Sammy needing her. She had become his cocoon.

Sammy had a bad night. He didn't have to tell her; she could see it on his face. He had dark crescents under his eyes that resembled bruises. They looked extra dark against his light blue eyes. He was exhausted and she knew it. Without saying a word, Ivy took Sammy's hand and led him to her bed in the center of her room. She made herself comfortable and pulled him next to her, pressing a kiss to the side of his face. In no time, Sammy drifted off to sleep safely in her arms.

Sammy's long, dark lashes feathered against his cheeks while he slept. He looked younger this way, all his worries lost to his dreams, his chest rising and falling in perfect harmony, his breathing making its own music, and it was her favorite song. She wished he could always be this at peace, wished some way she could give it to him.

Ivy let out a loud yawn. She reasoned Grams and Sammy had the right idea and closed her eyes for a short cat nap. Ivy had become close friends with the attic bed since she came to live with her grandmother. After almost a year of getting to know each other, her body had left a groove in the middle of the mattress that fit her body like a glove.

Ivy had just closed her eyes when her nose involuntarily twitched. She smelled a vaguely familiar scent, a scent from her past—a sweet, smoky fragrance that was as light as it was distinctive.

She opened her eyes to see Sammy still asleep in her arms. She pressed another kiss to his cheek. She couldn't help herself. He was so beautiful with his sun-kissed skin, his long lashes, and his dark hair that fell in whisps around his face. He really was a Spanish god. "I love you," she whispered in his ear.

He stirred, shifting in Ivy's arms to face her. "I love you too."

Ivy gasped; the air sucked out of her lungs in a hiss. Sammy's light blue eyes that rivaled tropical waters were brown.

"What's wrong?" Japhet Dean asked concerned. His large brown eyes searching for an answer in hers as they did that day he first came into being.

Ivy shot up in bed to find herself alone in the dark. Her eyes darted to her nightstand. The large alarm clock flashed 12:00 a.m. in bright red. It was the witching hour, or as Sammy had informed her the devil's hour. This was the time the jarred heart in Pastor Leeds's attic had beamed red, painting everything including her in her least favorite color.

A knot twisted in Ivy's stomach. She hated coincidences. She plopped back down on her pillow exhausted, her arms and legs tucked closely to her body. Taking deep calculated breaths, Ivy moved her damp hair away from her face. "Only a dream, Ives."

But it didn't feel like a dream; it felt real. She swore she could still smell the sweet, smoky aroma from her dream, but unlike her dream that was fading away, the aroma grew stronger engulfing the room. Ivy's eyes shifted to her bedroom door to find it ajar and to see a shadow standing at the threshold. The spark of light from the man's cigarette was just enough to highlight his well-formed lips—and well-formed they were, they were perfect.

Ivy's pulse quickened until she felt like she flatlined. She spoke in a whisper, unsure if the words left her mouth. "What are you doing here?"

She had often thought about what she would do if she ran into JD, and always concluded screaming was the best course of action. But now that he was so close, she lost her voice. She felt small. And she felt confused as if the kiss in her dream was really from him and the whispered words, *I love you,* were real.

JD stepped closer. His full face was momentarily highlighted by a stream of light coming in through her window from a passing car's headlights. Ivy held her breath and only released it when JD faded back into the shadows of her room. Her heart thudded in her chest, too hard and too quick. She felt it would give out soon.

This was the first time she had laid eyes on him in real time. She knew he looked like Mr. Lopez thanks to the portrait Jesse had painted of him. The portrait Sammy and she accidently stumbled across in Pastor Leeds's junk room. The face in the 1800's portrait of Japhet Dean Leeds was the same face she saw in her dream, but still, she felt an uncontrollable need to retch when she saw for herself just how much like Jeffrey Lopez, Japhet Dean Leeds was. He was even dressed like him, wearing a black button-down dress shirt with the arms rolled to his elbows and dress slacks.

Yet, as much as they were the same, they were different. She was never attracted to Sammy's father. Although she'd admit he was handsome and that Sammy inherited the majority of his good looks from his father, there was nothing between Mr. Lopez and her, as it should be. She had reluctantly looked into Mr. Lopez's eyes after her strange dream about resurrecting JD, his rebirth as he called it, fearing there would be something there, but she felt nothing. However, with JD, there was this tangible attraction, this friction in the air like electricity, as if the Midwife's feelings for JD were more real than her feelings for Sammy.

"I came to say hello," JD finally said in a sultry tone of voice.

"Leave now!" Ivy said in a hushed whisper. Terrified that he spoke. Terrified, his voice struck a chord in her heart—not the Midwife's heart, *her* heart.

"Come now, is that anyway to treat your creation?"

Ivy sat up briskly, she hated how he said that. It made her think of Frankenstein's creature. As if when the old her had helped him, she was playing God to only abandon him to the cruel, cold world.

"I don't know what you're talking about," she lied.

JD took another step toward Ivy's bed. He was so close now; she could see the whites of his eyes, the curve of his soft lips. "Hmm . . . Ms. Teller have you truly forgotten the part you played in my rebirth? Me, your greatest regret, and your greatest love?"

Ivy inched away from him, sliding her butt out of the groove in the center of her bed until she was clear on the other side of the mattress. His words frightened her. He frightened her. "Why are you here?" Her mind impulsively went back to JD replacing Sammy and kissing her in her dream, her confusion getting the best of her. Was it really fear she felt in his presence?

"I know something I think you may be interested in."

Ivy scoffed, "unlikely."

"Lindsey Lopez is pregnant again with another boy."

"Everyone knows that. She looks like she swallowed a watermelon."

"True, but does everyone know her cancer is back."

"What?"

"Lindsey and Jeffrey are keeping it a secret. Sammy doesn't know. Lindsey has forgone treatment until the baby is born, but by then it will be too late. She will die and with her, the baby."

"You lie!" Ivy's voice came out louder than she meant.

"I do not lie, and never to you Ms. Teller," he said, taking another step toward the bed.

"How do you know the future?"

JD took a long drag on his cigarette. "I listen, Ms. Teller. One can gather a lot by simply listening to the whispers."

Ivy's heart galloped in her chest. "Fine, you divined it from eavesdropping, but why are you telling me this?"

"Isn't it obvious?"

"No."

JD took yet another step toward Ivy. His legs now rested against the side of her bed. "I have the power to save Lindsey and baby Hugo. I want to save them. I want to do it for Sammy, but things get complicated. I cannot act on my own desires; I can only act on the desires of others, give them what they want and in return *I* get what I want. It's a give, take. A trade, a deal, a pact with a devil. I want that from you, Ms. Teller. In your possession, you have the key to helping them."

Her eyebrows scrunched together. "Me?"

"Yes. You. I understand you found a grimoire belonging to the Leeds family."

Ivy's mind went to the musty leatherbound book Sammy and she found after Pastor Leeds's mailbox suffered a hit and run. She recalled the three dragon-like creatures carved into the leather cover that gave her the creeps. "And if I did?"

"Well, *if you did*, I would like to borrow it. Offer you a trade."

Ivy hadn't given the book much attention since it ended up back under her bed. She hated the idea that she was a witch and did everything in her power to be what she considered a normal teenager. And that meant not reading spells from a spell book, but Sammy had gone through it thoroughly before his grandmother made him give it back to her. He'd reported his findings in grueling detail.

Ivy couldn't see why JD would want it. As far as she was concerned, the only spell worth anything was the *Beauty Spell*, but she had promised Sammy to never cast it and never to cast alone. Other than that one spell, the grimoire seemed obsolete, offering spells for things modern science could solve: hearing, sleep, hair-growth, and toe fungus. And then there were the strange food recipes, and healing spells; she reasoned the microwave was one button push away and triple antibiotic ointment would work better than a charm. If Sammy's mother was truly sick, modern medicine was the key not some musty book. Besides all that, she didn't believe JD. There was something about the curve of his lips that wouldn't let Ivy believe him. It was as if he was playing at something larger.

Her eyes narrowed. "You're saying there's something in the spell book that can help Lindsey? Well, if that's the case, and she's sick and I have the spell book, not saying I do, just talking hypothetically here, then I don't need your assistance."

JD didn't answer. The silence made her suspicious. "Why do you want to help Sammy's family anyway? You're the one who hurt him in the first place."

"One could make the argument, *you're* the one who hurt him, Ms. Teller. After all, it was you who forced poor brokenhearted Sammy out of the safety of his home and the loving arms of his family, to only send him into the night where a serial killer laid waiting."

"Get out now!" Ivy shouted, not caring if her grandmother heard her or not. She already carried around guilt over Sammy being kidnapped, he didn't need to rub it in. Jesse was JD's henchman; he was following *his* orders. If JD wasn't a psycho killer, Sammy never would've been kidnapped, but then again, if she didn't step in when JD's mother smothered him with a pillow, he wouldn't be alive to be a psycho killer.

"You're right Ms. Teller; let's not split hairs," he said calmly as if she hadn't just yelled at him. "We've both done Sammy wrong, and we both have the same goal when it comes down to it. Our goal being to make Sammy Lopez happy, to love him and give him what he needs." JD put out his cigarette on Ivy's nightstand. "I'm here to merely give you the chance to make it up to Sammy as I know you want to so badly. For there's nothing I wouldn't do for my sons, or for you. Can't you see, we both win in this Ms. Teller?"

"Son? Sammy's not your son," Ivy said, ignoring the fact that he said he'd do anything for her. She was not going to poke that bear.

"Not yet, but a man can dream, can't he?" For what is a man without dreams? We are no better than dirt without aspirations for something more, something grand."

"You can leave now. I'm not letting you borrow anything." Ivy was no longer confused. The touch of JD's lips from her dream no longer captivated her. She thought about Pastor Uriah Leeds and the deal he was tricked into making with Japhet Dean, how Uriah traded his son's life for thirteen lives for eternity. Ivy would not be bamboozled like that, even if the Midwife was. Her past did not determine her future.

JD walked around the bed, facing Ivy. Ivy put her hands up and crossed her index fingers to make the shape of a cross. JD laughed, a deep bellowing snicker. "Really, a finger crucifix, what child's play is this?!" JD grabbed Ivy, wrapping his arms around her. He talked in a low voice, his hot breath on her face. "Really now, Ms. Teller." JD drew Ivy closer to him, pressing her body against his as he rested his chin on her shoulder. Ivy was powerless to move. "You've forgotten how powerful I am." He ran his nose across her cheek. "But I haven't forgotten how powerful you are. We would make quite the pair, the two of us. Are you so sure your heart is set on young Sammy Lopez?"

Ivy squirmed in JD's strong arms. He loosened his grip. Ivy turned her body in a panic and pushed him away. "It is!"

"Well then Ms. Teller, the choice is yours. You hold the power in your hands to help Sammy—to protect him and save his mother and brother. But the question is how much do you *really* love Sammy? Would you do anything for him, even make a deal with me?"

Ivy's frame shook at the idea; she felt wobbly, her hand feeling for her bed to steady herself.

JD bowed his head, his eyes in shadows as if he wore a dark mask. Ivy preferred that; she didn't want to see those brown eyes of his. "I bid you good night, Ms. Teller. You know where to find me when your heart decides who it truly loves."

JD closed her bedroom door behind him. Ivy jumped over her bed and pushed her nightstand in front of the door. She ran to her dresser, taking out the perfume her grandmother bought her for Christmas and doused every inch of her bedroom. JD's alluring smell mixed with the sickly, sweet cotton candy scent of bargain basement perfume, making her head spin. She gagged, "I think I'm going to be sick."

Ivy opened the attic window to let some fresh air in. She took a pillow off her bed to use as a makeshift fan, fanning the pungent air out into the street like a matador egging on a bull.

Startled, Ivy dropped her pillow. From her window, she heard a bittersweet song. She scanned the dark, spying the whistler of the tune. JD was tucked under the shadow of Pastor Leeds's weeping willow tree across the street. He stared up at Ivy as he piped his song, the long branches blowing in the wind across his haunted face and sad brown eyes.

Ivy gave JD the finger and slammed her window shut. She crawled back in bed, pulling her blanket over her head. "I have to protect Sammy from him," she muttered to herself.

Ivy knew all too well JD's plans for her boyfriend. Sammy had confided in her what JD had told him in the church, how he freed him from Jesse's underground crypt because he wanted to be some weird, twisted stepdad to him. They knew JD fancied himself a father figure to Uriah and Jesse. Sammy was terrified JD would trick him into doing something horrible like he had done to Uriah. Sammy knew JD was not done with him, and now Ivy knew it to. She wasn't going to let Sammy make a deal with JD. She was on full guard. She couldn't help but think JD's warning about Lindsey and Hugo was a trap for Sammy. A merciless lie told to her in hopes that she would tell Sammy, and thus, send Sammy running into JD's demonic arms for help. That wasn't going to happen either. Ivy was going to protect Sammy and his family. She knew where her heart lied. It was with Sammy. She would do anything for Sammy Lopez, and she would start by not telling him about JD's visit. There was no reason to get him upset about the lie JD told about his mother and about JD calling him his son. Her lips were sealed.

From under her comforter, Ivy reached for her ear buds. She stretched, her fingertips just grazing the nightstand as she almost fell out of bed. She steadied herself on her nightstand and pulled it closer to the bed after having moved it as a barricade against JD coming back into her bedroom. She popped her ear buds back in, groaning in defeat as *Midnight Show* by the rock band The Killers played. She didn't need another reminder of the jarred heart that she'd kept under her bed last summer and how it came to life at midnight. Or, the little fact that it was MIA after it was mysteriously missing from where Sammy buried it in his back yard. "Not tonight boys. I've had enough hocus-pocus for the evening." Ivy skipped the song, letting her mind go blank as she shut her eyes tightly, snuggling into the groove in her bed and letting her rock music lull her back to sleep.

Leeds Point, New Jersey: 1735

The wind howled as the rain crashed against the windowpanes. Leeds Point hadn't seen a nor'easter like this in years. The newborn baby's cries were barely noticed amidst the storm that raged outside.

"A boy!" The Midwife declared, swaddling the baby. "Your first boy, Deborah. God has finally blessed you with a boy!"

The Midwife brought the baby to Deborah Smith Leeds so she could look upon him. Deborah glanced at the small, helpless baby in the Midwife's arms. "Another bad man in a bad world. Let the devil take him if he wants. I denounce it," she said, pushing the Midwife and the baby away.

"The baby is good. Born perfect in God's image. No ailments. He is healthy and strong," the Midwife said, smiling down at the baby. "Won't you hold him?"

"I will do more than hold it. Give it here," Deborah said as she sat up in bed.

The Midwife handed Deborah her son. The baby whimpered against her. Deborah placed a pillow over the baby, stifling his cries. "It was made in sin, and I need to send it back to Hell."

The infant let out a light cry that was quickly smothered by his mother with the pillow she held over his face. The Midwife tugged on her arm, but Deborah was determined to snuff out her baby's life. "Hurry, your wife means to hurt the baby!" She ran out of the room to get Japhet Leeds all along reciting a spell under her breath.

"Here my call
one or all.
God or Devil,
angel or serpent.

Save this babe with all your might,
give him wings so he can take flight.
Horns and claws that are sharp,
so that he can defend in the dark.

Sound the trumpets of rebirth,
let something new be spawned from the earth.
From God or Devil,
Angel or serpent.
Save this babe on this night."

Deborah removed the pillow. "There, my son . . . sleep. You will go to heaven now and not grow to be a monster like your father. Rest in peace."

The baby was cold and still in her lap, his countenance like marble. The silenced baby twitched. The infant's chest moved up and down. At first it was barely noticeable, but then the little chest filled with air, his chest and tummy rising as he breathed again. "What dark magic is this?!"

Deborah climbed out of bed, pressing herself against the wall in terror as her dead son reanimated. With every miraculous inhale, the perfect baby boy matured and changed before their eyes. The small, sharp tips of bony horns pierced through the baby's forehead. Veined wings sprouted from his back unfolding like a dark cloak. His skin turned as red as a ripe tomato and his back arched over his thick, strong arms. His toes and fingers fused to form cloven hooves as a forked tail sprouted from his back and whipped around the room.

Japhet stormed into the room with the Midwife behind him.

"What have you done?!" Japhet yelled.

"It's a devil!" Japhet shouted. He went to get his rifle. A direct shot pierced the back of the beast that now stood taller than his father. The shot had no effect. The creature lunged at Japhet Leeds, killing him at will and feasting on his warm body. The creature turned his attention to his mother who had smothered him.

The now looming demon jumped on top of his mother. His hands clamped her chest, tearing through flesh and bone to rip her heart out. Through cloudy eyes, Deborah could see the creature standing in front of her with her still beating heart in his hand. "Just like your father," she said, spitting in his face with the last of her strength. "You're just like your father. You're no good. You should have never been born." Japhet Dean licked the spit off his face and kissed his mother's lips as she faded away.

The Midwife stood paralyzed in fear as she was spattered with the blood of Deborah and Japhet Leeds. She could taste the salty tang of their demise in her mouth.

When the Leeds Devil had finished with his mother, he made his way to the Midwife, his mother's heart still in his hand. He stood directly in front of her and breathed his hot breath on her face.

"Please, Japhet Dean, don't kill me," she struggled to get out in a shaky voice as she cowered in the corner of the room.

The beast's glowing red eyes changed. They turned a soulful brown. "You gave me a name," the creature said, his voice wavering.

The Midwife couldn't believe her eyes. She watched as the beast became a man, his transformation working in reverse. His curled horns shrank until they were gone. His cloven feet separated, forming perfect fingers and toes. His tail and wings folded into his back, disappearing with the crimson color of his skin. In front of her now stood a young man with dark hair and dark eyes. His fair skin and handsomely chiseled face were bespattered in the blood of his parents. It didn't take away from his ethereal appearance, only strengthened it. The Midwife had never seen someone so beautiful.

He ran his bloodied hand down the Midwife's cheek. "I will not kill you. You showed me kindness when I was born. You tried to make my mother love me. You said I was perfect. The likeness of God." He looked her over very closely, studying her young face. His nose grazed hers.

"You are different," he said, smelling her. He buried his face in her hair rubbing the side of his face against hers as he took in her pleasant aroma. "It was you, wasn't it? It was you who brought me back to life after my mother smothered me."

Tears beaded on the Midwife's lashes. "I only meant for you to be alive, not for you to turn into—"

"A devil," he said, finishing her sentence.

She nodded her head slowly.

"What are you, girl?" Japhet Dean asked.

"I'm a child of the woods. I put my faith in the land and the trees . . . a Wiccan by religion, a witch to others . . . it's a secret."

"Your secret is safe with me. How do you yield such power?"

"I don't know . . . I was born with it, same as your mother."

"Her magic was different," he said, looking back at his dead mother slumped on the floor. "Dark . . . and you brought me back with light magic."

"You died before I could help you. I fear the Devil has already claimed your soul, and I merely reanimated you."

He looked at his human arms and hands. "So you have, Ivy."

The wild, primal red eyes of the beast were long gone without a trace. Japhet Dean's eyes now burned with a profound sadness no man should know. He glanced at his mutilated parents and turned away ashamed. Tears rolled down his face, trying to wash away his sins.

Japhet Dean looked to Ivy for absolution. He looked so fragile in that moment, helpless and alone—this demon of the Pine Barrens, remorseful for what he had done. His beauty was not from this world, but from Heaven. She saw that in him, this grace, that went beyond his beautiful face and eyes.

The Midwife placed her hand on the side of his face. She had no choice, she felt compelled to touch him, to know the feel of his skin on hers. She had never been so close to Heaven. She burned for more, inclining her chin so that their lips touched. It was electric. Japhet Dean scanned Ivy's eyes unsure as she deepened the kiss, his lips trembling under the burden of his kills.

His breath felt like velvet on her skin, silken and smooth, and she wanted more—she needed more. She lifted her skirts, pressing herself to him like he was the only thing that mattered. He pushed her against the wall, his hot body on hers, and for that moment they were one.

The Midwife turned her face as his free hand traveled up her neck, his muscled arms locking her against the wall where she wanted to be pinned for eternity. His eyelashes fluttered against her chest as his lips traveled downward. She opened her eyes to see the mirror on the wall. To see Ivy Teller in the arms of the Jersey Devil as he held his mother's still beating heart in his hand—Mother Leeds's heart keeping the beat of their unexpected love affair in the air.

Ivy woke up in a panic, sweat streaming down her temples. She grabbed her heart to stop it from jumping out of her chest. "Oh my God," she muttered into the darkness of her room. "It's true. I loved him."

CHAPTER SIX
The Promise

Jesse Richards casually sat on Rosa Littleton's bed, leaning against the headboard as he bounced a stress ball off the wall. "He's up to something . . . He tell you anything?"

"He's always up to something, and no," Rosa said, sitting at her vanity and brushing her long, dark hair.

Jesse chuckled to himself, his laugh not quite reaching the high-pitched titter Rosa loved. "Yeah, true enough. I'm just worried."

"Worried Ivy's gonna get hurt?"

Rosa turned to look at Jesse when no reply came. Rosa was Ivy's best friend and she'd seen the drawing Jesse had given to Ivy tacked to the back of her bedroom door. Rosa tried to tell herself it was just a drawing, that anyone could've drawn it, but when she spotted Jesse's initials her blood boiled. She'd thought she was the only one Jesse drew pictures for. She thought his drawings were proof he liked her. Rosa had been waiting for the perfect moment to bring up Jesse's feelings for Ivy, and felt satisfied now, having thrown his affection for her in his face. She parted her hair down the middle and braided her hair in her usual style.

"Yeah, that," he said with a smirk, not letting Rosa get under his skin. "That and other things. I'm worried about you too."

She raised her eyebrows. "Me?"

"With Devan gone that means you're fair game for whatever JD has planned. It was your grandfather that made a deal with JD all those years ago, not you. You were just his security policy to make sure Devan did what he was supposed to. That is, if he wanted his granddaughter's sight to be restored. And we both know there was nothing Devan wouldn't do to protect you."

It was true, Rosa had gone blind last summer but had regained part of her vision back thanks to the deaths of Zachary Lewis, Tyrone Jones, Louie Grindhouse, and Timothy Chen. With four of the thirteen souls promised to JD by Uriah collected, she was able to lose the ID cane and just wear thick glasses.

Rosa smiled a large grin of satisfaction. "You're really worried about me?"

"Damn it Rosa, of course I am."

Rosa got up and sat next to Jesse on the bed. "Funny enough, I was going to say I'm worried about *you*. Just do what JD says and soon you'll be able to leave this town and your past behind you."

"What choice do I have? I'm a wanted man and we both know I can't leave Pleasant Mills until JD collects his thirteen souls." Jesse bounced the ball off the wall again. "I just don't want Ivy to get hurt in all of this."

Rosa's cheeks blushed, heat running from her neck to her ears.

Jesse noticed. "I don't have a lot of friends Rosa. It was only you and her. I just don't want to see her get hurt that's all."

"She's not your friend now."

"No," he said, squeezing the stress ball. With vivid detail, he could still recall the look on Ivy's face when Jeffrey Lopez put a gun to his head and demanded he tell him where he was hiding Sammy. Ivy was disgusted by him, scared of him, there was no changing that. Those feelings ran too deep, but he couldn't stop feeling what he felt for her. "No not anymore, Ivy's not my friend. I only have you." Jesse smiled at Rosa. "I guess it's always been just you. I just wish JD would get on with it already. So I could leave."

Rosa reached for Jesse's hand and held it, his stress ball rolling onto the floor. "When it's time, take me with you?"

"This is your home."

"Not anymore. My grandfather's dead and he's not coming back. This whole house feels like a tomb. I only have you."

"What about your parents? You'd leave them?"

"We both know they're smothering me. I need a chance to have my own life and so do you, but we don't have to do it alone. You have to know what you mean to me. Take me with you?"

He stared at her unblinking. "Rosa . . ."

Rosa's eyes watered. "Don't I mean anything to you?"

Jesse took off her glasses and wiped her tears with his thumbs. "Of course you do. I just can't be responsible for you."

"You don't have to be. I'm not a child anymore." She pointed at the drawings of flowers Jesse had given her that hung from her walls in black frames. "You can't tell me you don't have any feelings for me."

"I never said that."

"My grandfather's gone. He can't stand in our way anymore. I know I was off limits to you before, but all that changed when he died. We can be together now."

"You really want that?" Jesse asked unsure.

"More than anything. Don't you?"

Rosa leaned in and pressed a kiss to his lips. "I love you, Jesse. Promise me you won't leave me behind."

Jesse pulled out her hair ties, freeing her braids. Cupping the back of her head, he pulled her toward him, gazing into her brown eyes as her heart fluttered. "JD is a monster. I won't leave you to him." Rosa pushed her lips to his, they locked and so did their bodies.

CHAPTER SEVEN
Trust

Sammy Lopez sat in his usual spot at church with his family and Mr. and Mrs. Chen and their daughter Anna. The church was full of people Sammy didn't know personally. Most of the attendees were Timothy's family. They had traveled from all over the globe to come to his wake and funeral. The sounds of his family whispering in their native tongue made Sammy feel uneasy. He couldn't shake the feeling they were talking about him.

Sammy turned around from the first pew to look for Ivy. She sat where she did for most Sundays, in the back with her grandmother, Mary Teller. Ivy smiled at him. Sammy gave a faint impression of a smile. He could feel the weight of Timothy's relatives' eyes on him. They stared with blank faces, while others pointed. He turned around and focused his attention in front of him, which didn't help. Behind the pulpit lay Timothy's closed casket. Lines of relatives continued to walk past it, caressing the mahogany lid as if they were running their fingers through Timothy's dark hair.

Sammy pulled up his shirt sleeve to look at his watch. They still had fifteen minutes before service was to begin. He shifted nervously in the pew.

Jeffrey looked past Alba and Maria who were sitting on his lap thumb wrestling, to Sammy. He knew better than to ask his son if he was okay. Instead, Jeffrey gave him a head nod before sliding the twins off his lap and going over to Detective Pearl Steele who had just passed Timothy's coffin. It seemed strange to see Pearl out of her black suit and camisole top that marked her as a detective and see her in a black dress the same shade of her long hair. She looked beautiful in a sad way. Today, wearing black made her skin look like porcelain. Sammy watched as his father hugged Pearl. She'd had a rough few months. She not only couldn't find her cousin Timothy, but she'd also suffered a great loss when Chief of Police Devan Rainier died. It appeared they were more than just coworkers and the news that he was an accomplice to murders shook her constitution, now, more than ever with Timothy being discovered dead. It was another blow to know her little cousin was murdered, and her lover was a part of it—a man she had looked up to and loved. She received just as many stares from her family as Sammy did.

Hoping his grandmother wouldn't notice, Sammy loosened his tie, rubbing his clammy hands together anxiously as the whispers behind him grew, filling the small church with an incessant humming.

In broken English someone said: "That's the boy who lived. The only boy they rescued."

Sammy swallowed hard, his survivors guilt stopping him from taking another breath.

"Not fair," another voice said. "Why him? It should've been our Timothy."

Pastor Uriah Leeds made his way to the pulpit just as Sammy stood up. "No, it's not fair!" Sammy yelled at them. "Sorry I didn't die!" The church went silent. All eyes were on Sammy. He could hear his heart beat in his ears. He ran out of the church through the double doors, the doors slamming hard behind him. Pearl chastised her family in her native tongue.

Lindsey went to get up. Jeffrey put his hand on his wife's shoulder. "Give him a moment."

Grams said the same thing to Ivy where her eyes were still glued to the church doors.

Sammy leaned against the side of the church with his hands on his knees breathing heavily. It felt good to be in the fresh air and he concentrated on that—on the tightness in his throat being relieved as he gulped air.

Sammy heard a voice from behind the church. "Psst . . . Sammy."

He turned, his entire body tensing. It was Jesse Richards. Sammy would know that voice anywhere. Jesse stepped out of the fog, putting his finger over his mouth, signaling to Sammy not to yell.

For a frozen moment Sammy stared at Jesse. Jesse's was a face he hoped never to see again. "What do you want?" Sammy asked, taking a large step back. His voice echoed in his ears, but he knew he spoke in a whisper.

Jesse looked around cautiously and walked closer to Sammy. Sammy's body trembled as he attempted to stand tall. He fought the urge to run, sliding his hand into his pants pocket where his Swiss Army knife was. He always carried it with him now. He was ready for a fight if it came down to it, but after the letter left on his bed from Jesse, he needed to know what JD was up to. The only one he feared more than Jesse was Japhet Dean Leeds. Jesse was just a pawn; JD was the chessmaster. Knowing JD's next move was the only thing that was going to keep his family safe. Whether he liked it or not, for the moment, he was going to have to trust Jesse Richards.

"Easy Sammy," Jesse said, noticing the change in Sammy's stance. "I came to warn you."

"I could scream right now, and the whole church would come running." There was no threat in Sammy's voice. He already felt defeated. It was as if God was answering his apology for not dying by sending Death for him.

"Your grandmother," Jesse said, "don't trust her."

"What?" Sammy asked, his eyebrows furrowing.

"You heard me. She's not who you think she is."

Sammy, more than anyone, knew Anita Gomez could be eccentric and cruel at times, but she was his grandmother, and he didn't doubt she loved him.

"I trust her with my life."

PLEASANT MILLS CEMETERY

"Well don't."

"Why's that?"

"I'm not sure yet," Jesse admitted, scanning the tombstones on the side of the church as if he was looking for something or someone.

Sammy snickered, "Well Mr. Richards, if that's all you have to tell me, you wasted your time."

"No there's more. JD's working with someone he calls the Midwife."

"Midwife?" Sammy asked rhetorically.

"Yeah, beats me," Jesse said with a shoulder shrug. "You're the smart one. Figure it out for both of us, won't you?"

They heard footsteps approaching. Without hesitation, Jesse ran into the fog toward the woods. Sammy didn't know why he did it, but he walked toward the footsteps, making sure Jesse wasn't seen.

Anita Gomez walked up to her grandson and took his hand. She gave it a tight squeeze. "No one wishes you would have died Samuel Cameron."

Sammy nodded, fighting back his tears, she seemed so much like her old self in that moment.

Anita lifted her head as if scenting the air like a wild dog. "Something's in the air."

"Uh, yeah, fog. It's been that way for a while now Abby," Sammy said, trying not to sound too condescending but attempting to buy Jesse time.

Sammy didn't trust Jesse, not really. He wasn't sure why he was protecting him. He trusted his grandmother, she had always been there for him in her own way, but as she continued to squeeze his hand, he felt an uneasiness course through him.

Anita narrowed her eyes. "By something's in the air, I mean someone's near. Someone who has scared the birds away, someone who has silenced the very trees and breeze."

"Come on Abby," Sammys said, protecting Jesse Richards once again. "We better get inside. I'm sure Pastor Leeds is starting soon."

CHAPTER EIGHT
A Bump

A small repast was being held at church after the funeral where the ritualistic coffee hour took place on Sundays. Ivy and Grams entered the church addition through the side door. Ivy searched the repast's buffet line for Sammy. He wasn't there. She checked her phone, finding a text from him: My mom's not feeling well. We're not making it back to the church.

"What is it?" Mary asked, noticing the change in her granddaughter's countenance.

"Lindsey's not feeling well. Sammy's not making it to the repast."

"For the best," Mary said, filling her plate with pasta salad and coffee cake.

"What's that supposed to mean?"

"Just that it's been a rough day for Sammy."

Ivy exhaled like a bull. She hated when her grandmother was right. Ivy had wanted to run after Sammy when he left the church and wanted to comfort him at the cemetery. They felt like they were worlds apart, both standing on opposite sides of Timothy's casket, locking eyes over Sammy's soon to be buried friend.

Mary bit into a store-bought crumb cake. "Not like Lindsey's." The crumbs were bland, and the cake was dry. It stuck to the side of her mouth forcing her to cough. She covered her mouth with her handkerchief while she moved her tongue across the top of her denture trying to ease the tickle in her throat. When the coughing wouldn't cease, she chased the bit of stale cake with a cup of coffee. "Coffee's also, not like Lindsey's," she choked out with a coarse voice. Ivy handed her grandmother a water bottle. Grams guzzled it.

Ivy giggled. "Easy Grams, you're not wearing your Depends."

Mary nudged her granddaughter. "Easy kid, or you'll be walking home."

"I meant to tell you the old girl looks good," Ivy said, fixing her grandmother's hair for her.

Grams swatted her hands away. "I meant the car, not you."

Mary proudly raised her chin.

"Danny detailed it for me," Mary said with a big grin.

"I hope he gave you a senior discount. If you keep spending our money at Titan Tires, we'll never afford to get me my own car."

"Our money, that's cute. And if you consider free a discount, then yes."

"Wow, you two are getting serious," Ivy said with a nudge to her grandmother's arm.

Mary responded with a large smile as she eyed the desserts, looking for a moister cake to accompany her lunch. "Lindsey must be feeling pretty tired these days. I never thought I'd see the day . . . not one homemade dessert."

Ivy walked beside her grandmother robotically, her mind trailing off to what JD had told her. She scrunched a napkin in the ball of her hand and squeezed.

"I'd like to see Lindsey put on a little weight. She's the skinniest pregnant woman I've ever seen. There're more men in this room that look further along than her."

Ivy agreed, Lindsey Lopez looked like a skeleton dressed in skin. She had exaggerated when she told JD she looked like she swallowed a watermelon, but Lindsey did have a bump.

"She has a bump," Ivy said positively. Hoping some positive thinking will do some good. She was one of Pastor Uriah Leeds's positivity pushers after all.

"A bump? Please, I have more of a bump, and I haven't been able to get pregnant for over ten years. Not to mention, I do sit-ups every day."

Ivy rolled her eyes. "Try thirty years Grams, and please you haven't done a sit-up a day in your life."

"Well, I'm starting today," Mary said, turning her nose up at her smart-mouthed granddaughter. "Now that I'm dating a younger man, I need to keep up my girlish figure."

Ivy had to smile at the thought of her grandmother dating the mechanic from Titan Tires. "You and Danny are not dating. You took the station wagon in for a tune up. That's a professional relationship, not a romantic one."

"Not yet my dear. A classy lady plays hard to get."

"Oh, is that what you were doing when you let the air out of the tires last weekend . . . playing hard to get?" Ivy chuckled. "Or was that damsel in distress mode?"

Mary turned away from her granddaughter. "No idea what you're talking about."

Ivy would have loved to tease her grandmother some more about her fictional relationship with Danny the tire guy, but she was distracted. She was really worried about Sammy.

Ivy's phone vibrated; it was a text from Sammy: Gonna stop by in a bit, I need to see you.

"Let's go Grams. Bring the cake home and dunk it in your own coffee."

"Fine by me, I have to call Danny anyway."

Mary finished making up her plate to take home. Ivy didn't bother, her grandmother's coughing fit after taking a bite of the coffee cake convinced her nothing was worth eating. She was struggling to maintain her weight loss from last summer and decided to go home on an empty stomach.

She knew when she felt how she did, she would just feed her feelings, and eat as a distraction.

Once Mary secured tinfoil over her lunch, they hugged Mr. and Mrs. Chen and their young daughter goodbye before leaving. Ivy spotted Detective Steele standing in the cemetery next to Jesse Richards monument as they got into her grandmother's station wagon. She was alone and stood as still as a monument herself, staring at it as if to ask why.

CHAPTER NINE
Childhood Fear

When Sammy and his family got home from the cemetery his Aunt Francine was already there." Hey Aunt Fran," he said with a hug and a kiss.

"Hi sweetheart."

Anita came out of the house with her overnight bag gripped in her two hands.

"The twins and Abby are staying with me the next couple of days."

"Oh, okay," Sammy said, surprised to see his father with an overnight bag already packed for the twins.

Sammy and Jeffrey walked to Fran's car and said their goodbyes. They waved to the twins as Fran pulled out.

Sammy nervously turned to his father. Jeffrey's face was pale and blank, like he was going out of his way to try to look stony. Sammy could tell he was deliberately trying to hide something. "Dad, is something going on that you're not telling me?"

Jeffrey met his son's stare, trying to hold back his tears. Sammy watched his father's eyes glass over, his pulse surging.

"Dad, what is it?!"

"I'm taking your mother to the hospital. I should've taken her last night, but she wanted to be there for you today."

Sammy's eyes grew large. "Mom . . . is she okay?"

"I tried putting off telling you . . . "

Sammy knew what was coming next. It was his childhood fear, the fear his mother would get sick and die. He had seen the signs and shrugged them off as morning sickness. He told himself time and time again that's all it was. He couldn't handle his mother being sick again.

Sammy had fought for the last year to climb out of his dark mind, as if his body left Jesse's underground crypt but his mind never did. He knew the suffocating feeling that came with being in the dark and he felt it so poignantly now that it made him want to scream. Every second his father remained silent was another second a crushing pressure made each breath harder to take as his lungs fought against his ribcage for air.

Jeffrey's eyes confirmed Sammy's worst suspicion, but still he had to ask. "It's back, isn't it?"

Jeffrey ran his hands through his hair, tucking his dark locks behind his ears. "Yeah Sammy, it's back."

Sammy immediately dashed into his mother's room. Lindsey sat at the end of her bed. She looked as fragile as one of his sisters' china dolls. He rushed to her side, sitting down next to her. He took her hand in his. "Mom, are you going to be okay?"

"Sammy," Lindsey said as her eyes swelled with tears, "I wish I could tell you I was, but I'm not. I want you to make me a promise."

"Mom, don't do this." Sammy felt the tears forming in the corners of his eyes as sobs stung the back of his throat. He tried not to blink, his only defense against the advancing tears.

"Sammy, I want you to promise me you'll look after your father and your sisters for me."

"Mom, you know I always will."

Lindsey squeezed her son's hand. "I am so proud of you. I couldn't have asked for a better son."

Sammy hugged his mother. "I love you, Mom." He could feel her bones poking out of her skin, feeling a xylophone of vertebrates as his hand moved over her back. He knew then how truly sick she was. "I promise, Mom. I'll watch over them and Hugo too."

Lindsey wept; it came in a whirlwind of emotion. "Yes, and Hugo too."

They heard a knock on the door, their eyes lifting to see Jeffrey. He sat next to Sammy and hugged him along with his wife. "We're sorry we didn't tell you. We wanted things to be as normal as they could be until they weren't anymore."

CHAPTER TEN
Heart Lies

Mary Teller sat in her kitchen and dunked a church donut in coffee. She patiently waited on hold to the sound of instrumental pop to schedule maintenance for her station wagon at Titan Tires. She was too busy humming along between donut bites to hear Sammy's knock on the front door.

Ivy ran down the steps at the second knock. "How's your mom feeling?" Ivy asked, opening the door and leading Sammy to the living room couch.

Sammy sat down and looked at Ivy with devastated blue eyes. She had never seen them look like that, seen them so dull, like the life was zapped from them.

"Sammy, what is it?"

His lips trembled. "My dad drove her to the hospital."

Ivy raised her eyebrows in concern, JD's voice ringing in her ears like an ambulance's wail. "The hospital?!"

"Yeah, my mom is really, really sick. My family doesn't want anyone to know . . . but you're family, Teller. Her cancer is back, and it's spread." Ivy hugged Sammy, his hot tears falling the moment her arms encircled him. "I feel so helpless. I don't know what I'll do if I lose my mom."

"It's okay Sammy. She'll be okay."

"You don't get it," he said with no bite in his tone. "My mother's dying." He swallowed hard, pushing everything down. "My mom, she had a talk with me. She asked me to watch over everyone. She didn't say Hugo's name and when I said his name, she started to cry. I don't think he's gonna make it. They won't say it out loud, but I know it."

Ivy squeezed him harder. "Oh Sammy."

"I think they're both going to die."

Ivy couldn't think of anything to say that could comfort him. There are no words for occasions like these, but she wondered if there was something she could do. JD hadn't lied about Lindsey being sick. If he didn't lie about that, maybe he *could* help. JD had asked her just a few nights ago if she would do anything for Sammy, even make a deal with him. The thought of it had rocked her body harder than hard rock, but now as he cried in her arms, she thought she would do just that—make a deal with a devil.

Sammy buried his face in Ivy's chest to stifle his cries, ensuring Grams couldn't hear from the kitchen. "What am I going to do?" His hot breath on her skin made her quiver in fear. She could feel his pain cut through her like a knife. She wanted to make it stop, and she would. She knew that now. She was corruptible and she would pay JD's price.

"It's not gonna be okay Ivy. I'm never gonna be okay again. That's what my dad told me. He said he'll never be okay again. And that goes for the both of us. He's so right. He's always right. I hate that about him. My mom is everything to me. She's the heart of our family. We can't lose her . . . not like this. And not Baby Hugo too. It's not fair."

"Sammy, believe me when I say things are going to be okay."

Ivy knew where her heart lied, it was with Sammy Lopez, and she would sacrifice herself, her soul or whatever else JD required of her for Sammy and his family, because that was what it meant to love.

CHAPTER ELEVEN
A White Haze

Ivy watched through the living room window as Sammy pulled out of her driveway and headed to the hospital. Mary was still on the phone when Ivy let herself free fall onto the couch. She folded her hands over her heart. It ached for Sammy. She detested that JD was right about Lindsey's cancer, and more so, that he was right about her, she would do anything for Sammy, even hunt down the Jersey Devil.

"*You know where to find me,*" Ivy muttered to herself, looking up at the ceiling as if staring at it hard enough would open a portal directly to him. Ivy felt like her brain was turning into mush and pouring out her ears, and with it any clues to where she could find Japhet Dean Leeds. "Thanks brain," she mumbled to herself. She rubbed her temples in a circular motion, hoping to spark an idea. "I have no clue where to find him." Letting out a huff of air, she thought out loud. "He's the Jersey Devil . . . he lives in the woods stalking people or something like that according to Pastor Leeds." She thought for a moment before blurting out, "the woods. I can find him in the woods."

Ivy rolled off the couch and sprinted up the stairs to her bed. She scraped her knees on the uneven hardwood floor, snatching the grimoire from underneath it. She'd combed over it after she got home from church, looking for the spell that would magically make Lindsey better, fearing the worse after Sammy's text message, but there was none. So that meant she couldn't save Lindsey without his help, and it also meant JD wanted the grimoire for another reason. She didn't like the idea of handing it over to JD, but it was worth the risk, besides most of the spells seemed silly to her.

She lied to herself as she headed downstairs, thinking JD had supernatural toe fungus modern medicine couldn't cure and that's why he wanted the spell book.

The old stairs croaked under Ivy's feet.

"Where are you going now Ives?" Grams asked as she twirled the phone cord and giggled into the receiver.

"Taking a walk around the neighborhood. You know Grams, exercise," she said, placing her hands on her belly.

"Hold up Missy. You know Jesse's still out there."

"I'm meeting . . . umm, I'm meeting Elsa and Tammy."

"You're hanging out with the girls?" Mary asked a little more than surprised.

"They're youth group members Grams, don't get yourself all worked up. I still have only one friend and am miserable to the core."

"Oh good," Grams said sarcastically with a chuckle. "Have a good time being miserable deary. Misery loves company you know."

"I know Grams, thanks, and you better make sure Danny isn't charging you for a phone consult."

Ivy walked out the front door before her grandmother could rebuttal. She headed down Pleasant Mills Road in a near jog and entered the entrance to the historical park of Batsto. Thanks to the dense fog, Ivy could hardly see her feet as she took the trail labeled *Red Path.*

The farther Ivy went, the narrower the dirt path felt, making her tense. The trees seemed to close in on her. Ivy imagined the trees uprooting themselves by tugging on their roots and moving closer to her when she wasn't looking, standing still to avoid detection when her eyes darted to them.

FOREST OF SECRETS

Before too long, Ivy got herself worked up into a panic and felt safer going off the path. She had no idea where she was going or how to find JD, even though he seemed to think she could. She had decided to go to Batsto because Pastor Uriah Leeds told them he first met JD as a child at Batsto's sawmill. Ivy reasoned it was a good place to start her search. The problem was Batsto Village was nestled in Wharton Forest, New Jersey's largest state forest, spanning over 120,000 acres. But as Ivy walked through the foggy woods, something about it seemed familiar to her. The unseen path under her feet washed over her like a case of déjà vu. Ivy felt like she had walked this path before, many times. She felt like her hands had graced the tops of the budding shrubs she now walked past. A strange feeling overcame Ivy. She couldn't shake the idea she was traveling back home after being away for a long time, a longingness in her growing.

Ivy stirred from her nostalgic state when a wild blueberry bush gripped unto her shorts. The rough branches felt like tiny little teeth biting her bare leg. She rubbed her knee. "Should've put pants on stupid."

Ivy tended to her bleeding kneecap as four walls of fog rose from the ground surrounding her. Ivy was painfully aware of the silence. Without her footsteps, the woods were still—too still. She felt like the fog was swallowing her up. She could no longer make out her own hands in the white haze.

Frightened, Ivy spun around in circles, straining to see an inch in front of her nose. The familiarity of the unseen path disappeared in the fog. She was lost. She had no idea what direction she came from and where she was going.

Ivy stretched her hands out in front of her and took baby steps. She stopped when her sneaker hit something. She ran her hand across the rough bark of a tree lying across the ground acting as a natural barricade, stopping her from moving forward.

She felt a light touch on her shoulder. "Hello Ivy."

Ivy turned in surprise, the combination of fear and dread making her heartbeat faster. "Jesse?!"

Jesse put his hands on Ivy's shoulders. "Ivy, please listen to me. Whatever you think you're doing to help Sammy, you're not. JD will twist it. Do something bad."

Ivy pushed Jesse off of her.

"Please Ivy, I care about you. I don't want you to get hurt."

"Care about me?!' Ivy scoffed. Ivy could just make out Jesse's defining features in the fog, his face punching through it, a face once upon a time she found handsome. "Jesse, you kidnapped my boyfriend and killed his friends!"

"He was your ex-boyfriend at the time, and it wasn't me that killed those boys. It was JD, the very someone you're looking for."

"Excuse me, Mr. Attention to Detail! You're still an accessory to murder."

"You don't understand," Jesse pleaded with his hazel eyes that looked like two golden moons.

"I understand perfectly fine. You were helping yourself and I'm helping Sammy."

Ivy stormed off into the fog trying to put as much distance between her and Jesse as she possibly could.

Jesse grabbed Ivy's arm to stop her. "He'll turn it around on you. I know Ives. I've been in your place. Trust me."

"Trust you?!" she said, her voice like a whip. "I'd trust JD before I'd trust you! I don't even know you, Jesse. You're one big lie!"

"And you know him?!" Jesse asked shocked, tightening his grip on Ivy's arm.

Ivy didn't answer. She owed him nothing. She pulled her arm out of his grasp and ran. Jesse grabbed Ivy and wrapped his arms around her as he wrangled her in. "Ivy," he said as he tried to restrain her. "He's evil."

"Aren't we all!" Ivy shouted. "You're a sicko! Stay away from me!"

Ivy fought against Jesse's hold, using her legs to kick at his knees. Her foot met his crotch. He released his grip, standing nearly buckled over. Ivy took a step closer to Jesse and kicked him in the chest, sending him lunging back.

Jesse stumbled over a fallen tree branch, falling backward. "IVY HELP!"

Ivy heard the quick succession of branches snapping. They crunched and cracked for a few moments before a loud bang ricocheted off the trees.

The woods were silent again. "Jesse?!" Ivy called into the fog. The panic in her voice was evident, it shook like her hands. "Jesse where are you . . . are you okay?" Ivy took out her phone and shined it through the fog. "Jesse!" she yelled. Ivy saw a steep drop that gave way to a ravine. She slid down the hillside on her buttocks to look for Jesse.

Ivy found him at the bottom of the ravine near a small stream. She raced to him. His body lay where it fell. He was propped up against a thick tree trunk, his face covered in blood from where his head smacked it. The smell of metallic rust overpowered the scents of leaves and fresh water, slapping Ivy in the face with the brutalness of reality. "JESSE!" Ivy screamed. She shook his shoulders. His head rolled back, his neck fully exposed as his golden eyes looked to the heavens. "Jesse wake up! Please Jesse, wake up! I'm so sorry!"

"He's dead," Ivy heard JD say in a low voice from behind her. She turned to see him standing in the fog like an unholy apparition, more fake than real—otherworldly. His face seemingly made of fog while his dark eyes pierced through her.

Tears streamed down Ivy's face. "He can't be dead!" Ivy was on the verge of hyperventilating. "Oh my God, I killed him. He was my friend and I killed him!" She struggled to exhale. She put her hands on her knees before falling to them.

JD crouched next to her and hugged her. "It wasn't your fault," he whispered in a sincere voice in her ear.

She breathed in the sweet, smoky scent left from his cigarettes and the fresh smell of the outdoors trapped in his dark tendrils. She buried her face in his chest, the smell of his hair was too familiar for her to be that close to. "He's dead because of me."

JD put a hand on Jesse's knee. "Don't worry, he will be reborn."

"Then why are you crying?" Ivy asked confused, lifting her face to see tears roll from the corners of JD's eyes.

"I love Jesse more than he will ever understand. It hurts me to see him like this. I never wanted to hurt him or cause him pain. When I took Jesse in, my goal was to help him, but he never saw it like that. No matter what, no matter how many lives he lives, Jesse always suffers. He's a good man, Ms. Teller. I hope you won't be too hard on him when he comes back."

Ivy sniffled. "Back, now?" Ivy knew when JD said reborn, he wasn't talking about Jesse being reborn in the afterlife. Like he said, Jesse had lived many lives and would live many more, but she didn't know exactly what that entailed.

"Soon. Very soon. Jesse will be reborn younger . . . the age he was when he satisfied our contract. He will be arriving at Uriah's house with no memories of what he did in his last life. No memory of what he did to our Sammy. Jesse will not remember collecting the boys for me. He will not remember you killing him. No one will know. It's our secret."

Ivy didn't like the way he said that and regardless of if only they knew, she would always know. "It was an accident," she said, wiping her tears on the sleeve of her T-shirt."

He gently moved aside a loose strand of her hair, tucking it behind her ear. "I know it was. You could never hurt anyone. You're the champion of those who have no voice, as you were for me when I was born. You will always be my savior, Ivy."

Ivy avoided his gaze, sitting knee to knee with him on the forest floor as if they were praying to each other, she his savior and he her—she didn't know what. He was a lot of things, but he wasn't her savior.

Ivy watched as Jesse's body disappeared into the fog. The last thing she saw was a glimpse of his yellow-gold eyes. It was as if he just faded out of existence.

"If you need to hate someone, Ms. Teller, hate me." JD's voice lowered. "All of this is my fault, and I'm sorry. So very sorry. Jesse was only doing as his father asked. He's a good boy, following his father's every whim. It's not his fault, it's mine. Jesse has always known it's best to give me what I want. I am a loving father, but I'm tyrannical at heart. There is too much bad in me to ever do good."

Her eyes locked with his. She saw the same soulful brown eyes the Midwife had seen. "That's not true. There's good in you. I saw it."

A blush bloomed across the bridge of his nose and cheeks. He bowed his head, no longer able to look into her eyes. He seemed so helpless to her like the infant that'd cried out for help all those years ago. It made her heart ache for him. In that moment, with his cheeks colored rose and his brown eyes in shadows, while the fog embraced them in its shadowy arms, he was not a monster or a murderer, he was something more—something beautiful, that wasn't supposed to be there but somewhere else, Heaven maybe—maybe Hell, but not there in the woods with her.

Ivy wiped the tear that fell from his eye, his face lifting to hers. Her eyes went to his lips as they parted as if he was going to say something but said nothing. Her lips mirrored his, their eyes locking again. Ivy felt like there was electricity in the air or maybe it was magnetic plates under the Earth's surface, that nudged her closer to him, their noses grazing as they'd done in her dream.

In his eyes she saw what she had seen in Pastor Leeds's eyes when she first arrived in Pleasant Mills last summer—Heaven. She knew it was crazy to think it, but that was what she saw. In his brown eyes, she saw beauty and grace, and happiness, but she also saw desperation and sadness and loneliness. More than that, it was as if his eyes were calling out to her for forgiveness. She couldn't look away, she felt entranced as she had been when she first saw the red glow of the jarred heart shine out of Pastor Leeds's attic. No, she couldn't look away, she could only move closer. Their lips touched; a jolt of energy passed between them. She pulled away from him, her chest heaving. His eyes seemed wild now, his blush deepening. He pressed his lips to hers, cradling her in his arms, her back forming to his hands.

JD looked at Ivy mystified; it was the same look he'd given her long ago. "Please tell me you remember me. Please, I've waited so long for you."

Her heart pounded fiercely in her chest. Ivy tried to speak, but her voice got lost in her throat. A strange sensation came over her. It was more than a passing familiarity of a déjà vu moment. She felt like she belonged there in the woods with JD.

"I remember wanting to help you," she managed to get out.

Urgently, as if she could disappear into the fog like Jesse, he kissed her again, her lips forming to his now. They fit perfectly together like they were meant to be. He smelled of the woods. His skin had the scent of a freshly cut pine tree oozing sticky sap from its woody flesh, nature's sweet thick clot perfuming his hair. She loved the familiar scent of his hair more than anything, her hands going to it, tugging on his locks to bring his head closer to her. She could almost remember it. Remember the first time she smelled him. She felt like she was living a lie as Ivy Teller as she kissed her creation in the fog laden ravine—she was the Midwife. She was as helpless as JD's eyes—defenseless, and JD was her savior.

CHAPTER TWELVE
The Mistake

Ivy turned away from JD, her eyes focusing on his suit jacket where it lay on the ground next to her. She honed in on the dandelion tucked in his suit pocket. The bright yellow flower shone like a miniature sun in the fog. It too was reminiscent to her. But of what and of when? Her mind traveled back to the vase of dandelions in her friend Rosa's house, the ones she said were from her uncle, and shuddered. For a brief instant, she wondered if somehow Rosa was involved in all of this, but dismissed it at once, her mind bouncing to the dandelion crushed in the palm of her hand when she awoke from her screaming nightmare of an eyeless Rosa. She wondered if it was from him. A gift from her past, from a man from her past. She wanted to ask him why she couldn't remember, why she only had bits and pieces of her memory, but she was too afraid to learn the truth, afraid she wouldn't like what he'd tell her.

Ivy nervously looked back at JD's face, glimpsing the more than human gleam in his eye and diverted her vision to the fog covered forest floor. She knew it to be true, the flower was from him.

Ivy's body quivered like a leaf in the wind as she adjusted her top. JD's fingertips reached for hers. "Are you alright?"

The feel of his skin on hers was too much for her to process, she pulled her hand away from his. The reality of what just happened sunk in, her betrayal ripping through her, leaving her raw. "Please," Ivy said in a whimper. "Don't touch me. Don't ever touch me again."

JD withdrew his hand confused, his eyes searching. "I thought . . ."

"You thought wrong," she said sharply, refusing to look at him. She couldn't look at him, it would make everything that just happened too real. "It was a mistake." Ivy wiped her tears on the back of her hand. "This can never happen again. I love Sammy."

The words stung, striking JD's heart like a bolt of lightning. He resisted grabbing his chest. He too loved Sammy, but Ivy's words meant she didn't love him.

"What happened to Jesse and this, what just happened, is a secret."

He silently nodded, finishing buttoning his shirt before sliding on his jacket.

"I came looking for you because I need your help." Ivy reached for her oversize purse and pulled out the grimoire.

That brightened JD's mood; the corner of his lip twisted into a grin. "It's been many years since I've laid eyes on my mother's spell book. It went missing some time ago."

Her eyes darted to him. "Your mother's?"

"Yes, whose did you think it was?"

"Um . . . Pastor Leeds's," Ivy guessed, tucking her hair behind her ears. They had found it in Pastor Leeds's mailbox although it hadn't been mailed to him but to Pastor Steelmen, the pastor Uriah replaced after she died of a heart attack.

Ivy had never thought that the spell book, at some point, belonged to Deborah Smith Leeds. Jesse had told Sammy that JD's mother was a powerful witch, but the last name Leeds was as common as they came in South Jersey. Even Grams's big crush's surname was Leeds. Somehow, she never made the connection and neither did Sammy, and he was all about conspiracies.

JD chuckled. "Uriah's book is the Bible. It's been that way since he was a small child. He was born to spread the good word of his Lord. He's always believed in a higher power to a fault. His faith is the very reason I was able to make a deal with him in the first place; he mistook me as his guardian angel."

Ivy withheld her judgment for the moment, tricking children didn't seem so bad next to murdering them and devouring their hearts. Nevertheless, it made her sick to her stomach to think she thought he was anything more than a monster.

JD tapped on the worn cover of the grimoire. "This book, this book was my mother's pride and joy. It's a compilation of my family's secrets."

"That's why you want it then?" Nostalgic reasons?" There's nothing in here that can help Lindsey, I checked."

JD ran his hand over the binding of the grimoire. "This is precisely what I need. May I borrow it?"

She didn't like that he dodged the question. She'd try to get a straight answer out of him another way. "I was thinking you could just tell me what spell you were going to use, and I'd cast it, but like I said I didn't find anything in there that cured cancer. So, maybe if you could just point to the spell, I'd be on my way and out of your hair."

JD's grin became a smile. "You're thinking about it all wrong Ms. Teller. Now may I borrow the spell book?"

"What does that mean? 'Thinking about it all wrong?'"

"It is I, who will be curing the cancer not the spell book."

"Oh," she said, twirling a lock of her hair around her finger anxiously. "You want to borrow the spell book because you can't just cure the cancer without some sort of a trade or deal, and you want the book back because it was your mother's, and you want it from me because I happened to be the one who has it at the moment. Am I right?"

He beamed. "You're on the right track. Now if you don't mind, time is of the essence."

"I need to be more than on the right track. What are you going to do with the spell book?"

"Borrow it."

"Borrow implies you're going to give it back."

"And I will. I promise."

Ivy tried to collect her thoughts but being so close to JD distracted her. "You're not tricking me?"

"Tricking you . . . How so?" he asked, raising an eyebrow.

Ivy's pulse raced, her eyes darting to his again. The sadness in them was masked with something else, something dark. "I'm not sure, but I won't help you kill kids. I won't." Her voice wavered in and out. "And I won't help you hurt Sammy's family."

"Understood," he said with a smile. "I would never ask you to kill anyone, and you have my word no harm will come to a member of Sammy's family. I came to you to help Sammy and his family, Ms. Teller, and that's what I plan on doing. Are there any other terms before I borrow your spell book?"

Ivy thought about it. "It's not mine, but yeah that sounds good. I do want it back though, okay?"

JD leaned in close to Ivy and whispered in her ear, his breath making her break out in gooseflesh. "Of course, Ms. Teller. You have my word and whatever else you want of me."

She trembled at the feel of his lips so close to her. She turned her face, her lips just grazing his cheek. "So that's it? You borrow the spell book then you heal Lindsey and the baby, then give it back."

"That's it. It's that simple."

"That's not how deals work," she said with panic traveling up the back of her throat. Ivy was worried JD was getting something over on her. She'd hoped he would be willing to help Sammy with the spell book without any strings attached, as his new goal in life was to have Sammy like him, but she doubted he would. "This sounds too good to be true. What do you get out of this?"

"I get to borrow the spell book of course Ms. Teller."

"Oh, duh," she said. "Okay deal."

He took her hand and kissed it above her knuckles. "Deal it is."

Ivy looked up toward the sky as water droplets struck her forehead. Her eyes returned to JD, but he was gone. Spreading over the fog like a melancholy symphony as the rain came down was a low whistling. The music notes sent a shiver down her spine, forcing her to her feet. It was as if he was serenading her.

As his song moved into the chorus, she cried. She cried for so many reasons. Out of confusion, out of being alone, out of being lost, for Jesse, for JD, for Sammy, and most of all for herself.

She ran. She ran as fast as her shaky legs could carry her, not knowing and not caring where she ran too. She fought through the brush with her hands, ignoring the branches that scratched at her soft flesh.

When Ivy came to the side of the road she collapsed on her hands and knees. She looked around. She knew where she was. She forced herself to her feet and ran down the sidewalk to her grandmother's house.

CHAPTER THIRTEEN
Baths Salts

"What happened to you? Grams asked when Ivy came in the front door covered in mud.

"I fell."

"I'd say. It looks like you were mud wrestling."

Ivy grumbled, "taking a shower."

Ivy quickly made her way to the bathroom and locked the door. Throwing her clothes in the hamper, she hopped in the shower. She didn't wait for the water to warm up. She rinsed off the mud as the ice-cold water made her pant.

Once most of the mud was down the drain, Ivy shut the shower off and went to the sink vanity. She got down on her knees and rummaged through the cabinet. Anita had given Ivy something like a witch care basket. She filled it with all sorts of things Ivy had never seen before and some things she had. She could make out incenses, bath-salts, and dried herbs, but the rest of it looked like it came from outer space. Anita's hopes were that Ivy may be more inclined to practice her craft in private, being that she refused to join Sammy in any lessons in witchcraft, healing, spell casting, or potion making.

Ivy had taken the care basket from Anita and shoved it under the bathroom sink and forgot about it.

It was just another step taken to be a normal teenager. Normal teenagers don't have witch care baskets and normal teenagers don't have dreams about legendary demons, and so she never told anyone about the dream she had about Japhet Dean Leeds and about her being the Midwife. She wanted it to just be a dream, all of her dreams about him to be just figments of her restless brain, and not a gateway into her past. Denial was a powerful thing and it had gotten her this far, but if she didn't find the bath salts from Anita soon, there would be no way of hiding what she'd done from Sammy and definitely not from his grandmother.

"Where is it?!" she asked, her search becoming frantic as she tossed everything on the bathroom floor. Tears rolled down her cheeks. "Come on . . . come on, where are you?!"

Ivy was about to give up hope, when she found the bath salts in the very back of the cabinet under the extra toilet paper. She hastily went to the claw foot tub. Having rinsed away the dirt residue, she let the tub fill. After sprinkling Anita's homemade bath salts into the water, she got in to soak.

Ivy was going to perform her own soul cleanse and wash away all traces of JD—all traces of her betrayal. She wanted her secret to remain between her and JD. If Sammy found out it would destroy their relationship and her life. Sammy meant everything to her. She shook her head at herself, trying to understand why she would jeopardize what she had with Sammy for a monster.

Ivy scrubbed with her loofa. She wished she had Anita's scrub brush, but with a little extra force, she was still able to scrub her skin red. This made Ivy feel better about what she had done, despite her scratches burning under the burden of her scrubbing and the bath salts.

When Ivy's soul cleanse had left her skin raw, she leaned back in the tub and closed her eyes. She may have washed away JD's magical residue, but she couldn't get him out of her head. In that twinkling in the woods, she had never wanted someone as badly as she wanted him. She could lie to herself, and tell herself it was otherwise, but her body ached for his and she gave into temptation. He seemed so special to her in that moment, as he did long ago when he was first brought back from the dead. But now that Ivy was alone and back in the comforts of her home, she struggled to understand her actions. She knew who and what JD was, but it was like she'd said to Jesse, she would trust JD before him. He didn't deserve that, she owed him nothing, just like she owed Jesse nothing. She wasn't the Midwife; she was Ivy Teller. Tears flowed from her closed eyes when she thought about Sammy. She couldn't bear to think how deeply she'd betrayed him. Ivy knew her heart belonged to Sammy Lopez forever.

CHAPTER FOURTEEN
Sweet Relief

Ivy was listening to music in bed when her phone went off. It was Sammy. Just seeing his name on her phone made her stomach tie in knots. She turned off her playlist, answering her phone, and pressing her cheek to the screen.

"Ivy great news! Hugo's here!" Sammy was talking a mile a minute. Ivy didn't have a split second to respond. "He's way early, but he's good! Better than good, he's great! And so is my mom! You're not gonna believe this—she doesn't have cancer. Her doctors say the pregnancy must've thrown off her bloodwork. My dad says if he wasn't so happy, he'd sue the crap out of the hospital."

Ivy exhaled slowly into the phone, relieved JD kept up his end of the bargain. "That's great news."

"I can't wait for you to see Hugo. He's so cute. Can you come to the hospital? I wanna see you."

There was silence on the phone.

"Ivy? Ivy are you there?!"

"Uh yeah Sammy, I'm here. I'm just so happy . . . I don't know what to say." She was happy, but it was mingled with so many other feelings: regret, shame, fear.

"Say you're coming to the hospital."

"I am. I'll be there soon."

"Kay. I love you."

Ivy's words were still stuck in her throat when Sammy hung up. "I love you too."

Sammy wrapped his arms around Ivy the moment she came off the elevator. She sniffed in his cologne as he squeezed her. She was happy he smelled nothing like the outdoorsy scent of JD. She felt like she hadn't seen him in days. She missed him. He was a sight for sore eyes.

Thanks to Sammy's cherry-red bloodshot eyes, Ivy could tell he'd been crying, but now, as he pointed at his baby brother from behind a large viewing window, he wore the largest smile she had ever seen. "Right there," he said, with a tap on the glass, "that's Hugo."

"Why is he in a hamster cage?" Ivy asked curiously.

"Teller, you're funny."

Ivy smiled awkwardly, giving him one of her funny faces.

"It's cause' he's a preemie. The doctor said he has to be in there for a little bit." Sammy scratched his head as he thought. "I'm not really sure why . . . I think it's like a heat lamp or something."

"He's so small."

"Yeah, crazy right, but he's four pounds even and healthy. The nurse said they have way smaller."

"Wow really?" Ivy said as she kept her eyes on baby Hugo. "Hard to believe."

Sammy nodded, taking Ivy's hand. "It's true, but uh, we can go see my mom now. She's feeling great."

CHAPTER FIFTEEN
A Surprise Visit

Uriah Leeds had just finished brushing his teeth when he heard a knock on his front door. "Early," he said to himself. He closed the medicine cabinet and quickly made his way downstairs. He opened the door to see a teenage boy with dirty blond hair. He had hazel brown eyes that burned with a golden intensity and a pleasant smile.

Uriah threw his arms around the boy, recognizing him at once. "Jesse?!" Uriah said shocked. I've been so worried about you." Uriah looked Jesse over with wonder. "What's happened to you?"

"I don't know." Uriah gave him an evaluating look. "I don't even know how I came to be on your doorstep. Just that I'm here. I must've died and been brought back." He looked at his small hands. "I'm a teenager again."

Uriah had never expected Jesse to show up on his doorstep, let alone as a teenager. Sammy had told them what Jesse said about him being reborn when he dies to come back to Pleasant Mills at the age of sixteen, the age he was when he made his deal with JD, with no memories but the memories of his first life. Therefore, although Uriah was surprised to see him, it wasn't a complete shock.

Uriah gave him a warm smile. "You're so—"

Jesse cut him off, "young."

Uriah let out a light laugh. "I was going to say short. Come in. Let's talk while I make you breakfast."

Jesse walked into the rectory and looked around. His eyes darted from one thing to the next as he followed Uriah into the kitchen. He ran his hand over a crocheted table runner on the kitchen table. "You dating an old lady Uriah?"

Uriah laughed. "Same Jesse. No. Furniture came with the house. And, as for the crochet pieces, they were gifts. The ladies at church love to crochet me things, especially doilies."

"It's okay to give things away Uriah," he chuckled in his high-pitched laugh.

Uriah smiled at that. He opened the refrigerator and pulled out a carton of eggs. "I don't know . . . I think they make this old place feel homey."

"You always did have an old soul."

Jesse pulled out a chair and took a seat at the kitchen table. He fixated on Uriah's centerpiece, a white ceramic vase that housed plastic daisies. Jesse pulled the table runner closer to him so he could see his reflection in the vase. He touched his youthful cheeks and thought about what he just said as he nibbled on his lip nervously. "Um. . . Uriah how much do you know about my past?"

Uriah turned away from the hot stove to look at Jesse. "Nothing. You never told me. But you told a boy in town some things about yourself."

"Like?"

"That like me, you made a deal with JD, and you like me, will keep being reborn. That little insight is probably the only reason why I didn't fall over when I saw you at the door."

"I know the feeling. Luckily, I came back with a general sense of awareness, otherwise I would've thought cars were UFOs."

Uriah laughed. "I guess part of me expected something unexpected like this. Sammy, the boy you told, said when you come back you have no memories. Is it true? You can't remember anything about the last couple of months?"

Jesse looked down at the hardwood floor as he anxiously touched the small, gray stone that hung from a necklace around his neck. "I remember only my first life."

Uriah nodded. "So, you don't remember anything, not even bits and pieces?" Uriah asked, forking eggs onto a ceramic plate, thinking of his own scattered memory.

"No nothing at all. Just my first life and I think I better tell you this time around."

"Of course," Uriah said, putting two plates of scrambled eggs on the table and taking a seat next to a young Jesse Richards. Uriah pushed a plate of eggs closer to Jesse. "It's the only thing I can make without starting a kitchen fire."

"Smells great. Thanks Uriah." Jesse moved his undercooked eggs with his fork. They jiggled like gelatin on his plate. "I've always trusted you Uriah . . . You were the pastor when I was a boy. You always had a good heart." Jesse paused to pull out a piece of an eggshell.

"Good to know," Uriah said with a kind smile. He put his hand on Jesse's shoulder. "It's okay Jesse, you can tell me."

It was hard for Jesse, but he told Uriah everything. Jesse told Uriah about the deal he made with JD that brought him back to life as a sixteen-year-old. Jesse told Uriah how his pride blindsided him to enter into a contract with JD, a contract that had him take ownership of his father's possessions, and what it had cost him.

Jesse confided in Uriah about murdering his wife, Mona Wolff, on their wedding night. With great difficulty, Jesse told Uriah how he carved out Mona's heart for JD. Jesse left out the details, they were private. They were too hard to say out loud. He had never told anyone about killing his first wife. In his wedding chamber that faithless night, long ago, two people lost their lives. Mona to Jesse's blade and Jesse to himself. He was never the same.

Jesse's eyes swelled with tears. "Can we keep my dealings with JD between us Uriah. I don't want people to know. I'm ashamed."

"Of course. This will stay between us." Uriah could see the stress on young Jesse's face, all his regrets. He hugged him. Jesse tried to hold back his emotions, but he couldn't. Being a teenager again brought his old feelings for Mona to the surface. Young Jesse was lifetimes removed from Mona's murder, but he felt like it just happened. When he saw his reflection in the vase on the kitchen table, he felt like he was that young eager-eyed boy all over again, about to make the biggest mistake of his life. His nerves felt like a live wire.

"Thank you for your understanding. I wish everyone was like you Uriah."

Uriah squeezed Jesse's shoulder. "I will always be here for you. Now you better eat up before your eggs get cold."

Uriah was happy Jesse was back, but he knew not everyone would be. When Jeffrey Lopez knocked on his door a few months ago and claimed it was Jesse who had kidnapped Sammy, Uriah felt his heart crack. He couldn't imagine the Jesse he knew to be capable of anything he was accused of.

Uriah knew in his heart, the man helping the Jersey Devil was not the real Jesse Richards. Uriah had known the real Jesse, a kind, caring friend. He had seen a different side to him while Jesse had cared for him when he was ill. Jesse had indeed become a good friend and Uriah valued that friendship.

Uriah watched Jesse slowly eat his eggs, grateful a teenage Jesse Richards scarcely resembled his older self. He was surprised how short Jesse was for a man that would grow to be so tall. He hoped this disparity would help pass Jesse off as a different Jesse, his nephew.

Jesse took another bite of his runny eggs. "You're not eating?" Jesse asked.

Uriah took a deep breath in. He knew Jesse had no recollection of what the 'old Jesse' did just a few months ago, but he had to tell him. Uriah was committed to Jesse getting a fresh start in Pleasant Mills and that meant helping him make amends for the 'old Jesse's' past crimes whether he remembered them or not.

Uriah nervously drummed his fingers on the table. "Jesse, I need to tell you something . . . Please know I don't judge you."

Jesse put his fork down. "Okay."

"A few months back an older version of you stayed with me."

Jesse nibbled on his bottom lip again, he already didn't like where this was going. "Um . . . okay."

"I know you were only doing what JD asked of you. I know that . . . And I know my hands are not clean in all of this, but I need to tell you what happened, so you don't make the same mistakes twice."

"It's okay, tell me what I did."

It was hard for Jesse to listen. He felt his heart ache in his chest as his long-standing friend told him the part the 'old Jesse' had played in Sammy Lopez's abduction and the deaths of Zachary Lewis, Tyrone Jones, Louie Grindhouse, and Timothy Chen.

"Oh my God, what was I thinking?" Jesse asked, covering his face with his hands. "What's wrong with me?"

Uriah hugged Jesse again. "Things will work out differently this time. I'm here for you."

Jesse couldn't respond.

"You mostly kept to yourself when you came to live with me last year. I don't think most people will recognize you and if they do, they'll just think they're seeing things. The Lopez family are good friends of mine. It's my hope we can all be friends. They're very loving people. I'm sure they'll forgive you Jesse, if you ask."

Jesse lowered his hands and stared into Uriah's sky-blue eyes. "Do you forgive me?"

"You don't have to ask. You're like a brother to me. JD was right about that."

JESSE RICHARDS

CHAPTER SIXTEEN
Breakfast for an Army

Lindsey woke up feeling better than she had in a long time. She came home from the hospital just yesterday and already felt like herself this morning. She couldn't wait to get back to the hospital to see Hugo, but first it was time to make her family breakfast. She kissed her still sleeping husband and quietly went downstairs.

When Jeffrey awoke to find his wife missing, he panicked. He had nightmares of just that, life without his wife. He jumped out of bed and opened the bedroom door. Smelling bacon cooking, he leaned in the doorway and sighed in relief before going downstairs in his pajamas, which was not his usual.

"You're doing too much," Jeffrey whispered in his wife's ear, hugging her from behind. Lindsey was already dressed. Her hair and makeup were done perfectly. She had her favorite apron tied around a flowered sundress. She greeted her husband with the tilt of her head, planting a kiss on his cheek.

Jeffrey released his hug but not before stealing another kiss. He looked over the food waiting to be cooked on the kitchen island. "Do you think you should be doing this? You just got home. And you're making enough food to feed an army."

"I feel great."

He wrapped his arms around her again and playfully pulled her away from the stove. "You keep saying that, but I think you should take it easy."

"I just want to make breakfast for my family. Let me do this," she said defensively.

"Okay." He kissed her cheek, not wanting to press the issue. He took a seat at the kitchen island. "I'm not going to lie. I miss your cooking and you look great," he said, his eyes traveling up his wife's long legs. "How long did the doctor say we have to wait before we can work on baby five?"

Lindsey beamed, ignoring her husband's question. "I'm going to invite Pastor Leeds and Mary and Ivy for breakfast. It's been a long time since everyone shared a meal."

"Sounds good. I'll call Uriah and I'll let Sammy call Ivy."

Lindsey gave her husband a quick peck on the cheek before going back to the stove.

Uriah had just gotten up to start a pot of coffee when his phone rang.

"Morning Uriah, Lindsey is making a big breakfast and wants to have you over. Hope you haven't eaten yet."

"Got room for two?" Uriah asked as he watched Jesse busily pick out more eggshells from his breakfast.

"Yeah of course. Who you bringing to breakfast?"

"This is going to sound crazy, but Jesse Richards."

Jeffrey went silent, rage taking over him.

"It's not what you're thinking Jeffrey. It's Jesse, but it's not him. He showed up at my door this morning, a teenager with no memories. —Well some, but none from the last year."

"A teenager?!"

"Yes, he's sixteen."

"Sixteen?" Jeffrey asked confused. "Uh . . . so how is it possible Jesse is a teenager now? That just doesn't make sense."

"Remember what Sammy said?"

"Yeah, I remember," Jeffrey said, his hand raking back his hair. "That doesn't mean it makes sense."

"Perhaps not, but I'm telling you a sixteen-year-old Jesse Richards is sitting at my kitchen table right now."

Jeffrey closed his eyes, trying to wrap his mind around the impossibility of it all. "Uh . . . even if everything you say is true, it still doesn't change what he did."

"I know that, I do. And so does Jesse. I told him everything that happened during his last life here in Pleasant Mills, what he did to Sammy and the rest of the kids. He wants to help us bring JD down."

"Can we trust him? He was helping JD before. What's stopping him from doing it again?"

"We can trust him, Jeffrey. I know it. Jesse told me he's bound to Pleasant Mills and can't leave unless he does JD a favor. I assume the old Jesse collecting the children for JD, was the favor that would grant him his freedom. The 'old Jesse' always wanted to leave Pleasant Mills. I just thought the town was too rural for him. I didn't know he was trapped here."

"Abducting kids is a steep price for a ticket out of town. If he was that desperate before, what's stopping Jesse from buddying up with JD again to gain his freedom?"

"The 'old Jesse' was a loner. He had no friends besides me and I wasn't in the state of mind to be much of a friend. I know if this younger Jesse makes good friendships like I have; he won't fall prey to JD again. He'll be content in Pleasant Mills if he has a sense of family."

"I don't know Uriah . . . this is a lot."

"I know. But please have faith that our futures are not written in stone, and we can change. Look at your own life." Jeffrey fiddled with a button on his pajama top anxiously as Uriah continued. "Maybe it's because I'm a pastor, but I'm willing to give Jesse another chance. I too was ensnared by JD, and you all welcomed me into your hearts. I hope you will do the same for Jesse. Jesse has lived a full life and died many times to find himself back in the body of a child once again. He can help us Jeffrey and he needs us. He has no one. I will not leave him to JD, besides its safer for us all if he's on our side."

With hesitation, "Uriah, I'm sorry I don't want him near my son. Make that my entire family. You do what you need to do, but know that if I even see him near Sammy . . . Well, I don't know what I'll do." Jeffrey counted down from ten like his therapist had told him to do when he felt his anger spiking.

"I only ask you to be open-minded."

"It was my son he kidnapped, not yours."

"I understand, but *if you do not forgive others their trespasses, neither will your Father forgive your trespasses.*"

"Don't quote the *Bible* at me Uriah," Jeffrey said annoyed.

"Sorry, habit. But maybe in time?"

"I doubt it. I'm an investor, not a pastor. I don't forgive or forget."

Jeffrey hung up the phone before Uriah could say another word.

"What's wrong?" Lindsey asked when Jeffrey walked back into the kitchen slouching in the closest chair, letting out a loud sigh.

"Uriah's got some nerve."

"What happened?" she asked, slicing bananas for banana pancakes.

"Jesse Richards is back."

Lindsey stopped chopping. "What? The police found him?"

"No. He's at Uriah's now and he's changed."

Turning around to face her husband, "changed how?"

"How . . . that's what I'd like to know. He's a kid again, about Sammy's age."

His wife gave him a curious look.

Jeffrey ran his fingers through his long hair before tucking it behind his ears. "Apparently, he showed up at Uriah's doorstep a teenager with no memories of his past, or so Uriah wants me to believe. Uriah wanted to bring him to breakfast."

"What did you say?"

"No. And he had the nerve to lecture me. Gave me the old 'we all deserve a second chance' speech." Jeffrey looked at his hands on his lap. "Sometimes I really want to hit that man."

Lindsey shut off the stove and sat in the chair next to her husband.

"Crazy, right?" Jeffrey didn't wait for his wife's response. "It's hard to believe. I'm not sure if I believe any of it, but if that boy that showed up at Uriah's doorstep is somehow the real Jesse Richards, I don't want him anywhere near Sammy. Uriah can't expect us to just forget what Jesse did to him. Seeing Jesse, no matter how old he is, could cause Sammy to have an anxiety attack or worse, a breakdown. We've come too far with him to let him regress now." Lindsey gave Jeffrey sympathetic eyes. "I don't care what your mother says. Sammy has come a long way in a few months. None of us know how bad it really was for him."

Lindsey held her husband's hand while the sound of bacon sizzled on the stove. "You're right, Sammy has come a long way. He's strong and will be okay. I think we should follow Pastor Leeds's example."

"Christ, Lindsey," Jeffrey said, standing up to pace. "There's no good that can come from this. Maybe we should just move. Pack up and just move Sammy away from everything. I don't want the family around this craziness, and we have Hugo to worry about now too. I've been thinking about it for some time but haven't insisted because I didn't want to move Sammy his senior year." Still pacing, "But now, I don't see we have another choice. How about Florida? You love Florida. Your mother will fit in with all the leathery alligators, and there will be lifeguarding all year round for Sammy."

Lindsey gave her husband a look of disapproval, her lips flattening to a straight line.

"Shit, I'll move the family back to Spain," Jeffrey continued. "That will make Anita happy. I just think it's time to go." He stopped pacing and looked to his wife. "Well, what do you think?"

Lindsey took her husband's hand, forcing him to sit. "It's not like you to run away from your problems."

He grinned. "What can I say, these aren't exactly normal problems."

"I thought you were committed to protecting this town from Japhet Dean Leeds."

"I am. I was . . . but I can't if I have no back up. Sammy's one step away from a breakdown, and Uriah's heart is too big. This whole Jesse thing proves that. What am I supposed to do Lindsey? No matter how many books I read on demons, it doesn't make me a demon hunter. Hmm. . . maybe I can find one on Google."

Lindsey drew her husband closer. "We have to stick together. If we run now, Sammy will never recover. We will always be running. We need to be strong for him."

Jeffrey exhaled loudly. "You're right. You're always right," he said, leaning in and kissing her forehead. "But I don't want Jesse around the kids. Sixteen or not, Jesse Richards deserves to be rotting in a prison cell where he can't hurt anyone."

"I think Jesse deserves another chance."

Jeffrey couldn't believe his ears. "You're on Uriah's side?!"

"It's not about taking sides. We've all done things we're not proud of."

"I'm not moving on this Lindsey. If Uriah wants to play caregiver to some brainwashed kid, that's on him. He can't guarantee me he's still not in JD's pocket and that's not good enough for me."

"I don't think Jesse had a choice before."

"Okay, let's say for argument's sake, he didn't have a choice. So, what's the difference now? All of a sudden he has a choice? Not buying it. I think JD is relying on us trusting Jesse because he's a child. We've been waiting for him to make his move; this could be it and we're falling right into his hands. I bet you this is part of some master plan, and Uriah is too naive to see it."

Lindsey squeezed her husband's hand. "I need to tell you something."

Jeffrey's eyes narrowed. "Tell me what?"

"It's hard to say."

His eyebrows furrowed. "What is?" he asked, not sure what his wife was getting at.

"When I was kidnapped, Devan tried to take advantage of me."

Jeffrey's voice became a whisper. "Advantage?" Devan's words came back to him. *'I helped murder those boys. And I raped your wife.'* Jeffrey had thought Devan was lying, trying to get under his skin, trying to make Jeffrey kill him before Anita banished his soul to Hell. He could hear Devan's voice in his head. *'She cried for you to help her, but where were you?! Come on, kill me; you know you want to!'*

Jeffrey's blood ran cold. "Tell me what happened Lindsey."

"His first attempt, he got a phone call and left, but later that night he came back." Lindsey took a deep breath, letting the air fill her lung chambers. "Jesse helped me. There's good in him Jeffrey."

Jeffrey felt chilled to the bone despite his increased heart rate. His anger had no outlet. Devan was dead. He wished it was Devan that was resurrected, not Jesse, so he could kill him—then kill him again. Jeffrey counted down from ten to get control of himself before he spoke. "Okay," he said in a low voice. "I'll give Jesse a second chance for you, but I'm going to be watching him like a hawk."

CHAPTER SEVENTEEN
A Young Jesse Richards

Jesse stood perfectly still in the Lopez foyer chewing on the inside of his cheek nervously as everyone's eyes fixated on him in awe. Jesse knew showing up a teenager was anything but normal, and everyone needed a moment to come to terms with this supernatural matter. However, he wished they'd stop staring.

Jesse was honestly surprised when Uriah said he was invited to breakfast at the Lopez house after Jeffrey had initially said no. But he'd called back, apologized, and insisted they come over.

In truth, he didn't want to go. Jesse didn't want to see the faces of the people the 'old him' had betrayed. But he knew he had no choice. Uriah was right. He was stuck in Pleasant Mills whether he liked it or not and needed a fresh start; and his fresh start began with apologies, at least to the people who would recognize him.

After several awkward minutes, Jesse's eyes lifted to meet Uriah's. Uriah gave him a reassuring smile.

"Now or never," Jesse muttered to himself.

Jesse extended his hand to Sammy for a handshake. He figured the straightforward approach was the best course of action and it was Sammy who he'd hurt the most. He reasoned his apologies should start with him.

"I'm sorry for what I did to you Sammy. Uriah told me everything. I don't know what I was thinking when I did what I did. I wasn't always a bad person. I hope you'll give me another chance."

It was true, all eyes were on Jesse, all eyes except Anita Gomez's, her eyes were on her grandson. She studied Sammy, waiting to see how he would react. Sammy was aware of his grandmother's penetrating stare but wasn't sure what his grandmother wanted him to do or how he was supposed to respond to having Jesse in his house. One thing was for certain, there was no way he was going to have a meltdown; he wouldn't give his grandmother the satisfaction.

He was glad he had run into the 'old Jesse' at the church before Tim's funeral. In a way it had prepared him for this. That Jesse was the real Jesse, the Jesse that stood before him now looked like a kid—just any boy that he would see in school. He had similarities to the Jesse he had known, like the dirty blond hair and hazel eyes, but he was smaller than Sammy now, a lot smaller. Sammy wasn't afraid of him, if push came to shove, he could take this Jesse Richards.

Sammy shook Jesse's hand, noticing something in his eyes. He thought he had seen it months ago when the 'old Jesse' had kidnapped him but was sure of it now. It was the same look he housed in his own eyes—he was scared.

Sammy rationalized they were a lot alike. Jesse caught the eye of JD and so did he. Sammy could have very well ended up like Jesse if he didn't have his family. He was desperate to get out of that underground crypt. He thought about that desperation often after he was returned to his family safe and sound. He wondered if JD had offered him a 'get out of jail free card', if he too would have made a deal with JD, like Jesse had. He never admitted it out loud, or even to himself, but he thought he would've and that had frightened him more than anything. He was one bad decision away from being Jesse Richards.

Sammy, still shaking Jesse's hand, "Sure Jesse, I can do that. I can give you another chance."

Jesse shook Ivy's hand next. All the while, her heart beat fast as a hot flush traveled up her neck. She hoped no one noticed. Jesse may not have remembered Ivy, but she remembered him, more precisely, killing him. Ivy kept getting cinematic flashes of a bloodied Jesse in her head. She was grateful this new, younger Jesse looked different. She tried to tell herself he *was* different but as she looked into his warm eyes and his smile cocked off slightly to the left, she knew he was the same. She shuddered as she remembered liking him, liking the way he flirted with her. Everything about him caused the little hairs on her arms to stand up. She felt like she was looking at a ghost. She wished Jesse would've stayed lost.

Ivy had hoped that whole thing in the woods was just one bad dream. Just another nightmare thanks to Anita Gomez's soul cleanse. As much as she tried to deny it, Anita had awoken something in her. The memory of her being the Midwife was just the tip of the iceberg. Sometimes Ivy's dreams were so real she swore they were. She was having a hard time ascertaining where her dreams ended, and reality began. Teenage Jesse being at the Lopez house for breakfast was proof—what happened in the woods did happen. Jesse did die. And her rendezvous with JD was real.

"Nice to meet you Ivy," Jesse said with his crooked smile. Ivy quickly withdrew her hand when a shiver went down her spine.

"Hi," she said, playing it off.

Jesse shook Mary's hand followed by Anita's. Next, Jesse shook Jeffrey's hand. Ivy's eyes followed their handshake up Mr. Lopez's muscled arm to his face. His outgrown bangs fell in whisps at the angle of his cheek bones. She stopped when she got to his eyes, she didn't want to chance seeing anything in them. She looked away, she couldn't believe how much JD and Jeffrey resembled each other. Guilt swarmed inside her, stinging her belly until she felt like she would pass out.

Jesse bent down to say hello to Alba and Maria who could care less about him. They just wanted to eat so they could play outside. Lindsey Lopez put an arm around Jesse as she led him to a seat at the kitchen table. "I hope you're hungry Jesse?"

"Um . . . yes Mrs. Lopez."

"Please, call me Lindsey."

After breakfast, everyone went outside. The sun was shining, and the fog was a mere haze. It was almost a normal summer day, besides Jesse Richards coming back from the dead.

Sammy and Jesse hit it off right away, which left Ivy sitting with the adults as Sammy and Jesse played horseshoes and Maria and Alba splashed around in the pool.

Ivy could tell the adults were happy Sammy didn't have a meltdown when he saw Jesse resurrected. In fact, they were pleasantly surprised how well Sammy responded to Jesse's rebirth. She could tell Jeffrey wasn't thrilled to have Jesse over. She noticed he kept glancing their way, only half listening to Grams talk about the great service she got at Titan Tires.

Ivy had to shake her head at Sammy's naivety. She wasn't surprised Jesse and him were getting along. Sammy had to be the most trusting person she ever met, to the point of idiocy.

"Keep your enemies close," Ivy mumbled to herself. That's what she was going to do. Ivy pretended to be happy to see Jesse and pretended she was happy Sammy made friends with his former kidnapper. But the truth was, Ivy hated Jesse for what he did to Sammy and to her. She had trusted Jesse, even had feelings for him and he betrayed her. It didn't matter to Ivy he was reborn. Rebirth did not equate to absolution in her eyes.

When it came to nurture vs nature, Ivy believed in nature. She thought Jesse would do it all over again, and welcoming Jesse into their friend's circle was a waste of time. As Grams always said: 'Leopards don't change their spots.'

Ivy almost let out a groan when she overheard Sammy ask Jesse if he wanted to sleep over. "What am I missing?" she muttered to herself.

Sammy was talking to Jesse like he just met him for the first time. Which Ivy guessed was accurate to Jesse, but Sammy should know better, he was almost Jersey Devil food because of him.

Ivy squirmed in her seat. She wished they would stop playing horseshoes. With each horseshoe thrown, Jesse fell down the sloping hill to his death. If ever a sound could produce an image, it was horseshoes. They uncannily rang in the yard like the smack of Jesse's head hitting a tree trunk.

"What do we make out of all this?" Grams whispered to Ivy.

"The weird keeps getting weirder," Ivy said as she glanced at Jesse.

Grams's eyes drifted to Uriah. "Not surprised Uriah's all unicorns puking glitter. And I suppose Jeffrey and Lindsey will do anything to keep Sammy happy. But I will say, too bad Jesse's a sociopath. He's a good-looking kid."

"You said it, Grams. About the sociopath part, not the good-looking part."

"You think he'll still play dominoes?"

"Grams!"

Sammy and Jesse went up to his room after Ivy left with her grandmother, and Uriah went home. The door shut and Jesse found himself pinned against the wall by Sammy. "Knock off the shit Jesse, what's your game?!" Sammy demanded to know through clenched teeth.

Jesse's eyes grew large. "Game?"

"Yeah, what are you playing at?!" Jesse was scared, Sammy saw it in his eyes. Turning the tables, to his shame, made him feel good.

"The whole forgiveness thing was just an act?"

Sammy tightened his grip on Jesse's shirt. "You think?!"

Jesse shrugged his shoulders and lifted his palms up in a gesture of innocence. "Sammy, there's no angle. To be honest, I'm a little confused—a lot confused. Everyone's telling me about myself, and I have no clue what's going on. I showed up at Uriah's not knowing how I got there or what I did the day before. I swear."

Sammy's hands tensed. "What about JD?"

"What about him?"

"What's he planning?"

Jesse exhaled loudly through his nose. "I have no clue, haven't seen him. Honestly. But uh, your dad's practically a dead ringer. I thought it was him. Uriah had warned me before I came over about your dad's likeness to JD to prepare me but damn they're really alike."

"Tell me something I don't know," Sammy said, releasing Jesse's shirt and going to his bed. He knelt to pull from under it his tote on wheels that stored his personal belongings. He opened the clear plastic lid and pulled out a folded piece of paper.

Jesse stood still, not sure what he should say or do.

Sammy walked back over to Jesse and handed him the folded piece of paper. "What's this?"

"A letter from you. Well, the other you. See if it jogs anything in your memory."

Sammy waited quietly while Jesse read the letter he'd left on his pillow. Jesse's gaze lifted from the page.

"Well, remember anything?" Sammy asked, fidgeting, an anxious energy travelling over his extremities.

Jesse folded the letter back into a small square and handed it to Sammy. "No sorry. But I told you to throw the letter out."

"Yeah, you did," Sammy said, taking the letter back and shoving it in his pocket. "No one knows, so it's okay. Do you think you dying had anything to do with what you were warning me about?"

Another shoulder shrug from Jesse. "You think JD killed me, don't you?"

"Maybe, what do you think?"

"I have no idea . . . He's capable of anything. I guess if I was getting in his way, he could've just reset me."

"Reset you—wow—when you put it like that, that seems more than possible," Sammy said, taking a seat on his bed. "From what the 'older you' told me you two were kinda on the outs. You were trying to get your hands on his mother's heart so you could use its power to live forever and retain all your memories."

"His mother's heart, that I remember. JD would carry it around with him."

Sammy nodded. "Maybe he found out about your betrayal or maybe you found out what he was up too. Or, maybe both. Either way, the easy solution would've been to reset you."

"Well, whatever he's up too, I'm on your side. I want to help."

"An easy choice to make since all signs point to JD killing you."

Jesse chuckled a nervous laugh. "Yeah, I guess so. But I do want to help. And I want to truly earn your forgiveness. I had a feeling a handshake and an apology wasn't going to cut it."

Sammy grinned. "You've got your work cut out for you. I just said what I thought my parents and grandmother wanted me to say, so they'd give me a little space. They've been overanalyzing everything I do. Especially my grandmother."

Jesse hung his head. "Sorry for that."

"It's not your fault."

"Isn't it though?"

Sammy ran his hands through his hair, like his father always did. "In a way. It's the 'old you' I don't like. I can't really blame you for all that. Shoot, you don't even remember what you ate for breakfast yesterday. It seems stupid to hold some grudge against you. Especially now that I know JD most likely killed you himself."

Jesse took a seat next to Sammy on his bed. "It's probably a good thing I don't remember that part."

Sammy smirked. "The 'old you' was an asshole, and the moment you become an asshole again, I'm going to be the one to reset you."

"That's only fair," Jesse said with something like a smile. "Well then, what are we going to do to make sure I don't become that asshole again?"

"For starters, no secrets between us. If we're going to be friends, we can't have any secrets. The moment JD contacts you or asks anything of you, you need to tell me. Can you make me that promise?"

"Yeah, I can do that. I promise. I give you my word."

Jesse shook Sammy's hand.

"I got an idea," Sammy said, his face lighting up. He went back under his bed and pulled out a marble notebook. "I think you should keep a diary."

"Diary?"

"Yeah, like a journal, so if you get killed again you can just read it and be up to speed."

"Grim thinking, but smart."

"We need to stay one step in front of JD." Sammy's eyes narrowed. "That's if we both want the same thing?"

"I *want* the same thing. I want to get rid of him, even if my immortality goes with him. I'm going to make amends with everything this time around, things are going to be different for me."

"Great," Sammy said. "I think we'll be good friends then."

CHAPTER EIGHTEEN
Questions

Detective Pearl Steele rang the doorbell at the Lopez house. She listened to the chimes ring from behind the closed front door and smiled politely at the doorbell camera. It wasn't long until Jeffrey answered the door. He was wearing business attire, slim-cut dress pants, dress shirt, and a tie.

"Caught me on a good day Pearl," he said, opening the door. "Working from home."

She stepped over the threshold. "You always dress like that when you work from home?" she asked with an inquisitive smile.

Jeffrey looked down at his tie featuring cats in bowties. "Yep. I would never wear this tie out," he said with a grin. "The girls gave it to me for Father's Day last year and trust me when I say the only time this thing comes out is a work from home day."

Pearl smiled. "I don't know, it suits you."

He snorted air loudly, ushering her into the kitchen and making his way to a half full coffee pot. "Coffee?"

She shook her head.

"Water?"

"No thank you."

"Something stronger?"

She laughed.

He poured himself a cup of coffee, left it black and took a sip. "You said you'd like to ask me a couple of questions, but it looks like you're off the clock."

Pearl looked down at her sweatshirt. "Yeah you could say that, but I'm always on the job."

"I can relate. Let's head to my office. I'm waiting on an important email."

Pearl followed Jeffrey to the last room off the hall. "I don't think I've ever been in this room," she said, looking around.

The room was filled with books neatly placed on rosewood bookcases that wrapped around it. Ladders on wheels gave the home office a warm library feel. A pair of leather club chairs, worn to look old and were no doubt expensive, were placed in front of an executive desk situated in front of a large window.

"I think this is my favorite room," Pearl said, still glancing over the books.

"Mine too. The kids know if the door's shut, not to bother me," Jeffrey chuckled. "But yeah, decorator did a great job."

"Should I shut the door?"

Jeffrey shrugged. "Depends on what brings you here, I guess? The house is quiet for now. Lindsey's out with the kids." He glanced at his Breitling watch. "Hugo's coming home tomorrow, and Lindsey wants to make sure she has everything. Not sure when they'll get back, but I think we have some time. She wants to get a few more outfits and apparently, the kids all miraculously need new swimsuits." He shrugged, "What can I say, Lindsey will look for any reason to go shopping."

Pearl gave a polite smile and shut the door. Jeffrey raised an eyebrow and motioned her to sit down. She sat in a club chair, unsure if she should put her arms on the armrest or on her lap. She settled for her lap. Jeffrey took a seat in the black leather chair behind the desk, putting up a finger before typing on his open laptop. "One minute Pearl, just have to get this out."

Pearl waited quietly. It had been a long time since she was alone with Jeffrey. She would come to the Lopez's on occasion when Devan was stopping by and the few parties she attended with Devan as his guest, but her and Jeffrey went way back. They attended the same high school. Pearl had joined Pleasant Mills High's debate team because Jeffrey was the captain. There she could admire him up close. They became good friends. Jeffrey was impressed with her tenacity when it came to making a strong argument. They had even slept together. He was her first, and she was pretty sure she was his. It ruined their friendship, but Pearl didn't care, she was after more. It was Lindsey Gomez that ruined the *more*. She transferred to Pleasant Mills High their junior year and Jeffrey got her pregnant.

As Jeffrey finished his email, Pearl noticed the only picture she had ever seen displayed in the house. It was a family portrait. The family was dressed in white on the beach. It sat in a wooden frame on his executive desk at just the right angle so she could see it. She wondered if she would've gotten pregnant if all this would've been hers—the house, the kids, Jeffrey.

"Sorry about that," Jeffrey said, closing his laptop.

"Don't look so nervous," Pearl told him. "This is a friendly visit."

Jeffrey laughed, leaning back in his chair. "You're the one that closed the door." It was his nervous laugh, and she knew it. It was the laugh he made when he was unsure. "I was just thinking about you the other day," Jeffrey said, deflecting.

Blood rushed to her cheeks. "You were?"

He had been thinking about her a lot. The day Sammy and Ivy found Tim, he'd come running through the woods at the sound of Ivy's screams. He'd seen the corpse and thought it was Pearl. He'd seen that slim face and dark hair and eyes and thought *Pearl is dead.* A sharp pain had pierced his heart that buckled his knees. A flood of old memories and feelings for his first girlfriend came rushing to the surface. He had almost cried out her name, that was until Ivy said Tim, and he realized the corpse wasn't hers, it was her cousins. He hadn't been able to shake that feeling he had on thinking Pearl died since that day. It brought up so many unresolved feelings, it made him feel awkward to be near her, and yet he wanted to be.

He found himself sending her a message every day since to check on her.

"Yeah, there's a junior debate team. The twins are joining next year." He chuckled, "We were hardly twins but we made a good team. We sure did carry the rest of them."

A smile bloomed across Pearl's pinkened cheeks. "We sure did."

"Not surprised at all you became a detective."

Pearl exhaled. "If only the high school debate team would've taught me how to ask the right questions."

"Questions," he said, tucking his hair behind his ears. "You have questions you wanted to ask me?"

"Like the new hair," she said ignoring him, she wanted to continue talking about the past, their past.

"You do?" he asked, re-tucking it behind his ears. "It's finally past the awkward stage."

"It reminds me of how you wore it at Pleasant Mills High."

Jeffrey laughed again, a real laugh this time. "Yeah, that's because I couldn't afford a decent haircut."

"And now?" she asked.

Jeffrey was done with the small talk. His smile flattened out. "*And now,* I just needed a change." He couldn't tell her there was a half-demon-half man walking around with his face and his hair—well not his hair, he fixed that.

"I waited to talk to you because I know Lindsey's been ill."

"Cancer scare," he said, swiveling in his chair slightly so he could look out the window onto his Koi pond in the backyard. "But that's all past."

"Good," Pearl said, meaning it. "I want to ask you about the day Timothy was found."

He turned in his chair to face her, steepling his hands on his desk as he repressed the feeling burning in his chest. "Of course?"

He had already talked to the police the day Timothy's body was found. Pearl hadn't been in the right frame of mind to take his statement after seeing her cousin's body and officer Wes Weston had stepped in.

"The woods where Timothy was found were searched repeatedly and had never turned up anything. Then, all of a sudden, your son and his girlfriend find him."

Jeffrey nodded, not pleased with her accusatory language.

"We know Timothy was killed somewhere else, and the body was moved."

"Forensics get anything?"

"I'm not at liberty to say."

"Come on Pearlie girlie, what'd they say?"

She rolled her eyes; he hadn't called her that since high school. "Nothing. No fingerprints, no DNA—nothing. If there was any evidence linking the killer to Timothy, the rain and the forest critters took care of that." Pearl looked at Jeffrey through slitted eyes. "Jeffrey, we have a problem."

"Besides the obvious?"

"Yes. The only thing forensics was good for was an estimated time of death." She spoke as if she didn't have a personal interest in the case, trying to sound professional. "Devan Rainier and Lois Ball were pinned with Zachary Lewis, Tyrone Jones, and Louie Grindhouse's murders, but Timothy died after Devan and Mrs. Ball were killed. So, there's no way they murdered him."

Jeffrey nodded in agreement.

"That would leave Jesse Richards," Pearl said.

"Anything on his whereabouts? Jeffrey asked, unsteepling his fingers and laying them flat on his desk.

"No, he's a ghost. He's disappeared. We assume he ran for it when his face was plastered to every streetlight. Sure, if we want to pin Timothy's death on Jesse we could. We could say Jesse stayed hidden for months hiding himself and keeping Tim captive while all along we had daily search parties scouring every inch of the woods. And sure, we can say that Jesse killed Tim in the same exact way Devan and Mrs. Ball killed the other boys and moved the body. That's what the department wants to say at least. They want the case closed. They want to bury the case, forget all about Jesse Richards, and those boys who were tortured and murdered." Pearl took a deep breath in to collect her thoughts, looking at her hands before looking back to Jeffrey. "The whole thing doesn't sit well with me, and it has nothing to do with Tim being family. If Jesse's smart, which I think he is, he ran when he had the chance. I think Devan and Mrs. Ball were part of something bigger and we never caught the real killer. The bastard's still out there."

Jeffrey leaned back running his hands through his hair, itching his scalp. She wanted to help him, wanted to feel his soft hair between her fingers. She had never been able to shut off her feelings when it came to Jeffrey. After all these years she still carried a torch for him. Devan had been her best friend and a distraction. She respected Devan and he was her mentor and lover, but she never loved him. She had only ever loved Jeffrey Lopez. Her feelings for him were raw after being cradled in his arms after Tim was found.

"Sounds like good detective work. You make a strong argument."

Irritated, lust gone, she snapped. "It's called deductive reasoning."

He raised his eyebrows surprised by her tone. "I wasn't patronizing you, Pearl. The town's lucky to have you. You're dedicated to keeping everyone safe. My family and I owe you a debt."

Her cheeks blushed. "Sorry, I just want to end this and clear Devan's name."

"Pearl," Jeffrey said, leaning toward his desk, "Devan was not who we thought he was."

She hung her head, looking at her nails that needed to be cut. "All those years," she said.

"I know what you're feeling, he was my best friend too. I was there, remember. He tried to kill Lindsey, the twins, and Mike Handover."

Pearl glanced at Jeffrey. "It just doesn't make sense. He was a darn good cop. Devan taught me everything I know."

Jeffrey could see Pearl's eyes glassing over. "I'm going through the same thing you are, I am. You have to trust me on this, Devan was living a double life."

"And you?" she asked.

"Me?" Jeffrey said, sitting up in his leather chair. "You think I had something to do with those murders?

"Not directly."

"What does that mean, Pearl?! I would never hurt a kid. Never." Jeffrey's mind went to the day he grabbed Sammy's arm, sending him tumbling down the stairs. Devan may have been a darn good cop, but Pearl was a darn good detective. He hoped she couldn't see through his lie. He had never been violent with her; she should have no reason not to trust him.

"Of course not," she said, sensing his anxiousness. "I didn't mean it like that. It's just I've been combing over the case again since Timothy was found, and the more I look at this, everything points back to your family."

Jeffrey held his breath as he spoke. "My family, how?"

"Sammy is the one thing that connects everyone together. All the boys."

"Tim," Jeffrey said, breathing a little easier. The idea that Sammy was at the center of whatever was going on set him on a razor's edge. "Sammy didn't know him until after he was kidnapped. He hadn't spoken to him before that."

"Oh crap," Pearl said, leaning to the right and pulling out a small notepad from her back jean pocket. "You're right." She wrote a note to herself and put it back in her pocket. "We could really use someone with your memory on the force Jeffrey." Pearl's cheeks shone a bright pink. "Sorry for wasting your time. I thought I was on to something. I came here to ask you if you knew anyone who would want to hurt your family. —If you had any disgruntled clients, maybe someone whose money you lost?"

Jeffrey laughed his real laugh. "If I lost clients' money, I wouldn't have a job. And no nothing like that. No friends. No enemies."

Pearl looked up at Jeffrey. "I'm still your friend."

He smiled. "Well then, you're the only one. And you didn't waste my time, not mine. His eyes stayed locked with hers. "Thank you for looking out for my family, and for me."

They sat in silence for a moment staring at each other. They heard a car pull up and the twins yelling as they came barreling down the hall like rabid dogs.

The twins knocked on the office door. "Daddy can we come in?" They asked together.

"Yes," he quickly answered.

Alba and Maria ran in holding up their new bikinis. "Daddy, look what we got!"

Pearl stood up to leave.

Jeffrey picked up his daughters and looked at the garments they pushed in his face. "Very nice."

He put his daughters down after he hugged them and walked with Pearl to the door.

"I'm dedicated to this," Pearl said in a low voice to Jeffrey. "I'm going to find the real killer and put him behind bars. Keep an eye on your family, Jeffrey. I got a gut feeling this isn't over."

They made it to the foyer as Lindsey came in with a barking dog in her hands. "What's that?" Jeffrey asked. Lindsey put the dog on the ground to say hello to Pearl with a hug. Jeffrey's eyes narrowed in on the small, wiry dog on the marble floor.

"Daddy, it's Hot Dog," Maria said proudly. "Isn't he great?"

Jeffrey pulled his wife aside, "I thought we agreed on getting a dog that was going to make the kids feel safe."

She whispered back, "Hot Dog was on death row."

The intuitive Alba told her father: "They were gonna kill him, Daddy." She gave the mangey mutt a big hug.

"Okay fine, Hot Dog Lopez it is."

The twins cheered, throwing their hands in the air, and waving them around.

The doorbell rang. Jeffrey opened the front door to a kid wearing a baseball cap holding a brown box.

The boy pushed the box toward Jeffrey. "Last kitten, could be yours sir for only twenty dollars."

Jeffrey peered into the box to see a solid black kitten. The boy picked up the kitten and handed it to Jeffrey. "Um . . . take it back now."

Sammy came into the foyer. His eyes lit up when he saw his father holding a kitten. "Dad, you're the best!" Sammy at once took the kitten from his father. It let out a light meow.

Jeffrey tapped his son's shoulder to get his attention. "Uh, Sammy."

"Thanks Dad. I always wanted a cat. Jeffrey watched in dismay as Sammy gave the kitten a kiss. He let out a loud sigh of defeat.

The boy in the baseball cap put his hand out. "That's a twenty."

Jeffrey pulled out a hundred-dollar bill from his wallet. "Here's a hundred, if you promise to never bring another kitten to my house again."

"Deal!" The boy took the money and the empty box and ran down the driveway to his mother.

Pearl smiled. "I told you the tie suits you."

"Jeffrey, a dog and a cat. What has gotten into you?!" Lindsey asked, rubbing her husband's arm tenderly. "You're in such a giving mood."

"I must be losing my mind."

Sammy put the small kitten next to the dog. "Look Dad, they're friends already!"

"What's her name Sammy?" The twins asked.

"We got Hot Dog . . . what about *Cat*chup?

His sisters giggled at that.

"Well, I better get going," Pearl said.

"Is it too late for me to take your offer and join the police force?"

Pearl patted his arm. "It's never too late," she said, meaning much more.

Jeffrey watched Pearl walk to her car before he shut the front door.

Alba wrapped her hands around the disheveled pooch and squeezed.

Hot Dog responded by peeing on the floor. Jeffrey's face turned bright red.

Alba gave her father a sheepish smile. "Oops . . ." She affectionately smoothed down the fur between the dog's ears. "Sorry if I squeezed you too tight, Hot Dog."

"It's okay, I'll clean it up," Lindsey volunteered. She went to the sink to get bleach.

"Let me hold Catchup," Alba squealed. "Here kitty, kitty, kitty," Alba hollered as she chased the kitten across the kitchen. Maria joined in on the chase, running after the kitten who weaved in and out of the furniture.

Sammy picked up Catchup. His sisters jumped up and down reaching for the kitten. "Calm down you two, you're scaring her."

"There's no way I'm getting any work done from home today. I'm going to go for a long jog," Jeffrey said, talking to himself more than anyone specifically. He made his way upstairs to get changed. "A nice, long, quiet jog all by my lonesome."

"Okay honey," Lindsey shouted over the twins. "Everything will be cleaned up by the time you get back."

Jeffrey jogged down the road to historical Batsto Village, looking forward to hitting one of the trails. He didn't make it far before the fog became a hinderance. He stopped when he could no longer see the path. "You've got to be kidding me. Where is this stuff coming from?"

Jeffrey heard a light whistle ring out of the fog straight ahead before he heard a voice very much like his own. "What a lovely face you have Jeffrey Lopez." Jeffrey felt a hand touch his cheek. He turned, freezing when he saw his likeness bleeding through the fog. "It's true!" Jeffrey said in amazement. "Your face, why do you have my face?" It was like he was looking in the mirror. JD's face was just like his, they had the same warm brown eyes, the same sloping nose, the same curved lips, the same square chin. The only thing setting them apart was Jeffrey's long hair.

Jeffrey had heard the accounts of JD being his doppelganger from Sammy, his girls, Uriah, and Mary. But seeing JD with his own eyes made him real. And it terrified him. He took a step back, keeping his eyes on JD.

"I wanted to ask you the very same thing. Why is it that you have my face, Jeffrey Lopez?"

Jeffrey took another step back. "This is *my* face."

"Yes, it is, for some reason unknown to me we share it."

"What do you want?"

"Nothing at the moment. I was just watching you. I like doing that. I have learned so much from just blending into the background and keeping a vigilant eye on the man who shares my face. I have learned how to talk like you, learned all of your hand gestures, all your kinks . . . How you think, how you take your coffee, how you screw. You are an interesting man to watch . . . It's not often you see someone like you."

"What do you mean?"

"You are a lucky man, Jeffrey Lopez. Dare I say, you have a beautiful face, a beautiful wife, and beautiful children. I want what you have."

"Stay away from my family," Jeffrey said in a stern voice.

JD didn't respond with words, he just stared at Jeffrey analyzing him. Jeffrey wasn't sure what to say or do. Any threats he made would be empty. The only choice he had was to run and fight another day, and he did. Jeffrey abruptly turned around and jogged home. He looked back just as JD's face faded into the fog. Like he had told Lindsey, he was no demon hunter. He was in over his head and didn't know how to handle it. He was a control freak, controlling every little detail in his life and his family's, but when it came to JD, he had no control and no idea how to gain it.

Jeffrey walked into his house and locked the front door behind him. Lindsey walked into the foyer and kissed her husband hello. "That was a quick jog."

"Too dangerous to jog now, the fogs really thick."

The dog and cat walked up to Jeffrey and looked at him.

Lindsey smiled. "They like you."

He rolled his eyes. "Great."

"You're a lucky man, Jeffrey Lopez."

"Yeah, so I've been told."

CHAPTER NINETEEN
Moon River

"Hurry!" Maria shouted as she pulled Sammy's and Jesse's hands. It was Hugo's first day home and the girls wanted to celebrate with a tea party.

Lindsey, with the help of Sammy, had transformed the girl's room into a tea house to welcome Hugo home in style. They hung pink and blue streamers from every inch of the room including the chandelier.

When Sammy and Jesse entered the twin's bedroom, they found some of the seats around the child-size white, wooden table were already occupied by Alba's and Maria's stuffed animals.

"Distinguished guests of honor," Maria informed Jesse when he gave the plushy animals a strange look.

"Of course," he said with a smile. "I feel lucky to be here. Thank you for inviting me."

"You're most welcome," the twins said together.

Sammy groaned, he hated it when his sisters spoke at the same time, it creeped him out.

"Wow," Jesse said to Sammy as his eyes darted from the decorations to the variety of fancy cookies laid out on the table.

"My mom loves when they throw tea parties." Sammy chuckled. "Not sure how excited Hugo is though." Baby Hugo was lying on a floor mat staring up at a mobile, not interested in the slightest to be at a tea party.

"Do you like tea Jesse?" Alba asked. She waited for Sammy to pull out her chair before she took a seat.

"Yes Alba," he said, taking a seat in a free chair.

"Just your size," Sammy snickered to Jesse, trying to get comfortable in his small chair.

"Suppose it is," he said with a grin.

Maria dumped sugar cubes into Jesse's cup. "How many sugars?"

"I think that's good," he said with raised eyebrows.

Sammy laughed.

"Your sisters are hams," Jesse whispered.

"If that's old fashioned for ridiculous, you're right."

Sammy picked up the stuffed wolf that sat in the chair next to him. "This is a new one."

"Yes, and her name is Moon River," Alba said proudly.

"Moon River?" Jesse asked startled. Jesse could hear his wife's voice in his head as if she was sitting next to him, as if he never cut out her heart for Japhet Dean Leeds.

"I thought you detested calling me Moon River."

"No, I love it . . . It's just that . . . —"

"Mona goes over better with your high society friends."

"Yes, but when we're alone, you are my Moon River. Every time I see the beauty of the moon or the beauty of the river, I think of you. But not even mother nature can compare to you, my Moon River."

"You can call her Mona," Alba told Jesse. "She says that's what you like to call her at parties."

The color drained from Jesse's face.

"You ok?" Sammy asked, noticing Jesse's color change.

"Uh . . . it's just too much sugar," he mumbled.

Sammy put the wolf back in its seat. "Just pretend to drink it."

"More tea?" Lindsey asked, coming in with a tray of sandwiches and a fresh tea pot.

"Yes, waitress that will be most welcome," Maria said in a grownup voice.

Jesse watched Lindsey play the part of waitress with a smile. She poured the girls more tea before kneeling next to Hugo. She pretended to pour tea into an empty teacup that was on the side of his blanket.

"Would you like tea sandwiches to go with your crumpets?" Lindsey asked the stuffed wolf.

Alba answered: "Moon River says no thank you, but I think Sammy would like some."

"Yes, please," Sammy said excitedly. "I'm starving." Lindsey artfully put the bitesize sandwiches on his plate.

"Jesse?"

"Um, sure thanks."

Jesse kept his eyes on the stuffed wolf while he ate. He had a bad feeling about Alba's toy. He couldn't wait to get out of there. He popped the bitesize sandwiches into his mouth as quickly as he could, then nudged Sammy, motioning to the door.

Sammy cleared his throat. "Well, Alba, Maria, and Hugo thank you for lunch."

Alba coughed and pointed at her stuffed wolf.

"Excuse my rudeness, you too Moon River, but we have to get going."

"Whatever for?" Maria asked like a lady, taking a sip of her tea.

"Well, you see we have to . . . do um . . . help me out Jesse," Sammy said with a nudge of his own.

Jesse blurted out, "boys' stuff."

"If you must," Maria said regretfully. "We do not partake in *boys stuff.*"

"Thank you for the tea ladies," Jesse said, showing his obeisance with a bow of his head.

"Always Jesse," the twins said together while Sammy groaned.

That night Jesse slept over. The boys camped out in the living room watching movies and eating popcorn until they passed out. Sammy couldn't take the cramped feel of the theater room, not after being abducted, making the living room his go to spot in the house. Thanks to the open concept he could see the kitchen and had a full view of the backyard and front door.

Hours later Jesse woke up to the sound of static on the television. Half asleep he got up, shuffling to the big screen. He ran his hand along the side of the television feeling for the off button. A loud exhale, he found it. Shutting the TV off, he shuffled back to the couch and plopped down.

His eyes went to Alba's stuffed wolf on the coffee table. "What are you doing down here?" he muttered, rubbing the sleep from his eyes before fixating on the stuffed wolf's black plastic orbs. Hesitantly, he picked up the stuffed toy, bringing it in closer for examination. He squeezed the stuffed wolf, whispering in its ear, making sure Sammy couldn't hear. "Mona, are you there?"

Alba and Maria jumped on the couch, "Boo! Did we scare you?!"

"You rascals," he said as he tickled them. "You're supposed to be asleep."

"We couldn't sleep, and Moon River thought it would be funny to scare you," Alba reported.

Jesse looked at the wolf, his mood shifting. "Not funny." He gestured for the twins to get upstairs. "Come on you two, get back to bed."

"Ask," Maria said to Alba.

"Ask what?" Jesse questioned, keeping his eyes on the stuffed animal Alba now held close to her chest.

"Would you ever hurt us?"

"Of course not," he said troubled.

"I told you Alba," Maria said to her sister like a know-it-all.

"I know, but Moon River said so."

"Told you she was just trying to scare us," Maria said, happy to be right.

Jesse glared at the stuffed wolf. "Moon River, don't scare Alba and Maria. That's not nice, they're only children."

Alba put the stuffed wolf to her ear as if it was whispering to her. "She says sorry, Jesse."

"It's okay. Now you both get some sleep," Jesse said with a faint smile.

Alba held out her stuffed wolf. "She wants a kiss goodnight first."

He anxiously kissed the wolf's cheek. "Good night."

The twins headed to the staircase. He listened to their footfalls until the house was silent again. Feeling on edge, Jesse lay back on the couch forcing his eyes shut.

Jesse woke up confused, his mind dulled with the cobwebs of sleep and memories long since passed. He was still in the Lopez's living room. It was morning. He heard pancake batter sizzling in the pan as Lindsey busily made breakfast.

Jesse rubbed his eyes. Slowly his warm hazel irises gravitated to the coffee table and narrowed in on Moon River, the stuffed wolf. "Déjà vu." It sat perfectly still as a plush toy should, but Jesse swore its reproachful, beady black eyes judged him, knew what he had done and hated him for it.

His blood pressure surged; his heartbeat sounded in his ear. He whispered to the wolf: "Mona, is that really you?"

"There you are!" Alba said. She picked up her stuffed animal and hugged it. Maria spoke to Jesse as if to chastise him. "You're finally up."

Jesse breathed out slowly, attempting to get a grip on his nerves. "Yeah, I'm up, but you know who's not? Sammy. I think we should jump on him."

"Good idea!" The twins shouted in unison. They ran over to Sammy and leaped on top of him.

Sammy let out a loud groan of disapproval and put his pillow over his head. "Go away!"

"Mom, we have any more ketchup?" Sammy asked, trying to squeeze ketchup onto his hashbrowns. He pounded on the bottom of the container. For his effort, all he got was one small drop. He went back to squeezing.

"Yes Sammy. There's a new bottle in the refrigerator."

Sammy looked toward the refrigerator, releasing his grip on the bottle, sending the dregs of the ketchup squirting all over his plate and Alba's stuffed wolf.

"Look what you did! You got ketchup all over Moon River!" Alba shouted, tears streaming down her face like tributaries.

"Shit," Sammy's said remorsefully.

"Language Sammy," Jeffrey scolded as he burped Hugo.

The Lopez kitchen was filled with pandemonium. The twins yelled while Sammy apologized. Hugo chimed in with a high-pitch cry of his own and Jeffrey pulled on his hair.

Jesse remained silent; his eyes fixated on the wolf's white chest that was now doused in ketchup. The scene was all too reminiscent of the night he took his Moon River's heart. The smell of the ketchup became something more to him. He swore he could smell blood.

Lindsey took the stuffed animal from her daughter and brought it to the sink and scrubbed away.

Jesse excused himself from the table and went to the bathroom. He was breathing heavily as he leaned against the closed door. He clutched his heart, trapping the necklace that hung from his neck close to his chest. His eyes watered. "Mona . . . Moon River why are you doing this to me? . . . You know I'm sorry. You know that. Please, I love you. Forgive me. I had no choice. I had to kill you."

There was a knock on the bathroom door. "Jesse, are you alright?" Lindsey asked through the door.

"Uh, yes," he lied, drying his tears on his shirt.

"Jesse, if you need to talk to someone you know you can talk to me."

"I know."

Jesse opened the door to find Lindsey waiting for him. She wrapped her arms around him like he was one of her own children, comforting him like his 'older self' had done for her in her time of need. Jesse let her hug him, not able to understand her kindness and not able to speak. Her compassion brought forth the tears he fought against. He swallowed the lump in his throat.

Lindsey took Jesse's hand in hers. "I just finished a fresh batch of pancakes, come on."

Jesse looked behind him to see Anita. She silently stood in the hall watching him. Her stare weighed heavily on his haunted soul. He felt like she could see through him, see what he'd done to Moon River—see her innocent blood on his guilty hands.

Jesse went back to the kitchen and took his seat. Alba's stuffed wolf sat on her lap. It was all cleaned up and so were Alba's tears. There was no evidence ketchup ever got on it. Lindsey had saved the day.

Anita took a seat across from Jesse. They locked eyes for a split second before Jesse's guilt forced him to look down. He cut into his chocolate chip pancakes, keeping his eyes on his plate.

CHAPTER TWENTY
Hugo's Baptism

"Come on Grams, stay to the right before you end up roadkill!" Ivy kept her eyes on the painted white line on the road as they made their way through the fog to church. Hugo's baptism had caused a shortage of parking, forcing the Tellers to park down the street from Pleasant Mills church. "This is bizarre," Ivy moaned.

"You're telling me. I never realized this church doesn't have handicap parking." Grams stopped a moment to rub her good knee, made bad after getting shot by Mrs. Ball a few months ago.

"Why couldn't they just do something small? If you have to have the police direct traffic, that should tell you to stop with the invites," Ivy said, waving to Detective Pearl Steele who was motioning for a car to keep moving while a gruff officer, she came to know as Weston, kept yelling "Go!"

Grams waved to the officer. "You tell'em, Weston."

"I wish I could tell Jeffrey Lopez where to go. He thinks he owns the police department. Abuse of power if you ask me."

Pearl groaned. "No one asked you."

Ivy shook her head at her grandmother as if to say don't add your two cents.

Ivy wondered with Devan gone, if Pearl would be made Chief of Police or if it would be Weston. The mantle had remained vacant while the two parties jockeyed for it. Devan left big shoes to be filled, big, ominous shoes. Ivy couldn't understand why anyone would want the job.

"I see why we had to park on the street," Ivy said to her grandmother, when she saw half of the church parking lot had been turned into extra seating. Hugo's baptism meant the Sunday regulars and the extended family and friends of the Lopezs' would be in attendance and the church just wasn't big enough.

Mary complained, winded, "I guess us getting inside seats isn't happening."

Ivy pushed the fog out of her face. "I told you to hurry."

"Yeah, yeah, yeah, you're not the one with—"

Ivy cut her grandmother off. "I know, two bad knees. Wait here Grams, let me check inside."

Grams waited in a chair in the parking lot catching her breath while Ivy went to look for an open pew. It wasn't long before Ivy raced back to her grandmother and pulled her arms. "Come on Grams, there's still room inside."

They squeezed into the last row. Sammy, from his seat in the first pew, turned around and smiled at Ivy. She smiled back, his contagious grin reminding Ivy of when she first met him last summer. He was already sun kissed from lifeguarding at Poor Richard's Community Pool and looked every bit of the Spanish god she'd fell in love with. Ivy's smile quickly disappeared when she noticed Sammy was sitting next to a very attractive girl. She had a familiar look, like Ivy had seen her somewhere before but couldn't place from where. The girl had raven-dark hair and blue eyes, not the same light shade as Sammy's but a gray, blue color that was just as dazzling. She could have been on television, with her full lips, the kind women pay to have, and tiny nose, and she was skinny, very skinny.

"Who's that Grams?" Ivy whispered through clenched teeth.

Mary scanned the church for something or someone out of the ordinary. "Who's who?"

"Keep it down—the dark-haired girl sitting next to Sammy."

"How would I know?"

"Shh," Ivy hissed at her grandmother. "Sammy's coming."

Sammy gave Ivy a quick peck on the cheek. "You look great," he whispered to her. Ivy's cheeks flushed red when the dark-haired beauty turned around and looked at them. Ivy wanted to ask who she was but as quick as Sammy said hello, he said goodbye and headed back to his seat.

Sammy's little sisters waved to Ivy. She waved back as her blood boiled under her fake smile. Sammy had never asked her to sit next to him at church.

Ivy spotted Pastor Leeds. He went up to the dark-haired girl and hugged her. Ivy was steaming. She was sure Grams could see the smoke coming out of her ears like you see in the Saturday morning cartoons.

Ivy felt a little better when Uriah made his way to her and Grams.

"Hey Uriah, I think it's time you get a bigger church," Mary said matter-of-factly.

He smiled. "We are blessed. It's so nice to have a large turn out like this."

"I'd say. This is a baptism. Imagine Sammy and Ivy's wedding."

"Grams," Ivy grumbled embarrassed.

Uriah put his hand on Ivy's shoulder. "Can't wait."

"Where's Jesse?" Ivy asked. It was hard to imagine them getting married when he was sitting next to someone else. She was no fan of Jesse Richards. He may have dropped Richards for Leeds on Uriah's suggestion, but he would always be the 'old Jesse Richards' to her. Still, she would rather see him sitting next to Sammy than the dark-haired girl. And since Jesse's rebirth he'd been glued to his side. Ivy wondered how Mike Handover, Sammy's oldest and best friend, was taking being replaced, she wasn't taking it so well.

"Jesse's at the Lopez house in case guests arrive early." Uriah let out a light laugh, leaning into Ivy. She saw a sparkle in his eye, and it made her think of JD. Instinctively, she held her breath. "I think he's there to make sure no one parks on Jeffrey's grass."

"Good thinking," Grams said sarcastically. "We wouldn't want the mayor to have ruts in his front lawn."

"Definitely not," Uriah smiled. "I'm going to go check with Pearl and make sure things are settling down. I'm going to be starting soon."

Ivy watched Uriah walk out the church doors while she thought.

"What's that look for?" Mary asked, examining her granddaughter's face that had more wrinkles than a hound dog.

"I was thinking."

"Don't hurt yourself."

Ivy rolled her eyes. "You said it's a good thing Jesse's at Sammy's. I think it's more like weird. The 'old Jesse' never came to church either.

"Ivy Belle Teller, mind your conspiracies before breakfast."

"I'm just saying Grams, it's weird." Ivy did think it was weird. For a second, she was hoping if they pushed Jesse into church he'd burst into flames and she'd be rid of him forever, but that hope was short lived. Both Devan Rainier and Mrs. Ball had come to church; Mrs. Ball had practically lived there, and JD had also stepped into the church unscathed. She chalked it up to Jesse just not liking church, but it was still weird since he was besties with Pastor Leeds and Sammy.

"I'd be more concerned about who showed up to church than who didn't," Grams whispered. She motioned to the dark-haired girl adjusting Sammy's shirt collar.

Despite that Pastor Uriah Leeds's words at the baptism were beautiful and left the church regulars and newbies alike in awe, Ivy couldn't wait to get out of there. Or more accurately get Sammy away from the dark-haired girl. She thought her head was going to fall off and roll down the aisle when she saw her whisper in Sammy's ear. Ivy pretended to fix her hair, making sure her head was still in place and exactly where it was supposed to be.

When the baptism concluded, Ivy practically dragged her grandmother out of church to the car.

"What's the rush, Ives?"

"Just want to get good parking at the Lopez's. Now, how about you show me some of your world-famous drag racing and break a record."

If Ivy had been keeping time, Mary would have in fact broken her record. But little good it did them, they still had to park on the side of the street and walk up the long, winding driveway to the house. No amount of tugging could will Mary Teller's legs to move quicker. By the time they made it to the backyard, the party was already in full swing. Music blasted over chattering people, some people she knew, some she didn't, everyone's voices were washed out over the noise. The Lopezes had gotten lucky; the fog was minimal and the fog that was there clumped in cloud-like patches low to the ground not obscuring the decorations that festooned the back yard. It was a sight. Ivy had never seen an outside party look so nice, not even on television. There were fresh flower centerpieces on large tables under tents, balloon arches, a DJ, from what she could see three open bars, one of those blowup fun houses for kids, and a magician literally pulling a rabbit from his hat. This was all in addition to the everyday Lopez backyard amenities.

"There you are," Sammy said, coming up to Ivy and hugging her. Sammy pressed a kiss to Ivy's cheek. "You ok, Teller? Your cheeks are all red."

"Dragging a lot of dead weight," she mumbled.

"Watch it!" Mary barked. She sat down on the first seat available and went to rubbing her knees.

Ivy saw the dark-haired girl talking to Uriah. This was her chance. Her pulse raced as she tried to play off her jealousy with curiosity. "Oh, so uh, who's that talking to Pastor Leeds?"

Sammy followed her line of vision. "Trudy Grindhouse."

That was why she looked familiar; Ivy knew that name. Trudy was Louie Grindhouse's older sister, they looked alike, his hair and eyes were just a few shades lighter, but they had the same smile. It had looked kind on Louie; on Trudy she wasn't so sure. Trudy was also Sammy's ex-girlfriend. Zachary Lewis, the night he went missing, had told her Trudy was a knockout and Ivy would have to agree. She didn't know who was better looking: dark-haired Trudy Grindhouse or light-haired Elsa Tilton.

Ivy balled her hand into a fist. "I noticed you saved her a seat upfront with you."

Sammy flashed her his iconic grin. "Oh my gosh Teller, you're jealous." He wrapped his arms around her and chuckled a low laugh. "With Hugo and Abby, you know there was only room for one more. You and Grams both wouldn't fit in the pew."

"I'm not jealous. I knew that. I was just pointing out the obvious," Ivy said, trying to keep her dignity, but she thought her and Grams would've both fit. Somehow, the Lopezes had managed to fit the Chens with them in the front row for Timothy's funeral and they were a family of three. Grams was thinner than her. It made Ivy feel like Sammy thought she was too large to fit. She pushed down tears, putting her nose in the air like a snob. "Just saying, I never sat with you at church."

Sammy took Ivy's hand and placed it over his heart. "You're much closer to me, Ivy Teller."

She pushed him away, partly because she was mad at him and partly because touching him, just holding his hand, made her guilt churn in her stomach. "Urgh, you're such a cheeseball."

He laughed, finding himself hilarious. "I can't help myself."

Ivy rolled her eyes. "I can see that."

"Let me introduce you to Trudy. You'll see you have nothing to be jealous of."

"That's okay, I'll pass."

"Come on, Teller." It was Sammy who now tugged on Ivy. He marched her right up to Trudy Grindhouse. "Trudy, this is my girlfriend, Ivy."

"Nice to meet you," Trudy said politely, shaking her hand as her brother had when Ivy met him at the church lock-in last summer. They both had good manners.

"Hi," Ivy said back.

"Ivy is a wonderful neighbor and friend," Uriah added.

Ivy was out of her element. Everyone's eyes were on her. She wondered if she had something on her face. She wiped her lips with her hand just in case. That didn't seem to do the trick, everyone's attention was still on her. Ivy wasn't sure what to say or what she was expected to say to be socially polite. She wished passing out was an option.

"Well," Sammy said, taking Ivy's hand. "We better go say hi to everyone."

Once they were away from Uriah and Trudy, Sammy laughed out loud. "You're too funny."

"I am?"

"Your faces. Boy, oh boy, do you make a lot of silly faces." Sammy imitated Ivy's face of distress, scrunching his eyebrows together until his eyebrows met.

"I do?!" she said, mortified she'd looked stupid in front of Trudy and Pastor Leeds.

"Yeah."

"What did I just say with my face."

"You yelled, Sammy rescue me."

Ivy held her chin up high. "Maybe you're just good at reading people."

"Maybe, or you *just* make a lot of silly faces."

She knew she did, there was no point in arguing. "Trudy seems nice."

"Despite your call for help?" Sammy teased with a squeeze to her hand.

"Yes, despite my call for help."

"Trudy *is* nice. I think she really likes Pastor Leeds and I think he may like her too."

Ivy looked back at Uriah and Trudy for confirmation. "Oh," she said, happy to hear that and even happier to see it. Ivy was so caught up on Trudy being Sammy's ex-girlfriend, she missed what was right under her nose. She watched satisfied as a flush faced Uriah anxiously pulled a loose string on his shirtsleeve, teasing it out like it was a dangerous rattlesnake, while Trudy touched his arm, tucked a strand of hair behind her ear, and touched his arm again. Trudy was enamored with Pastor Leeds, struck by an angel, and looking for any excuse to touch him and was more than happy to help him with the frayed string hanging from his sleeve hem.

"Wow, Sammy, you *are* really good at reading people."

He smiled proudly.

Lindsey approached them with Hugo in her arms. "Sammy, can you hold him for a minute? I need to make him a bottle, and he's being fussy."

"Of course, Mom." Sammy took his baby brother from his mother. Once Lindsey's hands were free, she gave Ivy a big hug. "You look beautiful Ivy. White is your color."

Ivy blushed, and for once she didn't mind the color red. "Thank you. So do you."

Ivy had bought a new dress for the special occasion. She had spent grueling hours trying on every dress at the mall until she got just the right one. She had spent close to an hour between her two favorites, a strapless white dress with small blue flowers or a strapless white dress with small pink flowers. Ivy went for the blue flowers. She was glad Lindsey took notice of her new dress.

While Lindsey hurried toward the kitchen, Sammy sat down with baby Hugo. Ivy pulled out the seat next to him and took a seat. "So, how you like being a big brother again?"

"I love it. Alba and Maria were so excited, but they got bored with him in under five minutes. They just don't understand why he can't do anything. I think Jesse and I have been having more fun with him. Hugo's part of the boy's club. Isn't that right buddy?" he gushed, making a silly face at his little brother.

Ivy rolled her eyes again. "You and Jesse have been chummy."

"We just get each other. We're a lot alike."

"You're an evildoer kidnapper?"

Sammy shot Ivy a dirty look.

"Sorry," she grumbled.

"That wasn't him, Ivy. This Jesse wouldn't do that. He's like my best friend."

"Better not let Mike hear that."

Sammy laughed. "You're right. Mike *is* my best friend. Jesse . . . he's more like a brother."

Ivy choked on her saliva. "Say what?!"

"I know what you're thinking. You don't trust him, but I do. It's hard to explain. We just clicked. He clicked with the whole family. Even my dad likes him now."

"I noticed, he practically lives at your house," Ivy mumbled under her breath. She wasn't really mad about Sammy hanging out with Jesse nonstop, in fact she was secretly glad he was his shadow. It was true, Ivy didn't like Jesse and didn't trust him, not fully, but she needed him to act as a barricade between her and Sammy. After what happened with JD, just the idea of sitting in a room alone with Sammy terrified her. She wasn't sure why. She didn't think being alone with him would give anything away. She had gotten away with it. Only she and JD knew, but the thought of being intimate with Sammy after cheating on him seemed wrong. Part of her wanted to come clean about it, but she knew if she did, she'd lose him. Ivy hoped if she gave it time, things would go back to how they were.

Sammy went on, ignoring Ivy's funny face. "He understands what I went through with JD, 'cause he did too. He's just generations removed from it."

"I just think you're rushing into the whole Jesse brothers' pact a little quick. You just met him . . . again."

Sammy adjusted Hugo on his lap, moving him to his right leg. "I know that, Teller. What happened to Jesse would've happened to me if you didn't tell my dad Jesse kidnapped me."

"Always glad to take credit for saving you. But you were going to be JD chow not Jesse 2.0. You see what I'm getting at. Please, don't be stupid again."

"We both know JD was going to do more than eat me."

Ivy rolled her eyes again. She wished she hadn't brought JD up. She gave a slight nod.

Sammy smiled faintly. "Just give Jesse a chance, for me."

"Okay. Fine, I will," Ivy mumbled, watching Sammy tickle Hugo. She knew he was not taking their conversation seriously anyway.

"You want to hold him?" Without waiting for her response, Sammy got up and handed her Hugo.

"Um . . . sure," she said, hoping he would read her 'rescue me' face. He didn't. Ivy held Hugo out in front of her. His chubby legs squirmed as they dangled in the air.

"Not like that. Hold him against your body. Support his neck."

Sammy helped Ivy reposition her arms. Ivy could feel her face turning bright red with embarrassment. She was thinking, for a midwife, she was pretty awful with babies.

Baby Hugo terrified her more than JD and Jesse combined. Sammy had told her a dozen times how he wanted a big family. He had dreams of being a proud owner of a luxury minivan with a handful of screaming kids. Sammy had their future all planned out. They would get married after college and start filling their minivan with Hugos of their own.

Ivy wasn't so sure if that was how she saw her future. She knew she wanted Sammy in it, but she didn't see herself being a mother. She didn't think she had it in her. She couldn't even keep a succulent alive and they need next to no attention.

Sammy teased, "good practice for the future."

Ivy faked a smile. "Why can't we just live in the present Sammy? I'm sick of thinking of the past and the future."

"We are." He leaned in, pressing a kiss to her cheek. "I can't help it, I'm a dreamer. Besides, what are we without dreams, Teller?"

"Just dirt," she muttered, quoting JD to her disbelief. "*We are no better than dirt without aspiration for something more . . . something grand.*"

Sammy laughed. She didn't.

Elsa Tilton walked over to Sammy and Ivy. "May I?" she asked, taking Hugo from Ivy. Ivy was instantly relieved to have Hugo out of her arms. But that relief was short lived. She watched Elsa swoon over Hugo. She held him just right, supporting his neck and holding his small body next to her chest. Ivy's cheeks flushed again when Elsa rubbed her nose against Hugo's chubby cheek.

"You're great with kids Elsa," Sammy pointed out to Ivy's dismay. She knew Sammy no longer had a crush on Elsa. Last summer was ancient history as far as Sammy was concerned, but Ivy wasn't so sure Elsa didn't still want him.

"Thanks Sammy."

Ivy tried to act normal. "Of course, she's great with kids," she muttered to herself.

Elsa rocked Hugo in her arms. "I want to have a big family someday."

Sammy smiled. "You'd be a great mother."

"Of course, she would. Elsa Tilton is perfect," Ivy mumbled under her breath. That was it, Elsa beat out Trudy for the title of Knockout of Pleasant Mills.

Ivy couldn't believe she was jealous of Elsa's dream to be a mother. But she was. And to make matters worse, Elsa had on her runner up dress. It was just like Ivy's but in place of the small blue flowers, were small pink ones. Elsa looked better in the dress than her. It wasn't hard, Elsa was taller and had a better figure, and for some reason the shade of her blonde hair was the perfect complement to everything she ever wore.

Hugo was happily nestled in Elsa's arms when Lindsey approached with his bottle. "You're so good with him," Lindsey told Elsa proudly.

Ivy clenched her teeth, a muscle jumping in her jaw. She thought if one more person complimented Elsa, her head would explode.

Elsa took the baby bottle from Lindsey and dribbled some of the milk onto her wrist to check the temperature before giving it to Hugo.

"Impressive," Jeffrey said, walking by.

That's it! Ivy thought. *I'm going to kill Elsa Tilton and write on her tombstone: She would have been a good mother!*

CHAPTER TWENTY-ONE
The Angel

Pleasant Mills, New Jersey:1744

"Miss Lilly, are you okay?" A young Uriah asked wide-eyed as he sat by ten-year-old Lilly Baker's bedside. Pastor Baker had given his dying daughter the elixir Uriah had brought to heal her from his guardian angel and now they waited. Her eyelids fluttered for a moment before she opened her blue eyes. She looked at the boy sitting next to her curiously. Lilly reached her small, frail hand to his face and rested it on his cheek. "My angel."

"No Miss Lilly, I'm just a boy. It is I, Uriah Leeds. My face has been healed, just like you've been healed."

"I knew it was you before I opened my eyes. You are so much more than a boy Uriah Leeds. I always knew it." Lilly sat up and hugged Uriah tightly. He felt her warm tears on his face. He never wanted her to let go. "You saved me Uriah when no one else could." Lilly squeezed him harder as she brought her lips to his ear and whispered: "I love you, always." Lilly tenderly pressed a kiss to Uriah's cheek before letting him go.

LILLY BAKER: 1744

Uriah sat dumbfounded, his hand brushing over his cheek. He could still feel where Lilly's moist lips had touched his face. It was a wonderous feeling. Different from his mother's kisses. It was magical and he knew it. He kept his hand over his cheek trying to keep the magic of Lilly's kiss on his face. He wished he could keep it forever.

Pastor Baker walked into his daughter's sickroom. "Glad to see your up Lilly."

"Yes father."

"We can thank young Uriah Leeds for that, God smiles on him."

"Thank you, Uriah," Lilly said with a kind smile.

Uriah smiled back. "You're most welcome but it was not my doing, it was my guardian angel's."

Pastor Baker put a hand on Uriah's shoulder. "I have finally found my understudy. I want you at church first thing in the morning, Uriah."

Uriah's face lit up. "Me, Pastor Baker?"

"Yes, Uriah. Your faith and devotion are like no others. God turned away from you when you were born, leaving you disformed and crippled, but still you had faith. And it is your faith in God Almighty that has restored you and saved my daughter. You, Uriah Leeds, will make a fine pastor. For it is what God wants, and me too. You, Uriah, will bring nonbelievers back to his church. They will look upon your face and follow the path of the light."

"Thank you, Pastor Baker." Uriah said, shaking his hand vigorously. "Thank you so much. You won't be sorry."

"Till tomorrow, Uriah."

Uriah looked back at Lilly sitting up in bed, still smiling at him. He rubbed his cheek again. The magic was still there. "Goodbye Miss Lilly."

"Till tomorrow, Uriah," she said.

Uriah ran home with his two good legs as fast as he could.

"Mama, are you home yet?!" Uriah yelled, barreling through the front door.

Uriah's mother was at the kitchen sink peeling potatoes. "Mama, I met my guardian angel today! He healed me!" Uriah tugged on his mother's skirt. "Mama, please look! I'm all better. I'm not irregular no more! And Miss Lilly, he saved her too. And Mama, Miss Lilly kissed my cheek, here,"

Uriah exclaimed as he pointed to his cheek with his free hand and continued to tug on his mother's dress with the other. "Pastor Baker wants to teach me to be a pastor! All my prayers have been answered! Today is the best day of my life. I thanked God and my guardian angel over and over. I know Mr. JD will watch over me. Mama did you hear me?!"

Uriah's mother put her knife down, turning around to hug her son feverishly. "Oh Uriah, I have waited a long time for everyone to see how special you are—see what I have always seen."

"Mama, why are you crying?" He gently put his hand under his mother's chin, slowly lifting her face to his and tenderly tucking her dark hair behind her ears.

Before Uriah's mother came into focus, he woke up to his cell phone ringing. He blindly reached for his phone. With a dry mouth: "Hello?"

"It's Elsa," Mrs. Tilton said, her voice cracking. Uriah held his breath. He knew what was coming. The dream he had just awoken from was more than a dream. It was a repressed memory. That could only mean one thing, JD collected another soul. One of the thirteen he was owed from his congregation. The price Uriah had to pay to save his son, Joseph, all those years ago. JD's words rang in his ears, making his body tremble. *It does seem a fair price to save your first son, thirteen souls for his. Is he not worth it to you my sweet Uriah? Would you not do anything for your son?'*

"Is she okay?" Uriah managed to get out with some difficulty. He knew last summer every time he got a memory back a child was found dead. That was how it went. Four children were taken last year, and he had gotten back four memories from his past life.

"She's in a coma. The doctors don't know what's wrong with her."

Uriah sighed into the phone. He was relieved, he thought for sure Elsa was dead.

"I'm heading to the hospital now. Don't lose faith Mrs. Tilton."

CHAPTER TWENTY-TWO
Tragic Events

"You hear about Elsa?" Sammy asked Ivy. He was leaning against the headboard of his bed staring up at the ceiling, his phone pressed against his face.

"Yeah," Ivy said into the receiver, turning down her music. She knew it was only a matter of time before Sammy called about Elsa. "Pastor Leeds stopped over and told us."

"It's JD."

"Umm . . . what's JD?"

"Elsa's coma. JD did it."

"Ivy pressed her cell phone firmly to her face in a slapping motion and exhaled loudly. "What makes you think that?"

"Pastor Leeds said he got a memory back right before Mrs. Tilton called him about Elsa."

"Yeah, he told Grams and me that too. It's just a coincidence."

"How can you say that?!" Sammy asked, sitting up in bed, his voice slightly raised. "It's just like last time. With everyone who went missing last year, Pastor Leeds got a memory from his past. Remember?"

"I'm not stupid Sammy. I remember. But I remember things a little different."

He scoffed. "How so?"

Ivy didn't want to upset Sammy, but the scoffing pushed her to lose her temper. Sometimes she was a little too much like her grandmother for her own good. "Uriah didn't get a memory back when someone went missing. He got a memory back when someone died. *Remember?*"

Sammy's mind went to Tim rotting in the woods. He instantly felt sick, the smell from that day filling his nostrils again.

Sammy's heavy breathing into the phone receiver made Ivy instantly regret her tone. "Don't worry about Elsa," Ivy said optimistically. "Elsa's not dead and she's not going to die."

"You're right, she's not dead," Sammy replied in a low voice. "But that doesn't mean JD has nothing to do with her getting sick." Sammy thought about the letter he received from Jesse on his bed the day they found Timothy's body. *'JD is up to something big.'*

Ivy's voice was a near whine. "Oh Sammy. I want to support you, I do. I know you need closure on this Japhet Dean Leeds thing, but JD kills kids, putting them in a supernatural coma is hardly demon like. People get sick. Elsa got sick after Hugo's party. It could just be really bad food poisoning. That's all. She'll come out of this; you'll see."

"I'm not convinced."

"Just breathe in Sammy, everyone we know is out of danger. Everyone's over thirteen, besides your sisters, and it'll be years before you have to worry about that. Can we both just agree that for the time being, everyone is safe? There's no weird double thirteen on some international calendar no one besides you has heard of. Or some leap year that corresponds to thirteen, or the alignment of thirteen planet's suns, or whatever your imagination can think up. Everyone is safe and that includes Elsa."

"JD picked kids who were linked to the number thirteen last year because it was a game to him. He's sadistic. He can take anyone at any age, when he wants, as long as they're members of our church. Jesse remembers him choosing people that had no connection to the number thirteen during his first life but Uriah's contract with him specifies they must be part of his church. Meaning no one we know is safe, including Elsa."

Ivy made a disapproving grunting noise into the phone. "There you go trusting the wrong people again. Who cares what Jesse remembers from the 1800s!"

"I do."

"Only because it coincides with your thinking—justifies some crazy idea you have in your head."

"I'm not crazy," Sammy said sharply into the phone.

Ivy sighed. "I know that. I didn't mean it like that."

"How do you explain the memory Pastor Leeds got back then?"

Not that Sammy could see her, but she shook her head at him. "Not giving you an inch Sammy Lopez. It's like Uriah said, it was a dream, and I think that's all it was. I'm sorry, but it's not like before. When Zac, Tyrone, and Louie died he got these huge chunks of memory back that showed him something about himself. He already knew he saved Lilly when she was a little girl, and that JD fixed his face and leg. This new dream didn't show him anything he didn't know. Think about it Sammy," Ivy said, switching the phone to her other ear. "The memories Uriah got back last summer were these tragic events that let him piece his former life together. Him making a deal with JD when he was a boy, JD forcing his hand to trade thirteen lives for his son's life forever, and then the horrible one where JD eats his wife's heart. I mean these are all crazy. I just don't think Uriah's latest dream fits the pattern of his repressed memories. Him having a boyhood dream about his crush just seems worthless to me."

"What about when Tim died?" Sammy asked with great difficulty. Just saying Timothy's name hurt him, made the guilt tie knots in his stomach. "What memory did Pastor Leeds get back with Tim's death?"

"I don't remember him saying."

"Me either," Sammy admitted, "I don't think he did. I'm not surprised he didn't bring it up after how Tim was found. By then we all knew Tim was dead, and I don't think I would've wanted to hear it. But . . . maybe Pastor Leeds already got back all of his life defining memories and the memory he got back after Tim's death was just like the one he had after Elsa slipped into a coma, not life defining, just a lost memory. I'm gonna ask him about it the next time I see him." Sammy paused. "Actually, he's dropping Jesse off later for a sleepover, gonna see if I can talk to him about it tonight."

"Ask away Sammy, but it's not going to change the truth. I know we're all a little jumpy waiting for JD to make his next move. But with Devan and Mrs. Ball gone and Jesse a literal born again Christian; I think it's going to be a long time before he pulls anything. Remember, JD has all the time in the world. You can't let him rule your life. You need to get over it."

Her words stung Sammy into silence.

Ivy realized how she sounded. "Not like that, Sammy. I just don't want you to . . ."

"To have a breakdown," he said finishing her sentence.

"No not that. I don't want you to forget to live." Ivy sighed. "Well, what does Abby say about Elsa's coma? What does her almighty ancient wisdom tell us?" Ivy asked with a laugh trying to cheer Sammy up.

"I don't know," he said. "I didn't ask."

"The two Lopez witches aren't conspiring over a boiling cauldron? I'm shocked."

"She's been busy with the baby and all." Sammy was not in the mood to talk about the problems with his grandmother.

"And your dad?"

"My dad acknowledged my concerns like I was one of his clients giving me his polite work face and taking down notes. He doesn't think a coma is supernatural."

"I know I've said this before, but I'm really starting to like your dad."

Ivy swallowed hard, she wished she hadn't just said that. Thinking of Mr. Lopez made her see his face, her mind skipping to his doppelganger, Japhet Dean Leeds. Ivy had tirelessly been trying to keep JD out of her head. Talking about him didn't seem to trigger his face, but for some reason talking about Mr. Lopez did.

Ivy quickly changed the direction of the conversation. "Well at least you have Jesse to talk conspiracy theories with all night."

"What can I say, he's the only one who believes them. And it's not like I can talk to Mike about it. I wish we could tell him the truth about what's going on. I think he's starting to feel left out.

"Nothing is going on Sammy. Save your hocus-pocus rants for

Jesse."

"I wouldn't want you to get jealous," he teased. She could just see him wearing his sideways grin she loved so much.

"Jesse's not nearly as cute as me."

"We finally agree on something. Gotta go, my mom's calling me for dinner. I'll see you tomorrow at the hospital for Elsa's prayer service."

Sammy leaned against the windowsill waiting for Pastor Leeds to drop Jesse off. As soon as he saw the headlights cut through the fog, he was outside. He was at the passenger side door before Pastor Leeds turned off the engine. Jesse gave a quick smile and got out of the car. "Hey."

"Hey," Sammy said back to Jesse as Jesse grabbed his overnight bag from the back seat of the car. "I'll be right in."

"Kay," he said, making his way to the door where Lindsey was waiting.

"Pastor Leeds," Sammy said, sitting in the passenger seat, "can I talk to you for a moment?"

"Of course. What's on your mind?"

Sammy shut the car door softly. "I wanted to talk to you about Tim," he said robotically. Sammy was trying to say the words without actually thinking of his friend.

Uriah nodded. "I spoke to his parents this afternoon. Everyone's doing well, all things considered. They asked about you. When you're ready, they would like you to reach out to them. They would like that very much."

Sammy swallowed the lump in his throat. "I actually wanted to talk about the memory you got back when he died. Tim was dead for a while when Ivy and I found him, but I can't remember you ever telling us you got back another memory. That's how it works, isn't it? Someone dies and you get a memory?"

Uriah nodded again. His right hand left the steering column and went to the button on his cuff sleeve. He rubbed the plastic button between his thumb and index finger. "Yes, that's how it works. I did get a memory back some time before Tim was found."

"And you said nothing?" Sammy said, his pulse picking up tempo.

Uriah put his head down, his dark locks falling over his forehead. "I didn't want everyone to lose hope. The memory was no reason to stop looking for Tim dead or alive."

Sammy agreed but he couldn't say it out loud, not without thinking of the promise he made to Tim, the promise he would be rescued. Sammy leaned back against the gray upholstery, his eyes coming to rest at the front door where he could make out his mom and Jesse waiting for him in the doorway, worried. He turned to Uriah, ignoring their stares. "What was your memory about, Pastor Leeds?"

Uriah lifted his head up slightly. His skin looked a sickly pallor under the outside spotlight. "I remembered burying my wife."

Sammy tried to recall Ivy's words to him earlier that evening. "Was your memory a tragic event that helped you piece your lost life back together?" He knew that wasn't quite what Ivy had said to him, but he thought it made the point.

"Tragic—yes. My son asked me how I could let his mother die. But as far as piecing my past back together. I'm not sure . . . I don't think it or I will ever be fully put back together."

"I'm sorry," Sammy said.

"Nothing for you to be sorry about, Sammy. My life is made up of my choices, same as everyone else's."

Sammy looked out the front windshield toward the house again, exhaling loudly.

"What's really on your mind, Sammy? Where are these questions going?"

"Elsa—do you think her coma is due to JD, even though she's not dead and your memory is less tragic?" Sammy asked, not able to think of a better way to phrase his thoughts.

"Yes, I do. I got the feeling your father and Mary and Ivy Teller think it was a harmless dream, but when I dream it's like I'm there, like I'm transported through time. I've never had a dream that wasn't a memory from my past, so I suppose they're all memories. I guess they could be right, and my dream was just a dream. Yet, I have this gut feeling that I can't explain. It's at my very core. I hope, I pray that I'm wrong and Elsa will come back to us soon. But I also feel better. It's true, I feel remarkably better than last summer, but my energy has still been very low and today I feel, well I feel great today. The best I've felt since I came to Pleasant Mills. I think my health is also connected to the memories. I started feeling better last summer after I got the first one back, but I can't know for sure."

"What can we do?" Sammy asked.

Uriah shrugged looking much younger than he was. "I don't know. But for now, try not to think of it. You and Jesse have some fun. It's summer vacation, enjoy yourself."

Lindsey knocked on the passenger side window. Sammy opened the door.

"Hello Pastor Leeds, is everything okay?" she asked, glancing to Sammy.

"Hi Lindsey. Yes, Sammy and I were just catching up. I visited the Chens this afternoon."

Lindsey gave a warm smile.

"Thanks for everything Pastor Leeds," Sammy said, hopping out of the car.

"Good night," he replied, starting the car engine, and putting the car in reverse.

Lindsey walked with Sammy to the front door, her hand placed on his back.

"Where's Jesse?" Sammy asked before Lindsey could ask if he was alright.

"In the kitchen. He was still hungry. I'm going to have to make up some trays for Pastor Leeds to keep in the freezer and just pop in the oven. I don't want them starving."

Sammy smiled at his mother. "You're the best Mom."

She smiled back, she never tired of him telling her that.

Lindsey made her way into the kitchen at the sound of the phone ringing while Sammy took off his windbreaker. He opened the coat closet pulling out the first hanger.

Anita grabbed his arm. "What are you up to Samuel Cameron?"

He yanked his arm away from his grandmother and put his coat on the hanger, shoving it into the closet. "Nothing."

She snatched his arm back and clutched it in a tight grip meant to hurt him. "Be careful where you stick your nose. Don't start something you're not prepared to finish."

"I *will* finish it, without your help." He pulled his hand free, slammed the closet door and headed into the kitchen. He could feel Anita's gaze still on him. He took a seat next to Jesse where he was forking mashed potatoes into his mouth.

"Everything okay?" Jesse asked, reaching for his glass of iced tea.

"Yeah. Just thinking."

Uriah's mind weighed heavy on his shoulders all the way home. He hoped he would never have to share the memory Sammy asked about, so he kept it to himself even though that meant Tim was dead and the search for a missing child was now a murder investigation. When Sammy asked, he could only tell the gist of his memory, not the full rendition. If he could even call it a full memory; it was only part of something—something tragic.

Pleasant Mills, New Jersey: 1769

Day light was fading fast, but Uriah didn't care. He kept digging. He stood waist deep in his wife's grave. No hole would ever be deep enough to bury his pain. He would have to dig to the center of the Earth, and he was fine with that. The blisters on his hands stopped him from thinking about Lilly, who lay dead waiting to be entombed.

"So it's true," a man said from behind a nearby tree.

Uriah paused, thrusting his spade into the dirt floor, and turning around to see Rupert Hanson. He knew Rupert and his brothers all too well and tried to always keep a comfortable distance from them. It had been a long time since the Hanson brothers had put a beating on him at Batsto's sawmill, but the memories of being teased, punched, and kicked were still fresh in his mind.

The Hansons hadn't touched Uriah since Pastor Baker claimed it was God that healed Uriah's cleft lip and stiff leg and saved his daughter, Lilly, from her death bed. The town believed Pastor Baker, all apart from the Hanson family, but Uriah's newfound celebrity status made him untouchable to the town bullies.

"I knew it was only a matter of time before you'd killed Lilly. I tried to tell her you were no good."

Uriah glanced upward at the woolen blanket covering his wife's dead body. A gust of wind pushed his hair onto his face, the hair sticking to his icy sweat. Uriah took a deep breath in to calm himself, tucking his stray clumps of hair behind his ears. "I have had a very rough day, Rupert. Leave me to bury my wife in peace."

"No, not this time Uriah Leeds. I shoulda finished what I started when you got Lilly sick the first time. My brothers and me shoulda beat you till you didn't move—till you were dead." Rupert took off his felt hat and ran it across his face, to wipe tears. "I could have saved my Lilly."

"Those words on Rupert's lips summoned an anger in Uriah he felt in his marrow. "Your Lilly?!" he shouted. "She never cared for you. She chose me. She loved me. Accept it."

"All the good her loving you did. She's dead now." Rupert took big strides toward the covered Lilly, ripping the blood-stained blanket off her with a flourish. "Animal attack, that's the rumor heard," he said in a low voice, unblinking as he stared at Lilly's corpse. "No. This ain't no animal attack. Not one scratch, not one bitemark on her." He crouched next to her, to further his examination. "Her heart's missing . . . this looks surgical, doctor like." Rupert's eyes left Lilly and locked onto Uriah. "Wouldn't you say parson?"

"Rupert, I'm warning you."

"Are you now," he said in a taunting voice, standing upright and pulling out the pistol he had tucked into his pants. "You fixin' on doing to me what you did to her, is that right?"

"I didn't do that to Lilly." The wind blew her hair, catching his attention. Her golden tendrils danced in the wind around her beautiful face, making her appear as if she was just sleeping. His eyes drifted to the ruddy stain on her chest, his own chest constricting in pain, he knew better, his beloved was dead.

Rupert brought the pistol closer to Uriah, "Admit what you did. Admit what you are. Maybe then God can forgive you." Rupert motioned with the gun for Uriah to get out from the grave. "Admit what you are," he said again.

Uriah planted his feet, his hand tightening around the handle of the shovel.

"Admit that you're a witch like your mother. I know you and your kind are in bed with the Devil," Rupert spat with venom in his voice.

Uriah shook his head in frustration. "What are you talking about?!"

"My nana told me stories about your mother and her family. We know what you are, always have."

"My mother is a good woman and a Christian, same as you and I, and I'm the pastor of Pleasant Mills. I was handpicked by Pastor Baker to be his replacement and marry his daughter."

Signaling with his loaded pistol, Rupert motioned again for Uriah to get out of the grave he dug. "Handpicked you say, we Hansons don't think so. You made him pick you. Made her pick you. Used your black magic, you did."

"Rupert, I don't have time for this. I need to bury my wife. Let me do that, then we can talk."

"Time for talk is over. You killed Lilly and it's time for you and your family to be put on trial." Rupert stood in front of Uriah, his pistol pointed at his face.

"You have no authority to do that."

"The hell I don't. Bud is getting your mother and Jeff is getting your little boy and then we going to have us a little test."

"Test?" Uriah asked, the wind picking up to a howl. He squinted his eyes against the onslaught.

"Yeah, heard a thing or two about that. Figure we take this to the lake, where I shoulda ended it years ago after you pushed Lilly in the water giving her that cut that got infected."

"That was an accident, and you know it. I slid because of my bum leg, I never meant to push her in the lake."

Rupert went on as if he didn't hear him. "If you drown, well, it looks like we made a mistake, if not we know what you are. Either way we will be cleansing the town from the likes of you and yours the way I see it."

Uriah looked down at the shovel wondering if he could use it to disarm Rupert. He pulled it from the cold dirt but hesitated. Before Uriah could react, Rupert's pistol cracked him on the side of the head, bringing him to the ground unconscious.

Uriah lay on his back. His hand reached up to his left temple, his fingers feeling something cold and wet. It took him a moment to remember what happened, to realize why his head pounded and that it was his own blood on his hand. Rupert Handson had hit him with his pistol, knocking him unconscious.

Uriah tried to make it to his feet. He was woozy, falling to one knee. Surveying his surroundings, his vision blurred from his migraine and the blood trickling down his face. He was no longer at his home, digging his beloved Lilly's grave after JD ripped out her heart. He was at Batsto Lake. A woman was sprawled out on the shore. She was wet, her damp, dark hair thrown over her still, pale face, her hands and feet bound. Uriah's heart pounded in his chest, sending a spike of pain to his head. He went to stand up again, making it to his feet slowly. He saw Bud and Jeff Hanson. They held onto his son by his shoulders, his son's small hands and feet bound with rope. Tears streamed down young Joseph's face. His eyes were on the woman who lay near his feet.

"Stop this!" Uriah shouted, his voice rough, cracking over the wind. "If you hurt one hair on my son's head . . ." His eyes darted to the woman on the ground again. He knew it to be his mother, but still he went on with his threat. "Or my mother, I will . . ."

"You will what, Pastor Leeds?" Rupert asked, coming from behind Uriah. He pulled out his pistol again, positioning it at Uriah's chest. "Cast a spell on my brothers and me? Cut out our hearts like you did to Lilly Baker? Admit you killed her. Admit it in front of your son."

Uriah glanced to his sobbing boy.

"Last chance Uriah Leeds," Rupert said through clenched teeth, his finger moving toward the trigger.

"Okay, okay," Uriah said, palms down, trying to defuse the situation. Tears mixed with the blood running down his face. He tasted its saltiness in his mouth, the taste making him nauseous. "Just don't hurt Joseph."

Rupert nodded.

"I am no witch nor is my son. I am just a stupid, stupid man. It *is* my fault Lilly is dead. But Joseph had nothing to do with it."

Joseph stopped crying and stared at his father shocked, his mouth agape, his blond hair, the same shade of his mother's, whipped around his face. "Poppa how could you let Mamma die?"

"I'm sorry Joseph. I'm so sorry."

Rupert smiled a satisfied grin, revealing a bottom row of crooked teeth. "Sounds like we got ourselves a confession boys."

Uriah glared at Rupert. His eyes so angry, they could kill. "You ignorant man, you don't know the powers at work here. You will be judged for this. God sees all. *No creature is hidden from his sight, but all are naked and exposed to the eyes of him to whom we must give account.*"

"Well then, we best not keep the good Lord waiting. The trial's over, time to deal out the justice." Rupert gestured to his brothers with the tilt of his head, and they tossed the rope-bound boy into the lake.

HANSON BROTHERS: 1769

Uriah sat in his car. The engine still running as he idled in front of the rectory. His hands gripped the steering wheel tight, his knuckles turning paper white. He swore he could still feel the burning sting of the wind on the open gash on his head and see his son's scared blue eyes before they disappeared into the dark lake.

CHAPTER TWENTY-THREE
Blue-eyed, Dark-haired Angels

Uriah jumped at the tap on his car window.

"Sorry," Trudy Grindhouse said with a giggle.

Uriah got out of his car. "Hi Trudy," he said embarrassed. "What can I do for you?"

"Actually, I was wondering if I could do something for *you.*"

"Oh!" Uriah said, putting his keys in his pocket and missing. He knelt to pick them up, a rose tint on his cheeks. "What's that?"

"I was talking to Lindsey, and I heard you burnt your dinner, so I thought I'd head over and cook for you, that is if you're still hungry?"

His blush deepened, a toothy grin blooming on his face. "Oh!" he said again. "That would be great. With Jesse heading over to Sammy's, we ate early, if you can call it that. I made pizza, I think next time I'll just order it. Poor Jesse ate the burnt cheese off the top, but not to worry, Lindsey informed me before I dropped him off, she had a plate of leftovers set aside for him." He was rambling now. "I was just going to come home and eat a pack of peanut butter cracker sandwiches Mary Teller had given me. She had this coupon and bought a whole bunch. I'm not crazy about them but—" Uriah stopped himself, realizing he was talking out of nervousness. Trudy did that to him. He tried to tell himself talking to Trudy was like talking to anyone else and there was no reason to get so nervous, but he knew that wasn't true. Trudy was special. "Yes, I'd love it if you made me dinner tonight. I'm not the best cook admittedly so, but I'm fairly good at chopping vegetables. And if not, I have a very comprehensive first aid kit that came with the house."

Trudy laughed. "You poor thing, I won't let it come to that."

He smiled sheepishly.

She mirrored his smile. "Want to help me with the groceries? They're in my car."

"Oh, yes, of course." He took the brown bag of groceries out of the trunk of Trudy's car. "What's for dinner?"

"I hope you like eggplant," Trudy said.

"One of my favorites, you must be a mind reader."

She giggled. "Close, I asked Lindsey."

Uriah helped Trudy in the kitchen. Placing her hand on his, she showed him the proper way to cut the eggplant, making sure the slices were the same thickness all the way through. He had never been happier to be a horrible cook.

"You're hopeless Uriah, you really are," she said as she breaded the irregular cut eggplant cutlets and placed them in the frying pan.

"I had hinted at my subpar cooking skills," he said grinning, cutting tomatoes for a salad. "Can't mess up a salad."

Trudy laughed. Her laugh sounded like a little girl's. "No conventional way at least."

"I'm very fortunate, Lindsey sends over lots of leftovers and the Henry sisters always drop me off baked goods. A pie one day, a cake the next, and sometimes cookies. Oh, and there have been some breads." His mind went to Mrs. Ball. She too had baked for him, but now she was dead. He'd shot her. He came down hard with his knife just missing his finger, the juice of the tomato squirting all over the counter reminding him of blood. He took a moment to steady his nerves.

Trudy grinned to herself, turning over a cutlet in the frying pan.

"Well, I'm going to outdo them all tonight. You're getting dinner and dessert."

"I'm feeling very lucky indeed," Uriah said, picking up the knife again.

She flashed him a smile. "Me too."

"Don't tell Lindsey this, but I think your eggplant parmigiana is better than hers," Uriah said to Trudy as they cleared the table after dinner.

Trudy beamed. "You're just saying that. I've had Lindsey's and its better."

"No, I really enjoyed it."

"Maybe it's the company," Trudy said, in a leading way.

He blushed. "You're the very best company indeed. Thank you for making me dinner. Please feel free to do that any time you have the urge."

Trudy put the dirty dishes in the sink. "And what about other urges?"

Uriah turned the hot water on, letting it pour over the dishes as his pulse raced, the gears in his mind turning. He wondered if she'd had just implied something or if he was making too much out of it. He had developed a crush on Trudy months ago, and thought it was blinding him now. He kept his line of vision on the dirty dishes, unsure of himself—unsure of what she meant.

Uriah had first met Trudy at her little brother Louie's funeral and had offered her grief counseling as he had offered everyone close to Louie. She took his offer and Uriah had been calling to check up on her ever since. He called her every day, like clockwork. He knew her schedule and would call her after her nursing classes concluded for the day. He never missed a call. As short as they were sometimes, it was the highlight of his day and as soon as he hung up, he would be anxious for his next call to her.

Uriah shook his head at himself, more embarrassed than ever, his ears burning. He had only just gotten her comfortable with calling him Uriah over Pastor Leeds. Lindsey cooked for him, that didn't imply anything, the Henry sisters cooked for him, that didn't apply anything, Mrs. Ball had cooked for him and that didn't imply anything, why did Trudy cooking for him imply something? He decided it didn't.

Trudy leaned in close to Uriah, their shoulders touching, and shut off the sink faucet. "I guess it would be a lot easier to clean these if I let them soak overnight," Uriah said, still not looking at Trudy. He tensely dried his hands on the sink towel, before facing her. She was smiling at him, with that kind smile of hers.

"So, what's for dessert?" Uriah asked, smiling back. "There's no way you're going to outdo the Henry sisters' apple pie. Even Lindsey admits defeat."

Trudy continued to smile, but there was an anxiousness to it. She nibbled her bottom lip as if she was thinking. "I'm just going to go for it."

"For dessert?" Uriah asked. "The custard stand is open, my treat."

She pressed a quick kiss to his lips then pulled away to wait for his reaction.

His hand grazed his lips, feeling the lingering sensation of her soft touch.

"Say something Uriah," she said in a low voice.

His voice was timid, but clear. "That's better than the Henry sisters' apple pie. So much better."

Her smile blossomed. "So . . . it's okay if I kiss you again?"

"Oh yes," he said in the same timid manner, his eyes darting to the floor than back to her. "I like to be kissed. I mean I like your lips. I mean I like you." His face was beet red; heat traveled up his neck in blotches. "I'm not very good at this."

Trudy beamed anew, her smile bright. "You like me?"

He made a noise in his throat before speaking. "Very much. You're a very good person. You remind me so much of . . ." He thought of Lilly. Of the memories he had of her kindness.

"Who?"

"An angel," he told her, not wanting to lie to Trudy. He lied enough to her already, consoling her for the loss of her brother whose death was his fault. Trudy reminded him of Lilly and Lilly was an angel.

Her smile widened. "That's funny, because I thought the same thing of you. I guess we're just two blue-eyed, dark-haired angels," Trudy said.

He shook his head. "Just one of us is," Uriah corrected. His entire body was on fire now.

"I like you too, if you didn't guess," she said.

I was hoping, but I wasn't sure as our relationship started out as grief counseling."

She looked down at her hands, her smile gone.

He took a step toward her, wanting to comfort her, but was unsure. He nervously nibbled on the inside of his cheek, almost biting through it. He couldn't believe he brought up Louie. She knew why they started talking, she didn't need a reminder her brother was murdered.

"I'm sorry," he said, "I didn't mean to make you upset." His hand brushed her elbow.

She lifted her head to meet his eyes.

"Please know how deeply sorry I am for Louie. If I could've done anything to prevent it, know that I would have for you, Trudy. Because I like you." He meant it. He never meant for anyone to get hurt because of him, and never Trudy. She, like her brother, was kind and good-natured. She was as rare as a perfect diamond, and he knew it. He felt guilty having these deep feelings for her because of Lilly and because he knew Louie was dead because of him, but he couldn't bury his feelings for Trudy.

When he saw her again at Hugo's baptism, after not seeing her for months, saw her blue-gray eyes the color of the sky, his feelings raced to his heart, taking his breath away. He liked her in a way he thought he could only like Lilly—he loved her.

He was so glad she was home for the summer. He had hoped she would come to church to nourish his crush, despite her family usually having to work on Sundays. His wildest dreams had already come true. Trudy was talking about him with Lindsey and stopped by to make him dinner. Then there was the kiss. That was beyond his imagination.

His breathing became increasingly strained as she planted another kiss on his lips. Her lips were so full and soft. They felt so good, his body temperature continued to rise. He wanted to reach up and touch her hair, touch her face, touch her lips, but he was too frightened to.

"I really appreciate everything you've done for my mother, grandmother, and me. I wouldn't have made it through last semester if it weren't for your calls of encouragement, not to mention all your help looking for my brother. You really have been a godsend to my family."

Shame bubbled up in his stomach at the mention of Louie.

Trudy moved Uriah's dark hair away from his face, their eyes locking. "It's okay if you kiss me back."

"Okay," he said in a timorous voice. Uriah placed his shaking hand on the side of Trudy's face pulling her closer until she rested against him. He bowed his head, his hair falling into his eyes as their lips touched.

"Now was that so hard?" she said playfully.

"No," he said with a boyish smile. "But if I faint, there's a nice pillow on the couch you can use to prop up my head."

Trudy took Uriah's hand, lacing their fingers together. "Which way to your bedroom? It's probably safer to kiss you there in case you do faint."

They made their way up the stairs together, Uriah's mind racing to catch up with what was happening. Just a few hours ago he was going to have crackers for dinner and now he was going to his bedroom with Trudy Grindhouse. His conscience gnawed at him. He wondered if this was right. Wondered if Trudy would be leading him to his room if she knew it was his deal with JD that caused her younger brother to be murdered. Wondered if this was right with Lilly laying undead in the room across the hall that used to be the junk room. He wondered if he should stop what was about to happen.

Still holding Uriah's hand, Trudy sat on his bed pulling him next to her. She brushed her long hair off her shoulder, leaning her neck to the side for him to kiss it. Uriah did as Trudy wanted and ran his hand down her neckline, cherishing the feel of her skin on his as his kisses spanned the distance. He was powerless against her, and he was thinking he was okay with that.

Trudy stood up and dropped her sundress. Her long, dark hair fell gracefully around her shoulders to her lower back. Uriah's eyes traced the majestic image of her naked. She really was a blue-eyed, dark-haired angel and with that his mind was silenced.

"I never thought I'd feel this again," Uriah said in a whisper as Trudy's head rested on his bare chest, her arm draped over him like a blanket while her finger traced the heart-shape birthmark on his chest.

Trudy tilted her chin to gaze into Uriah's cerulean orbs. His eyes captured the light from the hall, making them sparkle like stars and trapping her in the frame of his thick lashes.

He ran his hand up her arm. "Before you, there was Lilly. I thought there could be no one else but her. I loved her with all my heart, and we were married."

Trudy's body tensed. "You're married?"

"Was, Lilly died. I want to tell you about her because I want to share as much of my past with you as possible, so you can make your mind up about me. —I've already made my mind up about you."

She scrunched her eyebrows.

"I know making love doesn't have to mean anything in today's world, but it does to me." He touched his white sheets with his fingertips, before taking her hand. "This is all just an extension of what my heart feels. I love you Trudy Grindhouse."

"I love you too," she whispered in his ear.

Uriah's voice shook. "You do?"

"I do."

"Oh Trudy," he said as he held her tightly to his chest, their hearts beating against each other's. "I'm so happy. I don't deserve to be, but I'll gladly accept it."

CHAPTER TWENTY-FOUR
Anita the Strange

Sammy and Jesse sat on Sammy's bed talking in whispers, not entirely sure why they were whispering. "The 'old you', told me not to trust my grandmother."

"And?" Jesse asked.

"And that's all."

"Why would I say that?"

Sammy shrugged. "I don't know, but you got in my head. I could be making something out of nothing, but she's been acting funny—really funny even for her. I've always been close with her, her favorite. When she first came to live with us she was so great. She said she came for me and decided to stay for me. I was kinda emotional then."

Jesse elbowed him. "Then?"

Sammy rolled his eyes. "I mean I was really bad. I wasn't dealing with everything very well. It felt like I was talking to my therapist every day. I was sleeping in the living room in the family tent my dad set up so I wouldn't have to be alone. I had a few panic attacks and Abby was very supportive. Then my mom got pregnant, and things got strange. I feel like the better I got, the worse she treated me. No matter what I did, I couldn't please her. It was almost like she was deliberately pushing me away. Then she took the family grimoire from me when Ivy found Tim. It was the straw that broke the camel's back. I've been avoiding her ever since."

"Straw, camel?" Jesse asked, raising an eyebrow.

Sammy narrowed his eyes.

"Kidding," Jesse grinned. "Why do you think your grandmother would want to push you away?"

"No clue. Maybe she's up to something or got herself into something. I'm thinking maybe that's what you were trying to warn me about."

"You don't think her behavior has something to do with JD, do you?"

"Maybe. Possible. She just told me to be careful where I stick my nose after I was asking Pastor Leeds about Elsa. It's like she knows something I don't. But whatever she's hiding, you're going to find out tonight?"

"Me?" Jesse asked, pointing at his chest. "Tonight?"

"Yeah you. Sneak into her room and see if you see anything funny."

"Is this a joke?"

"No joke. I can't do it," Sammy said. "She'll sense me. The whole witch thing."

"Shouldn't we wait until she's not home?"

Sammy shook his head. "Can't, she locks her door if she goes somewhere."

Jesse let out a loud sigh, laying back on a pillow and folding his hands over his chest. "Great. What exactly am I looking for?"

"Something out of the ordinary, some sign she might be working with JD or a sign she might be in trouble."

"I'm going to be *in trouble* if I get caught."

Sammy nudged him. "Come on Jesse, you lived in the woods for months and never got caught by the police, you'll be fine. We'll wait until the middle of the night when she's fast asleep."

Jesse took a deep breath, mustering up nerve. "I can't believe Sammy talked me into this," he muttered to himself, his chin tucked into his chest. Slowly, he turned the doorknob to Anita's bedroom. He held his breath as he entered, closing the door softly behind him. The room was dark; he could hardly see. The smell of incense perfumed the room in scents of sage and thyme. Jesse's eyes darted around the room as they adjusted to the absence of light. Every inch of Anita's bedroom walls were covered with talismans and trinkets. Anita broke Jeffrey's rule of personality under the bed a hundred times over. Jesse felt like he was walking through a tourist trap selling witchy wares, from magic eight balls to healing crystals. "Stereotypes come from somewhere," he mumbled under his breath as he walked through a beaded curtain into the belly of the room.

"Hello, Jesse Richards."

Jesse sucked air, taking a step back, to scan the dark for Anita. He found her, sitting on the floor, legs crossed with small votive candles, their wicks barely lit, encircling her. "Anita I . . . I . . ."

Anita stood up, their eyes locked; the candles around her going out instantaneously as the light in the room turned on. They stood face to face. They were the same height. "You were just prying," she said, finishing his sentence.

"No. I was just looking for the grimoire for Sammy. I wanted to cheer him up. He said you took it back and I was going to—"

"Steal it."

"Borrow it and put it back before you noticed. Sorry."

"No need to apologize. I like you, Jesse."

"You do?" he asked shocked. "I'm pretty sure I just walked past a voodoo doll that bears a striking resemblance to me."

Anita dismissed Jesse's seeing her voodoo doll with a wave of her hand, as if that magically made it disappear. "You are tough, resilient. You are not afraid to say what's on your mind. Your soul was lost but it has found meaning again. That is a hard feat. Once you taste the darkness, it is hard to give up the allure of power, but you have. You are a good man, Jesse Richards."

Jesse didn't know what to say, he wasn't sure if she was being sincere or if this was one of her tests Sammy had been telling him about.

Anita inched closer, her nose now touching his. Jesse stood his ground. "You're not frightened, Jesse Richards?"

"No. I've seen pure evil. You don't scare me."

"Good. I could use your help."

"My help?"

"Yes. You have something that can help this family." She put her hand on his chest.

"My heart?" Jesse asked unsure.

"No, something deeper, something stronger."

"I'm not following."

"In time you will." She ripped open his shirt, sending the first few buttons of his dress shirt flying across the room. Anita moved aside the small, gray stone that hung from a hemp necklace and stuck her long fingernail into his chest as if she was wielding a small knife. Jesse flinched from the pain but stood steadfast.

"Here," Anita said. "He has claimed you."

Jesse looked down at his chest, blood trickling down his birthmark.

"My birthmark?"

"Not a birthmark. But the mark of the Beast. You bear it."

"I don't understand," Jesse admitted. "I've always had it. As long as I can remember."

"Then, that is how long you have been cradled in his arms."

Jesse stared at his birthmark. The shape of it always reminded him of a heart. Jesse recalled Mona tracing his heart-shaped birthmark and calling him the man with two hearts.

"This sets you apart from everyone else. This I can use." Anita dug her nail deeper into Jesse's chest, letting his blood fill the underside of her nail. She brought her finger to her mouth and sucked the blood from her fingernail as if it were a spoon. Anita stuck her nail back into Jesse's chest, then brought her nail to his mouth for Jesse to taste his own blood.

"Do you taste it?" Anita asked.

"It's sweet."

"Yes. The Devil's water usually is."

"What are you saying?"

"You are what you always feared Jesse Richards, but this doesn't have to be your fate. Help us."

"Us?"

Jesse saw a shadow behind Anita move, she wasn't alone, there was someone else in the room.

Anita wrapped her bony hands around Jesse's neck. "Know this boy, if you tell another living soul what I tell you, I will kill you. This is not an empty threat for you any longer. You like this new life you've built for yourself. You have friends and a family now. I will take it all from you and send you to the place you fear most, where you will be judged for all of your sins. You will lose everything Jesse Richards, but know this, if you don't help, they will all be lost anyway. Lost to him, the demon that stalks the woods. What will it be Jesse? Will you help us?"

Jesse swallowed hard. "Yes. I'll help."

Anita lowered her hands, sliding them down Jesse's chest. "Very good."

Jesse buttoned up his shirt the best he could and climbed the stairs to Sammy's room, mulling over what Anita had said.

"What took you so long?" Sammy asked in a hushed whisper, closing his bedroom door behind Jesse as soon as he entered. "I was getting worried."

"Well, you were wrong about me being Mr. Stealth, she caught me right away. She wasn't asleep she was . . . I'm not sure what she was doing . . ."

"Please tell me you didn't tell her I put you up to it?" Sammy asked, sitting next to Jesse on the bed. "

"I apologized for sneaking into her room and as far as my reason for being there, I said I was looking for the grimoire for you."

Sammy smacked the side of his face and dragged his hand down his cheek. "Urgh! You didn't?! She's gonna think I'm more pathetic than ever."

"Beats the alternative. I guess I could've told her you thought she was up to no good."

"Not me, the 'old Jesse' thought she was up to no good. So, is it true, is she up to no good? You see anything strange?"

"Define strange?"

"Uh . . ."

Jesse laughed, his voice coming out in a high-pitched hiccup. "There wasn't one thing *not* strange about her room. And no offense Sammy, I think your grandmother's more than a little crazy, but I don't think she's working with JD. She actually thinks he could be the reason why your uncle went missing. She hasn't said anything because she doesn't want to upset your mom.

Sammy sighed. "Samuel Cameron, the prodigy. I thought last summer when everyone started to go missing, that that was more than possible."

Like the rest of us, she agrees the town would be better off without Japhet Dean Leeds. The problem is your grandmother can't do it outright like she handled Devan. She's not strong enough. She can't kill him."

"What about with Ivy and my help . . . maybe we could overpower him then."

"I think that's exactly what your grandmother doesn't want you to do. I'm pretty sure you're right; she's deliberately pushing you away. I got the distinct impression, she wants to keep you safe, so let her Sammy. Let her worry about JD."

Sammy punched his bed. "I can't sit back and do nothing."

"I don't see what you can do."

"I'm going to confirm the link between Elsa and JD. I'm hitting the library tomorrow and gonna see if this happened before. If Pleasant Mills is really on repeat the library will have something."

"Is this a bad time to tell you I can't read?"

"What?!"

Jesse laughed, his hiccups stringing together. "Kidding."

CHAPTER TWENTY-FIVE
Ghosts

Jesse stirred in his sleeping bag next to Sammy's bed, stretching his arms out and hitting Sammy's leg that was hanging off his mattress. Usually when Jesse slept over, they slept downstairs in front of the big screen TV; however, the twins were watching a Disney princess marathon with their stuffed animals and the boys thought they better just sleep upstairs before they got wrangled into watching *Snow White* again.

Jesse sleepily went to the bathroom to get a drink. He used his hand as a cup and sipped a handful of cold water. His thirst relieved, he made his way back toward his sleeping bag. Seeing a young boy standing at the foot of Sammy's bed, he stopped dead in his tracks, instinctively feeling for the charm around his neck and noticing it was missing. He internally groaned, hoping it had only fallen off in his sleeping bag and he didn't lose it in Anita's room.

Jesse knew he was face to face with a ghost. Without his charm to block out his natural ability, he would see ghosts just as clearly as he saw the living. If he hadn't recognized the Jersey Devils Football hoodie with the fruit punch stain by the collar from Sammy's under-the-bed tote, Jesse would have thought someone broke into the house. That was how clearly, he saw Zachary Lewis. He saw the fine strands of his light brown hair, the glint in his brown eyes.

"Zac?" Jesse said.

The ghost's eyes widened. "Yeah . . . you can see me?"

"I can see you," Jesse replied softly, as not to wake Sammy.

"Who are you?" Zac asked.

Jesse was relieved Zac didn't know him or at least didn't recognize him. He wasn't sure if he did or didn't have anything to do with Zac's abduction.

"I'm Jesse. Sammy's friend."

Zac took a step closer to Jesse. "How is it that you can see me and no one else can? I've been trying to talk to Sammy forever, but he can't hear me." Zac sniffled, trying to hold back his tears. "I'm so lonely." As he wiped his tears with his sleeve, a crimson bloom spread over his chest. It started as a pinprick, quickly saturating his sweatshirt in blood.

Being taken off guard, Jesse took a step back.

Zac crossed his arms over his chest to hide the stain. "Sorry," he said anxiously, taking a step toward Jesse, "it bleeds sometimes. Please don't be scared."

Sammy's room grew cold, the temperature steadily decreasing until Jesse could see his own breath leaving his mouth like billowing phantoms. Zac's face looked as pale and placid as cold marble as if his heart had stopped and blood no longer flowed to pinken his cheeks. His dark eyes seemed searching, piercing as his cheeks sunk in. He looked every bit as dead as he was.

"It's okay," Jesse said in a calm voice, not moving. "I'm not scared. You just caught me by surprise. Try to calm down, okay."

He nodded, the room growing colder.

"Zac, listen to me. You need to calm down. You're making the room cold and you're the one making your chest bleed."

"Me?" Asked Zac, the blood from his chest now soaked the sleeves of his hoodie.

"Ghosts work on emotions, good or bad. Because you're upset, you're resorting back to how you looked and felt the last time you were emotionally taxed."

"How do you know?"

"It's the same reason I can see you. I was born with the ability. I've met a lot of ghosts. So just try to relax."

"How do I do that?"

"Um . . . um . . . Sammy's dad counts down from ten. Try that."

Zac closed his eyes moistened with tears. "Ten, nine, eight, seven, six, five, four, three, two, one."

"That's it Zac," Jesse said in a reassuring voice.

Zac opened his eyes, the blood stain was gone, just the fruit punch stain remained.

Jesse nodded. "You did it, Zac."

Zac went to hug Jesse, but instead Zac's hands went through him, giving Jesse a shiver that went up his spine.

"Oops, sorry. Sometimes I forget I'm dead."

"It's okay," he said, shaking off the cold.

The light from the window was suddenly blocked out. Jesse looked toward the window to see a dark shadow move across it.

"What's that?" Zac asked scared.

A voice moved through the room like a whisper on the wind. "No peace. No peace for me. No peace for you, Jesse Richards."

Jesse recognized the voice of his deceased wife. He reached for his necklace again, only to remember to his dismay, it was missing. The shadow moved past him slipping into the hall. Jesse's eyes followed it. His breathing returned to its natural cadence only after the shadow was out of sight.

"Zac?" Jesse called; he was gone.

Jesse heard light crying. He walked around the side of Sammy's bed to see Zac with his arms wrapped around his legs rocking himself. His chest was bleeding again. "It's okay Zac, she's gone."

"She? Who is she?"

"Just another ghost." Jesse unzipped his sleeping bag looking for his necklace, sighing in relief when he found it.

"What's that?" Zac asked in between counting down from ten.

"A charm that I've had since I was a child. It blocks out my natural ability to see ghosts and protects me from them.”

“Wait!” Zac said desperately, forgetting all about counting and trying to relax, his bleeding chest now sounding like a dripping faucet. “If you put it on, that means you won’t be able to see me. I’ll be alone again.”

Jesse hesitated, gripping his necklace in his hand, feeling the rough gray stone leaving an impression in the fat of his palm. “Zac, that ghost can’t hurt you because you’re dead, but it *can* hurt me. I have to wear the necklace.”

Zac looked at him with pleading eyes that made Jesse think of black olives. “Please Jesse, don’t.”

Jesse exhaled through his mouth. He pocketed his necklace and crouched down next to Zac. “I won’t leave you alone. I promise.”

Jesse lightly shook Sammy.

“Hmm,” he groaned.

“Sammy get up,” Jesse said, still shaking him.

“What time is it?” he asked, rolling on to his back and rubbing his eyes. “I know I said I wanted to go to the library first thing in the morning, but they don’t open till nine.”

“Do you believe in ghosts?” Jesse asked.

Sammy sat up as if Jesse had just said the magic word. “Ghosts . . . yeah why?”

“Good that’ll make this easier,” Jesse said, thinking of the best way to tell Sammy his friend was a ghost.

“Did something happen?” Sammy asked, all traces of sleep gone, anxiety building in his chest.

“Is it Elsa? Did she . . .” He couldn’t bring himself to say die.

“Elsa’s still in a coma as far as I know.” Jesse knelt and pulled out the plastic tote from under Sammy’s bed. He pointed to the Jersey Devils Football hoodie. “This is without a doubt your friend Zac’s hoodie and his spirit is without a doubt tethered to it. He goes where it goes.”

“What are you saying?!” Sammy asked, nearly shaking Jesse’s arm off.

“Zac’s a ghost, and he’s here. And I can see him.”

“What really?!” Sammy ran his hands through his hair. “Did he say anything. Does he have a message for me? Is he okay?”

"Um . . . well . . . he's dead . . . but besides that, he's okay."

"I've been dreaming about Zac a lot. I keep seeing him in my room. I think he's alive and then . . ." Sammy put his head down, his hair casting his eyes in shadows. "And then his chest starts to bleed, and it hits me like a Mack Truck that he's dead."

"Zac's been trying to communicate with you. Looks like he got through in your dreams. That's a pretty typical way for ghosts to communicate with the living."

"So cool," Sammy said. "Scary as all hell," he confessed. "But now that I know it was really Zac, so cool."

Jesse looked at Zac who sat at the end of the bed. Sammy followed Jesse's eyes. "He's sitting there, isn't he?" Sammy asked excitedly, reaching his hand out toward the end of the bed. "Hi Zac. Miss you man. Glad you're okay. But uh, I'm sorry you're dead."

Jesse chuckled. "Your finger is next to his nose, looks like you're trying to pick it."

"Wait!" Sammy said, retracting his hand. "If you can see him, why can't I?!" Sammy asked, forgetting that Jesse had said he could, in fact, see Zac in the first place.

Jesse shrugged. "I've asked myself that countless times. I'm not really sure why I can see ghosts, I was just born that way."

Sammy was brimming with excitement. "I thought we said no secrets between us."

Jesse took a deep breath. "Sorry, it was always kinda of top secret. I'm not sure if JD even knows . . . I never directly told him, and I don't want him to find out. This doesn't leave this room, okay?"

Sammy nodded. "Promise." Sammy's eyes were as wide as golf balls as he gripped his pillow. "Wow, what a cool ability. It's like a superpower."

"Not all the things I see are cool . . . and not all ghosts are friendly like Zac. Actually, more are not. They're ghosts for a reason, most are unhappy. When I was young, my father thought I just had imaginary friends, but they weren't, they were ghosts. It got so bad I couldn't tell if I was talking to the living or the dead, and some of them hurt me. My father thought I was possessed. He tried to cure me with some pretty extreme charlatan methods. He took me to countless tinkers for exorcisms with the hope they could remove the demon he thought was trapped within me."

"Crap," Sammy said.

"Yeah, remember we're talking about the 1800s here."

"How old were you?"

"I was around eight, I think. It was scary. I was scared of everyone around me and myself. I would've eventually been killed if it wasn't for Uriah."

Sammy raised his eyebrows in shock, "Pastor Leeds?"

"Yep, one in the same. Uriah was the pastor when I was a young boy. He was old, really old, but it was him. He stepped in and saved me. My father tried to rid me of my demons by having me bled out. I was bed ridden for weeks after that. Touch and go there for a little bit."

"Holy crap, Jesse!"

He nodded. "That's when Uriah took me to the Lenape Indians. He had heard about a medicine man he thought could help me. That's where I met Sky Wolff. His daughter and he made me this." Jesse pulled out the necklace he had tucked away in his pajama pocket. Sammy took it from Jesse and examined the rough gray stone attached to a braided hemp rope. "It's an amulet to protect me."

"Protection amulet," Sammy muttered to himself. He had seen spells for charms like this in Abby's grimoire and in the Leeds's grimoire too.

"I'm what the Lenape Indians call a dream catcher," Jesse told Sammy as Sammy rolled the necklace over in his hands. "I catch things from the spirit realm ... the nightmares. Let's me see ghosts. The necklace helps to block out my natural ability to see them, so they leave me alone. It works really well, but sometimes powerful spirits can still break through the charm's magic."

"Your amulet gave me an idea. Maybe a spell can help me see Zac!"

Zac nodded enthusiastically.

"Um, maybe a spell could work," Jesse said, "but Sammy, I can't stress enough how dangerous some ghosts are. If you can't see them, nine times out of ten they leave you alone. If you *can* see them, well that's a different story."

"I understand, but I don't want to see all ghosts, just Zac. We've got to try. Abby won't let me use the family grimoire but maybe there's a spell in the Leeds grimoire we can use. Tomorrow we're going to Ivy's and figuring this out."

"Before or after the library?"

"It's going to have to be after the library and the hospital. Don't forget Pastor Leeds is holding a prayer session for Elsa. We'll go to Ivy's right after that."

"Sounds like one heck of a day."

CHAPTER TWENTY-SIX
A Prayer for Elsa

Sammy and Jesse rushed to the hospital elevator, with Zac following close behind. The morning spent at the library flew by and they lost track of time. Sammy was on information overload, pleading for five more minutes when Jesse dragged him to the front desk. Sammy and his father had already read all of the books at Batsto's visitors center, figuring they have the best resources on all things local, by locals. He felt more than a little stupid he'd waited this long to go to the library when he saw how many books on the Jersey Devil the historical village was missing. Sammy checked out a handful of books, resentful he was the only one who could drive. He wanted to keep reading a book he found on New Jersey folklore, *The Man, The Myth, and The Devil* by Cameron Franklin.

He had completely forgotten his boss's son and coworker at Poor Richards Community Pool was more than a lifeguard in the summer, he was an author. It wasn't until Sammy saw *Cameron Franklin* in large print on the cover, did he recall that tidbit. Sammy never had an interest in folklore and had only half listened when Cam had talked about his books, which was very seldom. Cam was more of a listener than a talker. Sammy was surprised Cam had a few books published on folklore and the occult and one specifically on the Jersey Devil. He seemed too young to have so many. Sammy knew Cam was a pretty smart guy, tutoring kids in the summer along with his lifeguard duties and couldn't wait to get reading. He wanted to finish the book so he could ask Cam any follow-up questions he may come up with the following day at work.

Uriah stood up to greet Sammy and Jesse with a handshake when they entered Elsa's hospital room. "Jesse, Sammy, you made it."

"Sorry we're late," Sammy said, going over to hug Ivy.

"Where have you been," Ivy hissed. "You're almost a half hour late. Grams will be picking me up soon." She tugged on the stained sweatshirt wrapped around his waist. "I thought we had an agreement if you bought that thing, it would stay under your bed, never to see sunlight again."

Sammy flashed her his grin. "Some promises need to be broken," he whispered. "I'm coming over after this and will fill you in. I need your help."

"Sammy, I have plans."

"Change them. This is big," he said with a quick peck to her cheek.

"We're still waiting on one more," Pastor Leeds said, looking down at his watch.

"Oh yeah, Mike and Tammy are coming too Pastor Leeds. They should be here shortly." Sammy added.

"Perfect. The more the merrier. I know Elsa appreciates everyone being here. It's great the whole youth group could make it."

"I know Elsa would appreciate everyone being on time," Ivy muttered under her breath, glancing at the comatose Elsa. She looked like Sleeping Beauty, her blonde hair falling in ringlets, a slight blush on her cheeks. Ivy wondered if she would look that good in a coma and decided she wouldn't. Elsa could pull off any look, this proved it.

As soon as Mike and Tammy entered the room, Tammy threw her arms around Sammy. Ivy and Mike looked at each other. They were thinking the same thing. *"Hands off."*

Tammy took Tyrone's death hard and almost a year later was still outwardly grieving. Her parents, chiefly her father, told her young love never lasts and that she and Tyrone were due to break up when they hit high school anyway. Not the kind of tough love Tammy needed. Mike and Sammy had been there every step of the way through Tyrone's disappearance and burial. They were her main support system, but Mike was not so good with talking about his feelings. Tammy used Sammy for that—a lot, calling him at all hours of the day and night.

"I miss you," Tammy said as she hung from Sammy's neck. "I feel like I haven't seen you in so long."

Ivy thought she was going to be sick. Tammy reminded her of a bloodsucking leech, latched on for sustenance. "I thought you were needy," Ivy said, taking a jab at Mike. Mike ignored her; he had both eyes on Jesse. Sammy had introduced him to Jesse at Hugo's baptism, but they had only said hello, after that Jesse disappeared into the crowd. He was hoping to see him again.

Mike gave Ivy an idea. She resisted pulling on Tammy's fiery red hair to get her away from Sammy and tapped on her shoulder instead. "Have you met Jesse Leeds yet?" Ivy asked in a whisper, pealing Tammy off her boyfriend. "He's new and he's single."

"Single?" Tammy asked through tears.

"Yes, single and cute. Did I mention he loves redheads?"

Tammy wiped her eyes. "He does?"

Ivy nodded as her lips curled into a Cheshire cat grin. "Loves them." She pointed in Jesse's direction.

Tammy instantly perked up. She had walked right past the boy standing next to Pastor Leeds to get to Sammy. "You're right Ivy, he's cute. How's my makeup?"

"Uh . . ."

Tammy's racoon eyes reminded Ivy of the first time she met Elsa, coercing her to glance at her again, before taking her thumbs and dragging them under Tammy's eyes to wipe off her smudged makeup. "Much better,

Jesse needs glasses anyways."

Ivy pushed Tammy Jesse's way.

"That's Tammy Handover," Zac said to Jesse as Ivy and Tammy approached them from the other side of the small, sterile room. "She looks better when her makeup isn't all over her face, but still, you can tell she's pretty."

"Jesse this is Tammy," Ivy said nudging Mike over so they could get closer to Jesse.

"Yeah," Mike said annoyed, "my sister."

"Nice to meet you Tammy," Jesse said, going to shake her hand. He hesitated, thinking most boys his age wouldn't shake hands with a girl and slid his hand back in his pocket. "I think I saw you at Hugo's party."

Tammy smiled. "I was there, but I don't remember seeing you."

Jesse blushed. "I guess I just blended in."

"You mind Ivy?!" Mike hissed in a whisper.

"Barking up the wrong tree Mike, trust me."

He gave her a dirty look.

"Don't you think so Jesse, don't you think Tammy is pretty?" Zac asked, standing closer to her than he had ever stood when he was alive. "She's a cheerleader."

Jesse discreetly nodded to Zac and rubbed the back of his neck nervously. Jesse had, in fact, noticed her at Hugo's baptism from afar and thought she was very pretty. Her bright red hair and freckles made her stand out from all of the other girls there. Ivy was right, he liked redheads. Up close, despite the dark smudges under her green eyes, he thought she was beautiful.

"I would have really liked to date her," Zac said as what felt like his heart fluttered.

"But she was always with Tyrone," Jesse said, finishing Zac's sentence.

"What?" Tammy asked.

Jesse blushed again. "Uh Tyrone . . . you used to be with Tyrone. Sammy told me."

Tammy's eyes watered, tears threatening to spill over. "Tyrone was my boyfriend."

Jesse looked at Zac as if to say look what you did. "I'm sorry for your loss Tammy. Tyrone was very lucky."

Tammy wiped her tears before they fell. "So, you're new here?" she asked.

"Yep, got here just as summer hit. I'm Uriah's nephew. I'm staying with him."

"It probably gets lonely in that big, old house. Let me give you my number in case you get bored."

"Unbelievable!" Zac exclaimed. "I tried for years for that number. Mike wouldn't even give it to me. Some friend he was!"

"Um, yeah," Jesse said, fumbling to get his phone out. "Thanks Tammy." He texted her a smiley face emoji right away.

She smiled.

"Send her a heart. No, send her a kissy face!" Zac suggested.

Jesse cleared his throat in an attempt to block out Zac, he was very close to putting on his protection amulet and blocking him out for good.

Mike watched Jesse's complexion continue to pinken as he talked to his sister until Jesse was the color of a ripe tomato. Mike let out a loud sigh.

"Told you," Ivy whispered.

"Sometimes I hate you, Ivy Teller." Mike pushed his red curls off his forehead. "Jesse reminds me of someone, you?"

Ivy shook her head.

"I can't place it, must be someone from TV."

All eyes moved to Trudy Grindhouse as she entered Elsa's room.

"Must be the one more," Ivy mumbled under her breath.

Zac whispered in Jesse's ear: "Sammy broke up with her."

"Why?" Jesse asked.

"What?" Tammy asked Jesse.

Jesse rubbed the back of his neck again. He wished everyone could see and hear Zac so he would stop looking stupid in front of Tammy. "Why . . . are you still single?" Jesse asked, feeling beyond stupid.

"Good recovery, Jesse. Smooth operator," Zac said impressed.

"Not sure, but I got this feeling, I won't be for long," Tammy said, taking one of her tight curls in her finger and pulling it straight to only have it bounce back into a perfect ringlet.

Jesse swallowed hard. He could feel the heat on his cheeks.

"Sorry I'm late," Trudy said with a hug for Uriah. "I hit every light on my way here."

Uriah flashed an angelic smile. "You're right on time."

Trudy looked around to see everyone. "We got quite a party here."

"We certainly do." Uriah touched Jesse's shoulder, "let me introduce you to my nephew Jesse. I know you've heard all about him, but I don't think you two have officially met."

Trudy said hello to Jesse with a hug and followed it up with a hug for Sammy, her embrace lingering a little too long for Ivy's liking.

"Hello Ivette," Trudy said to Ivy.

"It's Ivy."

"What?" Trudy asked.

Ivy flushed; she was as red as Jesse. "My name is Ivy."

She giggled. "Of course, how silly of me. Sorry Ivy."

"What's Trudy doing here?" Ivy hissed to Sammy as Trudy sandwiched herself between Jesse and Pastor Leeds.

"She knows Elsa."

"I know, but shouldn't she be back at school or something."

"She's off for the summer. Said she's gonna be hanging around to help her mom with her grandmother, but I think it's more about hanging around with Pastor Leeds."

Ivy clenched her fists. "You've been talking to her?"

"A little. Text mostly."

"Text mostly? She's called you?!"

"I guess, a few times." Sammy looked Ivy directly in the eyes, to squash what she was thinking. "We're just friends."

"Uh huh," she grumbled in a low voice.

"You're jealous!"

"No. I just think it's funny your ex-girlfriend's calling you, that's all."

"There's nothing going on between Trudy and me. That's ancient history." Sammy grabbed Ivy's chin and gently directed it in the direction of Uriah and Trudy. "What are you blind, Teller? Pastor Leeds can't even pull out his prayer he's so lovestruck."

"I wish someone *would* help Pastor Leeds unfold his prayer, before

Grams shows up, whatever his issue."

"He's actually hard to watch. Poor guy," Sammy said into her ear. "Trust me, the only eyes he cares about are Trudy's and the only eyes I care about are yours."

Ivy wondered whose eyes Trudy Grindhouse cared about. Ivy surveyed Trudy. She wore Louie's good-natured smile, and a short white tube top sundress. Trudy's eyes didn't seem glued to anyone, in particular. In fact, Ivy saw Trudy look at Sammy several times and smile as if they were having a secret conversation.

CHAPTER TWENTY-SEVEN
Replaced

Sammy was just about to knock on Mary Teller's front door when she stepped out.

"Hey brat," she said, with her usual cheeriness.

"Hi Grams."

"Mary," Jesse greeted with a nod.

Mary opened her purse and handed Jesse folded twenties. "Owed you that from the last dominoes game."

Jesse put the money in his pocket, "thanks."

"Double or nothing next time."

"It's your money, Mary."

"I'm gonna win one day and when I do it's gonna be big."

"Where you off to?" Sammy asked, hoping she was going to be a while.

"Food shopping, got a coupon I have to use by today. Let yourselves in, have fun."

Sammy opened the front door and yelled for Ivy.

Ivy came out of the kitchen. "Sammy, what are you doing here?"

"What do you mean? I told you I was coming over."

She gave him a quick kiss, taking his arm and leading him back toward the front door. "And I said I had plans."

He leaned in and pressed a kiss to her lips. "And I thought I said change them."

Ivy pushed him back, harder than a playful shove. "The world doesn't gravitate around you Sammy Lopez. The sooner you learn that, the better off you'll be."

"Come on Teller, you're not doing anything. You were supposed to be shopping with Grams and she just left."

Ivy nervously looked at Jesse. "I have a friend over."

"Hi," Rosa said, from the kitchen doorway.

"Oh, hey Rosa," Sammy said, not happy to see her, his mood shifting.

"How long is she staying?" Sammy whispered.

"She just got here."

Ivy was nervous now. Dragging Sammy to the front door as if her life depended on it. Jesse was Rosa's big crush, all she ever talked about was him. She ignored the fact Jesse was on the Pleasant Mills most wanted list. To her, he could do no wrong. Ivy just hoped Rosa wouldn't recognize the younger version of her crush. She wouldn't be able to explain how and why Jesse was a teenager, let alone, admit to her best friend it was she who killed the love of her life. Ivy was grateful Rosa had poor vision. She felt ashamed at the thought, a feeling similar to a bee sting burned in her chest.

"I really need your help with something witchy," Sammy said in a whine, pressed against the front door.

"It's gonna have to wait."

"Hi, I'm Jesse," he said to Rosa as Sammy and Ivy bickered back and forth.

"Hi," she said, adjusting her glasses on her nose.

"Sammy told me you're one of Ivy's good friends."

"Yeah, that's right."

"I'm Uriah Leeds's nephew. I'm staying with him."

"Come on Jesse we're leaving," Sammy said, interrupting Jesse and

Rosa's conversation. "Nice seeing you again Rosa," he said with a wave. He whispered in Ivy's ear: "Call me as soon as she leaves."

"Will do."

"We could head back to the library," Sammy suggested as he started the hummer's engine.

"Please, no," Jesse whined, pressing his palms together as if he were praying.

"I got an idea," Zac said excited. "How about we go see my mom?"

"Zac wants to see his mother."

"Okay," Sammy said. "That's a good idea. I haven't seen her in a while. She left the church, goes to the one in Port Republic now. But I did run into her a couple of weeks ago at Shoprite with my mom. She looked well."

Zac was happy to hear that. He stared out the window as they passed the houses he remembered driving by every day of his life. It was surreal to see them again. He enjoyed comparing them to the memories burnt in his mind, pinpointing which homes stayed the same and which ones had been updated with new landscaping or a fresh coat of paint. It made him miss home and most of all his mother.

In truth, everything made Zac miss his mother. He thought about her all day, every day, when he was trapped in Pastor Leeds's junk room and in Sammy's room. When all he had was his thoughts, his mind went to his mother. She was his only companion in the dark.

Zac could barely contain his smile as he walked up to his front door. "Still hasn't gotten around to painting it," he said to Jesse. It was the same dull, canary yellow it had always been and that made Zac's heart happy. It was as if nothing had changed in the last year, and he was finally coming home.

Sammy pushed the doorbell. Mrs. Lewis opened the door wearing a wide smile, her dark hair pushed away from her face in a ponytail. Zac's face lit up. "Hi Mrs. Lewis," Sammy said. She hugged Sammy at once.

"It so good to see you, but please it's Mrs. Hanson now. I went back to my maiden name after the divorce was finalized."

"This is Jesse," Sammy said, gesturing to him.

"I don't recognize you, but I'm big on hugs."

"Uh . . . I'm one of Zac's friends from a different school. Was, was Zac's friend," Jesse quickly corrected as she hugged him.

"Well, come in boys."

They followed Mrs. Hanson into the small living room where a well-loved couch sat in front of a fireplace with a gas insert.

Zac's eyes settled on a picture of a boy he didn't know on the fireplace mantel. "Who's this?" Zac asked Jesse. He pointed at the little boy with dark hair that was now in the picture frame that used to display his picture. "Who's this kid?"

Zac quickly went to the hallway where his mother hung up embarrassing photos of him since he was born. The hallway was a collage of Zac's funniest moments, and with Zac that meant a lot of pictures. There was hardly space left for more pictures last year, a thing Zac was very proud of.

Zac froze in the hallway. All of his pictures were gone and replaced with a few embarrassing photos of the same boy as the one framed on the fireplace mantel. "Where's my pictures? Where are ALL my pictures?!" Zac yelled. "They've all been replaced!"

"Would you boys like some cookies?"

"Sure Mrs. Lewis," Sammy said with a smile. "Mrs. Hanson, I mean." She went to the kitchen.

Zac marched back in the living room. "Ask my mom who that kid is Jesse!"

"Okay," he whispered.

"What's going on?" Sammy asked Jesse.

"Zac's upset. Wants to know who the kid in the picture is. Do you know?"

"No," Sammy whispered back. "No clue, never saw him before."

Mrs. Hanson came back in with a plate of chocolate chip cookies. Sammy and Jesse each took one. "Um . . . who's this?" Jesse asked Zac's mom, pointing to the picture frame on the mantel.

"That's Aiden."

"Aiden come here honey," Mrs. Hanson called down the hallway. In no time, a small boy no older than eight came running to her. She wrapped her arms around the little boy. "This is Sammy and Jesse, say hi."

"Hi," the boy said with a large smile. He was missing his two front teeth.

"Who the hell is he?!" Zac yelled.

"Aiden, a relative?" Jesse asked, giving Zac a look as if to say calm down.

"Oh my," Mrs. Hanson blushed. She focused her attention on Sammy. "You know after what happened, I thought maybe I could give someone else a home. Aiden is my son. He's officially adopted as of last week."

"Son!" Zac shouted at the top of his lungs. "I'm your son. You better not have given him my room!" Zac ran down the hall to his bedroom.

Sammy and Jesse exchanged worried looks.

Zac ran back into the living room and stood in front of his mother. "I can't believe you!" He glanced at Aiden then back at his mother. "How could you do this to me?! You replaced me! You gave this kid my room and what about my pictures? You took them all down, like I never existed. Like you never cared about me . . . like I never mattered to you. How could you do it to me, Mom?!"

Zac's tears turned to sobs. The temperature in the living room cooled as if the air conditioner suddenly turned on, blowing a steady stream of cold air directly at them. Zac's face grew pale and thin. Dark shadows returned under his eyes. He covered his face with his hands to hide his tears from Jesse, the red spot on his hoodie growing.

"I hate you." He knocked the picture of Aiden off the mantel.

"Oh no," Mrs. Hanson said as she went to pick up the photo.

"I got it," Jesse said, quickly picking up the frame. The glass was cracked. "I must have knocked it off balance when I touched it earlier. I'm sorry."

Zac rushed to the hallway and knocked the photos of Aiden off the wall before disappearing through the front door.

They heard the frames hit the floor in a clamor.

"Must be at tremor," Sammy offered as an excuse.

Jesse whispered to Sammy. "Let's go, before Zac knocks down the house."

The boys quickly picked up the pictures in the hallway. "Well, we should get going," Sammy said, hanging the last of the pictures back on the wall as Mrs. Hanson came with a broom to sweep up the broken glass. "Just stopped by to say hello. We have lots of rounds to make today."

Jesse added: "Thanks for the cookies."

"You're welcome and good to see you Sammy and nice meeting you Jesse. Don't be strangers." She gave each of the boys a hug and walked them to the front door.

Zac was sitting on the front steps when they walked out. He had his hands tucked in his sleeves, pressing them against his face.

Jesse took a seat next to Zac. "I'm sorry Zac."

Sammy followed suit, sitting next to Jesse. "I had no idea about Aiden. I'm sorry."

"You're the only one Sammy," Zac said to Sammy as if he could hear him. "You're the only one that missed me. You couldn't get rid of my stupid hoodie, and you weren't even sure it was mine. You held on to it because it reminded you of me." Zac sniffled. "My mom wiped me from existence, like I was never born! My own mom . . . I missed her so much, I can't believe she would do this to me. I thought she loved me."

Jesse tried to comfort Zac. He really wished Sammy could hear him. "Your mom does love you, Zac. I think she misses you so much she couldn't be reminded of you." Zac whimpered as he listened. "It hurt too bad. It's just how she's dealing with the pain. She does love and miss you; she's just using Aiden to cope."

Jesse could relate to Mrs. Hanson. He had done that with Mona. Had pretended she didn't exist, pretended he didn't love her, pretended he didn't kill her and married another woman to help him forget.

Sammy chimed in. "He's a poor substitute for you Zac. You see those photos? They weren't even funny."

Zac cracked a smile and dried his tears on his sleeves. "This is no longer my home, it's Aiden's. Let's get out of here."

CHAPTER TWENTY-EIGHT
A New Spell

Sammy knocked on Mary Teller's front door in a quick rapid motion. Ivy opened it wearing a frown.

"Got your text," Sammy said, walking over the threshold and planting a kiss on Ivy's cheek.

"Um, yeah, what where you waiting in the driveway?"

Sammy smirked, "across the street."

"Hi again Ivy," Jesse said.

"Jesse."

"Hi boys," Mary called from the kitchen.

"Hi," they said one after the other like trained parrots.

"We need privacy," Sammy whispered. "You think we can distract Grams long enough to make it to your room?"

"Watch and learn." Ivy stuck her head in the kitchen, "Hey Grams, forgot to tell you Danny called. You better call him back, he said something about dinner."

"Is that a fact?!" Mary wasted no time taking the old rotary phone off the receiver.

Ivy whispered to Sammy and Jesse: "That will keep her busy for a while, come on."

Slipping their shoes off, they quickly made their way up the attic stairs. Ivy felt a little strange having Jesse with them. Sammy was the only boy that ever saw her room. She reasoned Jesse was no boy and she already broke Grams's golden rule of no boys in the bedroom close to a trillion times, but it was still weird. Her mind went to JD. He too had been in her room. He had stood by the side of her bed, she wrapped in his arms, struggling against his strength. Ivy shook the image of JD out of her head like she had water in her ears and closed the door behind them. She placed her hands on her hips. "So, when are you going to tell me what's going on?!"

Sammy smiled and pointed to his sweatshirt wrapped around his waist.

"Yeah. I see it. Hard to miss with the big red stain. Why is wearing that thing in public a promise worth breaking?"

"Long story."

"Not that long," Jesse said bluntly. "Zac's a ghost and is tethered to it."

"Of course," Ivy said disinterested. She took a seat at her desk, opening *Tamerlane and Other Poems by a Bostonian* and leisurely thumbed through it.

Sammy rested his head on her shoulder and whispered in her ear "And we need to do a spell so we can see Zac."

Ivy snapped her book shut, turning to him. "It's one thing after another with you Sammy Lopez! How could you possibly know Zac's a ghost and is attached to that old rag?!" She rested her head in her hand, "Oh Sammy, we've been through this before. That sweatshirt is just a sweatshirt. I feel like I'm starting at ground zero with you."

"Tell her," Zac said to Jesse. "Tell her, we need her help."

Jesse spoke up. "We know Zac's a ghost because I can see him."

Ivy looked at Jesse dumfounded. "Uh . . . okay, and you can see Zac and we can't because?"

Jesse looked at Sammy as he thought up a believable story. The less people who knew the truth about his ability, the less of a chance there was of JD learning about it and exploiting it. "Um . . . because I died before . . . so I can see him," Jesse lied.

"Oh," Ivy said, opening her book again, "that makes sense, I guess."

Ivy was nervous now, her eyes darting around her room looking for Zachary Lewis as she pretended to read. She was glad her cheeks were already flushed. She had died before too. She had lived as the Midwife and as countless other versions of Ivy Teller, but she couldn't see Zac. That could only mean Jesse lied to her. *Leopards don't change their spots.* Ivy wondered what he was hiding, but she was trapped. She knew she couldn't call Jesse out on his lie without coming clean about her own past.

"It's true, Zac just knocked pictures off the wall at his mom's house," Sammy said. "Show her, Zac."

Zac stood next to Ivy's desk and tried to turn the page of her book.

"Waiting," Ivy said frustrated.

"There!" Sammy said as a page turned.

Zac was concentrating hard, he felt like he was sweating even though he knew that was impossible. It had been a lot easier to knock the pictures off the wall when he was angry. With great effort he managed to turn another page.

Ivy slammed her book shut for the second time. "Okay, I get it," she said. "Zac's a ghost. So, what's the game plan?" Ivy's eyes freely danced around her room, looking for a shadow like the one she'd seen when she threw the jarred heart against the wall or maybe a cloudy apparition, anything that could be a ghost.

"I was thinking there may be something in the Leeds family grimoire that could help us."

Ivy turned around quickly and looked down at her desk. She was in full blown panic mode. She cathartically spun her bracelet from Sammy on her wrist. JD had promised to return the grimoire, but he hadn't yet. Ivy hoped Sammy wouldn't be able to read her face and see she was keeping something from him.

"There's nothing in the spell book to help you see ghosts," she said in a calm voice, once again opening her book of poems.

"You sure, Teller? I better take a look."

Blood rushed to her face. Her stomach tied in knots almost doubling her over. Her heart sounded like an electric drum kit. She turned in her seat to look at him. "Sammy, there's nothing, I combed through that thing looking for something to help your mom when she was sick."

Sammy slouched. He bought Ivy's excuse for the moment, but she wasn't sure how long that would hold him off wanting to see the grimoire. She could see the wheels turning in his head.

"I think we should write our own spell," Ivy suggested before Sammy insisted on seeing the spell book for safe measures.

"You think we could?" he asked, taking a seat on her bed next to Jesse.

Ivy held up her small book of poems. "Sure, why not, a spell's just a poem right?"

Sammy smiled, jumping up to take the book from Ivy. "I knew it! You acted like you didn't care and this whole time you were reading poems—working on spell casting."

Reading poems is accurate, Ivy thought. She loved poetry, relished reading Edgar Allan Poe, Emily Dickinson, Walt Whitman, Robert Frost, Lord Byron, William Shakespeare, and all of their contemporaries. It was part of the reason she loved music so much. It was all about the lyrics—powerful poems and prose made more beautiful with instruments. But practicing spell casting, Sammy couldn't be further from the truth. Ivy was not going to tell Sammy otherwise, at the idea of writing their own spell, he seemed to have completely forgotten about the Leeds grimoire.

Ivy let out a loud sigh of relief. Her cover wasn't blown. Sammy didn't know about JD and her, didn't suspect a thing, and she was going to keep it that way. If it was a spell they needed, then she was going to write it.

Ivy's clammy hands reached for a pencil and a spare notebook.

Sammy got down on his knees next to her. "Where do we start?"

"Let's start by deciding what we want the spell to do."

"That's easy," Sammy said, "we want to make sure we can see Zac. Well, you and me."

"Make sure I can go places without the sweatshirt," Zac said.

"Zac wants to know if you could make it so he's not tethered to his sweatshirt." Jesse said.

Ivy bit off her pencil's eraser, the pressure mounting. "Tall order

Zac," she said into the room. "This is not like ordering a fruit smoothie at the mall."

"Sure it is, Teller, they're all ingredients. Just got to get it right."

Jesse chimed in, "Make sure the only ghost you can see is Zac. You don't want every poltergeist in a ten-mile radius showing up at your doorstep. That would be welcoming all sorts of—"

Sammy cut Jesse off. "Hocus-pocus."

Ivy groaned. "Got it, acute spell." The Midwife had somehow brought the Jersey Devil to life with a poem, she just had to tap into her witchyness. It was the *how*, that she was caught up on. How was a poem going to make them see a ghost boy. She reasoned she was going to have to take a leap of faith, or believe in the power of suggestion, or just embrace the craziness.

"I like her," Zac said with a big smile. "I can't believe she's Sammy's girlfriend. What a lucky guy. The first time I saw her, she looked good, but now, now she looks wow. Way better than Elsa Tilton."

Jesse laughed. It made the hairs on Ivy's neck stand on end. It was that high-pitched titter Rosa liked so much.

Ivy griped, "What did he say now?"

"He said you look better than Elsa Tilton."

"Oh," Ivy said, sitting up a little straighter. "I knew I liked Zac. Thanks Zac."

Sammy pressed a kiss to her cheek. "I agree."

"In fairness," Jesse said, "Elsa's in a coma."

Ivy turned around and looked at Jesse with slitted eyes, and for a moment she was happy she pushed him down that ravine.

Jesse flashed a toothy smile. "I'm just kidding."

Ivy went back to her spell, not that she wrote down one word yet and anxiously tapped her pencil on her desk.

"I wish I could smell," Zac said. "I bet Ivy's bedroom smells amazing. What does it smell like Jesse?"

"Mothballs."

Ivy spun around and gave Jesse a dirty look.

He blushed. "Sorry . . . Zac was asking me a question."

"Mothballs?" Zac asked.

Jesse whispered, "helps deter mice."

"Oh," Zac said. "Maybe it's a good thing I'm dead." He giggled as he kicked his muddy sneakers against the side of Ivy's bed. "Plus, I get to sit on a girl's bed, that would never happen if I was alive."

"Glad you're enjoying the afterlife," Jesse said, getting up to stretch. After what happened at his mother's house, he was really worried about Zac. He was glad being in Ivy's room had made him forget.

While Zac attempted to smell Ivy's pillow, Jesse walked around Ivy's room looking at her posters, making sure to stay away from the desk where Ivy and Sammy were working on the spell.

Jesse noticed a picture of a drawn dandelion signed with his name tacked to the back of her bedroom door. He looked at it, then at Ivy, who was brutally slashing lines in her notebook and shrugged. He wondered when and why he had given it to her. He noticed the calendar she had hanging up next to his drawing was on the wrong month. Jesse took out the thumbtack, flipped it to June, and hung the Titan Tires calendar back on the door. He looked at the date, Ivy had it starred with a handwritten notation, *Anniversary of our first kiss.* Sammy's name was scribbled inside a heart. Next to the date it had a horoscope:

As Saturn collides with Pluto, the past becomes the present. Secrets become known as the moon moves to eclipse the sun. Be wary of an old love as a new romance moves in to take its place.

Jesse frowned. He hated horoscopes. He hated how they were always just vague enough to apply to anyone and everyone.

"Okay," Sammy announced, his smile contagious, "I think we got it!"

"About time," Jesse said, taking a seat back on the bed.

"You can't rush genius Jesse."

He laughed. "Is that what we're callin' you and Ives now?"

Sammy hugged Ivy. "Yep, sure am."

Zac was eager. "What do I do?"

"So, what do we do?" Jesse asked.

Ivy pointed to the ground. "Okay Sammy, take off the sweatshirt and place it on the floor.”

Sammy did as Ivy asked.

“Zac, stand on the sweatshirt please.”

“Kay,” he said, jumping off the bed.

“Jesse, let me know when Zac’s in position.”

“He’s on it.”

“Good. Now Sammy and I are going to wrap our arms around Zac. This will make sure we don’t see any other ghosts or ghouls besides Zac.”

“Perfect,” Jesse said, pleased.

“Ready when you are, Teller.”

“We call this the Zachary Lewis Spell,” Ivy said proudly, winking at Sammy.

“Catchy,” Jesse said sarcastically from the bed.

“It’s that genius you were going on about,” Sammy laughed.

Ivy shot Jesse an annoyed look. She cleared her throat and went back to business. “Ready Sammy?”

“Ready.”

Together they recited their spell, holding hands over Zac’s sweatshirt and Zac. It reminded Ivy of the first time they tried a spell in Sammy’s backyard. They had held hands as they did now. Their laced fingers made her heart pound with excitement. She wanted this spell to work.

“Zachary Lewis
is a ghost among us.
Lost to the world,
but still around us.

His spirit tied to his sweatshirt,
let him be free like the rest of us.

Let Sammy Lopez,
friend to all of us.
And Ivy Teller,
witch to bind us.

See the ghost boy now,
the both of us."

Little specks of color floated in the airspace between Sammy and Ivy's arms. Building momentum, the bright colors swirled, sticking to each other until Zac was left standing on his sweatshirt. He was in perfect detail as if he was just brought back from the dead.

Sammy's eyes grew wide. "Zac, I can see you! I can really see you!"

"Sammy!" Zac shouted. Zac went to hug Sammy, but instead fell through him landing on the floor. "Oops."

"He forgets he's dead," Jesse said with a high-pitched hiccup.

CHAPTER TWENTY-NINE
Sleeping Beauty

"Uriah, is everything alright?" Jesse asked, as Uriah left Lilly's room in tears.

Uriah couldn't bear leaving Lilly under the floor in the attic where he had found her, so he moved her magically preserved body into the room Tammy and Tyrone had cleared out, transforming the junk room into Lilly's bedroom. When JD and Uriah had struck the deal that saved Uriah's son Joseph, JD had promised Uriah that he could keep his wife and he had kept his promise. Now she served as a reminder of what he gave up to save his son and what he lost.

Uriah lay Lilly in a bed in her own room, pulling the covers up to her chest, her arms over the blanket, so he could hold her hand. Like Elsa Tilton, she too was Pleasant Mills's very own Sleeping Beauty. There she appeared to sleep, unmoved, unchanging, as if she was in a coma of her own. For that's how Uriah treated Lilly. Every morning Uriah would say good morning to his seemingly sleeping wife and every evening he would say goodnight. That was how things went since Jesse's return.

Uriah turned around startled. "Hi Jesse, I didn't hear you come in."

"Just got home. Sammy's taking Ivy out for their anniversary, then Mike and I are going to Sammy's for a sleepover."

Uriah wiped his tears. "That sounds like fun."

"What is it? Is Lilly okay?" Jesse asked concerned, glancing back at the closed-door Uriah had just come from.

"Oh yes, she's sleeping."

Jesse was used to Uriah referring to Lilly as sleeping, although they both knew she was dead.

"Then why are you crying? Tell me what happened?"

Jesse was more than a little worried about Uriah. He knew his old friend was depressed and was struggling with the guilt of killing Mrs. Ball. Jesse also knew Uriah held himself responsible for Lilly's death, and the deaths of Zac, Tyrone, Louie, and Timothy, but he was usually in high spirits after visiting with Lilly.

Uriah didn't need much coaxing. "Trudy spent the night here last night."

Jesse looked at him confused. "And, that's a bad thing?"

Uriah nodded his head in guilt. "No . . . Yes. At first, I was elated, but now I feel so guilty. Guilty I'm happy when I did that to Lilly." He pointed toward Lilly's bedroom door, shaking his head at himself. "Jesse, I'm sorry. I shouldn't bog you down with my problems."

Jesse put a hand on Uriah's shoulder, not sure how much of a comfort it would be. "I'm here for you. I'm no child. I can handle it."

Uriah buried his face in his hands. "What's wrong with me? I shouldn't be involved with Trudy. Her brother's dead because of me. And I'm committing adultery while Lilly sleeps under the same roof. Some pastor I am."

"If you want to harbor guilt for Louie, fine, carry that weight if it makes you feel better, but the situation with Lilly is unusual. Lilly is not sleeping Uriah—she's dead. And I'm sorry for that, but that's the truth of it. She's not sleeping and she's not in a coma. She's here to haunt you, don't let her. Lilly wouldn't want this for you."

Uriah sniffled, leaning against the wall for support as Jesse continued. "When I was a boy, you told me all about Lilly and your son

Joseph and how much you loved them. Lilly sounded like a wonderful person."

"She was."

"She wouldn't want you to be alone, Uriah. You don't deserve to be lonely. Lilly would want you to be happy. And if you find happiness with Trudy, then that's okay."

"But the promise I made Lilly."

"Till death do you part, and you both have died."

Uriah nodded.

"Listen," Jesse said kindly, leaning on the wall next to Uriah, "you honor Lilly every morning, noon, and night with your sermons. She will always be a part of you. Your being with Trudy, doesn't mean you love Lilly any less. Lilly knows that. You keep punishing yourself for what happened to her. You couldn't control her fate any more than you can change it now. You have to accept that."

Uriah pulled a handkerchief out of his pocket and dried his tears.

"You never married after Lilly. You could have time and again, but you chose to be married to the town. That's noble Uriah, but if you should be so lucky for love to find you again, you should embrace it."

"I didn't deserve Lilly then. How can I deserve Trudy now, after what happened to Louie?"

"I hope redemption waits for us Uriah. As you know, I played my part in his death too. I hope I deserve to be happy."

"You do, Jesse."

"So, that means you do too."

Uriah nodded again. "Yes, I guess it does."

"Do you love Trudy?"

Uriah lifted his eyes to Jesse. "Yes, I do."

"Then how can that be a bad thing?"

Uriah smiled. "You're very wise for a sixteen-year-old."

"What can I say, I used to be friends with this really old pastor."

Uriah laughed a warm laugh and put his handkerchief away.

"You might want to keep Lilly's door locked," Jesse said. "Might be a good idea if Trudy's going to be a regular."

"That's a very good idea. Come on, I'll make you dinner. How does

scrambled eggs sound?"
Jesse grinned, "crunchy."

CHAPTER THIRTY
Girl Problems

Jesse sat in his bedroom in the rectory with his phone in his hand. He couldn't get Tammy out of his head. He wondered if he should text her or maybe show a little more gusto and go for the call.

He couldn't ask Sammy; he was already out to dinner with Ivy. But Sammy owed him advice or anything else he wanted after he saved the day by reminding him today was their anniversary, well at least of their first kiss. Sammy didn't know there was such a thing as an anniversary for the first kiss, but he was going to make good on it and take her out to dinner, so Jesse was on his own.

Zac was also not available to give him some dating advice in the twenty-first century. Jesse would've most likely done the opposite of whatever Zac suggested, but at least it would've been a starting point. Zac had opted to go back to the Lopez's to practice moving objects, where his ghostly activity would be unobserved, taking up haunting one of the many guest rooms. He was using his anger over his mother to try to get a better hold on being a ghost. Knocking Aiden's pictures off the wall and turning a few pages in Ivy's book had opened a new world of possibilities for Zac. Distracting him from his heartache was just a bonus.

Jesse's face lit up when he received a text from Tammy: **What u doin?**

Jesse went to text back, but his fingers kept pushing extra letters. He wasn't good at texting yet. "She's gonna think I'm dumb," he griped. He opted for the traditional phone call, pushing the phone icon button. He held his breath, waiting for Tammy to pick up. Every second felt like a millennium in between rings.

"Hi," Tammy said into the receiver.

Jesse leaned back in his bed. "Hey Tammy."

"What are you doing?" she asked again.

"Nothing, just sitting in my room. Gonna eat soon, then I'm sleeping at Sammy's. Your brother's supposed to be heading to Sammy's too."

"Yeah, he said that. That should be fun."

"Yeah."

"What's Pastor Leeds making for dinner? My mom's making meatloaf."

"Sounds good. Uriah's not much of a cook, but he insists on cooking. He's making scrambled eggs. I can smell it burning from my room and my door's shut."

Tammy laughed. He liked her laugh, it made her sound like a little mouse.

"Well at least they won't be runny this time, but uh, um . . . I hope I didn't make too much of a fool out of myself earlier at the hospital. Sometimes I get a little tongue-tied."

"I can tell," she giggled.

"Hey, I wasn't that bad."

"No, not so bad. I thought it was cute."

"Cute is good . . . I thought you were cute too," he said into the phone, holding his breath.

"Maybe I can come over to Sammy's for a bit tonight with Mike?"

Jesse sat up in bed. "That would be great!"

"I have to be home at ten, so I won't be able to stay that long."

"Even a minute is worth it."

"Kay," Tammy said excitably. "Well, my mom's calling me for dinner. I'll see you later."

"Great." Jesse hung up the phone, finally releasing his breath.

A loud, singular knock sounded on the rectory door. Uriah, still busy in the kitchen, yelled for Jesse to answer the door. Jesse pulled himself off his bed and made his way to the front door and opened it. Before he could say a word, Rosa Littleton threw her arms around him. "Jesse, are you okay?! I've been so worried about you."

Jesse pulled away from her dumbfounded. "Um . . . worried about me?"

"I knew it was you when I heard your voice. What's happened to you? Did he do this to you?"

"He, who?" Jesse asked, trying to make sense out of why she was at his doorstep.

"JD."

Jesse's heart jumped a beat. "You know about JD?"

"Yes. You told me everything. I know you can't die."

"You better come in," Jesse said, closing the door behind her.

Uriah walked into the living room. "Hello," he said, shaking Rosa's hand. "My name's Uriah."

"Rosa Littleton," she said bashfully.

"Pardon me," Uriah said a little embarrassed. "We met at the church yard sale, didn't we?"

Rosa nodded.

"I thought you looked familiar. Forgive me, I wasn't well last summer."

Rosa smiled. "Nice to meet you again."

"Likewise. Have you eaten yet? I'm making breakfast for dinner if you want to join us."

"Sure," she said.

"Great. I'll let you two know when dinner's ready."

Once Uriah was back in the kitchen Jesse took a seat on the plastic covered couch. It crunched under his weight. Rosa sat next to him. "Rosa how do we know each other?"

"You were friends with my grandfather, and we became best friends."

"Your grandfather, what's his name?"

"Devan."

"Devan Rainier?" Jesse asked, feeling tension building between his shoulder blades.

"Yes."

"I do remember you."

She hugged him, pressing her face against his chest, her glasses smashing into her cheeks. "I knew you could never forget me."

"Rosa, I remember you as Devan's toddler granddaughter. Shy, always wearing pigtails."

Rosa sat up adjusting her glasses. "You don't remember us?"

"*Us?*" he mused, trying to read the eyes behind the thick, black rimmed glasses. This was a first, no one had hinted he had had a girlfriend.

"Yes us. You're my boyfriend. You love me. We were going to leave Pleasant Mills together once you were able to."

Jesse wasn't sure what to say. Not having his memories was a gut crushing feeling. He hated having to rely on what people told him and not his own experiences. "I'm at a loss for words. I'm sorry Rosa. I have no memories of us as a couple. My memories only date back a couple weeks."

Rosa sniffled. "Is there any way you can get your memories back?"

"No," he said. "I don't think so. I just have to start over."

She took his hand. "Okay, we can start over."

After a quick dinner of scrambled eggs, sausage, and burnt toast, Jesse offered to walk Rosa home. It was still light out and it would give them a chance to talk more in private.

"Uh . . . what direction?" Jesse asked.

"You really don't remember?"

He shook his head. "No."

Rosa pointed and they started walking down the road in the direction of the church. "Uriah's very nice."

"Yeah, he is."

"You always talked about him."

"He's a good friend."

"You had said that."

Jesse smiled. "So, we were good friends?"

Rosa moved closer to him, their shoulders almost touching. "Best friends. You were over all the time. You had a crush on me."

He blushed, "I did?"

"Yeah, but my grandfather would've killed you for even thinking my name."

Jesse smiled awkwardly. "I remember your grandfather and I could see that. He was very protective of you."

Rosa paused, taking Jesse's hand. She leaned in and pressed a kiss to his lips. It was easy to do now that they were the same height.

"Uh, Rosa," he said, pushing her away gently. "I know you have all these feelings . . . but think about how it is for me. Let's take it slow. I need to get to know you again, you know?"

"Okay."

"Okay," Jesse said back with a smile.

It wasn't long until they reached the stretch of Norway pines lining Rosa's driveway. "I remember this place."

"My grandfather's house."

"Yeah . . . I remember coming here a long time ago when JD first recruited him." Jesse looked around at the trees cautiously. The wind blew the pinecones where they hung low on the branches, clanking together like chattering teeth.

They started down the long driveway, passing under the pine trees that shrouded the path in a shade that seemed too dark. Jesse chuckled, "I never liked this house." He could see the old white farmhouse clad in pine up ahead and its many windows of hand-blown glass, giving the effect that faces were peering out of each one.

"There was one spot in the house you did like."

He scoffed. "Really? Hard to believe."

"I'll show you."

"I'll believe it when I see it."

Rosa opened the front door. "Looks like my parents are still out. I was supposed to stay put, but I had to see you. Besides, what they don't know, won't hurt them."

"You're a little bit of a rebel, I like that."

She smiled. "You always did."

Jesse followed Rosa down the long hallway adorned with old photographs. She led him to the door at the end of the hall and opened the door to her bedroom. His eyes opened wide when he saw his artwork hanging from her walls.

"See, told you we were best friends."

"You framed them all. That's nice," he said, rubbing the back of his neck anxiously.

"Yeah. This was the last one you did for me." She pointed to the drawing of a rose on her desk.

Jesse smiled. He didn't know what else to do, smiling seemed as good a thing as any.

"You know Jesse, you were always a little bit of a rebel too."

"I'm sensing that."

"You knew my grandfather would kill you if you and I were involved but that didn't stop you," Rosa said, bolstering their past. "I never told anyone about us. Not even Ivy. Ivy doesn't know Devan was my grandfather. I kept it a secret to keep you safe when the town was hunting you." Rosa took her shirt off and tossed it on the bed to reveal a pink lace bra."

"Um, Rosa . . . what are you doing?"

She walked over to where he stood near the doorway and kissed him.

"I . . . I think I should be going."

"What's wrong?"

"I told you. I want to take things slow. This is really weird for me."

"Jesse Richards never did anything slow, and this is his favorite bra."

It unnerved him, for Rosa to speak about him in the third person, as if he wasn't in the room. "Um, the bra is very nice," he said, glancing at Rosa's chest quickly before focusing his attention back to her face. He didn't know her; she was a stranger. He didn't love her as she loved him. Maybe the 'old him' did. The plethora of drawings hanging framed from her walls indicated that could've been the case. The problem was the 'old Jesse' died and no matter how much Rosa wished him to be her Jesse, he wasn't, and he couldn't pretend.

"I should get going, it's getting late, I'm supposed to be at Sammy's."

He went to leave.

Rosa grabbed his hand, "Jesse, please don't go."

"I don't mean to hurt your feelings, I don't. I'm sorry. But what we had died when the 'old me' died."

Breaking free of Rosa's hold, he walked out of her room.

"Jesse!" she yelled after him. "I'm the only one that's ever cared about you. I was the only one that protected you when you were pinned with those murders! Me, no one else. If they knew who we really were, do you think they would accept us. Do you think Ivy and Sammy would still like you or me if they knew what we've done? All we have is each other!"

Jesse paused, not turning around. "I'm sorry, Rosa."

CHAPTER THIRTY-ONE
Weirdness at the Teller House

Sammy walked up to the front door of Mary Teller's house with flowers in his hand and a big grin on his face, walking right past the red Mustang in the driveway. He knocked on the door expecting Grams's usual charm, but to his surprise a well-dressed man answered the door. He had blond hair and blue eyes and tan skin, the color you get when you spend a lot of time outdoors.

"Uh . . . is Ivy home?" Sammy asked unsure of what to say to the smiling stranger.

"Sure is. Come on in, she's expecting you."

Sammy walked into the house. "Danny Leeds," the man said as he shook Sammy's hand.

"Uh . . . Sammy, Sammy Lopez," he stumbled, caught off guard. He wasn't used to pleasantries at the Teller household. "Um . . . nice to meet you."

"You too, Sammy. I've heard a bunch about you, nice to finally put a face to the stories."

"Uh . . . "

"Hey nice Hummer," Danny said, looking out the bay window.

"Uh . . . thanks, my dad got it for me."

Danny pulled out a Titan Tires business card from his wallet. "If you need any work done, give me a shout. We do more than tires." He looked up to the ceiling in thought. "You know, I keep saying that, I think I'll add that slogan to the business card."

"Thanks Danny," he said, still clueless on who Danny was. He pulled out his wallet and placed the Titan Tires business card in an empty slot next to his cash and the old French coin dating back from 1735 his dad found in his room a while back.

"Wow Grams!" Sammy said, stunned when Mary came out of her kitchen dressed up. Sammy never saw her look so good. Her hair and makeup were done with an attention to detail, taking years off her face. "You look nice."

"Ivy's not the only one who has a date tonight, brat."

"Oh," Sammy said with a big smile. "Explains who Danny is."

Ivy came down the stairs wearing a dress which was not her go to for a date night, but Sammy was taking her to a fancy restaurant.

Sammy handed Ivy the flowers and gave her a quick kiss. "Wow, you look great. That dress is perfection."

Ivy smiled as she smelled the array of wildflowers. She took to heart what Lindsey had told her about white being her color and put on a tight white dress. It did the trick, Sammy followed Ivy into the kitchen like a lovesick puppy.

Ivy pulled out a vase for her flowers and filled it with water. She set her flowers on the kitchen table next to a vase of long stem roses. Sammy pointed to the roses. They stuck out like a sore thumb. If it wasn't labeled, it wasn't in Mary Teller's kitchen. "From Danny, for Grams."

"Oh," he said, a little embarrassed that Danny's flowers were nicer than his bouquet of wildflowers. Sammy was thinking about getting roses, but he did that on Valentine's Day and was afraid he would come off like a one trick pony if he went with roses again. But as he watched Ivy admire Grams's roses, he got the feeling he missed big with the flowers.

"Ready? Ivy asked, happily ecstatic Sammy remembered the

anniversary of their first kiss. She took Sammy's hand and led him to the front door.

He smiled. "Ready."

"Don't wait up for me Ives," Grams yelled from the hallway, mid argument with Danny over who was driving." Danny and I are doing an all-nighter."

Ivy made a face of disapproval. "Ew," she mumbled under her breath. "Wasn't going to."

Sammy chuckled hoping for an all-nighter of his own. If Grams was out, that meant there was no one home to guard the staircase to Ivy's room.

"Kay Grams, have a nice night," Ivy yelled back, shutting the front door.

"Way to go Grams," Sammy said as he opened the passenger side door for Ivy. He was going for gallant tonight.

"I know it's creepy . . . I'm pretty sure Danny is half her age."

"Nah."

Ivy gave Sammy a funny look as he got into the driver's seat. "*Nah*?"

He started the engine. "I mean Old Lady Mary looks good for her age . . . whatever age that is."

"Gross, Sammy."

"I just mean, at least I know you're gonna age well."

Ivy shot him a dirty look as she buckled her seatbelt.

"Come on, Teller, you know you look like her."

She groaned.

Sammy got the feeling he wasn't starting the night off on the right track. He had to recoup and fast. "It's no biggie. It's the same for me. You can't tell me you didn't think the same thing when you first met my dad?"

Ivy's pulse quickened. "What?!" The last thing she wanted to think about tonight was Sammy's father and more specifically how he's the spitting image of JD, and more specific than that, how much Sammy resembled them both.

Sammy smiled. "I just mean, you know I'm gonna age well 'cause I look like my dad."

Ivy lied to herself, she had to. "You don't look like your dad Sammy," she said sharply, as if saying it would make it true. She was trying to get all traces of JD out of her mind, which was proving to be difficult. He was constantly popping in uninvited. And after her most recent run in, Ivy felt like JD was always with her, part of all the anger she carried around. He was her albatross.

"Sure, I do," Sammy said as they stopped at an intersection. "Everyone says I look like my dad."

"Sammy, this is getting weird," Ivy said uncomfortably. Yes, she knew he looked like his dad—yes, she knew everyone said it, but she wanted to put as much distance between Sammy and Japhet Dean Leeds as possible.

Sammy grinned the smile she loved so much. Ivy lightened up, smiling back. She was powerless against that sideways grin of his.

"Speaking of weird . . . that guy Danny, he's kinda weird."

"He's dating Grams, that goes without saying. He must be bonkers." Her smile widened. "Here goes a mechanic pun—He's missing a few screws. —Get it?"

Sammy fake laughed. "Ha, real cute, Teller . . . but I mean, I get a weird feeling from him."

Ivy folded her arms over her chest, now she knew why he was grinning like that, he was trying to stop the volcano in her from erupting. "Don't even start Sammy Lopez! If you say it, I'll scream."

He grinned, that grin. "Hocus-pocus."

"Take me home."

He laughed. "Relax Teller. I'm just saying, I'm getting something witchy from him. You're not?"

"Urgh, Sammy, you've been doing a lot of *just saying* and no I am not. Can we change the subject please?"

"Sure. Let's talk about that dress you're wearing and how hot you look."

Ivy mirrored his grin. "Now, that's more like it."

After dinner Sammy pulled up to Ivy's house to see Grams's station wagon missing. Sammy felt a nervous energy heating up his body before he could even unbuckle. He ran over to the passenger side door to open it for Ivy. "Chivalry is not dead," he said, taking her hand and helping her out of his Hummer.

"Sammy, you're a goofball."

Sammy glanced at Danny's car. "Kinda looks like Jesse's old Mustang don't you think?"

"Can we please stop talking about Jesse. All through dinner it was Jesse. Jesse and Zac or Zac and Jesse."

"Sorry Teller, I only want to talk about you now." Sammy eagerly walked up to the front door holding Ivy's hand.

Ivy picked up the spare house key she kept under the doormat.

"I thought I told you not to keep your key there," Sammy said protectively.

Ivy huffed, unlocking the front door. She placed the key under a planter full of bright orange marigolds instead. "Happy?"

Sammy gave her a concerned look. "It's an improvement, but you have to come up with a better hiding place."

"I'll work on it," she said, eyeing the marigolds. They looked too much like dandelions for her comfort. They made her think of JD's suit jacket lying on the ground by the ravine, a dandelion serving as his pocket square. Just looking at the flowers made guilt bubble up in her stomach. The butterflies turned wasps that lived in her stomach were being eaten alive by stomach acid. She thought she was going to be sick.

As soon as they made it past the threshold, Sammy made a beeline to Ivy's bedroom. He kissed her at the top of the stairs. He couldn't wait any longer. He continued to kiss her as he fumbled to unbutton his dress shirt. Sammy got frustrated when he could only get the first two buttons unfastened. Giving up, he concentrated his efforts on Ivy. Sammy pressed her against her closed bedroom door. He kissed her lips feverishly before moving to her slender neck. He pressed kisses to Ivy's ears where diamond heart earrings sparkled like stars. "They look good on you," he said, kissing her earlobes again.

"I love them Sammy, thank you. The earrings were a nice surprise at dinner."

"Matches the heart bracelet I got you for your birthday," he said his hand running down her arm to the bracelet.

"I noticed," she said with a smile.

Sammy kissed the hollow of Ivy's neck. "Next, I have to get you a necklace, so I'll have an excuse to kiss your neck more."

Ivy giggled. "Really, you seem like you're doing just fine without any excuses."

Ivy discreetly sniffed Sammy's hair as he caressed her neck with kisses, checking for a sweet, smoky scent. There was none, just designer cologne. Since she dreamed of Sammy transforming into JD in her arms, she questioned her own eyes, her nose giving her much needed confirmation things were as they should be.

Sammy reached his hand behind Ivy's back and unzippered her dress.

"Easy tiger," Ivy said, thinking she sounded too much like her grandmother.

"You're right." Sammy gave Ivy a toothy grin, taking her hand in his and leading her to her bed in the center of the room. He jumped on the old mattress. The bed let out a loud groan of protest. "Nice not to have to worry about Grams hearing the bed rock." Ivy let out a nervous giggle. Sammy patted the bed, motioning for Ivy to join him. She took a bashful step closer, spinning her bracelet on her wrist. Sammy reached for Ivy's hand pulling her on top of him. Running his hand down her back, he finished unzipping her dress.

"Um, Sammy?"

"Yeah," he said, sliding the sleeve of Ivy's dress down and kissing her collar bone. Sammy felt Ivy's body go rigid in his arms. He stopped kissing her and sat up. "What's wrong?"

Ivy's cheeks blushed a bright red. Sammy tried to inconspicuously smell his own breath. He turned his head and breathed into the palm of his hand. He sniffed hard. Sammy had been careful at dinner to make sure he ordered a meal without garlic. But now that he smelled the palm of his hand, he wasn't so sure garlic didn't somehow find its way into his chef salad. He took a case of mints out of his pants pocket and popped one in his mouth. Unsure, he popped in another. "Fixed?" Sammy asked with an embarrassed smile.

"It's not your breath Sammy. I have my period."

"Still?!" he asked surprised. "I thought you had it last week?"

"Um, yeah. All the stress is getting to me. My hormones are out of whack," Ivy lied. She couldn't be with Sammy like that. Not after what she'd done to him. The guilt was too much for her. Every time she kissed him, her guilt grew and so did the biting pain in her stomach. She needed more time for things to go back to the way they were, for her to forget JD's soft kisses and gentle hands.

"Oh, okay," Sammy said disappointed as Ivy got up to change into something more comfortable. He watched from the bed doe-eyed as Ivy slipped out of her dress and put on an oversize T-shirt and Garfield pajama pants.

"You want to watch a movie?" Ivy asked grabbing her laptop off her desk.

"Uh . . . yeah, sure," Sammy said with a faint smile.

Sammy and Ivy leaned against her headboard, watching *The Three Stooges* on her laptop. They were Ivy's favorite. She sat there laughing as Sammy sat there staring at her.

He pressed a kiss to her cheek. "I love you, Ivy."

"I love you too," she said, not looking away from the screen.

"You know, in the past year I think this is the first time your grandmother hasn't been home." Sammy ran his finger up Ivy's arm. "Seems like a waste to just watch *The Three Stooges*." He chuckled to himself. "It's as if tonight is written in the stars . . . It's the one-year anniversary of our first kiss and Grams gets a date with a guy half her age—it's a sign—it has to be."

Ivy's eyes left the screen to find Sammy's eyes burning bright in the dim room as twilight cast the world in shadows. "Are you insinuating that the universe wants us to have sex tonight?"

"Yes, I am," Sammy said with a boy-like smile.

"Sammy, you're ridiculous. We're not having sex tonight." She pressed a kiss to his cheek, "Sorry Romeo, I think you got your stars crossed."

Ivy went back to watching *The Three Stooges*.

Sammy slid his finger under the elastic waistband of Ivy's pajama pants. "You know, I don't care that you have your period."

Ivy jumped out of bed. "Sammy, I said no!"

Sammy leaned back against the headboard and took a deep breath, his cheeks crimson with embarrassment. "Sorry . . . I just had tonight all worked up in my head. And then when Grams had a date—woah! My imagination went wild. I didn't mean to pressure you; I was just letting you know I didn't care. Now that little Sammy has calmed down, I realize I was acting like a jerk. I know, no means no."

Ivy groaned. "Please do not refer to your penis as little Sammy. I told you a hundred times, it's creepy."

Sammy chuckled, "sorry."

Ivy patted his arm, taking a seat back on the bed. "It's okay." She focused her attention on the laptop. She giggled at the screen when Moe hit Curly with a frying pan on the top of his head. Sammy wasn't in the giggling mood. He had a bad feeling in the pit of his stomach. He had it for some time. He tried to ignore it, pushing it aside. He never confronted Ivy about the feeling, he like her, blamed it on stress. Sammy tried to shrug it off again, but he just couldn't ignore it anymore. As he watched Ivy watch TV, it became clear to him, she was keeping a big fat secret.

Ivy pushed pause. "What are you looking at?"

"You."

"You're supposed to be watching the movie, Sammy!"

"Ivy, can I ask you something?"

Her eyebrows arched, twisting her face. "Uh . . . yeah."

"Are we okay?"

Ivy laughed nervously. "Of course we are stupid." She pushed play on her laptop.

"'Cause, I was thinking the other day how odd it was that we haven't been alone all summer."

Ivy kept her eyes glued to the screen. "Summer just started and how can we be alone when Jesse's your shadow."

"I think it started before that. The last time we were alone was the day I told you my mom was sick."

"Yeah, and right after that the new improved Jesse showed up," she said sarcastically.

Sammy nibbled on his bottom lip, not that Ivy noticed, she still refused to look at him. "I googled it, and it says you're either cheating on me or I'm bad in bed."

"You Dr. Googled our relationship?!"

Sammy exhaled out of frustration. "If you're doing the whole repackage your flower and give it to someone special thing they're preaching at church, then just tell me."

"No Sammy, that's not it."

"Do I not do *it* good? I'm open to pointers . . . *you know*, to make if better for you. Just say it delicately. Watch my manhood."

"No Sammy you're good. You do everything good."

"But maybe you need more than good . . . Maybe you need great and I'm not giving it to you."

Ivy's pulse raced, she wished she wasn't alone with him now, wished they weren't having this conversation. She felt like the truth was about to break through and ruin her life. She hated that Sammy was so good at reading people, especially her.

"No Sammy, it's nothing like that. I just have my period and am not in the mood. Mine is sporadic, you know that. I have it one day, then the next I don't. Hopefully, next time we're alone, I'm good. So, please stop listening to Dr. Google."

Sammy nervously attempted to button the buttons he had managed to get undone. "I just feel like we're having this disconnect and I don't know why. It's not just the lack of love making, you're pulling away from me all the time . . . I love you Ivy, I don't want us to disconnect. I know I've been all about Jesse since he came back and now there's Zac, but every time I want to hang out by ourselves, you say you're busy. It's like you're going out of your way not to be alone with me."

Her eyes cut to him. "I am not."

"For instance, today."

"I had plans with Rosa and besides you were with Jesse and Zac."

"Oh really? When did you make plans with Rosa? I asked you last week about hanging out today when I got my work schedule. You said you were going shopping with your grandmother and couldn't switch the day, but Grams went shopping without you and you had Rosa over. I didn't want to make a big deal out of it. It wasn't worth a fight, but you lied. It was a silly lie, but it was still a lie. And I was only with Jesse because you said you already had plans."

Her eyes moved into a half-lidded position. "I didn't want to hang out with Jesse, and I knew he'd tag along."

"I know you don't like him, but I think it's more than that."

"We're alone now, so I don't know why you're making such a big deal about this," Ivy said her tone laced with frustration.

Sammy bowed his head and spoke in a low voice. "The other two days I had off this week you said you had a dentist appointment and then you said you were job hunting. Then last week you said you wouldn't come to the Community Pool to see me because you had your period and didn't want to hang out after I got out of work because you had cramps. I'm not stupid Ivy, you're avoiding me."

"That's not true," Ivy said defensively.

"I guess I'm worried you only took me back after we broke up because I almost died and now that all the craziness around me being abducted is fading away, you're left with just me and that's not what you really want."

Ivy was relieved Sammy didn't guess at the truth, but what he thought seemed worse to her. She couldn't believe he could think for one second she didn't want him, didn't love him. "Oh my God, Sammy, no," Ivy said, clutching his hand and bringing it to her chest. "That's not it at all. I took you back because I love you."

They heard a croak coming from the stairs, it was as if someone stepped on a frog.

"Shoot Grams!" Sammy slid under Ivy's bed. "So much for an all-nighter."

Mary growled from the top of the stairs. "Ivy Belle Teller, Sammy Lopez better not be in your room!" She pushed open Ivy's bedroom door with a swoosh that sent papers flying off Ivy's desk. Her predatory eyes moved around her granddaughter's room. She took a deep breath in through her nostrils sniffing for Sammy's cologne like a basset hound. "Where is that boy?!"

"Uh Grams, overreacting much? He's in the bathroom. I just came upstairs to get my ear buds." It scared her a little, what a good liar she was. She could tell her grandmother believed her, Grams's stance relaxed, her demeanor softening.

Sammy thought he was gonna faint when Grams bent down to pick up a piece of paper that had landed bedside. He slid as far away from Grams as he could when his pants got snagged. He was stuck. Sammy peered out from under the bed, holding his breath. Mary picked up another piece of paper mere inches from Sammy, oblivious to the boy under the bed breaking her golden rule. She put the papers back on Ivy's desk before starting her way back downstairs.

Ivy hung her head upside down to look under the bed. "You can come out now, but I think we should head downstairs. Grams is on a war path."

She sighed internally; Grams had saved her. She always thought her grandmother's rule about no boys in the room was antiquated, but now she thought every girl should live by that rule.

"Sammy?" Ivy called when he didn't respond. She impatiently tapped her foot.

Sammy was preoccupied. He'd thought his pants had gotten snagged on a jagged floorboard but upon further inspection he learned that wasn't the case. "Hey Ivy, there's something under your bed."

"Yeah, like lost socks, now come on."

"Yeah socks, but there's a small trapdoor under here. I can open the top just enough to get my hand in."

"What's in it?"

"I can feel a box. It's too big to pull out. The door to the compartment is hitting your bed. I'm gonna have to slide the bed over."

Sammy climbed out from underneath Ivy's bed and pushed on one of the four bed posts. He chuckled. "Kinda embarrassing, but your bed is heavier than it looks. Wanna help me push, please?"

Ivy smirked. "Sure."

They pushed on the bed together, but still, it didn't budge.

"What gives," Sammy said to himself. He got down on his hands and knees pulling out his phone to use as a flashlight. "Hey Teller, check this out! Your bed's screwed to the floor!"

Ivy bent down next to Sammy to take a peek. "Maybe it helps the bed squeak less."

"Or maybe someone didn't want us to find what's hidden under the bed."

"Stop, you're making my head hurt! Why does everything have to be a big conspiracy with you?!"

Sammy smiled as he pulled out his Swiss Army knife. "I love this thing." He started unscrewing the bed from the floor.

"Maybe we should do this later . . . I'm sure by now Grams realizes you're not in the bathroom."

They heard the phone ring downstairs.

"Nope," Sammy grinned. "We got some time."

Sammy easily removed the screws anchoring the bed to the floor. "Quietly now," he warned Ivy. When they were both in position, he nodded and together they slowly slid the bed over.

Ivy looked at her floor then to Sammy. All she saw was a sock graveyard. "Uh . . . I thought you said there was a trapdoor." "There," he said, pointing. "See that nail."

"No."

Sammy knelt, touching his finger to a square nail head protruding from a floorboard.

"You're kidding me?!" Ivy said frustrated.

"Nope. At first, I thought it was just a nail, but look, you can see small brass hinges, making this unequivocally a trapdoor."

She admitted defeat with a nod, it was more than an old nail. "What are you waiting for?" Ivy whispered bewildered. "Open it."

"Just taking in the moment, Teller. It's not every day you find a secret compartment."

"Oh," Ivy said. She joined Sammy in staring at the trapdoor that was no larger than a sheet of paper. She was going to attempt to take in the moment with Sammy, though she was less excited than him.

Gripping the nail head with his thumb and index finger, Sammy opened the small trapdoor. They peered inside, their heads bumping. Ivy rubbed her forehead. The only thing in the floor's hidden compartment was a small tin box. It was so rusted, it looked like the box was made of rust. They couldn't make out any marks or labels on it. Sammy opened the tin, flakes of rust crumpling at his touch.

"Cool, looks like an old time-capsule," Sammy said to Ivy. He carefully picked up an old drawing on thick, yellowed paper. "Poor kid," Sammy commented, handing Ivy the picture.

"That's a sin," Ivy said, taking the drawing from Sammy. She ran her finger over the baby's cleft lip. It curled up distorting his face.

"Wow, this is weird! Check it out, she looks like you!"

"What?!" Ivy snatched the portrait from out of Sammy's hand, tearing off the corner in her haste.

"Easy," Sammy said, letting the torn corner fall into the tin. "She looks a lot like you, don't you think?"

"Uh . . ." Ivy felt like her heart stopped, her eyes fixating on a drawing of the Midwife—on a drawing of herself. It was just like the one she'd found in the spell book. It looked to be done by the same artist, maybe even the same day, she was wearing the same dress. In a panic, she glanced down at the other illustrations in the tin.

Sammy pressed a quick kiss to Ivy's cheek. "Of course, you're much prettier."

"Uh . . . must be an old family member or something." She felt like time was slowing down around her. Her voice sounded sluggish to her ears. She thought she was going to faint.

"Check the back of the portrait. See if there's a name," Sammy suggested.

Ivy froze, she couldn't move. Ivy felt like she couldn't breathe. She prayed it said nothing. Sammy took the drawing from her and flipped it over. She sighed in relief when she saw the back was blank.

Ivy knew she had to get the tin of drawings away from Sammy before he was able to piece her past together. She couldn't believe Sammy's need for everything to be a conspiracy didn't lead him to the truth. But she knew if he kept finding mysterious illustrations of a woman who looked like her, he would eventually put it all together, leaving her no choice but to come clean about her past and worst of all, her recent past with Japhet Dean Leeds.

DRAWING OF A BABY: IDENTITY UNKNOWN

"You should ask Grams if she knows who this is. It's wild. She really does look like you."

"I will."

Sammy's phone rang. He scrambled to get up and grab it where he left it on Ivy's bed before Grams heard it. Ivy seized the moment and quickly took the drawings out of the tin, looking for more pictures of the Midwife.

Ivy blinked her eyes in disbelief when she saw a drawing of her with JD. She quickly stuffed it in her shirt while Sammy talked on the phone. She sped things up, shuffling through the pictures like her life depended on it—because it did. Her life as she knew it was at risk. She pulled out any pictures that were not of the baby.

"Anything good in there?" Sammy asked, hovering over Ivy.

"Nope, just more pictures of the baby. That's it." Ivy tried not to move. She had stuffed several pieces of paper in her T-shirt and was afraid any movement would cause one of them to fall out.

"Who was on the phone?" she asked, trying to take Sammy's attention away from the tin.

"Mike."

"Wow, the boys' club couldn't wait till tonight."

"Yeah, him and Tammy are at my house already."

"Tammy's coming over?"

"Looks that way. I better get going."

Ivy's cheeks flushed when he didn't invite her to come along. She understood not getting the invite when it was just the boys for a sleepover, but now Sammy was leaving her house early to be with them and leaving her out. She didn't want to be alone with Sammy, that was true, because when she was, she felt like the third wheel between Sammy and her guilt, but a hangout at Sammy's house seemed fun. She felt like he made a distinction between her and his friends, like she was his girlfriend, and they were his friends and the two didn't mix. It made her feel like she didn't fit into his life as she should. Why should Tammy get to hang with the boys and not her?"

Sammy waited by the door. "Uh, you're not walking me out?" he asked surprised.

"Yes of course, silly," she said, turning slightly to look at him, her hands holding the drawings stuffed in her shirt in place as her cheeks burned. "We can't make it obvious you were in my room. Go downstairs and flush the toilet a couple of times so Grams hears it and thinks you were sick or something."

He grinned. "Good thinking."

Sammy took off his sneakers and headed downstairs. As soon as he disappeared, Ivy took the drawings out from under her shirt and put them back in the tin box. She closed the lid and slid the box under her bed before hurrying down the stairs.

Ivy walked Sammy to the front door. Mary waved goodbye from the kitchen, where she was still happily rehashing her date with Danny to Danny on the phone.

Sammy pressed a kiss to Ivy's lips. "I guess we'll try to figure out the mystery behind the tin later. Don't forget to ask Grams about the picture of the woman. Oh, and see if she knows who the baby is. And ask her why your bed was screwed to the floor."

Ivy nodded, faking a smile.

"Sammy, I will. Now go, Mike and Tammy are waiting," Ivy said, over emphasizing Tammy's name. "And I'm sure Jesse will be there soon, if he's not already there." Sammy gave Ivy a quick peck on each of her ears before she pushed him out the door. She was so mad at him, she could scream. He really was a stupid boy.

CHAPTER THIRTY-TWO
A Forgotten Family

I vy ran for the attic staircase. She was out of breath before she reached her room. She slammed her door and went back to the tin, taking off the lid and carefully looking at the drawings.

Ivy's hands shook as she examined the portrait of herself, JD, and the disfigured baby. They were posed like one big dysfunctional family, his arm clearly around her shoulders, she happy with the baby nestled in her arms. They were outside on a sunny day, pine trees behind them forming a living fence.

"This is not right," she said to herself. "Not right." She turned the illustration over, letting it fall to the floor as she impulsively covered her mouth with both hands to hush her scream. On the back of the drawing Ivy read: Ivy, Japhet Dean, and Uriah Leeds, 1736.

Ivy's body convulsed. "No, no, no, this can't be happening."

Ivy picked up several sketches of the baby and examined them. She brought them as close to her face as she could to get a better look. The drawings were fragile and worn from time. It was hard to see them clearly.

"Uriah," she muttered to herself in a daze. "Could this be Pastor Leeds? . . . He did say he had a birth defect."

Ivy had never given much thought to what the defect would've looked like or what it even was. It was hard for her to imagine him any other way than she knew him. "Why would a picture of Pastor Leeds be in a box hidden under my bed?"

"Come now Ms. Teller, you know the answer to that."

Ivy spun around on her butt to see JD standing in her doorway. His face was emotionless, hard to read, but his eyes gave him away. They blinked with rapidity, showing vulnerability, making him appear human. He wore what seemed to be his usual, a three-piece suit with a dandelion stuck in the breast pocket of his jacket, although Ivy thought it was a different suit than she last saw him in, but she couldn't be sure. She thought he looked like the cliché devil from old black and white movies.

"How did you get in here?"

"I took the stairs."

Ivy rolled her eyes. "How did you get past the locked door and my grandmother?!"

JD gave a boyish smile, holding up Ivy's spare key. "Under the flowerpot isn't a better hiding spot than under the doormat. If you're going to do something Ms. Teller, do it well." JD tossed the key to Ivy. "And to answer your second question, Mary didn't notice me. She really must be having a wonderful conversation. I think she's talking to her beau."

"May I?" he asked, taking the drawings from Ivy. She could smell the hint of cigarettes on him. JD brought them close to his face much like she had done, the paper grazing his nose. "Poor Uriah. He was cursed by God because of me. How dare he turn away from an innocent child. My poor, poor Uriah." JD looked down at Ivy where she sat on the floor and spoke in a soft voice just above a whisper. "For that's what they'd say back then when a child was born with a birth defect. When a child was born like Uriah was, they were irregular, God turned his shoulder to them, shunned them. I believe it. I have always known God to be cruel. To do this to an innocent baby is unforgivable. But Uriah, still he had faith."

"Why are these here?" Ivy asked, not sure if she wanted the answer.

"I imagine you put them there. You used to live in this house a long time ago with Uriah."

Ivy's voice shook like her body. "I did?"

"Yes, this house is one of the oldest houses in town. This was—"

Remembering what her grandmother had told her and Sammy, Ivy finished JD's sentence, "the original rectory."

JD nodded. "Yes Ms. Teller, the original rectory."

Ivy did her best to stay calm, taking slow breaths, her voice coming out in a murmur. "Why was I living with Pastor Leeds?"

"Don't you know?"

Ivy glanced down at a sketch of her holding baby Uriah. "I was the Midwife that delivered him, and he let me stay with him because I had nowhere else to go, because he was the pastor of Pleasant Mills and that's what pastors do."

JD shook his head. "Try again, Ms. Teller."

Ivy was in denial. She didn't want to say it out loud. She couldn't.

JD sat down on the floor next to Ivy and handed her the drawings of the baby. "Tell me why, Ms. Teller."

Ivy looked at JD with watery eyes, tears beading on her long lashes. "Because I'm his mother?" she said breathlessly, as if saying it out loud physically taxed her.

JD nodded.

She couldn't look at him, instead she diverted her gaze to the drawing of her, JD, and baby Uriah. "And . . . you're in the drawing with us because you're his father."

Ivy thought back to her dream, back to when she thought he was the most beautiful thing she'd ever seen, back to thinking he was an angel, back to kissing his blood bespattered face.

His voice sounded like velvet. "Yes, we're Uriah's parents."

Ivy knew that somewhere down the family tree Uriah had to be related to JD. They shared the same last name. But not even in her worst nightmares could she have imagined he was JD's son, let alone her son, even though Uriah and Jesse both had said he called them that. JD was not Jesse's biological father, and they assumed the same was true for Uriah.

The truth pushed Ivy over the edge. She felt like one more nudge would send her tumbling to her death or to insanity. She didn't know which one she'd prefer.

"You're lying to me," she gasped as if she couldn't breathe. "You're trying to get into my head so you can manipulate me." She found her voice. "It was you! You put these under my bed! That's why you're here, to see if I found them. Well, I did, but jokes on you—I don't believe it. You wasted your time, so you can leave and go torment someone else!"

JD wiped a tear from Ivy's face with his thumb, his touch surprisingly gentle. "I'm not lying to you. You asked me a difficult question and I answered honestly. You *are* Uriah's mother, and I'm his father. I always tell the truth, even if the truth isn't what's truly desired."

"But how?"

JD smiled his grin, looking too much like Sammy's. "I think you know the answer to that as well."

"Were we married?"

"No, we never married."

JD picked up the drawing of the three of them. "I remember the day this was done. The young artist came to your house and agreed to do a series of drawings, for a small fee of course. Not as detailed as Jesse's works but still very nice." He shuffled the drawings in his hand and looked at the next sketch of Uriah. "We agreed it was best Uriah didn't know who I was, in the hope that one day I would be able to make a deal with him and restore his health. You feared if he knew who and what I was, it would impact Uriah's life negatively and then I wouldn't be able to help him. I was new to the world then; my powers were not defined to me as they are now. I respected your wishes and stayed away from my son. I watched Uriah grow from a distance, waiting for the day he called upon me for help."

"You healed his face because he was your son?"

JD handed Ivy the drawing in his hand. "His face and his leg. And cured the girl he adored because I have always cherished my Uriah."

Ivy stared at the sketch of Uriah confused. "I don't understand, you did all this good for Uriah, so why would you hurt—"

JD put his hand up to stop Ivy from continuing her thought. "I am what I am—a demon. I just can't perform miracles; I'm not God. As I have told you, I need to make deals for my miracles. Everyone ends up worse for the wear, especially those I love. No good can come out of a deal with me.

Even a seemingly innocent act like healing Uriah's birth defects, I turned into something horrible in the end."

Ivy thought about the spell book she let JD borrow and worried. He still hadn't given it back. Was he going to twist her seemingly innocent act? She realized now, she should have set a date and time for it to be returned. She wondered if she asked for it back, if it would make him keep it longer. He was vindictive and figured that would be the case, she'd just have to wait.

"I love Uriah and I'm sorry for the pain I've caused him. But what's done is done. I can't change it any more than I can change the future, it's all part of the same contract."

Ivy took a deep breath in, letting the air sit in her diaphragm. It was easier to breathe now. "Why don't I remember any of this?"

"The day you created me, you unknowingly bound your fate to mine. You have never remembered your past or the many lives you have lived. You have never remembered me or Uriah." JD moved a stray strand of hair away from Ivy's face. "Your lost memories were your doing, not mine. I always assumed you didn't want to remember us. And because I love you, I respected your choice."

Ivy ignored JD's comment about loving her, she couldn't worry about that now, she had to focus on herself. "That makes no sense. Why would I do that?" she could see why she would want to forget about JD, after what he did to Uriah, but forget Uriah? She couldn't believe that was true. "Why didn't you come and tell me when I came back to Pleasant Mills? And don't tell me because you respect me, you're telling me now, so what stopped you then."

"I've always wanted more for you. I wanted you to have a life not weighed down by being connected to a demon." JD hung his head, staring at the floor. "You never meant to create the monster that sits before you, and I thought it was unfair for the rest of your days to be darkened by one act of kindness to a dead child. I have always wanted you to have a good life. There was nothing I could do to change what I did to Uriah and the fate that awaited him, but with you I could." His eyes lifted to hers, he held her gaze in the frame of his dark lashes. "Yet for all the lives you led after your first life, you were never happy. You never knew another day of happiness until this life. Until you met Sammy Lopez."

Ivy flinched at Sammy's name, the guilt bubbling up from deep inside her.

"It's funny . . . this time around things are different. You, Uriah, and Jesse, are all so close in age and are all friends. It's made its own magic. It has changed everything. This life is special, Ivy. I find myself excited by it all . . . happy even. It was your tears after all, that brought me to love Sammy. I was on the fence whether to spare him or not. His father was putting up quite the fuss, making Devan and Jesse's job quite difficult, but it was your love for him that made me take a closer look at Sammy. Something I will always be indebted to you for."

JD leaned close to Ivy. She could feel his warm breath on her face, smell its sweetness as if he breathed sugar and she was a hungry bee. "I thought your heart was set on Sammy, but when you came to me in the woods my heart soared." JD took Ivy's hand in his and put it over his heart, holding her hand there as he squeezed it. "When you remembered me, I thought how can this be . . . I don't deserve another chance with her."

Ivy's voice wavered, "JD, what happened in the woods was a mistake."

JD searched her eyes. "Was it now? Are you so sure? How can love be a mistake."

JD pressed a soft kiss to Ivy's lips, just letting them touch. His taste on her lips was euphoric. Too good to be good. Her lips moved with a mind of their own, parting to let him deepen the kiss, which he did with abandonment, pulling her entire body toward him, his free hand gripping her by the back of her head. She thought his kiss must be toxic, poisoning her from the outside in. In a moment of self-awareness, Ivy pushed JD away, panting. "I love Sammy and I'm committed to him. Please don't kiss me again."

JD released his hold on her, his lips parted. Lust glistened in his eyes like tears. She quickly withdrew her hand, folding her hands behind her back. Ivy wished JD didn't have those large, sad eyes of his. Her conviction buckled for a moment before she rose to her feet handing JD the drawings of their forgotten family. "You keep them," she said. "I'm not the person in those pictures anymore." Ivy opened her bedroom door and headed down the stairs, leaving JD sitting in her room all alone.

"I just came to tell you I'll be returning your spell book soon. Soon it will all be over," JD said into the empty room, wiping the solitary tear that ran down his cheek.

CHAPTER THIRTY-THREE
Call From Mrs. Grindhouse

Uriah was heading to his car to drop Jesse off at Sammy's when his phone rang. Uriah smiled, expecting it to be Trudy. She was coming over later to watch a movie. He pulled his phone out of his pants pocket looking at the number puzzled, it wasn't Trudy but her mother. "I better take this," he said to Jesse. "One minute." Jesse nodded and got into Uriah's Nissan.

"Hello Mrs. Grindhouse," Uriah said into the receiver.

From the rearview mirror, Jesse watched the color drain from Uriah's face.

"Are you sure? Okay, I'll see you soon."

Jesse opened the passenger side door and walked over to where Uriah was leaning against the bumper. "Is everything alright?"

Uriah felt dizzy, his legs acting as a wobbly support. "It's Trudy. Mrs. Grindhouse had to call an ambulance . . . She said Trudy fainted and wouldn't wake up. She wants me to go to the hospital to say a prayer." Uriah buried his face in his hands, a sob breaking through.

"Don't jump to conclusions," Jesse said, patting Uriah's back. "We don't know if she's in a coma."

"I know. I feel it," Uriah said. "This is all my fault. First her brother, and now her."

Jesse was more than out of his element; Uriah was the comforting one, not him. He thought he did a pretty good job with his pep talk over Lilly, but that was easy, it was logical. She was dead, it was time to move on. But this, this was different, a coma is perpetual—Uriah would never move on. "Did you get a memory back?"

Uriah shook his head.

"See, then there's no reason to be upset."

"I usually get them when I'm sleeping and if Trudy just slipped into a coma, I'll have a dream tonight."

"Let's not cross that bridge until we have to."

Uriah wiped his tears with the back of his hand. "You're right. I need to get to the hospital. I have to be strong for Mrs. Grindhouse."

"You're in no condition to drive. Let me see if Mary can take us."

Mrs. Grindhouse said her hellos and left with Mary to grab a cup of coffee from the hospital cafeteria. Jesse and Ivy waited outside Trudy's hospital room, giving Uriah time alone with the comatose Trudy.   "It's not fair Ives," Jesse said, leaning against the wall. JD has put Uriah through enough. Just today he told me he loves Trudy and now JD took her from him."

"Uriah said that? He loves Trudy?" Ivy asked. She knew Sammy thought something may be sparking between them, but love, that was more than a spark, that was a fire of the heart.

"Yeah, he does. He's been struggling with so much guilt over Lilly. He did back when I was a kid and even more now. But with Trudy, I thought he was finally in a good place. I was happy for him."

Ivy looked through the small window in the hospital door and watched Uriah dump all of his feelings bedside in a sad spectacle of lost love.

She really hated to see an angel cry. The thought made her heart skip. Her mind went to the past, to the Midwife thinking JD was angelic, made perfect in God's image. If she believed what JD told her, Uriah was their son. She really didn't see the resemblance, besides the dark hair. Uriah, like JD, was very handsome, but his face was put together very differently from JD's. She decided they had the same chin. The eyes were different and Uriah's full lips, well they were a lot like hers. The thought made her stomach clutch. She knew she was not Uriah's mother, she knew that, but in a past life she had been and seeing him cry devastated her in a way she didn't think possible.

"Uriah has everyone fooled," Jesse went on to say. "He walks around like he's Mr. Happy, like he drinks rainbows in his morning coffee, but the guy is a bundle of raw nerves and depressed as all hell. JD keeps kicking him when he's down. I just hope he can get up from this."

Ivy became overwhelmed, silent tears fell from her eyes. For a moment, Ivy wished Uriah knew the truth about her. Wished her past and the present could collide for just one moment so she could tell Uriah how much she loved him. Wished she could hold her son in her arms and tell him everything was going to be okay.

Ivy was more than a little surprised to find her maternal instincts racing to the surface as she was not a mother and didn't see herself ever being one despite Sammy's dream of a minivan full of screaming kids. Yet, she felt like a warrior princess, or she figured more accurately a warrior witch. There was nothing she wouldn't do for Uriah. It took everything in her to stay outside Trudy's room with Jesse and remain in character. More than ever, she felt like she was playing a part in a lie, like her whole life was one big lie. She reminded herself that she was not the Midwife, she was Ivy Teller, a student, not Uriah Leeds's mother. But regardless of all that, she was going to make JD pay.

CHAPTER THIRTY-FOUR
Confronting the Jersey Devil

As soon as Ivy and Grams made it home, Ivy sprinted to her bedroom. She put on long pants and a long sleeve shirt. She learned her lesson the last time she went tramping through the Pine Barrens. She still had the bug bites to prove it.

"Where're you going?" Mary asked her granddaughter as Ivy opened the front door.

"Meeting Sammy. Everyone's at his house."

Mary grabbed her keys off the kitchen table.

"I'm walking Grams."

"Walking? You?"

"Shocker I know, but I need the exercise. Gotta run, want to make it there before it gets too dark."

Mary looked over her granddaughter with an evaluating eye. "Grams it's fine. Tammy's waiting for me outside her house, we're walking together."

"My granddaughter making friends, never thought I'd see the day," Mary said releasing her clunky keyring back on the kitchen table.

"I like to keep you on your toes," Ivy said with a smirk. "Bye Grams."

"Be safe and hurry now, it looks like it's gonna rain," Mary said, looking out the living room window and scenting the air. "Yep, I can smell it. Rain will be here soon."

"I will."

Ivy quickly made her way down the sidewalk. Before she got to Sammy's house, she veered off into the woods. It was dusk, the last of the sun cast an amber halo over the trees. The fog hovered a few inches above the ground, making her phone flashlight very useful. Ivy moved through the woods as she did with Sammy that day on the shore, the day they found Timothy Chen's body. She let the woods guide her to her destination, let them pull her in. Ivy came across a tree that had been struck by lightning. She could see mushrooms growing from the rot, sprouting from the trunk like fungal fingers. It looked both tragic and beautiful to her.

Ivy looked onward, to see the fog rolling in from the north. She ran into it, crushing through the wild blueberry bushes until she came to a clearing in the brush. She took in the dead, twisted trunks of trees as swiftly and silently the viscous fog approached, choking out the light, just as she caught the glint of glass tucked into a tree trunk. She recognized the lid as a Lipton iced-tea container and new the jarred heart she and Sammy found in Pastor Leeds's attic was tucked away in the hole in the tree trunk. She was in the right place.

"JD!" Ivy called into the fog.

He appeared behind her as if by magic, his footfalls not detectable. "Hello, Ms. Teller."

Ivy spun around, finding herself a few inches from him. They locked eyes. The smell of a recently smoked cigarette was thick on his clothing. She wondered how he made it smell like that. Cigarettes were gross, they always smelled bad to her, but his smelled so sweet, it was like he was a flower, and she, one of many admirers.

"I know you're behind the comas. You've got to stop it now. You've got to wake them up, it's gone too far."

"Has it?" JD asked Ivy, studying her, his eyes not blinking as they took on an anamorphic quality. He seemed less human than he had in her room only a short while ago.

"Oh my God, yes! JD, please stop this!"

"You will find God doesn't have very good hearing. Me on the other hand, I do—nearly perfect."

"Good, then you know about Trudy Grindhouse. Uriah loves her, and you put her in a coma!" Ivy pointed at JD furiously, her finger waving in front of his face. "You broke his heart. You did it to him once before with Lilly and I'm not going to let you do it to him again!"

JD's tongue shifted around his mouth licking his teeth. Ivy pulled back her hand, balling it into a fist, thinking he could bite her finger off. She didn't like the twitch of his mouth. He was a demon after all and not to be trusted, regardless of the Midwife's old feelings.

"You should see him," Ivy continued, her anger making her voice shake. "Uriah can't even form a sentence. Please JD, wake Trudy up for him!"

JD didn't respond. He stood perfectly still like a deer in headlights, his mouth a flat line, his eyes large and unblinking.

"JD say something!" Ivy shouted, her voice ricocheting off the dead trees like a bullet, striking him in the chest—a kill shot.

JD spoke in a low, solemn tone. "Ms. Teller, I wish I could. But the spell has already been set in motion."

"Spell?!"

Ivy's frustration brought her to tears.

"Yes, Ms. Teller."

"Cut off the Ms. Teller shit! I was wrong about you! You *are* a monster! How could you do this to our son?!"

In a second, JD was upon her. He grabbed Ivy's chin forcing her to look into his eyes. "Don't play dumb with me little girl." His voice grew deep and menacing, she didn't recognize it anymore. "If you want to blame someone for our son's misery look in the mirror. Look at that very pretty face of yours. The face that's not good enough for you. It's your jealousy that has torn out our son's heart, not me."

Ivy whimpered. "What are you talking about?"

"Come now, Ms. Teller, you know. You have always known, but you've been too afraid to admit it to yourself." JD rubbed his cheek against

Ivy's, still holding her face in his hand. He moved his lips to her ears and whispered: "If you did, you would realize you're every bit as much of a monster as I am."

Tears rolled down Ivy's hot face. JD's grip was hurting her.

"First Elsa. Sammy's crush, the bane of your teenage existence. How fortuitous the lovely Elsa fell ill. Your next victim, Trudy Grindhouse—the knockout, Sammy's ex-girlfriend. So threatened you were by her looks and her past with Sammy, you let your own weaknesses corrupt you my dear. You put your insecurities before our son. Don't pretend you didn't know Uriah loved her."

JD released Ivy's face.

She rubbed her jaw. "What are you saying?"

"I'm not the one choosing the souls I receive, you are."

Her face twisted in confusion. "What?! How can that be?!" Her eyes grew large when she realized what he was hinting at. "The spell book? But all I did was let you borrow it. I never read from it or made a deal with you to hurt Elsa or Trudy. It doesn't make sense."

JD wrapped his arms around Ivy, bringing her close to him, his nose now centimeters away from her face. His grip made her feel safe and scared at the same time.

Ivy struggled to free herself. "You're a liar!"

JD pulled her closer. His face resting against hers, she stopped fighting. "Yes, *you* gave me the spell book."

"To help Sammy's mom," she said into his ear.

"And I did."

"You'd said borrowing the spell book was a technicality. That I had to give you something, so you would be free to help Lindsey. You said you wouldn't hurt anyone."

"I said I wouldn't hurt a member of the Lopez family and that I wouldn't kill kids, and I have kept my promises. No harm has come to Sammy and his family, and no children have died."

"You tricked me!"

"No, Ms. Teller. There were no tricks. You came to me remember?"

"I don't understand," Ivy said, trying not to breathe in the smoky aroma coming off his skin.

"You control the spell, because it's your grimoire. All spells read from that book answer to you."

"It's not mine. Sammy found that stupid thing!"

JD spoke agonistically slow. "Are you so sure Ivy? Doesn't it seem familiar to you?"

"I don't know," she said in a panic, wiggling, trying to fight against his hold. She could no longer stand to be that close to him. "I don't know!"

JD moved Ivy's damp hair away from her face. "I know there's so much you don't remember and even more you don't want to. I know this. I'm sorry for the turn the spell has taken. I had believed if you weren't the witch that read the spell, the spell wouldn't answer to you. But Ms. Teller, you hold so much power. The magic is helpless in your midst."

"Can you fix it? Can you wake her up?"

JD hugged Ivy tightly, pressing her so hard against himself she felt like she would suffocate.

He breathed in the smell of her hair. "For you and Uriah, I wish I could, but the spell has to run its course."

"Can I change it? Redirect it or something?" Ivy asked desperately, her words smothered by his chest.

"No, it's not your spell to change. Once I have collected the rest of the thirteen souls promised to me, the spell will have run its course."

Ivy sobbed into JD's chest. The warmth of her tears penetrating his shirt tantalized his skin. "I didn't know," Ivy cried. "Why didn't you tell me? Why didn't you warn me?"

"Look at me," JD demanded, loosening his grip.

Ivy did as she was told and gazed into JD's brown eyes. "You will not seek false comfort here witch. In the back of that devious little mind of yours, you always knew. But up until now, my soul reaping wasn't truly problematic for you, was it? It helped you knock off your competition. You never shed a tear over Elsa, and I imagine if Uriah wasn't crying now, you'd be pleased Trudy's in a coma."

JD put his hand over Ivy's heart. "Yes, there it is . . . the truth—you're happy. Listen to your little heart rejoice at their infinite sleep."

Ivy pushed JD away from her.

PLEASANT MILLS, NEW JERSEY: WHARTON STATE FOREST

"You're wrong about me! I didn't want this!"

"You can't lie to me or hide from me. I know you. We are both doomed to hurt those we love."

"NO!" Ivy screamed. "I don't want to hurt anyone! This is your fault. You did this. I trusted you and you turned it into something horrible. I HATE YOU!"

Ivy ran from JD, back through the fog and blueberry bushes as fast as she could. JD's face hardened. His lips thinned out and his eyes grew narrow. He clenched his fists. Rain poured down from a black sky as Ivy ran home. She looked overhead as thunder shook the trees and lightning lit the sky.

"Run all you want, Ms. Teller. You can't hide from who you are, none of us can."

CHAPTER THIRTY-FIVE
A Plan

Ivy ran to Sammy's house. As soon as she got to the Lopez's front gate, a floodlight on a motion detector turned on. She felt like a criminal, her hands clinging to the iron bars of the gate. She was waiting for the sirens. Ivy got a hold of herself; nervously, she hit the speaker button on the gate. "It's Ivy. Can you open the gate?"

"Opening it now," the voice said through the small speaker. She took a step back, for a moment she thought JD had followed her, beat her to Sammy's. Then she heard the voice again. "Come up the driveway, Ivy." She sighed, stealing a moment for herself as she recognized the voice to be Jeffrey Lopez's.

The gate to the Lopez estate opened, the two iron 'L's parting. Ivy ran up the driveway. Jeffrey was waiting for her at the front door.

"You walked here in the rain?" he asked concerned, as water from her wet hair ran down her face. Even soaked, he could tell she had been crying.

"Yes."

"Everything okay between you and Mary? You two have a fight?"

"No, nothing like that." She kept her head down; she didn't want to see his face.

"I just want to talk to Sammy. He's not answering his phone."

Jeffrey glanced at his watch. "It's pretty late. You shouldn't be out by yourself."

"Is Sammy still up? Can I talk to him?"

"Uh, yeah. I'm sure the boys are up. Come in, get dry, and I'll drive you home."

"Thank you, Mr. Lopez."

Ivy ran past Jeffrey and up the staircase to Sammy's room. She threw open the door without knocking. "Sammy, I have a plan!"

Sammy, Jesse, Mike, and Zac stared at Ivy wide-eyed from the floor where they were huddled around Monopoly, a small puddle of rainwater forming at her feet from the rain dripping off her drenched clothes. She had forgotten Mike was sleeping over, but she didn't care. She had to say what she came to say, before she lost her nerve. "Sammy you were right about the comas, it was JD! I know where the jarred heart is. Before anyone else slips into a coma, we need to steal it and destroy it!"

Sammy jumped to his feet, forcing Catchup off his lap with a hiss. "You really know where it is?!"

"Yes, we have to go now," Ivy said, desperately.

Mike looked at Jesse, "What's she talking about?"

Jesse's hand stroked the back of his neck, not sure if he should tell Mike. Jesse was thinking keeping him in the dark was probably for the best. "Uh . . . it's a long story."

Ivy grabbed Sammy's hand, leading him out of the room when she collided with Jeffrey Lopez. She was forced to look at him. His face was JD's. It was all JD, all but the eyes. Mr. Lopez's brown eyes were different, and she was grateful.

"I don't think so," Jeffrey said in a stern voice, sounding more like JD than he ever had.

Ivy took a step back, releasing Sammy's hand. Jeffrey handed Ivy a towel and a dry sweatshirt and sweatpants. She didn't take them.

"Mr. Lopez, we need to go now!"

"You don't need to do anything. Tell me what's going on and if there's any doing needing to be done, then I'll do it. But first you need to get changed."

Dry and frustrated, Ivy took a seat at the kitchen island. As she sat the room went quiet. She felt like she was on trial, everyone's eyes looking at her like she had done something bad, as if they could see into her guilty soul.

"I already told my parents about Zac when you were getting changed," Sammy said, taking Ivy's hand. "So, you can just start with what happened tonight."

"Everyone is freaking out I'm still alive, well that I'm a ghost," Zac told her proudly. "You think you and Sammy can do a spell so Mrs. L can see me. She really wants to see me."

Ivy's eyes went to Lindsey who was standing next to her husband rubbing his arm. "Yeah Zac, later, I promise," she mumbled.

"Well Ivy," Jeffrey said impatiently, looking at the face of his watch again. "What's going on? I tried calling your grandmother. I got the busy signal on the houseline and she's not picking up her cell."

"She doesn't know anything about it."

"About what precisely?" Jeffrey said, leaning on his elbows.

Ivy huffed. "There's nothing much to tell. I know where the heart is, the jarred heart Sammy and I found last year at Pastor Leeds's house." Her eyes flickered to Jesse who stood next to Jeffrey and Mike. Mike had a confused look on his face as if he was still digesting everything Sammy had told him. "It's the heart the 'old Jesse' thought was the source of JD's power. It's JD's mom's heart." She struck the countertop with the palm of her hand. "We only have a small window to get the heart. He'll know I know where it is and move it. We've got to get it now and destroy it before anyone else gets hurt. We need to go now, okay?!"

"Okay," Jeffrey said, "that's simple enough. Where is it?"

"In the woods."

He exhaled loudly, compulsively, running his fingers through his hair. "I'm gonna need more than that, Ivy."

"It's not like I can draw a map. I just have to take you there."

Jeffrey looked at Lindsey. She moved her shoulders in a half shrug. "Okay fine," he said. "We'll go."

"Me too," Sammy said, standing up. "I'm going."

"I don't think so Sammy. Stay here with your mother, sisters, and little brother. We don't want a repeat of last time."

Sammy knew his father meant his mother and sisters getting kidnapped. "Jesse will stay here with Mike, and I know you can't see him yet, but Zac's here too. He can help, he can move stuff."

"No Sammy."

Sammy talked with his father's voice. "Dad, I'm going with you and Ivy. You can't leave me out of this. I deserve to go."

Jeffrey avoided his wife's eyes, letting out a groan that sounded like a wild animal. "I would feel better if you stayed, Sammy."

"I want him to go," Ivy said. She didn't want to be alone with Jeffrey. She didn't want to look at him. She didn't want to hear his voice.

"Fine, he goes. Let's go."

Lindsey followed her husband to the coat closet. "Are you sure about this? Maybe we should call the police."

"And tell them what?" Jeffrey asked, putting on his raincoat. "Tell them there's a heart in a jar hidden in the woods?" He handed Sammy and Ivy a jacket. "The police will think I did it."

"Pearl won't."

"I'm not getting her involved."

Jeffrey went to the gun cabinet, unlocked it, and took out a handgun. He knew it wouldn't protect them against a demon, but it still made him feel safer.

Jeffrey opened the front door to pouring rain and gusts of howling wind. He sucked his teeth, "I don't know . . . maybe we should wait till morning."

"We can't!" Ivy pleaded. "What if he moves it?!" We have to go now!"

"She's right Dad."

Jeffrey reluctantly nodded. He went back to the coat closet and pulled a heavy-duty flashlight off a shelf. "Alright, let's do this."

CHAPTER THIRTY-SIX
Locator Spell

Jeffrey Lopez guided the flashlight in the direction Ivy pointed, and they marched on. The rain was so heavy it pulverized most of the fog, but it also obstructed their vision. It felt like they were looking through a shower door. Everything was out of focus and blurry.

Ivy almost slipped on wet leaves. Sammy kept her steady, taking hold of her hand as she led them deep into the woods. "How did you find out where JD was hiding the jarred heart?" he asked.

"*Locator Spell.*" The lie slipped off her lips. She didn't even have to think about it. Lying was getting easier and easier for her.

"*Locator Spell?*" he mused inquisitively.

"Yeah, it was in the Leeds grimoire. After seeing Pastor Leeds so upset at the hospital, I just found the spell and thought it could be useful. All the spell needed was a little blood over a map, a *bippity boppity boo*, and it showed up—'X' marks the spot."

"Nice Disney reference, but I thought you said a map couldn't take you there?"

She whispered in his ear: "I said that to your dad, so he'd let us tag along."

"Good thinking, Teller."

"How much farther?" Jeffrey asked, looking back to see only darkness. He didn't like that he couldn't see the house. He pulled out his cell phone, holding it in the cup of his hand to try to shield it from the rain. "Great, no service."

"Not much farther," Ivy said as a bolt of lightning lit the sky highlighting the woods and their faces before going dark again.

Ivy didn't know it could rain any harder, but it did. It pelted the leaves causing a crackling noise not dissimilar to popcorn popping in the microwave. She was losing her conviction. Ivy was worried JD knew she was coming and what she was planning. She worried she was walking Sammy and his father into trouble.

Ivy glanced to Sammy and took comfort in knowing JD promised he wouldn't hurt any member of the Lopez family. Whatever happened, Sammy and his dad were safe. But what about her? Could he hurt someone he loved? He had before, why should she be any different?

"There," Ivy said pointing, her voice washed out by the rain.

They entered a small clearing, their feet sinking into the mud like quicksand.

"Where Ivy?" Jeffrey asked as he spun the flashlight at the dead trees surrounding them. The mixture of the rain and the flashing light personified the tree trunks, giving them gnarled faces.

"Inside the trunk," Ivy yelled to be heard. "The jar is inside one of the tree trunks." Jeffrey shined the flashlight at the tree in front of him. He saw the hole in the trunk. Reaching in with his free hand, he felt around— nothing. He reached into another hollowed out tree as Sammy and Ivy did the same.

Jeffrey's fingertips brushed against something cold and smooth. He gripped his hand around the jar pulling it out of the trunk slowly so as not to drop it. His stomach twisted as he stared at the jar now in his hand, the knot in his stomach knocking the breath out of him. Seeing the heart was more than his imagination had prepared him for.

"You found it," Ivy said, quickly making her way over to Jeffrey and taking the jar from him, the heart sloshing around in its glass prison from being jostled about.

"Great. Let's get out of here." Jeffrey said, looking behind him as if he thought he was being watched. "Sammy, let's go, we got it!"

Sammy slowly walked toward them. Ivy could see something was in his hands. She took the flashlight from Jeffrey and handed him back the heart. She flashed it at Sammy. "Come on, Sammy!"

He held out the Leeds grimoire for her to see before tucking it under his jacket. "I thought you said you got the *Locator Spell* from the grimoire."

"I did," she said, pulling on his sleeve with urgency, her mind quickly thinking up a plausible lie. "JD must've stolen it. Now, come on, let's get out of here before he shows up."

CHAPTER THIRTY-SEVEN
Secrets

At the sound of the front door opening, Lindsey, Jesse, Mike, and Zac rushed into the foyer, Anita approaching slowly. "You find it?" Lindsey asked her husband, helping him take off his wet jacket.

"Yes," he said, holding up the jar for everyone to see.

Mike's face went pale. "There's no way that thing is real." He took it from Jeffrey, wiping off the rainwater to get a better look.

Jesse nodded. "It's real."

"This is crazy. We . . . we . . . we need to call the cops," Mike stammered.

Jesse shook his head. "No cops. The less people who know about this, the better."

"No cops," Jeffrey agreed, keeping his eyes on the jarred heart, happy to no longer be holding it. The knot in his stomach was already relaxing.

"I really wish I would've gone home with Tammy," Mike mumbled under his breath.

"Any sign of him?" Jesse asked concerned, glancing at Sammy who was pacing the foyer like a bull.

Jeffrey answered. "No, we got lucky."

"What's wrong honey?" Lindsey asked, going to help Sammy with his wet coat.

"I don't know where to start," Sammy said, opening the grimoire to where a stick acted as a makeshift bookmark, marking a spell.

"Sammy," Jeffrey said in a stern voice, "what's the problem?"

Sammy stopped pacing and faced Ivy. "You're helping him, aren't you?"

"What are you talking about?" Ivy asked, moving her damp hair out of her face to get a better look at him.

Jesse studied Ivy. Her eyes shifted around like a caged animal. "What would make you say that?" Jesse asked Sammy.

He held up the grimoire for Jesse to see.

"You're always trying to make something out of nothing," Ivy said frustrated. "I told you, JD must've stolen it."

Sammy snapped back. "In the last hour! I don't think so, try again."

"What's going on?" "Jeffrey asked.

"That's what I'd like to know, Dad."

"This page was marked," he said, flashing the page to everyone before reading it out loud.

"The Sleep Spell

Endless sleep.
Endless days.
Weary eyes.
Weary legs.
Eyes closed to night and day,
Day and night.
Endless sleep
Endless days.

Weary eyes.
Weary legs.
Eyes closed to night and day,
Day and night.
Endless sleep
Endless days."

Sammy closed the book and held it tight to his chest. "Dad, this is the spell that put Elsa and Trudy in a coma."

"You sure?" Jeffrey asked, still not sure where Sammy was going with this.

"Yeah Dad, I'm sure."

"Can you undo it?" Jesse asked.

"Sometimes you can, by reading a spell backwards," Sammy said, opening the grimoire again and glancing over the spell. "But it won't work on this one."

"Why not?" Mike asked.

"It's a looping spell," Sammy replied disheartened, closing the spell book again. "There's no way to break it, he made sure of that."

Jesse raised both of his eyebrows. "Looping spell?"

"The spell reads in a circle. The lines are the same lines over and over. Even reading it from the last line to the first line it reads the same—it's the same spell."

Anita nodded at Sammy proudly.

Sammy narrowed in on Ivy with cold blue eyes that looked like ice. "I need answers Ivy and I need them now."

"Not here, Sammy. Not now," she hissed, tightening her grip on the flashlight, her mind turning.

"Then when?" He demanded.

Zac interjected. "Shouldn't we do something with the heart before JD shows up?"

Ivy, ignoring Zac, turned to Jeffrey, "Mr. Lopez can you drive me home?"

"Yeah, of course Ivy."

"No Dad, not before she explains herself."

"Uh the heart," Zac said. "I think we should deal with the heart first."

"Think what you want to think Sammy," Ivy said, moving toward the front door.

Sammy pursued her. "I don't know what to think. Tell me the truth."

"Tell the truth child," Anita said from the kitchen threshold. Tell my grandson what weighs down your soul, cleanse yourself."

Sammy's eyes darted to his grandmother then back at Ivy. He motioned with his hand for her to speak.

Ivy felt everyone's eyes on her, judging her. She looked to the front door, wondering if she should make a run for it, wondering if she could scale the gate and make it home. But Jeffrey was blocking her exit.

"Ivy, please," Sammy said, his tone more pleading than angry now. There was a desperation present in his voice that made it sound hoarse. She glanced over him. His eyes were watering, at any moment tears would fall. She hated seeing him like this, hated knowing she was responsible for making him feel that way. Ivy looked to Anita, wondering how much she knew and if she would tell Sammy the truth if she didn't. There was a small chance Sammy would forgive her, but for that to happen, she knew she'd have to be the one to tell him the truth.

"Sammy, you have to believe me when I say no one was supposed to get hurt. I was only trying to help your mother. She was going to die and so was Hugo."

Sammy sucked air, waiting for her to continue. "JD came to me and said if he borrowed the spell book, he could save her. The both of them. He promised me he wouldn't hurt anyone in your family and that no kids would get killed. I thought lending it to him was innocent . . . your mom and brother were saved. You were happy. Then Elsa slipped into a coma and now Trudy." Her eyes found Mike. "I think Tammy is next, or it could be you, I don't know." Ivy's voice hitched, "We need to destroy that heart now, and stop all of this."

"Agreed," Zac said.

"Not Tammy," Jesse mumbled under his breath, as if saying it would stop it from happening.

"Ivy," Sammy said slowly, choosing his words carefully. "How did you know where JD's lair was? In all the books I've read on the legend of the Jersey Devil, no one knew where it was."

"I just did."

"No Ivy, you didn't. And you couldn't have used some locator spell from the grimoire because he had it, not you. Tell me the truth."

Sometimes she really hated how smart he was.

Anita fixed Ivy with a gaze, she tried to shrink from it, recoiling into herself. "I knew it from my past. I remembered it somehow." She glanced at Anita. "After your grandmother gave me that soul cleanse, I started remembering things. It's like your grandmother said, I'm getting stronger."

"Your past?" Jeffrey asked, the knot in his stomach returning.

She nodded. "I'm like Uriah and Jesse. I've been here before. Sammy, you know that picture we found under my bed, the one that looked like me?"

"Yes . . ."

"It *was* me."

Sammy was speechless, not sure how to respond. He dug his nails into the leather binding of the grimoire, feeling tension run through his arms and chest.

"I was there when Japhet Dean Leeds was born. I was the midwife that delivered him." Ivy was sobbing now, "I made him. I didn't mean to. His mother was killing him, suffocating him with a pillow and I just tried to help the only way I knew how." Ivy's voice carried in the large foyer with its high walls. "I'm sorry. I'm so, so sorry Sammy. I never meant to hurt you or anyone. I'm not a bad person."

Sammy and Jesse exchanged anxious glances. They'd found the Midwife, the person the 'old Jesse' claimed was working with JD when he had talked to Sammy outside the church at Timothy Chen's funeral.

Sammy's voice was barely a whisper, but each syllable felt like a rock striking her in the heart. "Is that all?" Sammy asked. He already got a confession of collaboration, proving the 'old Jesse' had told the truth, but there was something in the way Ivy cradled herself that led Sammy to believe there was more.

She looked at Sammy helplessly, the glimmer in her dark eyes gone. "No Sammy, that's not all." Covering her face with her hands, to avoid his judgment for as long as she could, she whispered her secret. "I slept with him. I'm so sorry."

There was a jolt to Sammy's heart. He dropped the spell book on the marble floor, it echoed in the large space as everyone held their breath in shock.

"You what?" he asked, hoping he heard wrong. Hoping he didn't understand what she meant. The room was spinning under his feet. It moved faster and faster, his heartbeat quickening to the tempo of the merry-go-round room. Sammy's mind moved to protect him from the truth. "He forced himself on you. That's why you've been acting so funny. Ivy, you should've told me right away." He went to hug her. "Are you alright?"

Ivy pushed him back. "No—it wasn't like that Sammy. I wanted to sleep with him." Sammy was stunned into silence and so was everyone else. "It just sorta happened in the woods after I . . ." She glanced at Jesse. "After I killed Jesse."

"You killed me?!" he gasped, shocked. "This whole time we thought it was JD."

"Jesse, you have to believe me, it was an accident. You were chasing me, and I pushed you. You fell and hit your head. I tried to help but it was too late."

Jesse fixed her with a cold stare.

"Don't look at me like that!" she yelled. "How many people have you killed! Don't act like you're so innocent."

"What's she talking about?" Mike asked Jesse.

"Holy crap Jesse, she hung you out to dry," Zac said. "See, told you we should've dealt with the heart first. Heart first, drama second."

"Tell him Jesse! Tell Mike who you really are," Ivy yelled through tears.

Before Jesse could say anything for himself, Sammy spoke up. "This is not about Jesse, Ivy. This is about you."

He looked at her in a way he had never before. His blue eyes were cold and lifeless as a corpse, the love in them gone forever.

"What do you want from me Sammy?! I made a mistake. I wish I didn't, but I did."

"I want to understand. I thought you loved me."

Jeffrey whispered to Lindsey: "This isn't a conversation they should be having in front of everyone. I'm going to break this up and take Ivy home and then we'll deal with the heart."

Ivy reached for Sammy's hand, he let her hold it. "Sammy, look at me." He looked at her, holding back tears. "I love you so much. I went into the woods that day because I love you. You have to believe me."

He pulled his hand away from her and shook his head. "How can you say that. How can you say you love me when you slept with him? He's not even a man. He killed my friends. Poor Zac can't even talk about it. You knew Tyrone and Louie—he killed them. And Tim, you saw what he did to him!"

"Sammy, it's hard to explain."

Jeffrey put his hand on his son's shoulder, attempting to stop his conversation with Ivy.

"Try it, Ivy. Try to explain," Sammy said exasperated. "Help me to understand. I'm really trying here. I feel like my head is going to implode. I just don't get it. You said you wanted to sleep with him. Why? Why would you want that?"

"Can we talk about this in private?" Ivy asked.

"I think that's a good idea," Jeffrey agreed.

Sammy seemed not to hear them. "Why Ivy?"

"I have a history with him."

"History? What the hell does that mean?"

Ivy wasn't ready for everyone to know Uriah was her son. She had said way more than she had wanted to already.

"I don't know Sammy. I didn't get it all back. I have less memories than Pastor Leeds. I just know that I made him and know that I was intimate with him in the past. That's why I keep coming back, I'm connected to him."

Sammy thought about last summer, how Ivy showed up out of the blue, not saying much about her past. In the last year, she never brought it up. Anytime he had mentioned her mother or sisters, she shot him down. Now he knew why, she didn't remember them. She had false memories like Pastor Leeds had when he showed up at Pleasant Mills Church and just like Pastor Leeds, as Ivy adjusted to her new life, those memories faded, and she was left with nothing.

"Ivy, I don't even know you," Sammy said with a spitefulness that made him sound like his father. The Ivy I know would never betray me like that. Everything I've gone through and the aftermath, the therapy, the panic attacks, the guilt—it's all because of JD".

Ivy wiped her tears. "What about Jesse? You forgave him."

"I've forgiven him and Pastor Leeds because they were both tricked by JD. They were both manipulated, but you already told me you weren't. You said you wanted to be with him. The thought of it makes me sick." Sammy raised his voice. "Do you have any idea what it felt like for me down in that hole in the ground, freezing and starving while I waited for your little creation to kill me? Do you?!" he yelled. "I felt like I was already buried alive. Then, to know that I was next at any second. Knowing that the next time I heard footsteps, it could be my time—afraid of that demon you have *a history with* was going to rip my heart out while I was still alive!" Sammy's voice wavered. "Because that's what he was going to do to me! What he did to my friends! And who knows how many others! Shit Ivy, he wanted to kill my baby sisters." Sammy held his head. "Oh my gosh, he was going to do that to Alba and Maria, and you slept with him."

Jeffrey and Lindsey exchanged another look, at this point there was no stopping it.

Sammy looked at Ivy with eyes that could have obliterated her where she stood. "What's wrong with you?!"

"I went into the woods to help your mother!"

"My mom wouldn't want Elsa and Trudy in comas because of her." Sammy shook his head. "Not my mom. She would rather die. She believes in God, if it was her time, it was her time. She would've accepted that."

Lindsey's face twisted in anguish. She wanted to say something but didn't.

"But Sammy," Ivy pleaded. "I didn't know about the *Sleep Spell.* No one was supposed to get hurt."

Sammy refused to look at her. "Dad, take her home, I never want to see her again."

CHAPTER THIRTY-EIGHT
Heart in a Blender

As Jeffrey drove Ivy home, she sobbed into her hands. He pulled into the driveway and spoke in a soft voice, a tone he seldom used. "Your heart was in the right place. I know you never meant for anyone to get hurt, Ivy." She nodded, choking on her cries, the grimoire on her lap. Sammy wanted nothing to do with her or the spell book. Her life was over. "Sammy's just upset, but I know he loves you. Give him time, okay? We have the heart now, we'll wake the girls up from their comas, and set everything right."

Ivy opened the car door, not looking at him. Jeffrey lightly touched her shoulder. "If it weren't for you, Lindsey and Hugo wouldn't be here. Thank you." His words brought forth another choking sob as she wondered why Sammy didn't see it that way. She hopped out of the SUV, rushing to the front door and disappearing behind it.

Jeffrey drove home with a heavy heart. He felt awful for Sammy and Ivy and above all, helpless. He should have been the one to help his wife and son, not Ivy. "Glad I didn't sue the hospital," he muttered to himself.

There was something else weighing heavily on him. It had been since he ran into JD on his jog and saw with his own eyes they share the same face. Ivy had said she had been in Pleasant Mills before, had a secret past, he feared, now more than ever, he did too.

Jeffrey pulled into the garage, shut the car off and got out. He heard screams coming from inside the house. The color drained from his face, his heart skipping a beat as he rushed to the side door, fumbling with his keys. "What's going on?!" he shouted, coming through the door in a panic.

The twins came running toward him still screaming high-pitched yelps. They hugged him. "Daddy, Zac's back." They each took one of his hands and led him to the kitchen. "Come see."

"Hi Mr. Lopez," Zac said, all smiles.

"Woah, Zac, it's great to see you," Jeffrey said, surprised Zac was standing in his kitchen. He'd heard what Sammy told him about Zac being a ghost, and even after everything he saw last summer, the skeptic in him struggled to believe it. He was also surprised and relieved Zac looked just how he had when he was alive. Jeffrey had seen Zac postmortem and struggled to get the image out of his mind. But the ghost that stood in front of him now was the Zachary they all knew and loved. He looked so alive.

Jeffrey turned to Sammy impressed and a little weary. "I see you made quick work out of that spell."

"Yeah Dad, Abby and I updated the one Ivy and I wrote. Everyone will be able to see him now. Well, us, Mike and Tammy, Grams and Pastor Leeds too."

"That's great," Jeffrey said still shocked, resisting pinching himself to see if this entire night was a dream.

Lindsey took her husband's wet raincoat and hung it in the closet for him. She called for the twins. "Okay you two, it's time to get back to bed."

"We can't go now, Mommy. We want to play with Zac." Maria, pleaded.

"Zac is sleeping over. You can all play in the morning. Now, say goodnight."

The twins did as they were told and kissed their father, grandmother, and Sammy good night. They blew kisses to Zac as they giggled and went upstairs with their mother.

"Wow, they forgot about me quick," Jesse said.

"How do you think I feel? I barely get a hello these days," Mike scoffed.

"Okay," Sammy said, once the twins were upstairs, "time to get to business." He took the jarred heart out of the refrigerator.

"Really Sammy, the refrigerator?!" Jeffrey said.

"What? I had to hide it from the twins. It was hard enough to explain why I woke them up with my yelling without them seeing this."

"Good point. So, what do we do with it now that we have it?" Jeffrey asked, taking a seat at the kitchen island next to Anita.

"Destroy it," Sammy said. "I'm thinking the blender. Chop it up and flush it down the toilet."

"Why not," Jeffrey said with a shoulder shrug, "but do it before your mom gets down here. If she sees you using her food processor to make a heart smoothie, she's gonna be pissed."

Sammy pulled out his mother's food processor. "You know I'm telling her you said it was okay."

Jeffrey chuckled, tucking his damp hair behind his ears. "I know."

Sammy hastily unscrewed the lid to the jar and dumped the heart in the food processor.

"Gross," Zac whined.

Jesse tensed, he wasn't sure what would happen when they destroyed the heart, he hoped it didn't take him with it. Anita was right, he liked the new life he built. He had friends. He braced himself for the worse.

"Here goes nothing," Sammy said, pushing the chop button.

They watched the heart get chunked into pieces, sloshing about in its own fluids.

"Double gross," Zac said when Sammy pushed the blend button.

After a few minutes Sammy shut the food processor off. "Okay, we got us a heart smoothie," Sammy said proudly, turning around to see his mother with her arms crossed over her chest. Sammy wasted no time putting the blame on his father. "Dad said it was okay."

"I use that every day for Hugo," Lindsey said irritated, taking the pitcher from Sammy and pouring the liquified heart down the garbage disposal.

"I think we have a problem," Jesse said from his seat at the kitchen island.

"What now?" Lindsey asked, scrubbing the plastic container with hot water and soap.

Jesse pointed. "It's back."

The heart was back in the jar, as it was, before Sammy fed it to the food processor.

"No way," Sammy said shocked. "That's nuts!"

"Let's try it again!" Zac shouted.

"No," Lindsey said.

"She's right," Anita admitted. "This heart will not be destroyed by kitchen appliances."

Jeffrey rested his face in his hand. His adrenaline was crashing, leaving him exhausted. "Maybe we can try something else."

"Burn it," Mike suggested.

"Run it over," Sammy offered as an option.

"Feed it to Hotdog and Catchup," Zac said.

"No, no, and no," Lindsey told them, giving her husband the evil eye. "Don't fuel their imaginations, Jeffrey."

Hotdog trotted into the room and put his paws on Jeffrey's lap.

"See," Zac said, "I think Hotdog is willing to give it a go."

Jeffrey flashed his wife a smile. She wasn't amused.

"Let me see that heart," Zac said, pulling the jar to him.

"Wow," Jeffrey exclaimed as he watched the jar slide across the kitchen island. "Sammy wasn't lying when he said you can move things."

"Yep," Zac said proudly.

"Wow, that's really something."

"Yeah, and you owe me an apology," Sammy said to his father. "The stuff lying around the house today was all Zac. He's getting good at moving things. Not so good at putting them back. I don't think he knows what a neat freak you are."

Jeffrey responded with a toothy smile. "Geez Sammy, sorry. You should've said it was the ghost in the house," he laughed. "And Zac," he said turning to him, his tone stern, "Sammy's right, I'm a neat freak, if you move something, move it back."

"Yes, Mr. Lopez."

"And we're not feeding the heart to Hotdog no matter how much he wants it," Jeffrey added, noticing the way Zac was still eyeing the family dog.

"Sammy, honey," Lindsey said, putting her hand on her son's shoulder, "it's okay if we don't figure it out tonight. It's very late and we've all had a rough day. Why don't you boys go off to bed and we'll work on this tomorrow after the special prayer service for Elsa and Trudy."

Jeffrey poured himself three fingers of whisky from a decanter on the counter. After tonight he needed a drink. "That's a very good idea Lindsey."

"We need to do this now. What if JD shows up?!" Sammy said concerned.

"That's what I've been trying to say since you guys walked in the front door!" Zac said exasperated. "No one knows how crazy he is more than me. We need to do something now before he kills everyone!"

Lindsey looked to Jeffrey. Mike was bright red; he didn't want to die.

"One more try," Jeffrey said, trying to appease everyone. "But let's try to relax. No one is going to get killed. JD doesn't know we have the heart, and even if he did, I'm sure he's aware it's hard to get rid of. That type of arrogance will buy us plenty of time. Try not to worry about him. If what Ivy says is true, he can't hurt any of us. We're all Lopezes and Mike, whether you agree or not, you're still a kid."

"I don't know how much I'd trust Ivy," Sammy mumbled under his breath.

Jeffrey took a steak knife out of the knife block and placed the heart on the cutting board. He sliced it in half. "What do you know about that, it worked!" He spoke too soon. He blinked, and the heart was whole again.

Jeffrey looked to Anita. "Any ideas from the witchery?"

Anita spoke confidently as if she'd come up against this kind of thing before. "It would take great power, power we don't have. I alone, can't do it."

Sammy bowed his head wishing he was his long-lost uncle, the magical prodigy, then maybe together they could've destroyed the heart and with it, JD.

"What about with Ivy's help?" Mike asked.

Sammy's eyes darted to his grandmother. Anita shook her head.

"Alright," Jeffrey said. "Maybe we can do what Sammy had planned to do last summer and use the heart as leverage. If JD wants his mother's heart back, then he's going to have to wake the girls from their coma and leave town. I'll call Uriah in the morning and see if he, along with Mary and Ivy, can come over after service and work out some sort of meeting place for the trade. Until then, let's get some sleep."

"We don't have to include Ivy," Sammy said.

"We do Sammy," Jeffrey told his son matter-of-factly. Sammy bit his tongue. "We at least have to invite her. It's up to Ivy if she joins us. We wouldn't be in possession of the heart without her and if your grandmother's right, and we're not strong enough to destroy the heart, she may be vital to setting up a meeting with JD."

Sammy nodded.

"What do we do with it until then?" Zac asked.

"It will stay with me," Anita said, taking the jar and going off to her room, but not before kissing Sammy on the temple. "I'm proud of you, Samuel Cameron."

Sammy smiled. His loving grandmother was back, first working on a new and improved *Zachary Lewis Spell* together and now the praise.

"Safest place in the house," Jeffrey mumbled. "JD would never find it in that room."

"Off to bed now," Lindsey said to the boys. They reluctantly went up the stairs to Sammy's room, the sound of their feet dragging on the stairs audible from the kitchen.

Jeffrey flopped down on the couch with his drink in his hand. Lindsey came and sat next to him. "It's all going to be okay Lindsey. I don't want you worrying about JD too. This is almost over."

She put her head on her husband's shoulder. He wrapped his arm around her.

"I know."

"Boy, am I glad the twins aren't freaking out over Zac being a ghost. I thought that would be a hard one to explain," Jeffrey confessed.

"We're calling him their imaginary friend."

"Smart," Jeffrey said, taking a sip of whisky.

"Not my idea. It was Sammy's."

"Poor Sammy, that was rough tonight."

"Very rough. Do you think they'll work it out?" Lindsey asked.

"I don't know. Her cheating with JD isn't going to be easy to get over. Honestly, I don't know if I'd be able too . . . but I know Sammy loves her."

"And Ivy, what do you think of her?" Lindsey asked, her face flushed.

"I don't know what to think," Jeffrey admitted. "She's always been hard to read, but I never doubted she loved Sammy. We weren't there, so we really don't know how it all went down. The insight into her past and her ever-growing abilities are a little scary. But at the same time, we owe her—big time."

Lindsey squeezed her husband. "I love you."

He kissed the top of her head. "I love you too. I love you and the whole family so much." He chuckled. "New additions included. If you would've told me last summer, we would have a new baby, a dog, a cat, and a Zac, I would've drove you to the loony bin myself."

Lindsey rubbed her hand over her husband's firm chest. "Don't forget about Jesse."

"True, he's here every day, he might as well move in. One big happy family."

Lindsey wiped a tear. "One big happy family . . . I wish things could stay this way."

"I'm not going to let JD hurt you or our family. I promise. I know I can't freeze time, and tomorrow the kids will be a little older, well minus Zac. And in a couple months Hugo will be crawling, then walking, but each day will bring something special. And we'll be there to enjoy it together. All of us, the whole family, Hotdog and Catchup included. And JD, well, he'll be gone, out of our lives forever."

CHAPTER THIRTY-NINE
Unbreakable Bond

Uriah insisted on staying with Trudy at the hospital, giving Mrs. Grindhouse the opportunity to go home to check on her mother and get some rest. The nurses' station didn't object to Uriah staying overnight, even though he wasn't a member of the Grindhouse family, and spending the night as he was, went beyond the privileges of a clergyman. Uriah was a hospital regular, and the staff all knew and liked him. It was the head nurse, herself, who wheeled a cot into Trudy's room.

Uriah, exhausted, never made it to the cot. He fell asleep in the chair next to Trudy's hospital bed with a book open in his lap. No sooner had he closed his eyelids, did his past begin to creep into his mind.

Pleasant Mills, New Jersey 1744

"Mama are you home yet?!" Uriah yelled as he barreled through the front door.

Uriah's mother was at the kitchen sink peeling potatoes. "Mama, I met my guardian angel today! He healed me!" Uriah tugged on his mother's skirt. "Mama, please look! I'm all better. I'm not irregular no more! And Miss Lilly, he saved her too. And Mama, Miss Lilly kissed my cheek, here," Uriah exclaimed as he pointed to his cheek with his free hand and continued to tug on his mother's dress with the other. "Pastor Baker wants to teach me to be a pastor! All my prayers have been answered! Today is the best day of my life. I thanked God and my guardian angel over and over. I know Mr. JD will watch over me. Mama did you hear me?!"

URIAH LEEDS: 1744

Uriah's mother put her knife down, turning around to hug her son feverishly. "Oh Uriah, I have waited a long time for everyone to see how special you are—see what I have always seen."

"Mama, why are you crying?" He gently put his hand under his mother's chin, slowly lifting her face to his and tenderly tucking her dark hair behind her ears.

"They're tears of happiness." She cradled his healed face in her hands. "I see your father in your beautiful face. You are truly whole now, go show the world how special my little Uriah is," Ivy said.

Uriah woke up startled, the image of Ivy Teller cradling his face burned into his head. He was hot and confused as he pushed his damp hair off his forehead. Ivy was his neighbor, but could she be something more? A migraine split his temple at the thought. The door to Trudy's hospital room creaked. His eyes shifted to the figure entering the room.

JD leaned against the closed door rubbing his chin as Uriah surveyed him. He wanted to light a cigarette, badly. His hands moved anxiously from his chin to his lips, missing having something to hold. Satisfied Uriah wasn't going to yell for help, JD walked over to the window on the far side of the room and leaned on the windowsill. His eyes flittered down at Trudy, "I'm sorry about Trudy, Uriah."

Uriah tried to control his breathing, which was difficult thanks to his racing heart. He spoke as normal as he could, his words coming out in gasps. "Then help her, please."

"I can't."

"But she's not thirteen. She's not even a child. I don't understand."

"No, she's not thirteen and she's not a child. Normally, I like to have a bit of fun playing with the whole Jersey Devil legend. It gives the locals something to speculate on. However, in the end, it doesn't really matter who I claim, a soul from your congregation is a soul. And to be honest with Devan gone and Jeffrey Lopez being a thorn in my side, I decided to work more discreetly. A coma raises less suspicion than dead children, and I ultimately still get what I want. My dietary needs can be met by the stray hiker.”

“What *you want*?” Uriah asked in a whisper. “I never understood what that was.”

“Yes Uriah, what I want. Soon you will have all your memories back, and soon you will be the ‘old you’ again. For this is what I live for, for you to be as you were all those years ago, for you to be my Uriah.”

Uriah fought to hold back tears. “Why are you doing this to me?”

JD tapped his cigarette case in his jacket pocket as he spoke. “When I first saw you, you were so perfect to me . . . This beautiful baby, with this beautiful heart. But your heart sang a bittersweet song. Ladened by the cross you were to bear as a son of a demon and a witch.”

“Son of a witch? . . . You mean Ivy Teller, don’t you?” Uriah asked, thinking of the strange dream he just woke up from.

JD nodded.

“How is that even remotely possible?”

“Through her, she makes everything possible—nightmares and fantasies and much more.”

“Son of a demon,” Uriah repeated, afraid to look at JD. “Are you telling me I’m your son?”

“Yes Uriah, you are indeed my biological son, the only one. You are special, very special.”

Uriah breathed in deep gulps. “Your son . . . why would you do those terrible things to me, your own son, your own flesh and blood?”

JD was silent.

Uriah looked at JD with his soft, blue eyes. “I need to know why. Why ask for Joseph’s life and kill Lilly? Why be so cruel to your own son?”

“Oh Uriah, if things were only easy when it came to me.”

“Why father?”

Hearing Uriah call him father made JD’s heart flutter, made him feel human, like he was just a man talking to his son. JD’s regret and guilt formed a lump in the back of his throat that would’ve brought a normal man to tears.

“I’m not proud of what I did Uriah, and I wish I could take back hurting you. Every day I live, I wish I could take it back.” JD hung his head.

"What I did, I did out of jealousy. I was so desperate for your love, to be loved by you. When Joseph was born, I saw how much you loved him, and it hurt me. I wanted you to look at me like you looked at Joseph. I wanted you to love me utterly, so absolutely. I thought I was losing you, and I panicked."

"I did love you," Uriah said earnestly "You saved Lilly and healed me. I thanked you every morning and night for your gifts."

"I know you did Uriah. The part of me that is man knew this. I would watch you through your window as you said your daily prayers. Thanking your guardian angel for your wonderful life. But when Joseph was born, something in me snapped. I was overcome with jealousy. The love he received from Lilly and you, the love of a mother and father . . . love, I never felt. The part of me that's wild and untamed, twisted those feelings in my head and brought me to ask you to kill your first-born child, kill your Joseph. It was my sadistic little way of giving you the opportunity to prove how much you loved me. I wanted you to prove to me you loved me above all. Above your God, above your wife, and above your baby boy that brought so much joy to your life. I wanted to be number one, your savior, your love, your reason you breathed."

JD stopped himself. His heart was thumping in his chest. He pulled out his cigarette case and lit a cigarette. He took a long drag before cracking open the window and exhaling.

"And when you wouldn't do what I asked, when you begged me to spare Joseph, your love for your son only made my darkness grow, twisting my love into knots, growing my jealousy like a strangling vine, and taking with it the last of my humanity. I wanted more from you now. I wanted to punish you for not loving me the way I loved you. I wanted to take it all away from you. All the things you cherished. And I did. I demanded thirteen souls from you to save Joseph. My way of sticking it to my mother and you, my son who wanted a large happy family—the family I never had. I took your unborn children's souls to fill the void in my own heart. And when you denied me them, I took Lilly."

JD's hand visibly shook as he brought his cigarette to his lips. "It happened all so quickly, in a rage. It was done before I knew it was over and she was gone. That day still haunts me. Your face . . . so tortured, like an angel with broken wings. I regret that day above all things. I hurt you so deeply, we have both shared the burden."

Silent tears trickled down Uriah's face.

"But my madness went deeper . . . I took more from you. I took your health and your memories. Those pretty little things you clung to, that kept you going after Lilly died and Joseph died. You held them so close to your heart, that I had to take them from you. Wipe you clean. And with each new life you lived, with each soul I reaped, I would let you feel the hurt as I viciously killed members of your church and tormented you by dangling lost memories over your head until you felt mad yourself. And when you couldn't take it any longer, I would swoop in as your guardian angel with razor sharp talons and restore you."

Uriah's lips quivered at his father's words.

"Every day I walk this Earth, I walk with regret. Me, the half man-half demon, that tells himself I love my children. I'm the biggest hypocrite of them all, bigger than your God, Uriah. I have hurt you in unspeakable ways. But I never meant to . . . I hope that you believe that and know that I'm sorry for the pain I've caused you and continue to cause you. I know you can never be who you were, things can never go back to how they were when you were a child."

JD took a drag of his cigarette to try to steady his nerves. "I know I can never go back." He had never made a confession like that before, he was rattled. Ivy's words had gotten under his skin. "For what it's worth Uriah, I'm truly sorry. You didn't deserve a monster for a father."

JD put out his cigarette on the window ledge. Not looking at Uriah, he walked out without another word.

CHAPTER FORTY
Wish

Ivy ran up to her room, not caring how loud she was as she took the old staircase to the attic. She slammed her door and threw herself in her bed dragging her blanket over her head like it was a coat of armor that could protect her from the outside world. But she was worried, what was going to protect her from herself?

With her covers over her head, Ivy reached under her bed feeling for the tin of drawings Sammy and she found in the secret compartment under her bed. Ivy felt the rough rust against her hand and brought the tin into her blanket cave. She opened it. JD had taken all the drawings but one. The picture of the three of them as a family lay at the bottom of the tin. She picked it up, ripped it in half and threw it back in the tin.

Regret tearing through her as if she was the picture she'd just torn, Ivy got out of bed in search of tape. Her hands shakily went through her desk drawer until she found it. Sobbing, she taped the portrait back together. She hated JD but she couldn't destroy the drawing. She wondered what that meant. She put the taped picture back in the tin and stared at it. She tilted her head to the side curiously when she noticed a small, dried flower at the bottom of the tin. Ivy picked it up, it was a dandelion. She twirled the dried stem between her fingers. Something about it was familiar to her. "When a dandelion dies it leaves you a wish. Don't be afraid to make yours," she muttered to herself.

Carefully, Ivy put the dandelion back in the rusty tin, closed the lid and slid it back under her bed. Lying in the groove in the center of the mattress, Ivy stared up at the cobwebs high above her. "When a dandelion dies it leaves you a wish. Don't be afraid to make yours," she repeated to herself. "I wish for Sammy Lopez to forgive me." Overcome with exhaustion, she closed her eyes and slipped into sleep.

Leeds Point, New Jersey: 1735

JD and Ivy stared into each other's eyes, talking in a silent language of elevated breaths and gasps. He rested his face against hers. "I love you."

"I love you too," she said, blocking out the sound of Deborah Smith Leeds's beating heart he held in his hand.

They heard commotion at the front door. Villagers had made their way to the home after hearing the screams.

"You have to leave now," Ivy whispered to Japhet Dean.

His eyes followed the sound of the knocks coming from the front door. "I don't want to leave you."

Ivy reached under her bonnet and pulled out a dandelion that was woven through her hair. She handed it to him. "When a dandelion dies it leaves you a wish. Don't be afraid to make yours." JD looked at her uncertain. "I've made mine Japhet Dean. I wish to be with you forever. Now run, before they hurt you."

Ivy could hear villagers in the house, but she also heard something else, a soft whimper. She scanned the room, Japhet Dean was gone. The sound was not from him.

She walked over to where Deborah Leeds Smith lay slumped against the wall. Ivy covered her mouth in surprise. On the floor amongst the blankets was a baby. She picked him up. Holding the infant close to her chest. "Another baby, a twin. —Shh now Jeffrey," she said. "It's going to be okay. I'm going to keep you safe."

CHAPTER FORTY-ONE
Mother

Uriah didn't get a wink of sleep after JD left. He took to drinking coffee and waiting for Mrs. Grindhouse to arrive back at the hospital. As soon as she did, he took his leave and drove home.

Uriah made a pot of coffee and with a coffee mug in hand, sat on his couch and stared out the living room window at Mary Teller's house across the street. Jesse had helped him pry open the old shutters weeks ago and he now had a convenient direct view of the Teller's front door from his living room window.

Mary had mentioned to him yesterday, at the hospital, she had a breakfast date in the morning before Saturday's prayer service and had asked him to throw in a good luck prayer for her when he was praying.

Uriah nervously checked his watch, hoping Mary didn't sleep through her alarm clock. He was desperate to talk to Ivy in private after his resurfaced memory and his surprise visit from JD. He knew all too well that Mary's hearing deficit seemed to miraculously clear up when gossip was in the air.

Uriah was on his third cup of coffee when Mary finally walked out of her front door and got into her old, white station wagon.

Uriah was out the door before Mary was down the street. He knocked on the Teller front door with shaky hands.

Ivy came to the door rubbing the sleep from her eyes. "Good morning."

"Good morning, Ivy. I was wondering if we could talk."

"Uh yeah, come in. You want a cup of coffee?"

"What's another cup?" he said with an anxious smile. "Sure, if it's not too much trouble."

"No trouble."

Uriah followed Ivy into the kitchen. He took a seat while Ivy poured him the rest of the coffee left in the pot from her grandmother's wake up cup. Grams had a cup first thing every morning before she got dressed, then at breakfast she'd have another one or switch to tea. —Something about coffee always giving her a jolt to her heart, which she claimed was essential to her starting the day off on the right track. With her grandmother having a breakfast date, Ivy was surprised there was any coffee left in the pot. She placed the mug of hot coffee in front of Uriah with a spoon and pushed the sugar bowl neatly labeled 'sugar bowl' to him.

"Cream?"

"Yes please."

Ivy worriedly looked at Uriah as she poured the creamer into his 'Best Grandmother' mug. She hadn't seen him look that bad since last summer. His body had the jitters and he had dark circles under his eyes from not sleeping.

"How are you doing Pastor Leeds?"

Uriah added a spoonful of sugar to his coffee and stirred. "I'm hanging in there."

"Any breaking developments with Trudy?" Ivy looked down guiltily, glad Uriah had not been at Sammy's last night and hoping the Lopezes hadn't phoned him yet.

"No. She's still in a coma." He anxiously stirred his coffee. "I did have a memory come back to me last night. So, we can be certain Trudy and Elsa are JD's victims."

"I'm sorry Pastor Leeds."

"Yes, me too," he said, looking into his cup of coffee as he spoke. "My memory from last night was quite strange . . . it was the continuation of the memory I had when Elsa slipped into a coma." Uriah paused to look at Ivy. "The memory of me telling my mother I was healed."

Ivy's heart felt like it stopped. "Oh," she said uneasily.

"In that first memory, I never saw my mother's face, but last night I did."

Ivy squeezed her hands under the table. "Uh huh," Ivy mouthed white knuckled.

"Ivy, the face I saw was yours."

Ivy didn't move a muscle. "Uh huh," escaped from her lips without her mouth giving way to the words.

Uriah laughed nervously. "I know it doesn't make any sense, but I think you're my mother."

Uriah looked to Ivy for reassurance, but her face had gone pale, and she appeared frightened. "Please, forgive me." Uriah said remorsefully, her face making him regret knocking on her door. He didn't mean to scare her. "I'm just tired. I must be wrong. It must be all the stress I'm under . . . and now with Trudy ill . . . I just feel like I'm losing touch. I'm just slipping away."

Ivy wasn't sure what to do, wondering if she should just admit it. Everyone hated her anyway, why not have Pastor Leeds hate her too?

She had held her secrets so close for so long. She had locked them away from everyone, hoping the key would be lost in time along with her past. She wasn't sure now, if she was ready for Uriah to know who she really was. Part of her was grateful he was already second guessing his memory. She could play it off like he was just losing his marbles, if she wanted; take advantage of his state of mind and broken heart and keep her secrets safe. But as Uriah sat there staring into his coffee cup, tears rolled down his face. Ivy couldn't bear to see him crying at her expense. She wasn't like JD, she wouldn't manipulate him, she was no monster. She put her hand on Uriah's "You're not losing it. You're my son. Well, not mine exactly, but in a past life."

Uriah embraced her at once, wrapping his arms around her and hugging Ivy as his mother for the first time.

Uriah hugging her felt natural, she knew she did the right thing. Ivy tried to hold back her tears, but she couldn't. It felt good to let the last skeleton out of her closet.

"I wanted to tell you . . . I just didn't know how," Ivy sniffled. "I found an old sketch of me holding a baby. I didn't know what to think. Or if I should tell you."

Uriah released his bear hug. "And my father, do you remember who he is?"

"Yes, but—"

He cut her off. "It's JD, isn't it?"

Ivy took a deep breath, then exhaled slowly. "Yes."

"Did you know what he was?"

She nodded. "I'm the one who made him, well not exactly, I made the call for help, and I think a demon did the rest. Your last to know, well besides Grams. It all came out last night at Sammy's . . . I'm the midwife that delivered him."

Uriah took a moment to digest what Ivy had just said, shifting his coffee cup between hands. He was very familiar with the legend of the Jersey Devil, having done research on it for last summer's lock-in.

"JD visited me last night at the hospital. I didn't believe him. I didn't want to believe him."

"It's true, he's your father."

"And you let him manipulate me?" Uriah's voice shook. "You let him take advantage of me when I was just a boy. You let me sign my life away to him. Let me think he was a guardian angel. You should have warned me about him, about who he really was."

"It's not like that Uriah. You were sick and he healed you." Ivy took Uriah's face in her hands like she had done in his dream. "You never deserved what you were given. This is the face you were always meant to have, and he made sure you got it. Your face is a gift from your father."

Ivy surprised herself a little, she didn't do anything to Uriah, but her words came out as if the Midwife was talking through her.

"I wasn't sick; I had a birth defect. People are born with birth defects all the time and live with them. I shouldn't have been any different. This face was no gift. It made me a prisoner to his will, and you let it happen."

Uriah stood. "I didn't know it then, but meeting him that day, as a boy, ruined my life. How could you let him do that to me? You're my mother; you were supposed to keep me safe."

Ivy grabbed Uriah's hand. "Don't be upset; you're not seeing things clearly." Again, her words surprised her. She wanted to tell him to blame someone else, that she hadn't let anything happen, but that's not what came out.

"No Ivy, I don't think *you're* seeing things clearly. I can see how it all unfolded now. You played a vital part in me meeting JD that day by the sawmill. You kept me away from him, so I wouldn't know him as my father; so, I would think he was sent to me from God. All, so that I could have this face. And for what? What good did it do me? Everyone I loved was murdered."

Ivy couldn't say anything, tears from the past choked out her words.

Without saying another word, Uriah tucked his chair in and let himself out.

Ivy slumped back into her chair and sobbed, everyone hated her, everyone besides JD. She hoped her grandmother would understand, but she had her doubts. She wished her secrets would've stayed buried with the dead.

CHAPTER FORTY-TWO
Witches in the Family

Mary Teller scolded her granddaughter as Ivy sat on the couch with her arms crossed over her chest. "Now get up to your room and get dressed. You're not going to church looking like that."

"You're right Grams, because I'm not going to church. I'm going to sit here in my PJs for the rest of my life."

"Where's this coming from Ivy Belle Teller? The whole town's going to be there for Elsa and Trudy, and that means you too. I'm not much for what townsfolk say about me, but we should be there for Uriah and Sammy. What will Sammy say when you don't show up?"

"I imagine he'll be quite happy."

"This have something to do with why you stampeded up the staircase last night like an elephant?"

Ivy looked away from her grandmother's icy gaze, her arms still firmly folded over her chest. "I don't want to talk about it."

"My house, my rules. Now talk."

There was a knock on the door.

"You gonna get that?" Ivy asked. "You wouldn't want the townsfolk to think you're rude."

Mary growled before going to the front door. Her face softened when she saw who it was. "Uriah, glad you're here. I'm having an argument with Ivy, I think you can help with."

She led him into the living room.

"Hello Ivy," he said.

Ivy's eyes were like slits. "Pastor Leeds."

"She's fighting me about going to church this afternoon for Elsa and Trudy's prayer service," Mary said with her hands on her hips.

"I think I know why."

"You do, do ya?" Mary said, taking a seat next to Ivy on the couch. "This should be good. Please enlighten me."

"It's because of me and I'm sorry."

Mary lifted her eyebrows, "*you?*"

Uriah took a seat across from Ivy on the La-Z-Boy chair. "Ivy, I'm truly sorry for the way I spoke to you earlier. I had no right to. You didn't deserve that." He fiddled with the button on his sleeve. I've been doing a lot of thinking since this morning, and I've come to realize something very important. You're not the Ivy from your past, just as I'm not the Uriah from mine. With a clear conscience, I can't blame you for things my mother has done because you're not my mother. You're Ivy Teller, my neighbor and my good friend, and I should've never gotten angry with you."

Mary scratched her head. "What the heck is going on here? I go on one date, which was very nice since no one asked, and the whole world falls apart without me. I always knew I was the glue that kept this town stitched."

"Oh Grams," Ivy said, turning to hug her. She buried her face in her chest. "Grams you're right, you go on one date and my whole world falls apart. Everyone hates me."

"No one hates you," Mary said, moving Ivy's hair aside.

"Sammy hates me."

"Poppycock, your grandfather and I used to fight like boxing kangaroos, and we always worked things out for the better."

"Not this."

Mary looked to Uriah for answers. "Better start in the beginning

Uriah."

Uriah told Mary everything, everything Jeffrey had told him about last night, including Ivy and Sammy's very public break up and the conversation he had earlier with Ivy. And Ivy told her grandmother and Uriah about Anita's soul cleanse, her strange dreams, and the drawings she'd found.

"Geez," Mary said when they finished laying everything out for her. "That's a lot of weight to carry on your shoulders. You should've told me Ives. I would've helped carry it. Was a hell of a linebacker in my hay day."

Ivy laughed, grateful her grandmother had a way of always making things seem not so bad.

"Grams, remember when you said there were witches in the family?" Mary gave her granddaughter an odd look. "You said I had something Elsa Tilton didn't have."

Mary cackled. "Yep, I said you had voodoo."

"Did you know all along I had magic?"

"All girls have magic. It's how we get the opposite sex to do what we want and have them think it was their idea."

Uriah smiled at that, not necessarily disagreeing.

A horrifying thought came to Ivy. She had no memories of her mother and sisters, and she had no memories of her grandmother that dated further back than last year. She worried Mary Teller wasn't her real grandmother.

Ivy took a deep breath in, taking solace in Sammy pointing out how much she and her grandmother resembled each other when Mary had gotten dressed up for her big date with Danny the tire guy. She could handle being the Midwife, and the part she played in making the Jersey Devil, and even everyone hating her, but she couldn't handle her grandmother not being her grandmother.

"Grams, I need you to be honest with me. Did you know about my past? Do you have any old memories?"

"Sorry Ives. I was just as much in the dark as you. Sure, I get a déjà vu moment from time to time, but I just thought it was my mind going," Grams chuckled, "or a glitch in the Matrix. It's part of the reason why I label everything. Just trying to keep my head straight. I'll be paying closer attention to those sorts of things from here on out." Mary hugged her granddaughter a little tighter. "But none of that really matters to me. I don't care who you were or what you did. No matter what, you're my granddaughter and I love you."

Ivy walked Uriah to the front door.

"Can I expect you at church?"

Ivy nodded. "I'll be there."

"Ivy, I hope you can forgive me."

She hugged him; she had wanted to do that the whole time he sat on the La-Z-Boy. "I do." She wanted to tell him she loved him but kept it to herself.

"Thank you," he said.

"But can you forgive me?" she asked with a sniffle, tears already beading on her lashes. Her face hurt from crying so much, she really hoped she could hold everything in.

"Ivy, like I said, nothing about the past is your fault."

Her lips, lips just like his, quivered. "But still, can you forgive me?"

"Yes," he uttered, holding back his tears. "I realized all my mother ever wanted for me was what she thought was best."

Ivy wiped her eyes with her pajama sleeve.

"Well, I better let you get dressed," he said, smiling at her SpongeBob pants. "I'll see you shortly and I hope Mary and you decide to join us at the Lopez's after church."

Mary was standing in the hallway when Ivy shut the front door. "I'm heading upstairs to get dressed," Ivy told her grandmother. "Not sure why everyone hates my PJs."

"Okay kiddo, and don't worry, we're going to join Uriah after church and help set everything right."

Ivy took a deep breath. "You're right, Grams. I think we should. Some things are more important than everyone hating me."

CHAPTER FORTY-THREE
The Haunting of Jesse Richards

Jesse missed a button on his dress shirt. He unfastened the buttons and tried again. He was so nervous his fingers wouldn't work, and he couldn't keep his mind on task. Jesse had agreed to go to church for Uriah's special prayer service, but as he got dressed in the Lopez's downstairs bathroom, he fully regretted telling Tammy he would come. But she had asked him last night at Sammy's to sit with her at church and he had said yes. He wanted to say no, knew he should have said no, but he wanted to please her and couldn't come up with one good reason why he wouldn't be at church the next day. Tammy had made such a big deal out of it, telling him that Elsa was her best friend, leaving him no way out of it.

Jesse put his hands on each side of the mirror and looked at his reflection. "Jesse Richards pull yourself together man . . . You can do this."

He was feeling a little better after reciting his mantra several times to himself in the mirror and was about to leave when a familiar woman's voice whispered in his ear.

"You belong in the dark."

Jesse instinctively turned around, finding himself alone. He was scared, his elevated pulse proved it. It made him feel like a child, a silly notion being that he was well over three-hundred-years-old. The image of the teenage boy in the mirror was a hoax. "You can do this," he said one last time to his reflection before leaving the bathroom.

Jesse could feel the sweat dripping off his forehead as they rode to church. He was nervous about riding in cars. He wasn't used to them. They were a far cry away from the horse and carriage of his day, but that wasn't what was bothering him. The screams of the Lopez twins and the car radio were mere static to Jesse. Everything was washed out by the fears whirling around in his head. Jesse had not stepped foot in a church since he killed Mona. Uriah had told him countless times God forgives all if we ask for his forgiveness and are truly sorry. Jesse was truly sorry, but he never asked God for forgiveness. He reasoned if Mona couldn't forgive him, he had no right to ask God.

When Jesse saw Pleasant Mills Church, the church his father built for Uriah as a thank you for helping him as a child, he felt immobilized by fear. The sweat now dripped down his cheeks like he had just completed a great feat of athletic prowess.

"You alright?" Sammy asked, unbuckling his seatbelt.

"You look like crap," Mike added.

"Yeah," Jesse said, wiping the beads of sweat on his shirt. "Just feeling a little nervous."

"Nothing to be nervous about. If JD can step in church, so can you. God's not going to smite you."

Sammy cracked a smile and so did Jesse.

"That's not why he's nervous," Zac teased, making a kissing face.

"If Tammy looked like that," Sammy laughed, "we'd have a big problem."

Jesse stepped out of the SUV. The late afternoon breeze felt good on his hot face. It was a clear day for the most part. The summer sun was out, and the fog was patchy, leaving little pockets of haze hovering close to the tombstones on the side of the old church.

"Come on, we sit up front," Alba said, taking Jesse's hand and leading him to the first pew.

"Jesse's sitting with Tammy," Sammy said, reminding his little sister.

"That's right," Alba replied. "So, that means Zac can sit next to me."

"Sounds good to me," Zac said, running to catch up.

Just as the Lopez family were taking their seats, the Handovers walked in. Mike waved to his family. Tammy, ignoring her brother, made her way over to Jesse and hugged him. She made a quick introduction to her parents before taking his hand and leading him into the pew behind the Lopezes. Mike followed.

The Lopez twins turned around and waved at Jesse. Hugo tried to do the same as he squirmed in Jeffrey's arms. Jesse gave a faint smile. He could feel his heart racing, each beat producing a tremor in him. His hands were growing increasingly moist and clammy in his lap. He wiped them on the side of his pants. Glancing down, he saw his hands were smeared in red. He could smell the salty scent of blood. He remembered it well—the scent of Mona's blood on their blood-soaked sheets, the texture of it on his hands.

Tammy squeezed his hand, the blood now on her palm, but she was oblivious to it.

Jesse closed his eyes. *It's not real Jesse. There's no blood.*

"You okay?" Tammy whispered.

Jesse opened his eyes; the blood was gone. As he looked at his spotless hands, he wished his conscience was as clean.

"Um, yeah, I'm fine. Just hot. Thanks for asking me to sit with you."

She smiled and squeezed his hand a little harder.

Uriah had finished saying his hellos and was about to start the service. He stopped at Jesse and Tammy before heading to the pulpit. He nodded at Jesse as if to ask if he was alright. He knew this was a big step for Jesse and was proud of him. Jesse smiled the best he could.

The church was full for a Saturday service. Every seat was taken, and people stood in the back. Jesse looked toward the door, toward the fresh air. He and Ivy glared at each other, before he faced forward.

Jesse was trying to focus on Uriah's sermon when he noticed something out of the corner of his eye. It was a dark shapeless shadow going in and out of focus hovering near Anita Gomez where she sat at the end of the first pew next to Sammy. He kept his eyes on the waning shadow, waiting to see if the poltergeist took form. Waiting to see if it was Mona Wolff, his dead wife. A silhouette of a boy materialized from the inky shadow. It seemed to become aware of Jesse watching it and vanished from sight.

Jesse swallowed hard. He wondered if the poltergeist was why his 'old self' told Sammy not to trust his grandmother. It made him doubt whether *he* should trust her. He deliberated on if he should tell Sammy his grandmother was haunted. For as he knew from experience, only those who have committed something terrible could be haunted like that, that's why Mona was haunting him in the first place—he was her murderer.

From behind him, Jesse heard what sounded like a dripping faucet. He turned around to see blood dripping from the hand-blown windowpanes, blocking out the sun. He and Ivy locked eyes again for a moment before he quickly turned back around. Tammy smiled at him. He attempted to smile back but he could still hear the blood splatter hitting the floor in rhythmic drips. Faintly, he could hear Mona humming along to the beat. He knew he was the only one who could see and hear the blood, it wasn't really there, but even with this knowledge he struggled to collect his nerves. He was starting to understand why the 'older him' was desperate to get out of Pleasant Mills. Jesse wondered if Mona would be forced to remain in town or follow him for the rest of eternity, no matter where he went.

Tammy released Jesse's hand, to itch her nose. Blood covered her hand from where Jesse had held it. She smeared blood on her face, before putting her finger in her mouth and chewing on her nail.

Jesse fished around for his protection amulet in his pants pocket. He knew it wouldn't block Mona out completely, she was too strong for that, but he was hoping for a little reprieve from the theatrics. "Crap," he muttered under his breath. He had left it in the bathroom when he got changed.

Tammy took her finger out of her mouth and smiled at him, her once white teeth painted red. A crimson stain bloomed on her chest; it looked just like how Zac's had looked when he had gotten upset. He knew what that meant. It meant her heart was gone. It was what he had done to Mona and now she was returning the favor.

Jesse stood up and lurched toward the end of the pew. The room spun around him as he stumbled to the exit. He spilled out into the parking lot onto his hands and knees. The white lace of a wedding dress came into view. He lifted his eyes ever so slightly.

Mona knelt next to him, grabbing his face with her hands, and forcing him to look directly into her dark eyes. "Look what you did to me Jesse Richards." His eyes flickered downward to her chest, the lace on her dress dyed a ruddy red. "God does not welcome you home. You have no home and deserve none."

"Mona I'm sorry, forgive me!"

She released his face. Jesse clung to her dress with both hands. He begged, "Please forgive me. Please?!"

"No peace for you, Jesse Richards. You deserve to be alone for all eternity. Everyone you touch, you destroy. The Lopez family will be no different. You will bring death to them. Heed my warning."

Mona knelt again and kissed his forehead as blood spilled out of her lips. She took his hand and put it on her bloodied chest. "If you would have asked for it, I would have given it to you. For it was already yours, husband."

"Oh God Mona, please I'm sorry!" Mona vanished, and in his hands he held her heart. He dropped it, letting it roll in the dirt. Sobbing, he covered his face with his blood-covered hands. "Please forgive me."

"Jesse," Lindsey said, crouching next to him. "Are you alright?"

"I can't go back in there."

She hugged him. "Jesse it's okay, calm down."

"No Lindsey, it's not. You don't understand, she doesn't want me to."

"Who?" Lindsey asked as she pushed his hair away from his face.

"Mona, she doesn't want me to know peace."

"Mona?"

Jesse was scarcely understandable through his tears. "My first wife. I killed her when I was sixteen for JD. She's haunted me ever since. She doesn't want me to save my soul. I can't go to church."

"Shh," she said as she rocked him. "It's okay."

Pleasant Mills Cemetery: Mona 'Moon River' Wolff

"I didn't want to do it Lindsey. I loved her. She doesn't realize that we both died that day. I died with her. And me being kept alive by JD is hell for me. Every day is hell. She doesn't know how I feel."

Jesse couldn't believe he had just told Lindsey that. He had never told anyone about Mona, besides Uriah. He had kept the secret from Sammy, despite he promised there would be no secrets between them.

"Shh, I got you," Lindsey said, cradling him. "Jesse, I know you're a good boy."

"I'm not."

"You are. What you did when you were sixteen was not your fault. You were only a child; put in an impossible situation you never should've been put in. There is a goodness in you that shines through. I saw it at once. And when the time comes, I know you will come through for all of us."

Lindsey helped Jesse to his feet. He nodded. "I will. I promise."

Jesse and Lindsey heard the ambulance sirens before they heard the commotion coming from inside the church. They ran to the door. Jesse gasped when they saw Tammy lying unconscious in a pew.

Jesse felt a cold hand on his shoulder. He knew who it was. He didn't turn around to look at Mona. The wind picked up around him, blowing the fog under his feet and into the church. He heard a soft voice calling his name. It was carried on the wind that whisked around him, causing the hair on his arms to stand on end. Still, Jesse didn't turn around. Instead, he crossed his arm over his chest and rested his hand on top of Mona's, his hand becoming icy cold as it rested on hers.

Jesse felt her cool breath on his face. "I know what you're up to Jesse Richards. I know what you're planning. You're a very bad man." Her voice cut through him like a winter chill.

Jesse felt her ice-cold touch leave him as Detective Pearl Steele rushed people out of the church to make way for the EMT's. Jesse looked to the cemetery. He saw the ghost of his dead bride walking through the graveyard on her way back to Batsto Village, the place they once called home.

Part of Jesse wanted to go with her, walk hand in hand with Mona behind the sun, but he feared his judgment day. He feared that he was damned. His fear had always conquered his love. "You're a coward Jesse

Richards.”

CHAPTER FORTY-FOUR
The Strange Case of Tammy Handover

Jesse stared at Tammy tucked into her hospital bed. She looked like she was peacefully asleep. He wished that were the case.

"Tammy regained consciousness on the way to the hospital for a couple minutes and then that was it," Mike said.

"She say anything?" Sammy asked.

"Nothing that made any sense. It sounded like a different language."

"What are they saying is wrong with her?" Jesse asked.

"No clue at this point. The doctors thought diabetes, but her glucose test came back normal. They did a whole bunch of blood work to see if anything shows up. They're thinking it could be a really bad case of Lyme disease."

"Lyme disease," Sammy whispered to Jesse, "that's what the doctors thought Uriah had last year when he got mysteriously sick."

"You think this has to do with all that stuff Ivy was talking about last night? Did Ivy do this to my sister?" Mike asked.

Sammy hesitated to answer. "I hope not." Mike hung his head. "But don't worry. We're dealing with the heart as soon as we get back to the house. Text me when Tammy wakes up."

"Okay, will do," Mike said, walking Sammy and Jesse out of his sister's hospital room.

Zac stayed behind. He felt sorry for Tammy. He wondered if she knew she was trapped, and if she did, if she was scared. He could relate, that's how he felt until Jesse saw him.

"I'm here for you Tammy. But hey, look on the bright side, you answered the old age question, gingers do have souls." Zac nervously chuckled. "Sorry, not the time for jokes. I just hope you're going to be okay." Zac went to put his hand on Tammy's hand. His ghostly fingers fell through hers and the bed until his hand reached his side again. Zac let out a loud sigh and tucked his hands back in his hoodie.

Just then, Tammy sat up in bed. Her eyelids fluttering before they slowly opened to reveal bloodshot eyes. "Tammy you're up! This is great!"

She slowly turned her head toward Zac, her eyelids rapidly flickering. She spoke as if she was in a trance, her voice hollow. "Beware the Leeds Witch."

"Uh, Tammy are you alright?" Zac asked in a panic.

"Beware the Leeds Witch."

Tammy's arm mechanically lifted, her finger pointing at Zac. Her eyes rolled back in her head until Zac could only see the whites of her eyes. "Beware the Leeds Witch."

Zac ran for the door. "Uh guys!" Zac yelled.

"What's wrong?" Jesse asked.

"I think Tammy is . . ." Zac looked behind him to see Tammy lying in her hospital bed as if she never moved.

"You think Tammy is what?" Jesse whispered to Zac.

"Um . . . nothing Jesse. "I just hope she's going to be okay."

Jesse nodded. "Me too."

CHAPTER FORTY-FIVE
A Witch's Loophole

Sammy, Jesse, and Zac were seated at the kitchen island huddled around the jarred heart with their backs to Ivy when she came in. "Hi Ivy," Alba and Maria said together, taking a break from their coloring to give her a hug. Grams walked into the kitchen with Uriah, Jeffrey, and Lindsey with Hugo in her arms, feeding the twins' hugging frenzy.

Uriah's eyes found Zachary Lewis. "Zac Lewis, it really is you," he said happy to see Zac in any form.

"Hi Pastor Leeds. You miss me?"

"Completely. You have no idea how quiet Saturday mornings are without you."

Sammy's eyes shifted to Ivy, then back at the jarred heart.

"So that's the infamous jarred heart," Uriah said, turning the jar to get a better look at it. "And we think it's JD's power source?"

"Think's the key word," said Jesse. "But after several attempts last night to turn it into cat food failed, I think it safe to say this heart is special."

Lindsey put the television on for the girls in the living room and moved their coloring books to the coffee table, keeping them away from the discussion in the kitchen. She put Hugo in his play pen near his sisters.

Anita made her way to the kitchen. She quietly rubbed her pointy chin as she listened in.

"So, you're saying you can't destroy the darn thing?" Mary asked.

"Pretty much," said Jesse.

"Better show them," Jeffrey said to Sammy.

Sammy took the heart and dumped it into the food processor. Lindsey, not convinced a demonstration was necessary, crossed her arms over her chest.

"Should we be doing that?" Uriah asked, feeling conflicted now that he knew JD was his father.

Sammy pushed blend and just as the night before, they watched it turn to puree to only have it appear unscathed in the jar.

"Now how do you explain that?" Mary asked.

"Hocus-pocus," Ivy said mockingly from where she leaned against the wall.

Sammy shot Ivy a dirty look. "Since you're so smart Ivy, why don't you destroy it. You made him, so I'm guessing you can destroy him. Unless your little crush on him is stopping you."

Blood rushed to Ivy's cheeks.

"Sammy," Jeffrey said sternly, "not now."

"I love *you* stupid," she mumbled under her breath.

Uriah seized the moment. "I think I've changed my position on JD," he said, taking a seat at the kitchen table next to Lindsey. He folded his hands anxiously to only unfold them.

"This is not an election, Uriah," Grams pointed out, pulling out a chair for herself at the kitchen table. "*Changed position?*"

Jeffrey leaned on the kitchen island, "Changed your position on JD, how so?"

"I found out JD's my father."

"He likes to call himself that and have you call him that, but he's not your father," Jesse said. "He does the same crap with me."

"That's just it, Jesse," Uriah said looking to his old friend. "He *is* my father. I found out last night Japhet Dean Leeds is my biological father."

Jesse was shocked. "What?!"

"Heavy," Zac said.

"It's true," Uriah said earnestly. "JD is my father."

"I had no idea," Jesse said in a low voice. In his first life he had always thought Uriah was chosen like he was. If he had ever learned the truth, it was lost when he was reborn. He turned to Sammy, "Looks like we got our answer to why JD's obsessed with Uriah."

"Hold up," Zac said. "So, that makes you part—"

"Demon," Uriah said, finishing Zachary Lewis's sentence. "And part witch."

Sammy's eyes darted to Ivy. She refused to look at him. He didn't need any more explanations. He had seen the picture of the baby hidden in the compartment under her bed. He knew the baby with the cleft lip had to be Uriah. And the woman in the portrait with the baby, the one Ivy admitted was of her, could only mean Ivy is his mother. Sammy's stomach tied into a pretzel when he realized the true scope of her relationship with JD, the history Ivy had alluded to. It was more than a crush and more than ever, Sammy wanted to kill JD.

"It makes sense," Uriah said. "My words seem to affect people . . . I always thought it was God's gift, not the tongue of the devil."

"No Pastor Leeds," Lindsey said, "you do have a gift from God. Half demon or not, you are the very best pastor."

"Thank you, Lindsey . . . When I was a child, I thought JD was a guardian angel that watched over me, but he was merely a father watching over his son, doing the best he could in his own strange way. Make no mistake, JD is twisted and warped, and he has done many horrible things, more so than even I know, but just as I couldn't hurt my own son; I can't hurt my father. I can't be part of this. I can't commit patricide. It's just wrong."

Jeffrey took a seat next to Uriah. "Unfortunately, we can't choose our father's," Jeffrey stated matter-of-factly. "You're not the one pushing the blend button. Nothing to feel guilty about, okay?"

He nodded.

"I think as his son, it's your duty, more than anyone else's, to stop him from hurting people."

"I didn't look at it like that," Uriah admitted.

"We all on the same page then?" Jeffrey asked Uriah.

"Yes, I want to wake Elsa, Trudy, and Tammy up."

"Good," Jeffrey said, opening the conversation up to everyone. "Any ideas? As you can see, the blender isn't cutting it. I was thinking a trade. JD has experience with that and will try to get the better of the deal, so we'd have to be very careful." He glanced at Ivy, "Ivy, maybe you could set up a meeting and we could start negotiating?"

Before Ivy could respond, they heard a knock on the front door. Alba ran out of the living room to get it with her stuffed wolf in her arms, Maria trailing behind her. Jeffrey was right behind them as Alba opened the door. "Daddy it's your twin."

Jeffrey's eyes met Japhet Dean's. An eerie fog trailed behind him, surrounding his feet, and giving him the appearance he hovered above the ground. He was not wearing his usual, a suit. He wore jeans and a T-shirt and looked utterly normal, his outfit very close to what Jeffrey changed into after church. Jeffrey couldn't help but think he did that to taunt him, an unease creeping into his bones.

Jeffrey pulled Alba's arm, jerking her toward him. She whimpered, "You hurt me, Daddy."

Jeffrey picked her up and rubbed her arm as Maria clung to his leg. "Sorry sweetie. I didn't mean it."

"What are you doing here?" Jeffrey asked, turning his attention to JD standing in the open doorway.

"I thought you wanted a meeting. Is this not a good time?"

Everyone dashed out of the kitchen. JD greeted them with a large grin. "Hello Ms. Teller and Mary. Uriah. Jesse. Is that young Zachary Lewis in the flesh?" JD chuckled to himself. "In the spirit," he corrected. "It's good to see you about. I've missed you. I've second guessed killing you, such spunk for a child. I really enjoyed your tenacity, that fighting spirit you had. Well, it seems it's all you have left. But chin up Zachary, it was the best part of you. I would know."

Zac crossed his arms over his chest, he knew it was bleeding again.

"Shut up!" Sammy shouted.

"Oh Sammy, it's good to see you too. Good to see you all. Everyone so alive and healthy and cancer free . . . You're welcome, Sammy. You owe me one, you know?"

"I don't owe you anything! I owe Ivy."

Sammy glanced at Ivy. Her heart fluttered.

JD smirked. "As much as I love house calls, I really should be on my way. Now if you would please give me my mother's heart back, I will bid you all good day."

"Wake the girls up from their comas and leave town and it's yours," Jeffrey said.

Grinning, JD took out his cigarette case and lit a hand rolled cigarette. "Mind if I smoke?" He blew a smoke ring toward Jeffrey. Alba swatted it with her hand.

"Like I have told Ms. Teller, I can't stop the spell once it's in motion. You have to wait it out." He exhaled, smoke escaping his lips like steam from a kettle. "Back to the pressing issue, you stole my mother's heart and I want it back."

"You stole it from me first," Sammy said, keeping his distance.

"Now that's just not true, Sammy. I traded you for it. Don't you remember, I gave you my father's coin?"

"What," he said confused.

"Yes, a rather large Persian silver coin dated 1735."

Sammy and Jeffrey exchanged glances. Sammy opened his wallet and looked at the coin his father found in his room and told him to put away.

"You still have it I see," JD pointed out. "Very good. Like I said, I gave you my father's coin and I took my mother's heart in exchange. A fair trade. So, if you would be so kind to hand me back my property, I'll let you get back to your plotting and planning."

"I don't think so," Jeffrey said. He handed Alba to Sammy and took his wallet from him, plucked out the coin and threw it to JD.

JD resisted catching it, letting the coin bounce off him and hit the foyer floor. "Clever Jeffrey, but I'm not falling for that trade." JD exhaled through his mouth. "We both know you can't destroy the heart. It's worthless to you, so give it back."

"Then why do you want it so badly?" Jesse asked.

"The heart is sentimental to me, Jesse. As you well know, I'm a sentimental kind of guy. I thought you would understand that. After all, you kept that necklace from Moon River and her father all these years even though it doesn't work very well. One could say it was sentimental to you. A memento from the first day you met your true love."

"Moon River?" Sammy whispered to Jesse, thinking of his sister's stuffed wolf with the same name. The same stuffed wolf she clung to now.

"The heart stays with us until you wake the girls, end of story." Jeffrey said, staying on task. "So, if you don't mind, we're busy *plotting and planning.*"

Jeffrey went to close the door. JD stopped it with his foot.

"That tone may work with the dregs you deal with at work, but you don't scare me, Jeffrey Lopez. It's you who should fear me. You have no idea what I could do to you and your precious little family."

Ivy spoke up. "You said you wouldn't hurt them. You promised you wouldn't lay a finger on any member of the Lopez family if I let you borrow the spell book."

JD smiled as he stomped out his cigarette with the heel of his shoe. "Correct you are Ms. Teller, and I'm bound to my promise. I'm a man of honor. My word is my bond."

Jeffrey attempted to close the door again. This was not going the way he thought it would in his head. But he meant it, he wasn't giving JD the jarred heart until they got what they wanted. He wouldn't be bullied. Closing the door on JD would show he was being serious; he too knew a thing about negotiating, even if he wasn't a trade wielding demon.

JD prevented the door from closing with his outstretched hand.

"Not so fast. It's true I can't hurt a member of the Lopez family, but I can hurt Mary Teller."

Ivy jumped in front of her grandmother. "You wouldn't?!"

"*I would.* I would do a lot worse for something less worthwhile. Hand over my mother's heart or I will kill her. This is not a threat Ms. Teller, but a promise. And as you know I keep my promises."

"Doggone it, figures this happens once I get a boyfriend."

"He's not touching you, Grams."

"I'm losing my patience," JD said. "And that's not good."

"That's enough," Lindsey said, speaking up. "This ends here."

He smiled at her. "What would that be my dear?"

"Don't call her dear," Jeffrey snapped.

"You're not hurting Mary and you're not putting any more children in comas."

JD laughed, the sound filling the foyer. "Come now, Lindsey, I don't think this is a conversation you want to have in front of your entire extended family, do you?"

All eyes and ears were on Lindsey. She turned to face her family. "I've been keeping a secret and I'm very sorry."

"What are you talking about?" Jeffrey asked.

Lindsey ran her hands over her pencil skirt, her hands shaking. "It was me who made the deal with JD."

"What?!" Jeffrey and Sammy said at the same time.

"Lindsey, what deal?" Jeffrey asked. In his head, he counted down from ten to calm himself.

"Ivy lent JD the spell book, but it was me who read from it. I cast the spell. I cast the *Sleep Spell* and in return JD cured my cancer."

Ivy's jaw dropped. She knew JD said the spell was being controlled by another witch, but she had assumed he just meant himself.

Sammy and Jeffrey were speechless.

Lindsey wiped her tears, trying to explain herself. "I was so desperate to save Hugo . . . he was going to die. I'm not proud of what I did, but I would do anything to save my son or any of my children."

"Why didn't you tell me?" Jeffrey asked in shock.

"It was my burden, Jeffrey. But I'm putting an end to this madness today. I've stolen enough days, it's time for those poor children to get their lives back and for me to say my goodbyes."

Jeffrey's throat was dry; his heart raced. "What are you talking about?"

"I only read from the spell book to ensure Hugo would live. I never intended on living longer than that."

JD smiled. "A deal is a deal, Lindsey. I'm sure your mother told you that."

"No, you're wrong. Our deal has conditions set by Ivy. No children die and no member of the Lopez family gets hurt. That's what you told me."

JD nodded. "No children were killed, and no member of the Lopez family will ever be hurt on my watch. We're all one big happy family," JD said with a large grin.

"You're not my family," Lindsey said. "But you do have two sons."

JD looked at Uriah and Jesse with pride. "Yes, I do."

"Jesse is an extension of your bloodline. As he is your son, you must take responsibility for his actions."

JD's eyes darted to Jesse.

"If Jesse were to hurt a member of my family our deal would be broken."

"Yes, I suppose it would be," JD said, thinking as his eyes shifted from Lindsey back to Jesse. "The girls would wake up, but you would be riddled with cancer and die."

"But Hugo, he'll be fine," Lindsey said. She looked at Jesse and nodded.

"No Jesse!" Jeffrey yelled, when he realized what was about to happen. He tried to get between his wife and Jesse, but it was too late. Jesse already had his hunting knife in his hand. He thrust his knife deep into Lindsey's chest, helping her to the floor. "I'm sorry, so very sorry," Jesse cried, his tears pouring down his face.

"Thank you, Jesse."

"I can't believe it," Zac muttered, his mouth hanging open in shock as everyone rushed to Lindsey.

"Ivy, quick call 911!" Grams shouted scooping Alba and Maria up and getting them as far away from Lindsey as possible.

Sammy looked at Jesse with destroyed eyes. "How could you, Jesse? I trusted you."

"I'm sorry. I didn't want to." Jesse bolted to the back sliding doors, unlocked them, and ran for the woods.

Sammy went to pull the knife out of his mother's chest.

"No Sammy, leave it in," his father cautioned. "She'll bleed out. We have to wait for the ambulance."

Lindsey looked into the faces of her husband and son. "It has to be this way my boys. I was always supposed to die. I'm okay with it." Lindsey's breathing became shallow. "Please watch over our family and forgive Jesse. He did this for us. For me, to save my soul. I asked him to do this for me at a great personal cost to himself. Forgive him." Lindsey squeezed Sammy's hand. "I would've asked the same of you, if it would've broken my contract with JD. Promise me you will forgive Jesse."

Tears blinded Sammy. "I promise, Mom. I forgive him."

Uriah put a hand on Sammy's shoulder and squeezed it, as he prayed.

JD stood shocked from the doorway for a long time before he stirred into motion. "No," he said in a low voice. "No," he said louder. "No," he yelled at the top of his lungs. "Not like this. It was not supposed to happen like this!"

JD walked toward Lindsey; Anita met him head on. He glared down at her with red eyes.

"We found a loophole devil. We've tricked you."

"Tricked me, witch?" JD said, touching his chest. "You sacrificed your own daughter. You're no mother!"

"I helped save my daughter's soul, a soul you would have dammed."

Anita went to slap JD's face. He grabbed her hand before it struck his cheek and squeezed.

"JD, let her go," Ivy pleaded.

JD kept his eyes locked on Anita. "Why should I?"

"This is not the time or place."

"On the contrary, Ms. Teller, I think it's the perfect time. JD squeezed Anita's hand harder forcing her to her knees. He whispered in her ear so only she could hear. "I know you were in the woods that day Anita. I know you sent Jesse after Ivy. I know you were the one that pushed him to his death, not her. You planned this all from the beginning. You killed my son and used him against me. You are more of a monster, Anita Gomez, than I will ever be, and I plan on showing your family just that."

JD had told Ivy Jesse's death wasn't her fault, but withheld it was Anita who delivered the final blow that sent Jesse tumbling to his death. Ivy's guilt made her malleable and to his shame he took advantage of it. He would do anything to have her in his arms again.

Ivy cried, "JD, you promised me you wouldn't hurt a member of the

Lopez family and that includes Anita!"

"Our deal is broken, Ms. Teller. I thought Lindsey bleeding all over the expensive marble floor would have made that clear to you."

"JD, let her go. The deal is broken but your promise was more. Your promise was to me."

JD released his grip, sending Anita to the ground in a heap.

He turned to Ivy and took her by the chin. "I did promise you that, but how many promises have you broken? How many hearts have you crushed, shattered into teeny, tiny pieces until there was nothing left—nothing left but a monster?"

Tears rolled down her face. "Please, JD."

JD pressed his moist lips to Ivy's ear and whispered: "I will spare her today. But know this my little enchantress, I will not rest until I have collected my third son and Sammy is in my arms."

JD pushed Ivy away from him and turned to Anita still on the ground. "This isn't over, witch." He glanced at Sammy by the side of his mother. "All bad mothers will meet bad ends. That is a promise and as Ms. Teller can tell you. I keep my promises."

JD clenched his fists in defeat and walked out the front door. Ivy's eyes went to Sammy where he sobbed at his mother's side as Uriah continued to pray. She knew Pastor Leeds's prayer wouldn't save Lindsey, nothing would. They would need a miracle from Heaven or Hell. She watched Jeffrey Lopez cry; his sad face so familiar to her. "*So much like his brother,*" she thought. She turned and ran after JD.

CHAPTER FORTY-SIX
Jesse's Torment

A raging storm blew through Pleasant Mills without notice. The rain poured down as if the heavens opened to weep for Lindsey Lopez. Thunder and lightning acted as God's voice, crying out in pain as lightning struck the ground around the Lopez house. The tree branches chattered in the wind like jawing banshees spreading tidings of death.

Jesse ran through the woods blinded by his own tears. The guilt of what he'd just done weighed heavy on his shoulders making him sluggish and cumbersome. He had betrayed his loved ones all over again. History had repeated itself. The small town of Pleasant Mills was in a state of constant replay. Jesse felt like he was doomed to relive his past no matter how hard he strived to be a better man. He was given a second chance, but he couldn't change his fate. He was a murderer and would always be one.

The sound of his hunting knife piercing Lindsey's chest was all too reminiscent of when he murdered his wife. It all came back to him in a tidal wave of emotion that acted to drown him: the feel of her skin as it fought against his blade, the smell of the fresh blood, the sound of her gasping lungs.

Jesse bumped into trees, their rough bark scraping his hands and arms. He strained to run from himself, run from the guilt that continued to compound in his treacherous heart. Guilt and he were no strangers. He always carried it around like a crushing boulder that got heavier over time, weakening his heart and soul. But now his guilt caused him to stumble as the disappointed faces of Sammy, Jeffrey, the twins, and Zac delivered the final blow to his resolve.

Jesse tripped over a tree branch and fell to the ground, mud splattering on his face. He wiped it off with the sleeve of his shirt and slumped against a tree. His guilt overthrew him, immobilized him. He couldn't make it back to his feet. Jesse gave into sorrow and sobbed.

"I didn't want to do it!" Jesse shouted into the pouring rain. "I didn't want to do it . . ."

But Jesse had told Lindsey and Anita, that night he got caught snooping in Anita's bedroom, that he would do it. He would kill Lindsey to save her soul and protect the Lopez family. Lindsey's death would not be like Mona's. He wouldn't kill her out of fear but for love. But it didn't feel any different. It felt wrong.

The heavy rain began to wash away the thick layer of mud from Jesse's hands. His heart burned when he saw the crimson blood of Lindsey Lopez still on his palms. "I'm sorry Lindsey," he whimpered. "I did it for love. I swear I did it for love . . . please forgive me."

The ghost of Jesse's dead wife appeared next to him. Mona Wolff was in her wedding dress, the front of her gown saturated in red, the rain washing the color to the forest floor. "You're a very bad man Jesse Richards. When will you have enough blood?"

Jesse looked up at the apparition of his wife with lost eyes. "Mona, I'm so very sorry . . . please forgive me. What must I do for you to finally know peace?"

Mona's body decayed in front of Jesse as time seemed to hasten around her. He watched in dismay as worms inched and crawled under her lifeless skin, devouring the woman he'd loved. Jesse reached out to help her as she turned to dust and fell through his fingertips. He collapsed in the mud, breathing in large mouthfuls of hot air.

After what seemed like an eternity, trapped in his personal hell, Jesse heard footsteps. He turned to see Ivy Teller run by. He stumbled to his feet. He could barely see her in the rain and fog by the time he'd gotten up. He took a deep breath in and followed her.

CHAPTER FORTY-SEVEN
For the Enchantress

Ivy ran as quickly as she could through the woods. The sound of ambulance sirens became a muffled cry washed out by the pouring rain.

Ivy was grateful she had stopped home and changed out of her church clothes before heading to the Lopez's with Grams, but the rain still bogged her down. A gale of wind bellowed the bittersweet song of the Jersey Devil from the depths of the Pines. She followed it, holding her arms close to her body as she ran. She knew she was racing against the clock.

Ivy took a deep breath in and willed her feet to move faster, crushing over fallen tree limbs as if she ran through a battlefield heavy with mortalities.

Ivy found JD in his clearing surrounded by death and rot. He sat on his knees and cried into his hands. She crouched down in front of him.

"I didn't want this," JD said in a low voice to Ivy. "I never wanted any of this . . . I didn't want Lindsey to get hurt."

"I know. I know that," Ivy said, putting a hand on his shoulder. "You can still do good, JD. Save Lindsey."

"You know I don't have the power to do that. I'm cursed. I'm a demon, a spawn of the Devil, not our Uriah's guardian angel. I have to make a deal to save her."

"Make one with me."

JD looked into Ivy's foolish eyes, seeing his eyes reflected in hers. "I can't do that to you, Ivy. I would spare pain today, but tomorrow there'll be agony. I can't do good . . . I will have you do something for me one day that will shatter you." Tears ran down his cheeks. "Don't you see, that's my way? I can't do that to you . . . not you. All the pain I caused you by borrowing the Leeds grimoire, in trade, will be nothing compared to a deal with me. I will destroy you. I don't want to hurt you like I hurt our son, like I hurt my Jesse. I can't do anything but be evil. I *am* a monster."

Ivy held both of JD's hands as she sat in front of him. She squeezed them tightly. "Look at me, JD." JD glanced up at Ivy before returning his gaze to the mossy floor. "That's not true. I never believed it and I never will. What do you want from me?"

"I've never wanted anything from you, Ivy Teller."

Ivy grabbed his face in her hands forcing him to look at her. "Make a deal with me. You can't let Lindsey die, not when you can save her."

"This is what she wanted."

"Think of Sammy," Ivy pleaded. "He can't lose his mother. Please do it for him!" JD remained silent as his tears mixed with the rain. "Do it for me Japhet Dean."

Hearing his full name spoken by her, as she had done long ago when she named him, brought back a surge of emotion. He felt redeemable. JD gazed into Ivy's dark, sad eyes that matched his own despair. "You called me by my name."

Ivy pressed her face against JD's. "Please," she whispered in his ear. "Please, Japhet Dean, save her. Do it for me. You said you would do anything for me."

JD cradled the back of Ivy's head in his hand "Will you do me a favor when the time comes?" He whispered in her ear, "Will you enchantress?" His breath smelled sweet on her face, enthralling her with every exhale.

"I will. I promise."

"Then it is done. Lindsey will survive." JD pulled Ivy's face closer to his. They stared into each other's eyes, their noses touching, as the rain dripped down their faces.

"See, Japhet Dean, you can do good. You're no monster." Ivy leaned in, their lips brushing against each other as delicately as butterfly wings.

"Ivy . . . please don't . . . I can't bear it."

Ivy's lips slid over his in a terrible dance she couldn't stop. She knew the steps and what came next. It was oddly familiar and foreign to her all in the same swoop. Ivy shuddered, not sure if she ever wanted it to end. Her hands instinctively coiled around his neck, drawing him closer. The sense of belonging washed over her, making everything else in the world disappear, even Sammy.

CHAPTER FORTY-EIGHT
Destroyed

Lindsey opened her eyes. She heard Jeffrey's voice from where he sat bedside. "Thank God, you're going to be okay." He squeezed her hand.

"Jeffrey . . ."

"Shh," he said, moving a blonde tendril away from her face. "Don't talk. You punctured a lung, but you're going to be okay."

"Jesse?"

"Don't worry about him right now. We'll find him."

"The kids?" she gasped, trying to take a deep breath in.

"The girls woke up from their comas and Sammy, the twins, and Hugo are fine. You're going to be fine. Everyone is fine."

Lindsey cried, the tears rolling from the corners of her eyes. Jeffrey planted a kiss on her forehead. "Hey don't do that. Try to stay calm."

"Everything is not fine. He will never let us be."

"For the moment we won. Let's celebrate the little victories, huh?" He kissed her forehead again. "We still have that heart, and he wants it. He can't just take it back, otherwise he would have. So as far as I'm concerned, we have the upper hand even if we're not sure what to do with it yet."

"Everything is not fine," she said again with great difficulty.

Jeffrey pressed his lips to his wife's cheek. "Lindsey, please don't get yourself upset."

"I need to tell you something."

"Shh now, it can wait. You need to rest."

"No, it can't. I can't keep it to myself any longer. Months ago, you came home like you always do, said hello to me, the girls, and we went into the bathroom like we sometimes do."

He grinned.

"But then you stepped out, and a few minutes later you came back in the house acting like you'd just got home, saying you had gotten a flat tire. You kissed me and the girls again, said hello to Sammy, and we went to the bathroom again. I didn't think anything of it at the time. I knew we were all under a lot of stress with the boys going missing and Sammy having been abducted."

Jeffrey knew the day Lindsey was talking about. He recalled his wife commenting on his strange behavior and remembered the funny look Sammy gave him when he went to say hello. Come to think of it, he realized it was the same day he spotted the coin on Sammy's dresser; the silver coin they now new JD had left for Sammy.

Lindsey continued. "When you told me about Uriah and Mary seeing a man that looked and sounded like you, and Sammy and the twins also said they saw the same man, it made me think back to that day."

Jeffrey held his breath; he knew where this was going. *'I have learned how to talk like you, learned all of your hand gestures, all your kinks . . . How you think, how you take your coffee, how you screw.'*

"I'm sorry Jeffrey. I don't know if Hugo is yours."

Jeffrey stood up, releasing his wife's hand. "Don't ever let those words escape your lips again," he said in a raised voice. "You hear me?! Never say that again. He's my son. So help me God Lindsey, if you say it again . . ."

Lindsey's tears gained momentum.

He ran his hands through his hair as he thought, forgetting all about what his therapist said about controlling his anger. "You mean to tell me you couldn't tell the difference between me and him? You expect me to believe that? Christ, we've been together since we were teenagers."

"He looks just like you, how was I to know," she sobbed.

"I don't know," Jeffrey hollered. "You just were!"

"Isn't that why you grew your hair out? You were worried people would think he was you."

"Yeah, I was worried about that. But I never thought my wife wouldn't know me."

A nurse walked in. "Is everything okay, Mr. Lopez?"

"I think she's in pain, can you see to her," Jeffrey said, before walking out.

Jeffrey held his face in his hand, resting his arm on his knee as he sat in the hospital waiting room. His once very structured life was now a three-ring circus, filled with a dog, a cat, a ghost, and a baby. But it was his sideshow and he loved it.

Jeffrey felt like he got more than a second lease on life when Sammy and his family survived the clutches of the Jersey Devil and again when his wife beat cancer for the third time. He was a lucky man, and he knew it. He didn't need JD to tell him that.

Now Lindsey was stabbed, she could've died, and he could do nothing to protect her. He couldn't do anything to protect anyone. And Hugo, his little boy, could be the son of the very man who tried to take it all from him. He squeezed his fist. He hated JD.

Jeffrey felt a hand on his shoulder. He looked up to see Pearl. "How are you doing?" she asked, taking a seat next to him on the bench.

"I'm okay," he said with a faint smile. "The doctors got Lindsey stabilized. She'll pull through."

"How about the kids?"

"The girls and Hugo are with Anita at Mary Teller's. Fran's on her way to pick them up."

"And Sammy?"

"He ran off."

"Want me to look for him?" Pearl asked concerned.

"No. He just needs some space. I texted him to come to the hospital when he's ready."

"You want to tell me what happened?"

"Is this police business?" he asked. He could really use a friend right now. Of course, his only friend was a cop.

"I'm not here in an official capacity, so you can relax. I heard what happened over the police blotter and wanted to check on you."

Jeffrey leaned back, resting his hands on the tops of his thighs. He took a deep breath in. "Lindsey had a knife in her hand and fell."

Pearl's eyes narrowed. "You don't actually expect me to believe that do you?"

He swallowed a laugh. "No, Pearl. I don't, but that's what I'm going to say happened. And that's what everyone else is going to tell you too."

She put her hand over his and squeezed. "I said I wasn't here in a professional capacity. Tell me what kind of trouble you got yourself into and I can help. I want to help."

He searched her eyes for a long moment not saying anything. "I don't want you near this. There's nothing you can do."

She could see the tears collecting in the corners of his eyes, about to spill over. She hugged him, bringing him close to her chest. She could feel his body tremble. She knew he was crying. He wrapped his arms around her.

"Jeffrey, let me in. I'm on your side, where I've always been."

CHAPTER FORTY-NINE
A New Beginning

The rain came down like invisible hands parting the fog, leaving JD and Ivy intertwined amongst the clearing in the Pines. Jesse watched them wide-eyed from his hiding spot behind a tree and so did Sammy. Sammy gasped, taking a step back, as if that simple action could protect his heart from the betrayal of it all, shield him somehow as if taking a step back removed him miles from the scene, transporting him somewhere his heart couldn't break. Sammy had imagined Ivy kissing JD since she had confessed to cheating on him; but, to see it, to see his worst nightmares come to life made everything too real: Japhet Dean, his mother being stabbed and dying, Jesse's betrayal, Ivy's betrayal.

Sammy's phone vibrated, pulling him out of his waking nightmare. His hand shook as he reached into his pocket for his phone. He wasn't sure if it shook out of fear or anger, his fingers clutching it, bringing the phone to life. It was a text message from Mike: Tammy's up! Everyone's up! Another vibration, a text from his dad: Your mother's going to be alright. Come to the hospital when you can.

Sammy glanced up from his phone noticing for the first time Jesse was on the other side of the clearing. They saw each other, each giving a thoughtful nod. Sammy assumed he got the same texts. Sammy quietly approached Jesse, taking his time as he stepped around low growing blueberry bushes shooting up in wild mounds from puddles, reminding him of reaching tentacles.

"I'm sorry," whispered Jesse as Sammy came to stand next to him.

Sammy let out the breath he felt he was holding for what felt like hours, his voice raspy. "I forgive you. My mom's going to be alright."

Both their eyes focused on Ivy and JD. "Because of Ivy," Jesse said.

"Because of Ivy," Sammy repeated. A rage boiled up from his stomach, turning his saliva to acid in his mouth.

To be continued . . .

Want more?

Read book three!
GET FOREST OF WITCHES NOW!

Thanks for reading!

If this book helped you escape, if only for a moment, please consider taking the time to leave a review or star rating on Amazon or whatever platform you use. It would warm the cockles of my little, black heart to hear from you.

Looking for something else to read? Don't forget to check out my other books on Amazon.

Follow me on social media (I'm on all platforms under Holly Knightley). Sign up for my newsletter for the latest news, glimpse into my wacky process, and occasional freebie. Stay spooky and happy reading!